'An elegant, fun page-turner' *Red*

'A multi-faceted tale of fading fame and shifting fortunes' *Grazia*

'This cleverly constructed, dark tale [is] dripping with dark humour, gritty realism, with a little bit of romance thrown in too. An absorbing read' *Star*

'The shallow LA of today is wittily satirised, and the more glamorous age of the 50s brilliantly recalled' *Sunday Mirror*

Also by Harriet Evans

Harriet Evans

Not WITHOUT You

HARPER

Harper
An imprint of HarperCollins*Publishers*
77–85 Fulham Palace Road,
Hammersmith, London W6 8JB

www.harpercollins.co.uk

This paperback edition 2013
1

First published in Great Britain by
HarperCollins*Publishers* 2013

Extract from *Bring on the Empty Horses* by David Niven. Reproduced with permission of Curtis Brown Group Ltd, London on behalf of The Estate of David Niven © Copyright David Niven 1975

Extract from *I'll Be Around*, composed by Alec Wilder © Copyright 1942 by Regent Music Corporation. Reproduced by permission of Boosey & Hawkes Music Publishers Ltd

Harriet Evans asserts the moral right to be identified as the author of this work

A catalogue record for this book is available from the British Library

ISBN: 978-0-00-735031-5

Set in Meridien by Palimpsest Book Production Limited, Falkirk, Stirlingshire

Printed and bound in Great Britain by Clays Ltd, St Ives plc

For Cora

I felt as though I had returned from far, far away.

David Niven, *Bring on the Empty Horses*

PROLOGUE

A BRIGHT SPRING day, sunshine splashing yellow through the new leaves. Two little girls stand on the banks of the swollen stream, which rushes loudly past their small feet.

'Come on,' says the first. 'There's magic coins in there. Gold coins, from the elves. I can see them glinting. Can't you?' She pushes the short sleeves of her lawn dress up above her shoulders; a determined imitation of the men they see in the fields beyond, backs curved over the soil. Her brown hair bobs about her head, sun darting through the bouncing curls. She grins. 'It'll be fun. Don't listen to *them*.'

The second one hesitates. She always hesitates. 'I don't know, Rose,' she says. 'They said it's dangerous. All that rain . . . Father said you weren't to do it again. He said you'd be sent away if—'

'You believe them, don't you.' Rose crosses her arms. 'I'm not doing all those things they say I do. They're making it up. I'm *not* bad.'

'I know you're not.' The younger one mollifies her sister.

'I didn't mean to break the jug. Something happened to me, everything went black, and I didn't know where I was.' She bites her lip, trying not to cry. 'I don't like it. I want Mother and she tells me I'm bad when I do.'

A tear rolls through the brown film of dust on her cheek. They're both silent, under the old willow tree. Eve speaks first.

She points at the gold coins, swelling and then vanishing in the water's rush.

'Come on, let's try to get them, then.'

'Really?' Rose's face brightens.

'I'll do it if you do.' She always regrets saying that.

Rose immediately clambers in. 'I'll go first.'

Eve watches her doubtfully. 'It's awfully strong. You won't get swept away?'

'I told you, it's fine. Thomas does it all the time,' Rose says, leaning over, confident again now, and Eve relaxes. Rose is right, of course. She's always right. 'There it is. I'm sure it's gold! I'm sure the elves were here – their kingdom is right under the ground, ancient noble soil!' She claps her hands. 'Golly! Imagine if it is! I told you, little Eve. You mustn't worry – they won't send me away. I'm not going anywhere.'

This is the last image of her that Eve remembers. Standing like a miniature pirate, legs planted firmly in the stream. 'We'll always be together. I'm going to be a famous explorer. You'll be a famous actress. We'll do different things for a couple of weeks at a time. I'll see some polar bears and . . . pharaohs. And you'll do plays and dine with Ivor Novello. Then we'll meet up in New York, under the King Kong building. You'll have that delicious robe on, the one Vivien Leigh was wearing in *Dark Journey*. 'Member?'

Eve nods. She joins in the game, smiling. 'Oh . . . yes. We'll stay in beautiful hotels and we'll drink milk stout.' This was a great obsession of theirs, after Cook had told them it was her favourite tipple. But Cook had left, like so many of the servants lately. Gone in the night, shouting, 'I'll not stay here with that thing in the house!'

Rose nods. 'We'll always be together, Eve, like I say, 'cause I'm not going anywhere, not without you.'

And she screamed, then jerked forward. I can still see it, as if something else, an evil spirit maybe, was knocking her over from behind.

* * *

2

Should I have stayed? Or gone for help and left her prostrate in the water, eyes wide open, small body rigid? I still don't know to this day if I did the right thing. I ran to the house, as fast as my legs would carry me.

But it was all over by the time they came back, by the time the doctor arrived. I stayed in the kitchen, with Mother; they wouldn't let me go out there again, and when they finally returned it was much later. Too late. You see, Rose was gone. My beautiful sister was dead, and it was my fault. I should have stayed with her. *Not without you,* she'd said. And I let her down.

That was my first mistake, though I couldn't be blamed for that, as everyone told me. I was only six. It was many, many years ago. But I know what I did was wrong. I left her when she needed me. I carried that mistake with me, maybe for too long. And when someone showed me a way out, a new life, I took it.

PART ONE

CHAPTER ONE

Los Angeles, 2012

> '*And . . . coming up next . . . Sophie Leigh's diet secrets! How the British beauty stays slim, and the answer is . . . you won't believe it! Chewing cardboard! I know, these stars are crazy, but that's Hollywood for you. That's all when we come back . . .*'

IT'S A BEAUTIFUL May morning. We're on the 101, on our way into Beverly Hills. I'm heading into my agent's office and I feel like crap. I'm super late, too. I'm always late, but when your most recent picture had an opening weekend of $23 million it doesn't matter. I could turn up at Artie's mom's funeral and demand to have a meeting and he'd clear the synagogue and thank me for coming.

I flip the TV off and chuck the remote across the car, out of temptation's reach. There was a time when a ten-second trail like that would have sent me into a tailspin. *They're saying I chew cardboard? But it's bullshit! People'll believe it, and then they'll . . . they'll . . .* Now I just shrug. You have to. I've never chewed cardboard in my life, unless you count my performance in that action movie. It's a slow news day. Sometimes I think they stick a pin in a copy of *People* magazine to choose their next victim and then make something up.

When you've been famous for a while, you stop reacting to

stuff like this. It just becomes part of life. Not your life, but the life you wake up to and realise you're living. People filming you on a phone when you're washing your hands in the Ladies' room. Girls from school who you don't remember selling your class photo to a tabloid. Being offered $5 million to sleep with a Saudi prince. Working with stars who won't ever take their sunglasses off, 'cause they think you're stealing their soul if you see their eyes. Sounds unbelievable, right? But there's been some days when I almost know what they mean. I know why some of them go bat-shit crazy, join cults, wear fake pregnancy bellies, marry complete strangers. They're only trying to distract themselves from how totally nuts being famous is. Because that's what fame is actually about, these days. Not private jets, diamond tiaras, mansions and free clothes, handbags, shoes. Fame is actually about how you stay sane. How you don't lose your mind.

I know I'm lucky. It could have been any one of hundreds of hopeful English girls from small towns with pushy mums who curled their hair and shoved them into audition rooms, but it was me, and I still don't quite know why. All I know is, I love films, always have done, ever since I was little. Lights down, trailers on, credits rolling; I knew all the special idents the studios use to open a movie by the time I was eight. My favourite was always Columbia – the toga lady holding the glowing torch like the sun. And I know I'm good at what I do: I make movies for people to sit back and smile at on a Friday night with their best friend and their popcorn, watching while Sophie Leigh gets into another crazy situation. OK, it's not *Citizen Kane*, but if it's a bit of fun and you could stand to watch it again, is there anything wrong with that?

Lately I've been wondering though: maybe there is. Maybe it's all wrong. The trouble is, I can't work out how it all got like that. Or what I should do about it. In Hollywood, you're either a success or you're a failure. There's no in-between.

The freeway is crowded, and as we slow down to turn off I look up and there I am, right by the Staples Center on a billboard the size of your house. I should be used to it but still, after six years at the top, it's weird. Me, doing my poster smile: cute chipmunk cheeks, big dark eyes peeking out from under the heavy trademark bangs, just the right amount of cleavage so the guys notice and don't mind seeing the film. I'm holding out a ringless hand, smiling at you. I'm cute and friendly.

Two years of dating. She's thinking rocks.
No, not those ones, fellas . . .
SOPHIE LEIGH IS
THE GIRLFRIEND
May 2012

My phone rings, and I pick it up, gingerly, rubbing my eyes. 'Hi, Tina,' I say.

'You're OK?' Tina asks anxiously. 'Did the car come for you?'

'Sure,' I say.

'The clothes were OK? Did you want anything else?'

Do I want anything else? The late-morning sun flashes in reflected rays through the windows; I jam my sunglasses on and sink lower against the leather seats, smiling at the memory of him asking the very same question, then taking my clothes off piece by piece, getting the camera out, and what we did afterwards. Oh, it's probably insane of me, but . . . wow. He knows what he's doing. I'm not some idiot who lets herself be filmed by a douche-bag who puts it on the Internet. This guy is a pro, in *many many ways*.

'I'm good. Thanks for arranging it all.'

'No problem.' Tina is the most efficient assistant on the planet. She looks worried all the time, but I don't think she actually cares where I was last night. 'There's a couple things. OK?'

'Go ahead.' I'm staring out the window, trying not to think about last night, smiling and biting my lip because . . . well, I'm exhausted, that kind of up-all-night skanky, hungry, and a little bit hungover exhausted. And I can't stop smiling.

'So . . .' Tina's voice goes into her list-recital monotone. 'The *People* interview is tomorrow. They'll come by the house. Ashley will arrive at eight a.m. Belle is doing your make-up frosty pink and mushroom – she says the vibe is Madonna eighties glamour meets environmental themes.' Tina takes a breath. 'DeShantay wants to drop off some more outfits for the Up! Kidz Challenge Awards. She has a dress from McQueen and she says to tell you you're gonna love it. It's cerise, has cap sleeves and it's—'

'I don't want to sweat,' I say. 'Tell her no sleeves.'

'DeShantay says it won't be a problem.'

'I'm not—' I begin, then I stop, as I can hear myself sounding like a bit of a tool. 'Never mind. That's great. Anything else?'

'Tommy's coming over later this week to talk through endorsements. And he's gotten *Us Weekly* to use some new shots of you doing yoga on the beach. And the shots of you grocery shopping are being run again, in *In Touch*. And *TMZ* want the ones of you getting the manicure, only they need to reshoot—'

'OK, OK,' I say, trying not to feel irritated, because it's so fake, when you say it out loud, but it's true, and everyone does it. You can so tell when someone doesn't want their photo taken and when they do, and those ones of me pushing my trolley through the Malibu Country Mart wearing the new Marc Jacobs sandals and a Victoria Beckham shift, holding up some apples and laughing with a girlfriend, came out the same week as *The Girlfriend* and I'm telling you: it's part of the reason that film has done so well. It's all total bullshit though. The clothes were on loan, and the friend was Tina. My assistant. And I don't go food shopping; I've got a housekeeper. Be honest. If you had someone to do all that for you, would you still go pushing a trolley round the supermarket? *Exactly*. Today stars have to look like normal, approachable people. Fifty years ago, it was the other way round. My favourite actress is Eve Noel; I've seen all her movies a million times, and *A Girl Named Rose* is my favourite film of all time, without a doubt. You didn't have photos of Eve Noel in some 1950s

Formica store buying her groceries in a dress Givenchy loaned her. Oh, no. She was a goddess, remote, beautiful, untouchable. I'm America's English sweetheart. Pay $3.99 for a weekly magazine and you can see my nipples in a T-shirt doing the sun salute on Malibu beach.

Another thing: I starved myself for three days to fit into that fucking Victoria Beckham dress. That girl sure loves the skinny.

We're off the highway, gliding down the wide boulevards of Beverly Hills, flanked on either side by vast mansions: old-looking French chateaux wedged right next to glass-and-chrome cubes next to English Gothic castles, Spanish haciendas, and the rest. My first trip here with my best friend Donna, both aged nineteen, driving round LA in a brown Honda Civic, these houses blew our minds – they looked like Toytown. It's funny how things change. Now they seem normal. I know a couple of people who live in them, and I haven't seen Donna in nearly seven years. Where is she now? Still living in Shamley, last time I Googled her.

We're coming up to Wilshire and I need to check my make-up. 'I'll see you later,' I tell Tina. 'Thanks again.'

'Oh – one more thing. I'm sorry, Sophie. Your mom called again.' I stiffen instinctively. 'She says you have to call her back.' Tina clears her throat. 'She says Deena's coming to stay with you. Tonight.'

The compact mirror drops to the floor.

'Deena? She can't just— Tell her she can't.'

Tina's voice is apologetic. 'Your mom said she has roaches and damp and it needs to be sprayed and . . . She's got nowhere to go.'

'I don't care. Deena is not bloody staying. Why's she getting Mum to phone up and do her dirty work for her anyway? No. No way.'

My head feels like it's in a vice. It always aches when I don't eat: I'm trying to lose ten pounds before *The Bachelorette Party* starts shooting.

'Her cell is broken. That's why. So – uh – OK.' Tina's tone

conveys it all. She keeps me on the straight and narrow, I sometimes think. I'd be a Grade A egomaniac otherwise.

I clear my throat and growl. 'Look. I'll try and call Mum and put her off. Don't worry about it. Listen though, if Deena turns up . . .' Then I run out of steam. 'Watch her. Make sure she doesn't steal anything again.'

'Sure, Sophie,' says Tina, and I end the call with a sigh, trying not to frown. There are wrinkles at the corners of my eyes and lines between my eyebrows; I've noticed them lately. The Sophie Leigh on the poster doesn't frown. She doesn't have wrinkles. She's twenty-eight, she's happy all the time, and she knows how great her life is. That's not true. I'm thirty, and I keep thinking I'm going to get found out.

CHAPTER TWO

'SHE'S HERE! MAJOR star power incoming, people!'

Artie's waiting for me as the elevator doors open, his arms open wide. 'Sophie, Sophie, Sophie!' The assistant on reception smiles, and someone whispers, 'I loved your last movie,' as I walk past, and Artie hugs me and kisses me on both cheeks. '*Hola!* She's here, people!'

It's all an act, and he knows I know it.

'You look. Amazing,' he says simply, and leads me through to his office suite, overlooking Wilshire Boulevard, the wide straight road lined with palm trees right along from Rodeo Drive where Julia Roberts went shopping in *Pretty Woman*. I like going into Artie's office, seeing what's going on, what's new. And though it sounds stupid, I like being in places where normal people work. Not that anyone at World Artists' Management is particularly normal, but I'm an actress. OK, I'll never be Meryl Streep, but part of my job is to play girls who work in offices and you don't get that realistic a view of the world living in the Hollywood Hills and having the kind of life where you have your own florist.

Once upon a time I used to be like everyone else. I'm beautiful, but so are many people. It's like being left-handed or having freckles – it's just a fact. Plus I freely admit that the facials, the clothes and the instantly recognisable bobbed hair do a lot of the work for me. Seven years ago you wouldn't have looked at me twice on the street.

'Sit down,' Artie says, gesturing to a thin, angled leather couch in the centre of the room. There's an armchair opposite, for him, and a box of Krispy Kremes on a glass table.

I stare at the doughnuts and my stomach rumbles. I'm so hungry. I'm always hungry but I haven't eaten since yesterday lunchtime, unless you count the *maki* roll I had last night and the handful of popcorn – we watched a film before we went to bed. A film he'd made of us.

Tacky, I know. At the new memory of last night, I blush àgain, and my stomach rumbles with a sharp pain. Which is good. I hold onto that dragging, tightening feeling, the one you get when your stomach is crying out for food and you feel like you might faint. I hold it close, and smile brightly at Kerry, Artie's assistant.

'Can I get you something? Some coffee?'

'That'd be great. No milk. And some water, please. Thanks so much, Kerry. Your top is so cute!' I say, and she glows with pleasure.

'Thanks, it's from this totally—'

But Artie gestures that she should clear out, and Kerry's mouth snaps shut. She retreats immediately, still smiling. Artie sits down, and stuffs a doughnut into his mouth. I watch him. I watch the crystals of sugar on his chin, on his fingers, watch his gullet move as he swallows.

When he pushes the box towards me with the tiniest of movements, I say nothing. I shake my head and give a regretful smile, though he and I both know, of course, I'll never take a doughnut. It's a test. I hate him just a little bit then.

'So,' he says, wiping his fingers and slapping his big meaty hands onto his black pants. 'It's great to see you, right? Everything's good, isn't it? It's great!'

'It's great,' I repeat.

He leans forward. 'Honey. You're being too British. The foreign numbers are in for *The Girlfriend*. We've already done forty million dollars – last week domestic gross was twelve million. That's four weeks on! It's killing everything else. It beat Will freakin' Smith! You are back on top, baby. Back on top.'

'Well, it's the movie, not me,' I say. This isn't really true. *The Bride and Groom*, my breakthrough, was a really good film. Since then I think it's been the law of diminishing returns, like *Legally Blonde* sequels. They're not terrible, just not amazing. It's not *Tootsie*: no one's going to be studying the script of *The Girlfriend* in film school any time soon.

'We're on top of the world, OK? Enjoy it.' His eyes linger on the doughnuts, and then he says, 'So, you got a couple of weeks off now? Gonna read some scripts, take some meetings? Because we need to get thinking about your next project after *The Bachelorette Party*, don't we? We're excited about that, aren't we? All good? You met up with Patrick yet?'

Artie put the deal together for *The Bachelorette Party*, the picture I'm due to start making in a few weeks. The male star, the director, the comedy-sidekick best friend, the scriptwriter and I are all agented by WAM. And Artie has got me a fantastic deal: I'm on a 20/20 – $20 million, 20 per cent of all revenues. If this film works, Artie will make a bomb.

'No,' I say. 'It's being fixed up.'

'OK. Well, you're gonna love Patrick, I promise you. He's a straight-up guy. Brilliant comedian. I think you two'll really get along.'

Patrick Drew is my co-star. He is a surfer dude with tatts who is always being photographed stoned or punching paparazzi. Last month they got him throwing up out of the side of a car, speeding along Santa Monica Boulevard. He's extremely hot, but dumb as a plank. Apparently, we're really lucky to get him because, you know, he's *authentic*.

Artie reaches forward for another doughnut. His large meaty fingers hover over the cardboard tray, touching the smooth, shiny caramel frosting of one, the plump slick of custard on the other. I close my eyes for a second, thinking about how the sweet, fluffy cream inside would taste on my tongue. *No. No. You fat bitch, no.*

'How about George?' Artie says heavily, and when I open my eyes his mouth is full and he's brushing sugar off his trim beard. 'You guys met last month, yes?'

'Yes. He's great.'

'George is a fucking great director.' Artie nods. 'The guy's a genius. You're lucky.'

'I know it. He is a genius. I'm very lucky.' I'm parroting it back to him.

Artie gives me a curious look. 'I'm glad you two are getting along. Tell me something—'

Kerry comes in with the coffee and the water. Artie nods at her then shakes his head, swivelling on his chair.

'Forget it.' He rubs his hands. 'What comes next, after you wrap on *The Bachelorette Party*. This is what we need to think about. The new Sophie Leigh Project, Fall 2013.'

Now's my moment. My palms are a bit sweaty. I rub them together. 'Actually, I've been wanting to talk to you about that.'

'Great!' Artie smiles happily.

I take a sip of the water 'Just . . . run some things past you.' I don't know why I feel nervous. It's crazy. I'm the A-Lister – a film with me in will always be a tent pole, something for the studios to prop up their profits with while they try out other, smaller, more interesting projects. 'I've had some ideas . . . been thinking about them for a while. I – wanted to find the right time to pitch them to you.'

Artie frowns. 'You shoulda told me. I'd have come over. Twenty-four/seven, Sophie, I'm always here. You're my number one priority.'

'It's OK, I've been crazy with promotional stuff,' I say. 'I only – I want us to think carefully about what we do next. I kind of want to move along a bit. Not make the same old film again.'

Artie nods violently. 'Me too, me too,' he says. 'Man, this is great, you're totally right! I totally agree.'

'Oh, good!'

'Sophie. You're a really talented actress. We have to make

16

sure we exploit that. Let me show you something.' He's still nodding. Then he stands up, strides to the other side of the huge office, picks up a pile of paper.

My gaze drifts out the window. Downtown Beverly Hills gleams through the glass wall. It's a beautiful day. Of course it is. The purple-blue jacaranda trees are out all over LA; they stretch in a line down towards West Hollywood. It's spring. Not like spring at home in the UK though, where everything's lush and green and hopeful. In northern California the wild flowers litter the canyons and mountains along Route 101, and the fog clears earlier in the mornings and the surf frills the waves, but in LA spring is like any other season: more sunshine. It's the only time I miss home. I was never a country girl, but you couldn't live in Gloucestershire and not love the bulbs coming up, the wet black earth, the freshly minted green everywhere. Sometimes I wish—

A loud thud recalls me to my senses as Artie throws a script on the table in front of me. 'This,' he says. 'This will blow your mind.'

I look down at the title page. '*Love Me, Love My Pooch*', I read.

'Yes!' Artie's rubbing his hands. 'It's getting a lot of heat. Cameron's interested, but she's way too old. Universal want it for Reese but I heard she passed already. And some people say Carey Mulligan is super keen. So we need to move fast. Do you want to read it tonight?'

I'm still staring at the script. 'Carey Mulligan wants to star in *Love Me, Love My Pooch*?'

Artie nods, looking amazed. 'Sure, honey. Why not? You think – oh, wait, do you think it's, ah, kinda silly? The title?'

'A bit,' I admit, relieved. 'It's—'

'No problem!' He waves his hands. 'Listen. We can change that. The important thing is the material. And the material is fan. Tastic.'

'What's it about?'

'I heard it's *Legally Blonde* meets *Marley and Me*. Schlubby guy meets hot girl, hot girl not interested, schlubby guy uses

17

dog called Pooch to get hot girl. Girl falls for schlubby guy.' He laughs. 'Cute, huh? It's so cute!'

I hear myself say, 'Yeah! Sounds good.' Then I correct myself. 'What I mean, Artie, is – sure it'll be great, but I don't know.' I take a breath. 'I'd like to do a movie that's – uh. Maybe not about some girl hanging out for a boyfriend and being ditzy. Something a bit more interesting.'

Artie nods enthusiastically. He brushes sugar off the front of his black silk shirt. 'Great. Sure. I'm with you. Let's talk about it. I can see you want a change. You're not just a beautiful face. You've got so much talent.'

'Well . . . thanks.' I nod politely; I've learned to accept compliments over the years. Not that everyone agrees with him. The critics are . . . hmm, how shall I put this? Oh, yeah, VILE about my films; the more money I make the ruder they are. 'Sophie Leigh's Sweetener Overload,' the *LA Times* called my last movie.

'Listen, I don't want to play Chekhov or anything. I'm not one of those annoying actors who tries to prove themselves on Broadway.' I can hear my voice speeding up. 'It's that I don't always want to be playing someone who's a dippy girlie girl who gets drunk after one cocktail, who's obsessed with weddings and babies and has a mom and dad with funny one-liners who live in the suburbs.'

There's a pause, as Artie tries to unpick what I'm saying. 'I guess you're right.' The smile has faded from his eyes and he's silent for a moment, tapping one foot against the coffee table. 'We don't want to get into a *Defence: Reload* situation,' he continues, suddenly. 'You're back on top. We shouldn't jeopardise that, Sophie, that's totally true.'

'No way,' I say warmly. Though I hadn't said anything of the sort, he's right. 'God, that was terrible.'

'Listen.' He grabs my hands. 'You were great in it! Astonishing! It's just America's not ready for you to do martial arts action.' He shrugs. 'Or hipster mumbly independent shit. You're with me now, OK? I am never gonna let you make the same mistake.'

18

'Sure.' Artie's right, as always. Anna was my old UK agent back from *South Street People*, the teenage soap that I had my first big role in. I left her after first *Goodnight LA*, the art-housey independent film I'd always wanted to make, disappeared without trace and then *Defence: Reload* totally bombed. Two flops in a row. Biiiiig mistake. Huge. As they say. I'm not made to wear leather and do high-kicks. The film was horrible and Anna was useless about it – everything seemed to take her by surprise and she'd flap and cry down the phone. It was time for a change. I went with Artie, and he put me in *Wedding of the Year*, and it spent three weeks at number one and was the fifth-biggest grossing picture of 2009. Anna understood I had to move. It's all part of the game – we're still friends. (Translation: I sent her a gift basket. We're not friends.)

'I'm not talking about doing another *Defence: Reload*,' I say. 'But . . . well, I don't always have to be the daffy girl who loses her engagement ring, do I? Look at that pile. There has to be something in there.'

Artie gets up. 'You don't want to see everything, trust me. Here's the highlights.'

He flicks the list over to me.

Bridezilla. Boy Meets Girl. Bride Wars 2. Two Brides One Groom. I glance down the list, the same words all leaping out and blurring into one huge inkjet mush of confetti. I turn the page. 'This is the rest of the scripts I'm getting sent?'

'Yeah, but you don't need to worry about that. These are not projects to take seriously.'

I scan the second and third pages. *Pat Me Down. She's So Hot Right Now. From Russia with Lust.* 'What's *My Second-Best Bed*?' I say wearily.

Artie takes the piece of paper off me and looks at the list. 'No idea,' he says. He gets up and goes over to his glass desk, taps something into his computer. 'Hold on. Oh, yeah. It's some time-slip comedy. They sent it to you because . . . there was some note with it. I remember reading it but I can't remember it. I think it was because you can do a British accent.'

'Well – yes,' I say. 'They're right there. What is it?'

'*Second-Best Bed* . . .' His finger strokes the mouse. '*Second-Best* – oh, yeah, here it is. She's a guide at Anne Hathaway's cottage and she dreams Shakespeare comes and visits her.' Artie shakes his head, then turns to the shelf behind him, picking a script out of a pile. 'Who'd wanna guide people round Anne Hathaway's cottage? Why's Anne freaking Hathaway living in a cottage anyways? She just got a place in TriBeCa. I don't understand, that's crazy.'

'Anne Hathaway was Shakespeare's wife,' I say. 'That's who they mean. Her house was outside Stratford-upon-Avon.' I've been to Anne Hathaway's cottage about three times. It was a short coach drive from my school. Closer than the nearest Roman fort or working farm, so our crappy school used to take us there every year – it was almost a joke. I remember one year Darren Weller escaped from the group and ran into the forest. They had to call the police. Darren Weller's mum came to meet the coach. She screamed at Miss Shaw, the English teacher, like it was her fault Darren Weller was a nutcase. I can picture that day really clearly. Donna and I went to McDonald's in Stratford and drank milkshakes – simply walked off while the others were going round his house or something. It's the naughtiest thing I've ever done.

It's funny – I never thought Donna and I would lose touch. We stopped hanging out so much when I moved to London for *South Street People*, then she had a baby. She wasn't best pleased when I told her I was off to Hollywood. I don't think she ever really believed I wanted to be an actress. She thought it was all stupid, that Mum was pushing me into it.

'OK, OK.' Artie isn't interested. 'Take them, read them through if you want. But will you do me a favour?' He puts his hand on his chest and looks intently at me. 'Will you read *Love Me, Love My Pooch* for me? As a personal favour? If you hate it, no problem. Of course!' He laughs. 'But I want to see what you think. They're offering pretty big bucks . . . I have a feeling about this one. I think it could be your moment. Take you Sandy–Jen big. That's the dream, OK?

20

And I'm working on it for you.' He takes his hand off his chest, and gives me the script, solemnly. 'Now, tell me what picture you'd like to make. Let's hear it. Let's make it!' He claps his hands.

I'm still clutching the pile of scripts, with *Love Me, Love My Stupid Pooch* on the top. I clear my throat, nervously.

'I want to . . . This is going to sound stupid, OK? So bear with me. You know I moved house last year?'

'Sure do, honey. I found you the contractors, didn't I?'

'Of course.' Artie knows everyone useful in this town. 'You know why I bought that house?'

'This is easy. Because you needed a fuck-off huge place means you can tell the world you're a big star. "Look at me! Screw you!"' Artie chuckles.

'Well, sure,' I say, though actually I don't care about that stuff that much the way some people do. I've got a lot of money, I give some of it away and I take care of the rest, I don't need to go nuts and start buying yachts and private islands. This was the place I always wanted. It's a beautiful thirties house, long, low, L-shaped, high up in the hills, kind of English meets Mediterranean, simple and well built. Blue shutters, jasmine crawling over the walls, Art Deco French doors leading out to a scallop-shaped pool.

I love it, but it has a special connection that means I love it even more.

'I bought the house because it belonged to Eve Noel. She lived there after her marriage.'

Artie's lying back against the couch. He scrunches up his face. 'Who? The . . . the movie star? The crazy one?'

'She wasn't crazy.'

Artie scratches his stomach. 'Well, she disappeared. She was huge, then she vanished. I heard she was crazy. Or dead. Didn't she die?'

'She disappeared,' I say. 'She's still alive. I mean, she must be somewhere. But no one knows where. She made those seven amazing films, she was the biggest star in the world for five years or so, and then she vanished.'

'OK, so what?' Artie puts his hands behind his head.

'I want to make a film about her.'

From my bag I pull out a battered copy of *Eve Noel and the Myth of Hollywood*, the frustratingly slim biography of her that ends in 1961. I must have read it about twenty times. 'So . . . it'd be a film about where she came from, about her starting out in Hollywood, what happened to her, why she left.'

'I never knew you were into Eve Noel. Old movies.' Artie makes it sound like I've told him I love anal porn.

'Sure,' I say. 'My whole childhood was spent on the sofa watching videos. It's a wonder I don't have rickets – I never saw the sun.'

Artie grunts. He doesn't much like funny women. 'So why the big obsession with her?'

'She's the best. The last real Hollywood star. And she . . . She grew up near me, a little village near Gloucester?' I can hear the edge of the West Country accent creep into my voice, and I stutter to correct it. 'It's crazy, no one knows what happened to her, why she left LA.'

The first time I saw *A Girl Named Rose*, I was ten. I remember we had a new three-piece suite. It was squeaky, because Mum didn't want to take off the plastic covers in case it spoiled. I was ill with flu that knocked me out for a week and I lay on the sofa under an old blanket and watched *A Girl Named Rose*, and it changed my life. I never thought about being an actress before then, even though Mum had been one, or tried to, before I was born, but after I saw that film it was all I wanted to do. Not the kind Mum wanted me to be, with patent-leather shoes and bunches, a cute smile, parroting lines to TV directors, but the kind that did what Eve Noel did. I'd sit on the sofa while Mum talked on the phone or had her friends over, and Dad worked in the garage – first the one garage, then two, then five, so we could afford holidays in Majorca, a new car for Mum, a bigger house, drama school for me. The world would go on around me and I'd be there, watching *Mary Poppins* and *Breakfast at Tiffany's*, anything with Elizabeth

Taylor, all the old musicals, *Some Like It Hot* . . . you name it, but always coming back to Eve Noel, *A Girl Named Rose*, *Helen of Troy*, *The Boy Next Door*. I even cut out pictures of my favourite films and made a montage in my room: Julie Andrews running across the fields; Vivien Leigh standing outside Tara; Audrey Hepburn whizzing through Rome with Gregory Peck; Eve Noel walking down the road smiling, hands in the pockets of her flared skirt.

Everyone else at school thought I was weird. It was weird, probably. But Eve Noel and that film opened a world up for me. It seemed magical. It isn't, any more, and I should know. Back then it was all about glamour and artifice, these gods and goddesses deigning to appear on a screen for us. Whereas I know what it's like now. It's a business, less profitable than online poker, but a profitable business still, until the Internet kills it totally dead.

Mum and I used to drive past Eve Noel's old house. It's in ruins now. It's funny – everyone knows that's where a film star grew up. But no one knows the film star any more, or even where she is now. Her last picture was *Triumph and Tragedy*, in 1961, and it was a big flop. There's a picture of her at the Oscars, the year she didn't win and her husband did. She's smiling, so lovely, but she doesn't look right. Her eyes are odd, I can't describe it. And then – nothing.

I try and explain all this to Artie. He nods enthusiastically. 'Give me the pitch then,' he says.

'The pitch?'

He's grinning. 'Come on, Sophie. You know it's you, but you're gonna have to get some big guys to put big money up if you want this thing made. Give me the one-line pitch.'

'Oh . . .' I clear my throat. 'Kind of . . . *A Star is Born* meets . . . um . . . *Rebecca*? Because the house burns down. I suppose maybe it's more *The Player* set in the fifties meets *A Star is Born*, or—'

'*Boorrring!!*' Artie buzzes. My head snaps up – I'm astonished.

'Listen,' he says. 'You are my number one client. You are

23

so important to me. This could be amazing. I'm talking Oscar-amazing. But it could be career suicide. Again. And you can't afford that. Again.'

He stands up again and pats his stomach. 'I'm a pig. I'm a pig! Listen to me, sweetheart. Go home. Think up a great pitch. We have to get this thing made.'

'Really?' I stand up, stumbling slightly.

'Really. But you're totally right. If we can't do it properly we should forget all about it.'

'That's not—'

'And you'll read the dog script? For me? Think about who'd be good, who you'd like to work with?' I must have nodded, because he gives a big smile. 'Thank you so much. Take the other scripts. Read them. I wanna know what you think of them all. I'm interested in your opinion. Sophie Leigh Brand Expansion. We're big, we need to go bigger, and you're the one who's gonna lead us there. *Capisce*?'

'Thanks, Artie,' I say, aware that something is slipping from my grasp but unsure of how to take it back. 'But also the Eve Noel project, let's think—'

'Sure, sure!' He pats me on the back and squeezes my shoulder. 'I think with the right project and a good writer we could have something wonderful. And listen, I spoke to Tommy, did he tell you?' I shake my head. Tommy's my manager, and he rings Artie roughly ten times a day with ideas, most of which Artie rejects. 'It's fantastic news!'

'What?'

'He tested the line we discussed for the Up! Kidz Challenge Awards on a focus group and it came back great. So that's what you're saying. OK? Wanna give it a try, for old times' sake?'

I smile obligingly, hold up my bare left hand, then scream, 'I LOST MY RING!!!'

This is the line I'm famous for, from *The Bride and Groom*. It's a cute film actually, about a wedding from the girl's point of view: bitchy bridesmaids, rows with parents – and from the guy's point of view: problems at work, a bachelor party that ends in disaster. The bride, Jenny, loses her ring halfway through in a cake shop, and that's what she screams. I don't say it often, because I don't want to have a catchphrase. Tommy would sell dolls that scream 'I LOST MY RING' and T-shirts by the dozen if I let him. I don't let him.

'Wonderful. Just wonderful.' Artie's clutching his heart. I push my sunglasses back down over my eyes.

'It's good to see you,' I say, hugging him. 'We'll talk soon. When are the awards?'

'Two weeks. Ashley will brief you. So you're OK? You know you're going with Patrick, yes?'

I hesitate. 'Well, and George,' I say. 'A bonding night out before we start shooting.'

'George? OK.'

I match him stare for stare and as I look at him I realise he knows.

'George is a great director.' For once Artie's not smiling. His tanned face droops, like a hound dog. His beady eyes rake over me.

'I know he is,' I say slowly.

'That's all.' He turns away. 'That's all I'm gonna say. OK?'

I can imagine what's going on in his mind. *If she's banging George, they'll be making trouble on set. Patrick Drew's gonna get difficult about his close-ups as it'll all be on her. George'll dump her halfway through and start fucking someone else and she'll go schizoid. This is a disaster.*

I know it's nothing serious, me and George. He's A-list, so am I; we won't squeal on each other. He's way older than I am, he's been around. Plus I don't need a relationship at the moment, neither does he. If we screw each other once a week, what's the harm?

Artie chews something at the back of his mouth, rapidly, for a few seconds, then claps his hands. 'OK, we'll regroup afterwards about your Eve Noel idea. I like it, you know. If not for you then someone. Maybe you're right! Could be big . . .' He pauses. 'Hey, you should be a producer.'

He laughs, and I laugh, then I wonder why I'm laughing.

Me, in a suit, putting the finance on a movie together, all of
that. Then I think . . . no. That's not for me, I couldn't do
that. I'm too used to being the star – it's true isn't it?

'Read the scripts, think it over,' he says, as I leave the room.
'Then we'll talk.'

CHAPTER THREE

AS I EXIT the building, I'm still thinking about Darren Weller and the day we went to Stratford, me and Donna escaping to McDonald's. I'm smiling at the randomness of this memory, walking through the glass lobby of WAM, clutching this bunch of scripts, and suddenly—

'*Ow!*' Someone's bumped into me. 'Fuck,' I say, rubbing my boob awkwardly and trying to hold onto the scripts, because she got me with her elbow and it is painful.

This girl grips my arm. 'I'm so sorry,' she says, her eyes huge. 'Oh, my gosh, that was totally my fault. Are you OK—?' She looks at me and laughs. 'Oh, no! That's so weird. Sophie! Hi! I didn't recognise you with your shades on.'

I'm trying not to rub my boob in public. I can see T.J. waiting by the car right outside. 'Hi there,' I smile. 'Have a great day!'

'You don't remember me, do you?'

I stare at her. Who the hell is she? 'No, I'm sorry,' I say, beaming my big megawatt smile and going into crazy-person exit-strategy mode. 'But, it's great to meet you, so—' She's still grinning, although she looks nervous, and something about her eyes, her smile, I don't know, it's familiar. 'Oh, my God, of course,' I say impulsively. I push my sunglasses up onto my head. 'It's . . .'

I search my memory, but it's blank. The weird thing is, she looks like *me*.

'Sara?' she says hesitantly. 'Sara Cain. From Jimmy Samba's.' She's still smiling. 'It's been so long. It's really fine.'

I stare at her, and the memory leads me back, illuminating the way, as scenes light up in my mind from that messy, golden summer.

'Sara Cain,' I say. 'Oh, my gosh.'

Back in 2004 I starred in a sweet British romcom, *I Do I Do*, during a break in *South Street People*'s shooting schedule. It did really well, better than we all expected, and LA casting agents started asking to see me, so I went out to Hollywood again the following summer. That was when Donna and I kind of fell out, actually; she told me it was a big mistake and I was in over my head.

She was wrong, as it turns out. It was a great time. I was young, didn't have anything to lose, and I thought it was pretty crazy that I was there anyway, to be honest. Jimmy Samba's was the frozen-yoghurt place on Venice Beach where my roommate Maritza worked and we all practically lived there: a whole gang of us, actors, writers, models, musicians, all waiting for that big break.

'Your twin, remember?' I stare at her intently. She gives a small, self-conscious giggle.

'Wow,' I say. 'The twins. Sara, I'm so sorry, of course I remember you.'

The thing about her was, we had a few auditions together, and every time people always commented on how similar we looked. She had a couple of pilots, and the last time I saw her it looked like things might be about to happen for her.

The sight of her is like hearing 'Hollaback Girl' – that was my song of that summer. Takes you totally back there to a time that I rarely think about now. It's gone and that's weird, because we were friends. Her dad was a plastic surgeon, I remember that now, an old guy who'd done all the stars; I loved hearing her stories about him. She even came up to the rental house in Los Feliz, her and some of the gang, after I moved out of Venice. But it was an uncomfortable evening. Sara especially was weird. And even though I called her and a few others a

28

couple of times afterwards, no one returned my calls. Turns out we weren't all friends, just people in similar situations, and I didn't belong in that gang, the clique of hopefuls. I'd passed onto the next stage, and they didn't want to know me any more.

Now I try to look friendly. 'That's so cool, bumping into you here. How's it going? Who are you here to see?'

She doesn't understand and then smiles. 'Oh. I'm not acting these days.' My face is blank. She smiles again, a little tightly. 'I – work here? I'm Lynn's assistant? She's in the same department as Artie.'

'I know Lynn,' I say. 'OK, so . . .' I trail off, embarrassed.

'It's fine,' she says, nodding so her perky ponytail bounces behind her. 'It's totally fine. Guess some of us have it and some of us don't. I don't miss the constant rejection, for sure. That time they told me no when I walked in the room, you remember that?'

I screw up my face. 'Oh . . . oh, yeah, I remember. What was it for?'

'It was *The Bride and Groom*, Sophie.' She grins. 'You *should* remember, we were totally hungover from being up all night drinking Bryan's tequila?'

'Oh, my God,' I say, shifting my bag onto my other shoulder. 'That night.'

'Some of us get the right haircuts at the right time, you mean!' Sara smiles, and says suddenly, 'That was a totally insane evening, wasn't it? You getting that bob, like . . . who was it? Eve Noel?' She looks at my hair. 'Still rocking it, right? You always said those bangs got you the part – maybe that's what it took!' She stops, and then looks alarmed. 'Sorry,' she says, flushing. 'I mean, of course . . . you're so good as well, you totally deserve it!'

'No way. I was probably drunk,' I said. 'I'd never have got that bob if I hadn't been totally bombed. I owe Bryan . . . it was Bryan, wasn't it?'

She nods. 'It was.'

My memory is so shit, it's terrible. Maybe the tequila

drowned my brain cells, because they were kind of crazy times. We behaved pretty badly, we didn't have anything to lose. I was still seeing Dave, my boyfriend back in London who I met on *South Street People*, but I knew he was cheating on me by then. (Turns out he was cheating on me about 80 per cent of the time we were together anyway.) It's the only slutty period of my life; maybe everyone has to have a summer like that. I'd always worked so hard and all of a sudden it was so easy. America was easy. Sunshine, friendly people, and I was young. I lived for the ocean, the cafe, the bars and the crowd I hung out with.

I loved acting, but I never thought I'd make it, to be honest. I knew I wasn't as talented as someone like Sara, knew I wasn't trained. I didn't know anything about stagecraft or method; I turned up and said the lines the best way I could. Still do, I think. I'd already got further with my career than I'd ever expected to without Mum by my side all the time, and I suppose I thought I'd ride it for as long as I was allowed to. They'd find me out and I'd be sent home and so for the time being, I reasoned, I should hang loose and enjoy myself – and for once, I really, really did.

I stroke my forehead and fringe, trying to remember. 'Bryan. He was hot, wasn't he? Kind of Ashton Kutcher-y.'

She smiles. 'That's him.'

'I think I slept with him,' I muse.

'Yeah, I know,' she says, then she adds, 'You know, I went out with him for a while. Maybe we *are* twins!'

There's an awkward pause. Sara clears her throat, and stares at me after a moment. 'Sorry,' she says. 'I'm being weird. But it's really good to see you, that's all. I never returned your calls. I suppose I was jealous. Brings back those days and it's crazy, remembering how it used to be, I guess.'

'You were really good,' I say, changing the subject. She looks uncomfortable, but I press her. 'Have you totally left it behind? That's a real shame.'

Sara knits her fingers together. 'Yeah. At my last audition, this guy, the director I think it was, stared at me and said,

"This girl's just an uglier Sophie Leigh. Next, please."' She's smiling as she says this, but there's an awful expression in her eyes. 'That's what made me give it up.'

'That . . . that sucks, Sara.' We're silent. I sling my bag over my shoulder again and as the silence stretches on, and Sara says nothing, blurt, 'So, Bryan! What's he doing now?'

'Bryan moved to New York. He has his own salon now – he's doing really well.' She recovers her smile again. 'Hey, I'm super happy for him. And for you! You totally deserve your success, Sophie! It's not only about the bob, so don't believe people who tell you it is!'

'Uh – thanks.' Maybe it's time to go. 'Great to see you, Sara.' I wave to T.J., my driver.

Sara calls after me, 'You look so great, Sophie. Sorry again!'

I stride out, smiling at another WAM minion who glows when she spots me and at the doorman as I exit the building, momentarily catching the wall of fierce afternoon heat.

I climb into the car, sinking into my seat. T.J. has got me a diet root beer and some carrot and celery sticks, and there's even a packet of crisps (which I'll never eat, of course), all nicely laid out in the back. Chips, I should say. I'm mostly American these days, but some things never feel right. Chips are the chips you have with fish and burgers.

'Mulberry sent you over some new stuff to pick out. Tina was unpacking it when I left and she told me to tell you,' T.J. says. He pulls the limo away from the kerb.

'Get Tanisha to come over.' Tanisha is T.J.'s daughter.

'I'll call her. That's kind of you. She did well on her test yesterday, Sophie, I'm real pleased with her.'

A thought occurs to me. 'Did Deena arrive yet?'

'I don't know,' T.J. says firmly. 'She wasn't there when I left.' He switches topic. 'So how's your day going?'

I have to think for a moment. 'Not sure.' Now we're gliding away from WAM, I recall what I wanted to say to Artie, and what in my hungover state I actually said. I said I would read that stupid script. I didn't really get to talk about Eve Noel, the film I want to make one day, the mystery about her that

31

I still don't understand. Not because it's complicated, because that's obvious. But because she was new in town once like I was, and it must have started out OK for her. And I don't know what happened to her, *no one* seems to know or care. I'm on every billboard in town but she was the last great film star, to my mind. Hollywood is about extremes, as someone once said. You're either a success or a failure, there's no in-between.

We're turning into Sunset, right by the Beverly Hills Hotel, and I glance over at the white italic scrawl, the palm trees that reach up to the endless blue. I pull my sunglasses on and lie back against the soft leather. For a few minutes I can be still. Don't have to worry about that wrinkle on my forehead, that bulge in my stomach, that crappy script, that feeling all the time that someone else, someone better, should be living my life, not me.

the avocado tree
Los Angeles, 1956

'NOW, MY DEAR,' Mrs Featherstone whispered to me as we entered the crowded room. 'Don't forget. Call everyone Mr So-and-So and be simply fascinated, no matter what they say. You understand?'

'Yes, Mrs Featherstone,' I answered obediently.

She put her hand on my back and smiled mechanically. 'And remember, what are you called?'

'Eve Noel.'

'That's it. Good girl. Your name's Noel now. Don't forget.'

Her thumb dug into my shoulder blade. I could feel the side of her ring pushing into my flesh and involuntarily I stepped away, then smiled politely, looking around the room.

It was a beautiful old mansion house in Beverly Hills; at least it looked old, though they told me afterwards it had only been finished last year. At the grand piano a vaguely familiar man sat playing 'All the Things You Are' and my skin prickled with pleasure: I loved that song. I had danced to it only two weeks ago, on our clapped-out gramophone in Hampstead. Already it seemed like a lifetime ago.

Mr Featherstone was at the bar, shaking hands, clapping

33

shoulders. When he saw his wife, he nodded mechanically, excused himself and came over.

'Hey,' he said, nodding at his wife, ignoring me. 'OK.' He turned to the three men standing in a knot beside us, and grasped the hand of the first one.

'Hey, fellas, I want you to meet someone. This is Eve Noel. She just arrived from London, England. She's our new star.' His arm was around my waist, his fingers pressed tightly against the black velvet. I wanted to shrink away.

Each man balanced his cigarette in the cut-crystal ashtray, then turned to shake my hand. I had no idea who they were. The third, younger, man narrowed his eyes, and turned away towards the piano player to ask him something. The first man smiled, kindly I thought. 'When did you get here, Eve?'

'Two weeks ago,' I said.

'Where are you staying?' He smoothed his thinning hair across his shiny pate, an automatic gesture.

'She's at the Beverly Hills Hotel at the moment, and Rita is chaperoning her where necessary,' Mr Featherstone said before I could speak. He cleared his throat importantly. 'Eve is our Helen of Troy, we're announcing it next week.'

'Good for you,' said the second man. 'Louis, you dark horse. You swore you'd got Taylor.'

'We went a different way. We needed someone . . . fresh, you know. Elizabeth's a liability.' His hand tightened on my waist and he smiled.

'That's great, that's great,' said the first man. 'So – you got what you wanted from RKO, Louis? I heard they wouldn't give you the budget.'

He and the second man smirked at each other. 'Oh,' said Mr Featherstone. He flashed them a quick, automatic smile. 'Hey, we all make mistakes, don't we.' His voice faltered. 'But they're coming around. We'll start principal photography in a couple of weeks – we don't need the money right now. It's only that – well, fellas, this thing is going to be huge, and I'd like a little extra, you know? I've been thinking, a big studio might like to share some costs. I assure you, they'd get more than their share back. MGM and David O. Selznick, ring any bells?' He winked at the first man, as though trying to make him complicit in something. 'But let's not talk business in front of Miss Noel.'

'Of course,' said the second man. He was short and greying where the first man was short and fat with black hair; they looked similar, and it occurred to me suddenly they must be brothers. 'How do you find LA, Miss Noel?'

'Oh,' I said. I moved away from Mr Featherstone's hand. 'I think it's wonderful.'

'Wonderful, eh?'

'Oh, yes, wonderful.' I could hear myself: I sounded dull and stupid.

He laughed. 'How so?'

'Oh, the . . .' I couldn't think of how to explain it. 'The sunshine and the palm trees, and the people are so friendly. And there's as much butter as you like in the mornings.'

He and his companions laughed; so did Mr and Mrs Featherstone, a second or two later.

'I'm from London,' I said.

'No,' the first man said, faux-incredulous. 'I would never have guessed.'

I could feel myself blushing. 'Well, it's only – we had rationing until really quite recently. It's wonderful to be able to eat what you want.'

'Now, dear!' Mrs Featherstone said. 'We don't want you talking about food all night to Joe and Lenny, do we! They'll worry you're going to ruin that beautiful figure of yours.' Again the thumb, jabbing into my back.

'Oh, no!' I tried to smile. As with everything else here I was constantly trying to work out what the rules were; I always felt I was saying the wrong thing.

'I'm sure that would never happen.' I jumped. The third man, who'd not yet spoken, had turned back from the piano and was eyeing me up and down, like a woman scanning a mannequin in a shop window. He smiled, but it was almost as though he were laughing. 'You look as if you were born to be a star,' he said.

35

It was all so ridiculous, in a sense. Me, Eve Sallis, a country doctor's daughter, who this time two months ago was a mousy drama student in London, sharing a tiny flat in Hampstead, worried about nothing so much as whether I could afford another cup of coffee at Bar Italia and what lines I had to learn for the next day's class: there I was, at a film producer's house in Hollywood, dressed in couture with a new name and a part in what Mr Featherstone kept referring to as 'The Biggest Picture You Will Ever See'. Tonight a beautician had curled my short black hair and caked on mascara and eyeliner, and I'd stepped into a black velvet Dior dress and clipped on a diamond brooch, and a limousine with a driver wearing a peaked hat had driven me here, though it was a 300-yard walk away and it felt so silly, when I could have trotted down the road. But no, everything was about appearance here. If people were to believe I was a star then I had to behave like a star. Mr Featherstone had spotted me in London. He had spent a great deal of money bringing me over and I had to act the part. It was a part, talking to these old men, exactly like Helen of Troy. And I wanted to play her, more than anything.

'Well, I'm Joseph Baxter,' said the first man, leaning forward to take my hand again. He really was quite fat, I noticed now. 'This is my brother Lenny, and this interesting specimen of humanity is Don Matthews. He's a writer.' He tapped the side of his nose. 'First rule of Hollywood, Miss Noel. Don't bother about the writers. They're worthless.'

The third man, Don, nodded at me, and I blushed. 'Hey there,' he said. He shook my hand. 'Well, let me welcome you to Hollywood. You're just in time for the funeral.'

'Whose funeral?' I asked.

They all gave a sniggering, indulgent laugh as a waiter came by with a tray. I took a drink, desperate for some alcohol.

Don smiled. 'Miss Noel, I'm referring to the death of the motion picture industry. You've heard of a little thing called television, even in Merrie Olde England, I assume?'

I didn't like the way he sounded as though he were poking fun, and the others didn't seem to notice. Nettled, I said, 'The

36

Queen's Coronation was televised, over four years ago, Mr Matthews. Most people I know have a television, actually.'

I sounded like a prig, like a silly schoolgirl. The three older men laughed again, and Mr Featherstone raised his eyebrows at the two brothers, as if to say, 'Look fellas, I told you so.' But Don merely nodded. 'Well, that's told me. I guess someone should tell Louis then, before he starts making The Biggest Picture You Will Ever See.'

Mr Featherstone looked furious; his red nostrils flared and his moustache bristled, actually bristled. I'd discovered in my whirlwind dealings with him that he had no love for a joke. I knew what Mr Matthews was talking about, though. Every film made these days seemed to be an epic, a biblical legend, a classical myth, a story with huge spectacle, as if Hollywood in its death throes were trying to say, 'Look at us! We do it better than the television can!'

'We'll come by and meet with you properly,' Mr Featherstone told Joe and his brother. 'I'd like for you to get to know Eve. I think she's very special.'

'We should . . . arrange that.' Joe Baxter was looking me up and down once more. 'Miss Noel, I agree with Louis, for once. It's a pleasure to meet you.' He took my hand. His was large, soft like a baby's, and slightly clammy. He breathed through his mouth, I noticed. I wondered if it was adenoids. 'Yes,' he said to Mr Featherstone. 'Bring Miss Noel over, we'll have that meeting. Maybe we'll – ah, run into you again tonight.'

'Bye, fellas.' Don stubbed out his cigarette, and winked at me. 'Miss Noel, my pleasure. Remember to enjoy the sunshine while you're here. And the butter.'

He touched my arm lightly, then turned around and walked out of the door.

'Who was that?' I asked Mrs Featherstone, who was ushering me towards another group of short, suited, bespectacled men.

'Joe and Lenny Baxter? They're the heads of Monumental Films, have you really not heard of Monumental Films?'

'Of course, yes,' I said. 'I didn't realise. That's – gosh.' I cleared my throat, trying not to watch Don's disappearing form. 'And the writer – Don?'

'Oh, Don Matthews,' she said dismissively. 'Well, he's a writer. Like they say. I don't know what he's doing here, except Don always was good at gatecrashing a party. He drinks.'

'He wrote *Too Many Stars*,' Mr Featherstone said absently, watching the Baxter brothers as they walked slowly away, to be fallen upon by other guests. 'He's damn good, when he's not intoxicated.'

I gasped. '*Too Many Stars*? Oh, I saw that, it must have been four, five times? It's wonderful! He – he *wrote* it?'

'She's got enough people to memorise without clogging her brain up with nonentities like Don Matthews,' said Mrs Featherstone, as if I hadn't spoken. 'Who's next?'

'Well.' Mr Featherstone scanned the crowd. 'I wanted to get the Baxters, that's the prize. If I could put her in front of them they'd see—' He nodded at me, his expression slightly softening. 'Honey, you did very well. Make nice with the Baxters if you run into them again, OK? I want them to help us with the picture.'

It was hot, and the smell of lilies and heavy perfume was overwhelming, suddenly. 'May I be excused for a moment?' I heard myself say. 'I'd like to use the – er –'

'What? Oh, yes, of course.' Mr and Mrs Featherstone parted in alarm; any reference to reality or, heaven forbid, bodily functions, was abhorrent to them. I'd discovered this the evening I arrived in Los Angeles, tired, bewildered and starving after a flight from London that was exhilarating at first, then terrifying, then just terribly tiring. When we got to the hotel I'd said I felt I might be sick, and both of them had reared back as if I was carrying the bubonic plague.

I slipped through the crowd, past the ladies in their thick silk cocktail dresses, heavy diamonds and rubies and emeralds and sapphires on their honey skin, in their ears, on their fingers – and the gentlemen, all smoking, gathered in knots, talking in low voices. I recognised one ageing matinee idol, his once-black hair greying at the temples and his face puffy with drink, and a vivacious singer, whom I'd read about in a magazine only two weeks ago, nuzzling the neck of an old man who I knew wasn't her husband, a film actor. But they all had something in common, the guests: they looked as though they were Someone, from the piano player to the lady at the door with the ravaged, over-made-up face. The party was for a producer, thrown by another producer, to celebrate something. I never did find out what, but it was like so many parties I was to go to. It was the first of a template in my new life, though I didn't know it then. Old-fashioneds and champagne cocktails, delicious little canapés of chicken mousse and tiny cocktail sausages, always a piano player, the air heavy with smoke and rich perfume, the talk all – all, all, always the business. Films, movies, the pictures: there was only one topic of conversation.

It was early May. In London winter was over, though it had been raining for weeks by the time I left. But here it was sunny. It was always sunny, the streets lined with beautiful violet-blue blossoms. The air on the terrace outside was a little cooler and I stood there, relief washing over me, glad of the breeze and of this rare solitude. There was a beautiful shell-shaped pool, and I peered into the shimmering turquoise water, looking for something in the reflection. The trees lining the terrace were dark, heavy with a strange green fruit. Idly, I reached up and touched one, and it dropped to the ground, plummeting heavily like a ripe weight. I picked it up, terrified lest anyone should see, and held it. It was shiny, nobbly. I turned it over in my hand.

'It's an avocado,' a voice behind me said.

I jumped, inhaling so sharply that I coughed, and I looked at the speaker. 'Hello, Mr . . .' I stared at him blankly, wildly.

'It's Don. Don't worry about the rest of it. You're very – er, polite, aren't you?' He finished his drink and put it down on a small side table. I watched him.

'What do you mean, "er, polite"?'

He wrapped his arms around his long lean body, hugging himself in a curiously boyish gesture. 'Oh, I don't know. I just met you. You're awfully on your guard. Like you're not relaxed.'

I wanted to laugh – how could anyone relax at an evening like this?

'I – I don't know,' I said. 'Back in London . . .'

But I didn't know how to explain it all. Back in London I was always late, I was always losing parts in class to Viola MacIntosh, I never had enough money for the electricity meter, or for a sandwich, and my flatmate Clarissa and I alternated sleeping in the bedroom with its oyster-coloured silk eiderdown that shed a light snowfall of feathers every time you moved in the night, or on the truckle bed in the sitting room, with the springs that pierced your sides, like a religious reproach for our sinful ways.

Whoever I was back then, I wasn't this person, this cool demure girl, and I knew I was always relaxed. This was my dream, wasn't it? Training to be an actress. And that's all I'd ever wanted to do since I was a little girl, playing dress-up with Mother's evening gowns from the trunk in her dressing room. First with Rose, then by myself after Rose died. There was a brief period during which my increasingly distant parents were concerned about my solitude enough to organise tea parties with other (suitable) children who lived nearby, but it never took. Either I wouldn't speak or I went and hid. A punishment to myself, you see. If I couldn't play with Rose, then I wouldn't play with anyone.

One night, when I was older, I had crept back downstairs to collect my book, and heard their voices in the parlour. I stood transfixed, the soles of my feet stinging cold on the icy Victorian tiled floor. And I remember what my father said.

'If she's as good as they say she is, we can't stand in her way, Marianne. Perhaps it's what the girl needs. Bring her out of her shell. Teach her how to be a lady, give up this nonsense of pretending Rose is still here.'

My father, so remote from me, so careworn. I looked down at the avocado in my hand. I found it so strange to think of him and Mother now. What would they make of it all? How would I ever describe this to them? But I knew I wouldn't. When I'd left the cold house by the river eighteen months previously to take up my place at the Central School of Speech and Drama it was as though we said our goodbyes then. I wrote to them and of course I had let them know about my trip to California. But I was nearly twenty. I didn't need them any more. I don't know that I ever had, for after Rose died we eventually shrank inwards, each to his or her own world: my father his surgery, my mother her work in the parish church, and I to my own daydreams, playing with the ghost of Rose, acting out fantasies that would never come true.

Mr Featherstone had called my parents himself, to explain who he was. 'Funny guy, your old pop,' he'd said. 'Seemed to not give a fig where you were.'

I couldn't explain that it was normal for me. I was alone, really, and I had been for years; I'd learnt to live that way.

I felt a touch on my arm, and I looked up to find Don Matthews watching me. He said, 'It's a culture shock, I bet, huh?'

'Something like that.'

He smiled. He had a lopsided grin that transformed his long, kind face. I watched him, thinking abstractly what a nice face it was, how handsome he looked when he smiled. 'It's also . . .' I took a deep breath, and said in a rush, 'Don't think me ungrateful, but I feel a bit like a prize camel. With three humps. Mr Featherstone and his wife are very kind, but I'm never sure if I'm saying what they want me to say.'

'They don't want you to say anything. They want you to look pretty and smile at the studio guys in the hope that they'll give Louis some money to finance the picture. Oh, they say the studios are dying a slow death, but there's no way Louis will be able to make *Helen of Troy* without a lot more money than he's got.' He reached out to the tree and twisted off another avocado. 'A camel with three humps, huh? Well, you look fine from where I'm standing.' He took a penknife out of his pocket, and sliced the thin dark green skin to reveal the creamy green flesh inside, then scooped some and handed it to me. Our fingers touched. I ate it, watching him.

'It's delicious,' I said. 'Like velvet. And nuts.'

'It's perfectly ripe,' he said. 'Enjoy it, my dear.'

I nodded, my mind racing.

'What's your real name?' he said, his voice gentle. 'It's not Eve Noel, is it?'

I swallowed, blushing slightly at being thus exposed. 'Sallis. Eve Sallis.'

'Eve's a nice name.'

'I hate it. I wanted to—' I looked around, weighing up whether to take him into my confidence. 'I called myself Rose at drama school. Rose Sallis, not Eve. But Mr Featherstone liked Eve, so I'm Eve again.'

'Why Rose?'

My hands were clenched. 'It was my sister's name. She died when I was six.'

'I'm sorry,' said Don, his face still. 'You remember her at all?'

'Yes,' I said. 'Very clearly.' Then, in a rush, 'She drowned. In the river by our house. It was a strong current and she fell over.'

'That's awful. What the hell were you kids doing in there anyway?'

'It was only her,' I said, and I blinked. 'We weren't allowed. I was chicken.'

'But she wasn't.' His tone was even, not judgemental.

'Rose was . . . naughty. Very wild. They said it was dangerous, there's a weir upstream and the current's too strong. But she never listened.' I scrunched my face up. 'I can see her if I really concentrate. She was older than me, and she'd get so furious with them, shouting, screaming, and sometimes she'd play dead . . . I thought she was playing dead that time, you see, and I left her to get help, and it was too late . . .'

It felt so good to be talking about something close to me, to share a piece of my real self with someone, instead of this artifice all the time. Don watched me, a sympathetic expression in his kind dark eyes.

'You must miss her.'

'Every day. She was my idol, my sister.' My shoulders slumped. 'And they never let me see her afterwards, to say goodbye, you see. I . . .' I shook my head. 'I used to go over everything we did together in my head. So I'd remember. I didn't have anyone else, you see. She – she was my best friend.'

'So Rose was like a tribute to her.' Don sliced another piece of avocado, watching me. 'That's nice.'

'Nice is such a little word, isn't it,' I said after a moment's silence. He raised his eyebrows.

'You're right, Miss Noel. It's not nice. Well, I'm sorry again. Rose, huh? Maybe I should call you Rose.'

'OK,' I said, sort of laughing, because it was a strange conversation, yet I felt more comfortable with him than anyone that night.

'OK, Rose.' I liked how it sounded when he said it.

'Can you tell me something?'

'Of course, Rose. What did you want to know?'

The noise from the party inside washed over towards us. A shriek of hilarity, the sound of men laughing, the distant ringing of a bell.

'What happens if I don't stay quiet?' I said. 'What about if I tell them I've made a mistake and I want to go home?'

'Do you think that?'

I breathed out. 'Um – no.' My throat felt tight all of a sudden. 'I'm not sure. It's been two weeks and . . .' I swallowed. 'This is stupid. I'm homesick, I suppose. It's such a different world.'

The sky above us was that peculiar electrifying deep blue, just before the moon appears. He took my hand. His skin was warm and his fingers on mine strangely comforting, even though he was a stranger. 'Hey,' he said. 'Look at the stars above you.' I looked up. 'And the fruit on the trees, the smell of money in the air. You're in California. You were chosen to come here. You're going to star in what could be the biggest picture of the year. I know Louis can come off as a jerk, but he knows what he's doing, trust me.' He shrugged. 'This is the break thousands of girls dream about.'

'I know,' I said. I wished I could put my head on his shoulder. I could smell tobacco and something else on his jacket, a woody,

43

comforting smell. 'And I can't go home. The thought of going back to London with my tail between my legs. And seeing my parents – explaining to them.' I stood up straight. 'I have to get on with it. Stiff upper lip, and all that.'

'You British,' he said. He released my hand. 'Where's home, then?'

How did I explain I didn't really have a home? 'Oh, it's a village in the middle of the countryside. But I was at drama school, in London. I was living in a place called Hampstead. That was really my home.'

'I've always wanted to go to Hampstead. Oh, yes,' Don said, smiling at my surprise. 'My father was a teacher. Taught me every poem Keats ever wrote.' I must have looked completely blank, because he said, 'Keats lived in Hampstead, you little philistine. I thought you Brits grew up on the stuff.'

I shrugged. 'He didn't write plays. I like playwrights.'

Don leaned his lanky body against the tree, sliced a little more avocado, and said, 'How about screenwriters?'

I smiled. 'I like them too, I suppose.'

'I'm glad to hear it,' he replied.

'There you are, Eve.' Mr Featherstone came waddling out onto the terrace. 'I was wondering where you'd got to.'

'I'm so sorry,' I said guiltily. 'I met Don – Mr Matthews – again, and we were—'

'I was monopolising your star,' Don said smoothly. 'I should let you go.'

'No, I don't want to interrupt,' Mr Featherstone said genially, wiping his moist brow with a handkerchief. 'Eve, I wanted you to meet the head of publicity for Monumental, Moss Fisher. He's a great guy, and if he likes you too I really think the Monumental deal's in the bag.' He smiled at me. 'Joe Baxter liked you, honey. Really liked you. He wants us to go out to dinner with him. So I'm gonna take you to meet Moss now and then we're going to Ciro's. You'll love it.' He looked at Don. 'Won't she, Don?'

'Depends,' Don said. 'But yes, I think she might like it. If she makes up her mind it's what she wants.'

The shade from the tree was black. I couldn't see his face. 'Well,' I said. 'Goodbye – and thank you.'

'It was my pleasure,' he said. 'Hey, do something for me, will you? Try and enjoy it.'

He moved away and I suddenly realised I might not see him again. I don't know why but I called after him, 'I loved *Too Many Stars*. It's my favourite film.'

He stopped and turned around, one half of his slim body golden in the light from the hallway, the party. 'Thank you,' he said. 'Thank you, Rose.'

He disappeared through the door and then he was gone.

'Did you tell Don Matthews to call you Rose?' Mr Featherstone said, a note of displeasure in his voice as he steered me back inside. 'Why would you do that?'

'I – it's – oh, we were having a joke.' But then the guilt I always felt deepened some more, as though I thought Rose was something to joke about. 'I'm sorry, I won't do it again,' I said, more to myself than to him.

'It takes time to learn these things,' he said. 'You've done very well, my dear.' His eyes ranged over my dress again. 'Now, here's Mr Baxter. And Mr Fisher. Be nice. Moss, hey! This is the little lady I was telling you about. Eve dear, this is Moss Fisher.'

Out of the shadows stepped another man, thin and even shorter than the Baxters. His thick curling hair was smoothed down with Brylcreem or something that made it look wet. His dark eyes darted from side to side, then stared coldly at me. He nodded.

'Hi,' he said, to no one in particular.

'Hello, Mr Fisher,' I said politely.

He didn't acknowledge this, but turned to Joe Baxter. 'The teeth need fixing, Joe.'

'Yes, I know,' Mr Baxter said under his breath. 'Still though—'

'How old are you?' Moss Fisher asked, almost uninterestedly.

'I'm – I'm nearly twenty.'

He nodded. 'Maybe it's worth it,' he said. He shrugged. 'The hairline, too. It's awful but they can change it. Do a screen test. I'm going, Joe. See ya tomorrow.'

Joe Baxter rose a hand in farewell as Moss Fisher walked away.

'Don't mind Moss,' he said jovially. 'He's all business. A great guy, a great guy, isn't he, Louis?'

'Oh, yes,' said Mr Featherstone. He stared at my hair in annoyance. I put my hand up to my brow, self-conscious.

Behind me, Mrs Featherstone had brought my velvet cape. With a quick flick of her wrist she twisted it up and around my shoulders, and I screamed, and she jumped. Mr Baxter was standing behind the cape. 'Sorry,' I said, clutching my hand to my heart, which was thumping ridiculously. 'I didn't see you, Mr . . . Mr . . .' Suddenly I couldn't remember his surname. I smiled in what I hoped was a charming, apologetic way.

'It's Baxter,' he said, putting his watch into his pocket and offering me his arm. 'Come, my dear. We'll ride to Ciro's together. I'd like to show you my Rolls-Royce. All the way from England. Louis, we'll see you there?'

We left the party, and I remember it clearly now, to this day, how the waiter bowed and said, 'Goodnight, Mr Baxter, congratulations on *Eagles Fly North*,' and Joe Baxter ignored him. I don't think it was because he was a rude man. It was because he simply didn't notice people like waiters. It was as if they were completely invisible to him. He could only see two things: stars and power.

'Here we are,' said Mr Baxter as we approached a powder-blue Rolls-Royce, waiting on the kerb for us. A driver jumped out and opened the door. I looked around for the Featherstones, but I couldn't see them.

'Oh . . .' I said, and I must have sounded wary.

'I'm sorry,' said Mr Baxter, smoothing his hair over the top of his head again. 'They're getting a ride with Lenny.' He looked around. 'Would you feel more comfortable with them here too? Yes, you would.' He signalled to the driver. 'Go and find Mr Featherstone.'

'It's no problem, Mr Baxter,' I said. 'I just wanted to make sure they were coming too.'

'Of course,' he said. He held the door open. I climbed in and he followed me. 'I don't want to do the deal with you, now do I? Or are you telling me you have a head for figures too, as well as a figure that turns a man's head?'

I laughed; I couldn't help it, and I wondered what Clarissa would say if she heard him. But Clarissa was thousands of miles away, asleep. I knew tomorrow was Thursday, and she'd have vocal classes first thing in the morning. Making ridiculous vowel sounds, sitting cross-legged on the floor and pretending to be farm animals. That was what we'd done, the final class I'd taken, before I said goodbye to her, to my friends, and left them behind for ever.

The seats were huge, the butter-coloured leather soft, sewn with tiny powder-blue stitches that matched the outside paint. 'What a beautiful car,' I said politely, trying to sound normal. The two of us alone together in the back was rather strange.

Mr Baxter put his hands on his knees, and sat up straight, looking ahead. He muttered something under his breath. 'Thank you, dear. Now tell me, where are you from in England?'

I answered, as I'd been told to by Mr Featherstone, 'Warwickshire. Shakespeare country.'

'Very good. Your father's job?'

'He's a doctor,' I said. 'He's a very good doctor.' I don't know why I said this. I ran my fingers along the polished walnut interior, tracing the clover-shaped whorls of the wood. We drove off slowly, and my stomach lurched. I was hungry, or nervous, I didn't know which.

'Any brothers or sisters?'

'I had a sister. She died.'

He nodded, eyes still fixed straight ahead of him. 'Sad. Anything else?'

The spot in the river where Rose drowned was next to a willow tree. The trunk was hollow and almost dead, but there were green tendrils creeping off it and eventually they might make another whole tree. When I was little I used to think she lived inside it, that she'd just come back one day. I'd play by the tree, and talk to it, until Mother said I wasn't to any more. I said, 'Anything else? I—'

'Any stories we need to know, any secret marriages to unsuitable actor boyfriends, kids, anything that the fan magazines or the gossips can dig up on you?'

'No,' I said, shaking my head. It was so strange the way everyone in Hollywood wanted to know about the secret past lives I'd lived before I'd got here. I wasn't twenty till November. I'd done nothing with my life, really. I'd never been abroad, unless you counted holidays in Scotland. 'Nothing at all.'

'Nothing at all? You're not lying?'

'No,' I said. 'I'm very dull, I'm afraid.'

Mr Baxter said something, to himself this time. He turned to me. 'I would disagree, my dear,' he said, and he moved across the seat towards me. He put his hand on my knee, then slid the palm up my thigh. I remembered again his clammy, hot skin.

The strange thing is I didn't do anything. I was so surprised I sat there, bolt upright. He was such an odd man, with his black comb-over, his fat, unexpressive face, his strangely babyish expressions. I thought he must have made some kind of mistake. But then he reached out and, with the other hand, squeezed my breast, then stopped and made a snuffling noise. His fingers started scrabbling at the neckline of my dress, flickering under the velvet to try and worm their way towards my bare skin as all the time his other hand scratched at my underwear, under the skirt. I pushed him away, a short sharp action, and he fell back against the seat.

'Mr Baxter!' I said, thinking how high and stupid my voice sounded, and what a silly thing it was to say, like a heroine in a melodrama.

He was breathing heavily, and his eyes darted around, avoiding mine. He reached for me again, only this time his clammy, horrible hands were under my backside, and he pulled me further down so that I was half-lying with my head against the door, then he lifted my skirt and pushed it up over my hips. I screamed, in indignation more than anything else, but he put his hand over my mouth. I bit him, and I heard the snuffling noise again, as he started nibbling at my ear, my neck, my jaw, with slippery wet movements, and the sound he was making was like the jeering newspaper boy I scurried past outside Hampstead Heath tube every morning: *heheheheheh, hehe-heheheheh*, only very soft.

'Pretty girl, pretty girl,' he said, in this soft, high-pitched tone. 'You're a very pretty girl. Now you lie still. The driver understands – he won't stop till we're finished.' He smiled at me, a little impatiently. 'Unzip the dress . . . unzip the dress . . .' Again the snuffling noise, as he licked my ear, juddering against me in excitement. He slid his hands underneath me, undid the zip and pulled the beautiful velvet dress down my shoulders, and I struggled to free my arms. I could see the driver through the glass. Did he drive him around every day, while he did this? He didn't move. His green cap, clipped hair. And I knew if I screamed he'd take no notice.

Joe Baxter pulled the dress further down, so it was ruched around my middle, the bottom half pulled up to my stomach. My neck felt as if it might snap. He pulled my breasts out of their brassiere, chuckling to himself, then buried his head between them, murmuring. *Heheheheh. Heheheheh*. It got faster and faster, and he started rocking against me. He took my hand and rubbed it up and down the front of his trousers. I could feel his hard penis. I knew that much, at least; my boyfriend at Central, Richard, and I would kiss for hours the week when I had the good bed in Hampstead, and I knew this was what happened to him after a while. But Richard was a vicar's son, a sweet gangly boy from Yorkshire. It wasn't like this with him, this undignified, frightening tussle, in which I didn't know where I was or who I was.

And so it was the first time then, I suppose, that I realised I had to pretend it was happening to someone else, not me. *Eve Noel. Pretend you're this girl called Eve Noel.* The indignity of it was worse than the force, the assumption of rights over my body. He was mounting me, in his own car, and his driver was ignoring us. I didn't know where we were. I didn't know where my hotel was, or how I'd get home. As I lay with him above me, looking out of the window at the blurred scenery, I could see palm trees flying past us, and a street light.

He pumped against me, holding my hand against his body, and then he said, 'It's time, you pretty little girl. I want to play with you. You're so beautiful. I won't hurt you . . .'

So I acted then. I knew suddenly that I wasn't going to lose my virginity to him. I wasn't going to start a baby because I'd been violated in a car by this fat, awful man, because he had power and I didn't. I pushed him back, in a different way this time. I caressed his neck and pushed my breasts into his gobbling face. 'Let me do something,' I said, sitting upright, playing bright and confident, laughing. Rose used to laugh, hiding and then appearing behind the willow tree. 'Catch me if you can,' she'd say, and then she'd vanish, her fleet steps taking her further and further away.

I kissed his neck, his oily, stubby neck, watching the palm trees over his shoulder so I didn't gag. And then I opened his trousers, and did what I used to do with Richard. Only two weeks ago, two weeks and one day in fact. I rubbed him with my hand, pushing my breasts against him rhythmically, until he groaned, spurted his stuff all over: all over me, all over him, all over the buttery leather. And then, God help me, I kissed him on the mouth, and told him how much there was of it, how big he was, and how it scared me. And then I zipped his trousers up as his head lolled forwards and he panted, still making that snuffling noise in his throat.

He patted my head after his breath was back. Squeezed my breasts again. But I knew he wouldn't be able to do it again, not for a while. He was old. I was young, I look back now and smile to think how extremely young I was. I wiggled myself back into my brassiere, slid the beautiful dress over my arms and shoulders again. I moved towards him. 'Mr Baxter,' I said, in a sweet, little-girl voice. 'Could you zip me up again now?'

I gave a little giggle. And he did too, girlish and funny, as if we'd just enjoyed a picnic in the woods, not a rape.

'You know some tricks, don't you, Eve?' he said. He zipped me up, and kissed the top of my neck. I held still. Now it was over, now he'd zipped me up, I felt sick. His hand stroked my thigh again. 'Pretty girl, but you're a clever girl too, aren't you?'

'Just like Helen of Troy, Mr Featherstone says,' I said in my best cut-glass English accent.

'Very good,' he said. 'Very good.' He stared at me. 'You're beautiful. He's right.' He ran his fingers over my forehead, and I tried not to flinch, hating him, hating myself.

'But I think you'd look better with a widow's peak. Change the hairline. Moss is right. He's always right, goddammit, the son of a bitch. I'll speak to Tyrone at the studio – he's the master. Smile?'

I smiled, automatically, too shocked to know what else to do. He was panting still, as if trying to regain his breath. 'Yes,' he said softly. 'The teeth, maybe the nose. But it's fine. I've seen worse. I've seen much worse. Well done. We'll arrive shortly. I tell you, I could use another drink.'

He gave another snuffling laugh and patted my thigh with his clammy hand. He didn't seem unduly pleased with himself, or to think that he'd done anything wrong or marvellous. It was, I realised, purely transactional. In a way that made me hate him even more.

On the door of the Rolls was a tiny silver vase, fixed into the walnut, with a spray of roses in it. Mr Baxter took a single stem out and gave it to me. It was a white rose, beginning to bloom, its waxy petals slowly unfurling, glowing in the dark of the car like something ghostly.

'This is for you,' he said.

I took it and smiled at him, and put the rose in the button-hole of my cape. I could smell its rich, heady scent. I knew that by accepting it I was accepting something bigger. I knew I shouldn't but I did. I went along with it because I was desperate for the part, and I realised it then. I wanted to act, that's all I'd ever wanted to do. But I know now I did it because my survival instinct is strong. Over the years, I convinced myself it was because I wanted to act. And so it became acceptable for me to do things that I'd never have done before, because I told myself I wanted to act. It came out of this night, the warm night that I met Don Matthews and he gave me an avocado; my first Hollywood party, the night I ended up in the back of

51

a car with bruise marks on my thighs and scratches and an angry red rash from his stubble on my breasts, marks I ignored as I'd ignored the indignity of the situation and got myself through it. It was the beginning of everything, and the end of something too.

CHAPTER FOUR

THE CAR WINDS through the dusty, shrubby hills, into Mulholland Drive, and begins its twisting final ascent towards Casa Benita. I'm staring out of the window, at nothing really, and so I jump when Denis, the security guard, taps on the glass and waves.

'Hi, Sophie, that was quick! You're back so soon!'

I wave at him, but don't correct him. Denis is not as young as he once was. He was a doorman at Caesar's Palace in the seventies. He's seen a *lot*; I like to think of this job as his reward in later years for services to excessive celebrity behaviour. My life's pretty boring: he just has to sit at the gate doing his crosswords and wave through packages and the occasional sushi takeout. No wrestling Frank Sinatra to the floor or mopping up Elvis's girlfriend's vomit.

As we pull up in front of the house Tina lopes onto the terrace. She is tall but her shoulders droop; the afternoon light catches her dark hair.

'Hi, Sophie,' she says as she opens the car door. 'How're you doing?'

'I'm good, thanks,' I say, hopping out. I stretch, looking up at the bougainvilleas and jasmine scrambling along the walls in a riot of purple and white. When I first came here to look around, all I knew was that it was Eve Noel's old house. I didn't expect to fall in love with it. The realtor stood by my

53

side, like a cat ready to pounce, as I gazed round at the light, airy rooms.

'If you knocked it down,' she told me excitedly, 'you could really build something beautiful here. I mean that hydrangea –' she gestured out at the wall beside the pool, where white flowers and green foliage smothered the white-wash – 'it's been here like half a century.'

'Why would you knock it down?'

She looked at me like I was crazy. 'It's old,' she said.

'That's why I like it,' I told her.

'Isn't it a beautiful day?' I ask Tina now.

'They say there's a storm coming,' she says sadly. Tina is not a positive person.

T.J. heaves out the box of scripts. 'Can you put those in my office, T.J.?' I look at Tina. 'How are you?'

'Good, good,' Tina mumbles. Her lips are like hard chipolatas. I don't know whether to offer to pay for it to be sorted out; I know a surgeon who could do it, but maybe she loves those lips, thinks they make her look like Nicole Kidman or something. She says awkwardly, 'Carmen said to tell you she has lunch ready – you're on week two of the diet already.'

'OK, great.' I take my sunglasses off and head into the sunny hall which smells of grapefruit, the floorboards gleaming in the midday glow. I breathe in. I love coming home. No matter how stupid the day, how cruel some studio exec has been, how spiteful some TV report about me is, being back here always makes things better. I control this environment and I feel safe here.

I decide to start on some of the scripts now: I'm so hungry, but if I hold out a while longer the lunch will go even further, though already I feel kind of faint. I'm glad I don't have any interviews coming up. You have to munch down a burger and chips to convince the (female) journalist you love food and you're just naturally this thin. I hate it. I wish I could just say once when someone asks, 'Candice, *no one*'s naturally this thin, for fuck's sake! I'm this thin because I eat bloody *nothing*!' I know a famous actress, an A-lister, who wanted a baby but was so terrified of putting on weight that someone else had the baby for her and she wore an expanding prosthetic belly for four, five months. I don't know how we got like this, but it's wrong, isn't it?

Tina follows me into my office as I sit down in the swivel chair and swirl around – I like the swivel chair for that very reason. I touch my fingers together, like when I was young and used to practise being a newsreader.

'Any messages?'

Tina starts and frowns, glaring at her BlackBerry. A vein pulses on one caramel-coloured temple. 'OK, well, while I remember, Sophie, Kerry from Artie's office called about finalising the time for you to meet up with Patrick Drew. They're thinking coffee, in a cool place in West Hollywood. He's on board.'

'Fine,' I say, without any enthusiasm. I'm sure he's going to be a massive douche. I wish I didn't have to bother. Maybe I could get George to come along too? He is the director, after all. The thought of George makes me sit upright – a cool breeze seems to slide over my face and down my neck. George. Mm.

'There are a couple of additional publicity days next week for *The Girlfriend*, you remember?'

'Yep,' I say. 'What do I have to do?'

'Ashley sent over the schedule. You're in NYC next week, going on *The View* and maybe *Today* if we can get it to work. And you're on *Ellen* in a couple weeks, I've sent the dates to your diary.'

I am twisting round in the chair. 'Great. You should come then – you love *Ellen*, don't you? You could meet her.'

'OK. Sure.' Tina looks mortified at my attempt to be friendly. She always does, so I don't know why I bother, except I hate the fact I work with her and have no other interaction with her apart from conversations about my schedule, my diet, my photo shoots, my security.

The door bangs open and T.J. appears with the box of scripts. 'Here?' he says, gesturing to the floor.

'No, on the desk, please. I'm going to start going through them now.' I try to sound businesslike.

'But you hate reading scripts,' T.J. says. 'You never look at them.'

'Thanks, T.J.' I shake my head and ignore him.

'Do you have anything on tonight?' Tina asks me.

I'm waiting for George to call. 'I'm not sure . . . I might slob out in the den. There's an Eve Noel season. *Lanterns Over Mandalay*'s on TNT tonight.'

'Oh. Haven't you seen all her films like a million times?' asks Tina with a shy smile.

'I don't care,' I say. 'It makes me happy.' It's true, it does, even when I'm sitting there sobbing my heart out at the end of *A Girl Named Rose* or *Triumph and Tragedy*, which is a strange film, and Eve Noel herself is strange in it. It's about a nurse who keeps having visions. I think they were trying to replicate the success of *A Girl Named Rose* but it didn't work. It was a big flop. She disappeared afterwards, left this very house and no one knows where she went.

The thought still makes me shiver. I look up at Tina, a wave of longing for something washing over me. Lolling on a couch having silly chats and eating cheesy snacks, dissing programmes on TV – all things I don't have any more. 'You should stay over, watch them with me. You'd love *A Girl Named Rose*.'

'I – well, I have to – sure, Sophie. Maybe.'

I say, embarrassed, 'Or . . . whatever. Of course. So, anything else?'

She hesitates. 'In fact . . . there's two more things. I need to talk to you.'

'What's up?'

'I'll – no, I'll ask you about it later.'

I put my elbows on the table. 'I might be out later, I don't know. Talk to me now.'

Tina puts her BlackBerry in her back pocket and twists her long, slim fingers together. 'I need to have some time off. It's not in my contract. You can – um, I'm gonna need two months.'

'Two months? Why?'

She flushes and looks furiously at her hands. 'I – medical reasons.'

I follow her gaze. She bites her nails; it's the first time I've noticed. 'Are you OK, Tina?'

'Sure. I'm fine.' She stares at me defiantly, her dark eyes flashing. I realise she's quite beautiful; like the nails, I never noticed before. She always looks so downbeat, and those terrible lips . . . Suddenly it makes sense.

'Are you having your lips done?' I ask, and immediately wish I hadn't. Tina is an unknown quantity. She worked for Byron Bay, the big action star, for several years before me and I think he was such a basket case she wanted a change. She's been here for three years, but apart from the fact that she has a mom in Vegas and she once got an infected finger from a cactus prick, I know nothing about her. I've asked, believe me. I'm nosy, and a little bit lonely, plus there's something about her I really like. She's kind of loopy, but cool. But there's some stuff you just shouldn't ask. I've lost a level of appropriateness, living in my bubble.

'I'd rather not say,' Tina tells me firmly.

'I'm sorry. Tina, I shouldn't have asked.' A wash of mortification floods over me. 'It's none of my business. Two months is fine – I guess we'll have to find someone to cover you, and—'

'I've already spoken to Kerry at WAM about it,' she says. 'In preparation. She's talking to Artie and Tommy and I've contacted the agency who covered me last time. You liked that girl Janelle, didn't you?'

'Sure . . . sure . . .' I'm looking at her now, wishing there was something else I could say, some way to cross the gulf between us. 'She wasn't as good as you, of course not, but – thanks, so . . .' I sound so over-keen, it's tragic. It's like a scene from *He's Just Not That Into You*.

'I'll leave you now.' She takes a big breath and her pink

tongue runs over her swollen lips. 'Um, hey. Just one more thing. Deena's arrived.'

My mind is still turning over the conversation, and it takes a moment before I catch up. 'What?'

'I warned you earlier, Sophie . . .' Tina looks like she's about to burst into tears. I wave my hand at her.

'I know, I know. Don't worry. Oh, jeez. Where is she?'

'In the guest house. Unpacking. Her pickup is in the garage.'

'She has a pickup truck?'

Tina gives the slightest suggestion of a smile. 'It's got three pairs of mannequin legs in the back.'

With anyone else this would be strange, not Deena. I give a small groan. 'Listen, can you go across to the guest house and take out the laptop and the projector? Just in case.'

'Sure,' says Tina. 'I'll – leave you then.'

She closes the door and I stare at the pile of scripts but my eyes dart towards the window, in case Deena's peering in, watching. My ghoulish godmother is here. When Mum was in London in the seventies, during her brief bid for fame as an actress, Deena was her best friend. They did everything together. Deena was always the star; my mother was dazzled by her, and still is. In the early eighties Deena moved to LA for a part in a TV soap and for a while she was doing well – Mum could boast to people she met in Woolworth's that she knew someone in *Laurel Canyon*, and that she might have a guest role in next season's *Dynasty* – but then she turned thirty-five and it all sort of petered out, like it does for hundreds of women here every year.

But I don't trust her and I don't think she's a good influence either. Mum behaves like a Bunny Girl when they're together, wiggling and giggling and batting her eyelashes at everyone, and telling anyone who'll listen that they used to 'rule London in the seventies'. Those were her glory days, she's always telling me. They can't have been *that* glorious though. I mean, she ended up moving to the middle of nowhere and becoming the wife of a man who runs garages in the Gloucester area.

Still, Deena's my godmother. I can't let her sleep on the streets, can I, but I wish she wasn't here. My shoulders slump childishly as Tina shuts the door, and I'm left alone gazing around my office at the markers of my career: the MTV movie award for Best Kiss, the magazine covers with my face on, the poster for *A Cake-Shaped Mistake* from Italy that looks a bloody piece of human tissue and not a wedding cake. I pull out the box of scripts, open page one of *Love Me, Love My Pooch*, and start to read.

CHAPTER FIVE

HALF AN HOUR later I put *Love Me, Love My Pooch* down and gaze around the room. I wish I had a cigarette. Or a gun. I pick some gum out of a drawer and chew three sticks in one go. *Love Me, Love My Pooch* is shit. Perhaps I've been blind all these years, just happily saying what people told me to say, but this is a new low. Sample extract:

Int. House.
SEAN IS TALKING ON THE PHONE.
SEAN (chuckling into phone):
Yeah, she's a bitch. And those puppies of hers . . .
man, they are cute!
MEGAN IS COMING IN FROM OUTSIDE. SHE HEARS SEAN
TALKING. SHE IS DISGUSTED.
MEGAN (in hallway, standing holding mittens in hand,
mouth wide open):
What kind of man am I dating! A man who calls
women bitches and talks about their puppies?
SHE WALKS INTO THE KITCHEN AND TAKES HER COAT OFF.
SHE BENDS OVER SEAN.
MEGAN:
I hate you, Sean Flynn! Get out of my life! You'll
never see these puppies again!
SHE SQUEEZES HER BREASTS IN HIS FACE AND LEAVES.

I keep thinking, *Oh, no, this is so bad, there'll be some pay-off, it's setting itself up for a secondary joke, it's not totally this one-note and crass and shit.* But I'm wrong. This is the movie Artie thinks is going to take me 'Sandy–Jen big'. Well, if Cameron and Carey Mulligan really are dying to do it, which I doubt, they're welcome to it. No way. No freaking WAY.

Carmen brings me my lunch in the end and I spend the afternoon going methodically through the rest of the pile. *Boy Meets Girl* is about a boy who meets a girl. Yep, you guessed it. She seems really sweet at first but then turns out to have a wedding album full of pictures of dresses she wants, and flower arrangements, so by accident he sleeps with a stripper. *From Russia with Lust* is an *American Pie* style frat-comedy: a cute local prosecutor marries a girl he has a whirl-wind romance with and she turns out to be a Russian prostitute! *Pat Me Down* is about a waitress who falls in love with a bodyguard after he strip-searches her at a nightclub and she takes secret stripping classes as a fun thing to do with all her girlfriends! Because being a stripper is every little girl's dream, isn't it? Then there's *Bride Wars 2* – seriously, who thought that was a good idea? Did they not see *Bride Wars*?

Not one of these girls has anything to say about anything other than boys, weddings, clothes and shoes. I mean, I like all those things, but is that all there is?

I scuff at the carpet and my toes kick something by accident. It's the Eve Noel biography which has slid out of my bag. I frown as I remember Artie's reaction. I know when Artie's playing me, and most of the time I just go along with it, because I trust him and I want an easy life. But I want to make that film about her. Or rather, I want to find out what happened to her.

I Google her again – "Eve Noel where is she now", "Eve Noel disappearance", "Eve Noel living in England" – but I get the same results I always do whenever I cunningly use my wiles to track her down, i.e. Google her. The same old stuff. A review of the biography, which in itself doesn't have any answers, it's really just a retelling of what we know anyway, but even so it's a good story. The only actual hard facts it has are that all her residuals and any monies from films are paid into a bank account by her agents in London, and they have no contact details for her, or none that they'll say. An article in the *Sunday Telegraph* last year about her films, which tails off at the end and asserts, kind of limply, '*She now lives anonymously out of the spotlight*' – yeah, thanks, crappy journalist, good one. An advertisement for a British Film Institute retrospective which says, '*It is a mystery that Eve Noel's whereabouts are not a greater mystery. One of the UK's most successful and talented post-war stars, she must surely know some of the esteem in which she is now held. Yet she chooses, for whatever reasons, to remain out of the public eye. A salutary lesson for many of today's young actresses.*' The rest of the results are stupid blog references or DVDs on eBay or people talking in discussion threads about her. The Internet is useless when you actually need to find something important. Perhaps she's dead? Her husband's dead, but she must have had some family? Well, maybe I should actually do some proper research. Like, call her agency and get them to give me her address. I bet they have it. I email Tina.

Can you track down Eve Noel's British agents and say I'm interested in talking to her?

Won't work but can do no harm, I reason, and I go back to my pile, flicking through to find something I might vaguely like. I'm relieved when I get to the bottom and see *My Second-Best Bed*, the Shakespeare script which I'd sort of been subconsciously hoping would be something special. As I start to read it I'm practically crossing my fingers.

And it's no good which somehow makes me angrier than ever, because out of all of these scripts this one could be great. The girl working at Anne Hathaway's house is OK, actually quite cool. She's a nice character, a bit chippy, funny. Even the bits in the past aren't too wacky, to start with – she hits her head on a low beam and passes out, and when she wakes up she's the younger Anne Hathaway meeting Shakespeare and it almost works because you don't know if it's a dream or not. But then she and Shakespeare and Elizabeth I – yes, she suddenly turns up – go on a treasure hunt to find this key to take her back to the modern day, and it turns into a weirdly crappy sort of trawl through history. All these historical figures keep appearing, like Jane Austen and Lord Nelson and the ones they didn't use in *Bill & Ted,* and it's ridiculous. In the end you sort of wonder if it's a piss-take.

It annoys me, because like I say it could be really good. Some of the scenes have a special sharp, cool charm, and I want to keep reading, no matter how ridiculous it gets. It'd be easy to whip into shape – if I had my own production company or some people on my side I'd get them to work with the girl who wrote it. But I don't and I can't take it back to Artie; it needs to be straight out of the ballpark good, this one.

Idly I look at the title page, wondering if there's an email address for the writer or her agent.

My Second-Best Bed
Tammy Gutenberg

I sit up straight. I know Tammy. Maybe it's because seeing Sara and thinking about those Venice Beach days is fresh in my head but it comes to me right away this time. She used to hang out at Jimmy Samba's; she got a job at Castle Rock, I think, and moved on from that scene before I did. She was half English: her mother was from Bristol and she knew some of the places I knew. It's a sign, I'm sure it is. Well. I type her an email, which I send to Tina to pass on, asking if we can have coffee some time to talk about it. I don't know what good it'll do but it's a start. I've done something, at least.

My neck hurts, my shoulders are stiff. I look up to see it's nearly seven. There's a framed photo of Bette Davis in *All About Eve* I've had hung on the wall next to the clock. No one ever sent Bette Davis a script called *From Russia with Lust.*

I think for a moment. Fatigue, adrenalin and excitement mingle in my stomach, making my blood pump faster round my body. I pick up the phone and dial a number I'm ashamed to say I've learned by heart.

A deep, gruff voice answers, smoky with promise. 'Hello?'

'Hi, George – it's me.'

'You? Hey, you. How are you?'

'I'm good.' I wriggle in my chair, pleased. Last week when I rang him he thought I was his sister. She's fifty-five and lives in Wisconsin; I remember everything about him.

'What you up to, honey?'

'Oh.' I don't know what to say. 'Just hanging out. Had the meeting with Artie.'

'Good, good,' George says. 'He tell you how good you're gonna be in *The Bachelorette Party*? How hot you are? How tight your smooth little buns are, honey? Did he tell you that?'

I laugh. 'No, he didn't.'

'Well, he's a fucking idiot,' George says. 'Tell him I'm taking that deal away from him and going to Paramount. What else?'

'Artie gave me a load of scripts for my next project, and they're kind of crap. I don't know, I want to—'

'Show 'em to me,' George interrupts smoothly. 'He should know what to put in front of you. He shouldn't be wasting your time with stupid art-house shit and sci-fi. He doing that to you?'

'No, the other way round,' I say. 'It's . . . Oh, never mind.'

'We'll get it sorted out.' There's a noise in the background, voices, an echoing sound, maybe splashing from a pool. George's voice gets closer to the phone. 'Listen, now's not a great time, sweetie. Listen to me. I have to fuck you today, honey, otherwise I'll lose my mind. Come over, later.'

I'm knackered, I realise. 'Well . . .'

He lowers his voice even further. 'I want to show you something, Sophie babe.'

'Really?'

'What we shot last night. I want you to see it. I want you to see how hot you are. There's one shot I got of you – mm.'

His soft, low voice rasps gently into the phone. I press myself against the leather chair, mad for him. 'Can you bring some different clothes? You got any babydoll nighties, that kinda thing?'

'Honey, what I've got'll blow your mind,' I say softly into the phone. I can hear him breathing. 'I'll come by this evening?'

'Yeah,' he says. 'Around eleven, eleven-thirty? I have to have dinner before with some friends.'

'Oh – OK,' I say.

He says slowly, deliberately, 'Will you be ready for me?'

'Yes,' I whisper. 'Yes . . . I will.'

He puts the phone down. I uncurl myself from the chair and stand up. I realise I'm flushed, and my heart is pounding. I've never been with anyone like George before. He is like a drug. It's a cliché but it's true. He's so powerful; it oozes out of him, and he knows it. He's not a megalomaniac, he's just . . . intense. When you're with him you know he's in control and he's so used to being in control you'll let anything happen.

I mustn't let him bite my tit again though. That fucking hurt. I don't care if it was hot on film or not. And that stupid girl bashing into my boob – humph. Sara. I open the bottom drawer to put the script of *My Second-Best Bed* away until I hear back from Tammy, and see a bag of Goldfish crackers I'd stowed for a day like today. I'm sick of doing what someone else says all the time. I tear open the bag and munch, and when the other scripts cascade to the floor I pay no attention. I close my eyes, imagining the night ahead. It's good to be bad sometimes.

CHAPTER SIX

UP IN MY white bedroom, I take off my clothes and stand naked in front of the mirror. I turn around slowly, appraising myself. I hate this part so much but it's my job, this delicate balancing act. You can't have any fat on you, yet you don't want to end up like Nicole Richie. It's not a good look for a bona fide A-Lister being scary-thin – unless you're Angelina, but Angelina's a basket case. I turn slowly. My butt is still high, and firm. When I turned thirty a couple of months ago, Tommy suggested I get it lifted before it needs to be, but I told him to fuck off in such definite terms I don't think he'll mention it again. My tits are good – I wish they were bigger, but bigger means you're fatter and so far I've had no complaints. Tommy's suggested having a tiny lift in a year or so. He says it just makes the job easier later on. I cup them in my hands, thinking about tonight, wondering what George will make me do, what I'll do to him. I shiver with anticipation and smile at myself in the long mirror, shaking my head at my stupidity; but it's so good to have someone to go and be this person with, someone who understands, and he does.

And then a shadow on the bed reflected in the mirror catches my eye.

At first I think it's just a crease in the sheet, but when I turn around and walk towards the bed, I realise it's not. It's a rose. A perfect, white, single rose. There's the faintest hint of cream in the soft buttery petals, and when I pick it up I cry out, sharply, because it has thorns. It smells delicious.

I suck my thumb and look towards the window, almost expecting to see a face there, but this side of the house looks directly over the hills and the road and they'd have to be suspended 30 feet above the road to get a good look in. I pull on some sweatpants and a top, hurriedly peering into the bathroom, then into my closet, but there's no one. A hair on my neck itches, as if there's something else there.

So I tell myself I'm overreacting. It was probably delivered to me and left here by Tina. Or maybe Deena stole it from somewhere and left it as a present. There've been guys in and out of the house all day, fixing the TV, steaming the carpets. Probably some loser trying to make a joke.

Why do white roses ring a bell though? There's something about them that makes a knot tighten in my stomach. I can't put my finger on why. I stand there for a moment trying to remember, then suddenly I pick up the rose and throw it out of the window. It loops awkwardly in the air and disappears. It will land on the road below me and be crushed by a car and it's nothing – I'm being stupid. I go downstairs, to try and find something to eat.

Carmen is clearing up, polishing the wood. 'Carmen,' I say. 'Did someone leave a rose for me on my bed?'

She frowns. 'What?'

'A rose. Single stem.' I sound insane; I wish I hadn't thrown it away.

Carmen gives me a curious look. She shrugs. 'No, Sophie, I have not seen a rose. No roses here.'

'Where's Tina?'

A slight spasm crosses Carmen's face. 'She on the phone outside.'

Tina is standing by the pool whispering urgently into her cellphone. I clear my throat and she jumps, automatically putting her spare hand on her head, like she's been busted in a police raid.

'Oh! Sophie. Hi there!' She kind of bellows this at me. 'Are you OK? Do you need something?'

'Sorry, I didn't mean to interrupt.' I feel stupid, even asking. 'Er – did you put a rose in my room?' I say.

She looks understandably confused at this question, though her rigid forehead remains immobile. 'Uh – no, I didn't, Sophie—'

She must think I'm going mad today. 'Not you personally,' I say impatiently. 'I mean did someone ask you to or did they drop it off there? I was just in there. There was a white rose on my bed.'

'I don't know,' says Tina. She narrows her eyes and then clears her throat. 'Do you think someone was in the house?'

When she says it like that, it sounds kind of sinister, and I don't want to hear it. 'I'm sure not,' I say. 'I bet there's a perfectly simple explanation.'

'Sure,' Tina says. 'Let me just call Denis.' She dials the gatehouse. 'Denis, can you read me the list of who's been checked in today? Uh-uh . . . sure. Sure.'

She ends her call. 'You, well, you and T.J., the carpet guys, Juan was here in the garden, me, Carmen. The Mulberry guy but he didn't come inside. A FedEx guy, ditto. We can go back to the carpet company too, see who came in, ask them if they left it. OK?' She sounds calm. 'I'm sure it's nothing.'

'Thanks.' I believe her. It could be any one of several things. There's something about Tina – she is totally capable and calm dealing with my shit. I know I can totally trust her. Yet anything to do with herself is a different matter. I chew the inside of my cheek. 'Look – Tina, I'm sorry about before,' I say, edging towards her. She looks suspicious. 'About you taking time off. It's just two months is a long time, and I wanted to make sure – you are OK, aren't you?'

She shoves her phone in her pocket and scratches her face. 'Of course I'm OK. I just don't want to talk about it much.'

'Right,' I say, and then fall silent.

'You are right. It is a surgical procedure,' she says eventually. 'It's my lips. Yeah.' She's looking at the pool and I'm looking up at the sky, both pretending this is a normal conversation. 'I was stupid. I got fillers from some quack doctor years ago. He screwed them up and I haven't been able to get them fixed.'

'Why?' I say. 'Couldn't you sue him?'

She smiles. 'That costs money. I don't have money. I wasn't properly insured when I did it and it's kind of impossible to fix unless you totally know what you're doing. I've finally found someone on my insurance who'll try and take some of the fillers out but it takes a few weeks to remove them. The surgeon's in Vegas, so I'm going to stay with Mom . . .'

'You should have asked me,' I say. 'I'd have helped you.'

'Helped me take them out yourself?' she says, with a glimpse of mordant humour. 'Right. No, I need to . . .' Tina looks across at the pool again, out to the city sprawled below us. 'Some guy at a seminar told me if I got them done then I'd get more jobs, and I listened to him. Biggest mistake of my life.' Her eyes fill with tears.

My heart aches for her. 'So . . . you were an actress?'

She takes a tissue out of a pack and delicately wipes her nose. 'A model.' She adds, with a rush of bravado, 'In fact I was Miss Nevada 1998.'

'No way!'

'Uh-huh.' She's smiling. 'They said I'd be a star, but I didn't want that. All I ever wanted to do was be a Victoria's Secret Angel. I loved those girls.'

'Wow.' I am amazed at how people give themselves up to you all in one go. 'I never knew that, Tina. You're beautiful. You should have—'

'It's a long time ago. And it didn't work out, did it.' Her shoulders slope again and she adds, with something more like her normal tone, 'I came to LA, so sure I was going to be a star, you know?' I nod. 'But nothing was really happening, and a year later I had this done. It ruined everything, I was broke and ugly. No one wanted me. That's when I started working for Byron.'

'Is that what you really wanted? To be famous?' I am fascinated at the idea of this new Tina, the gorgeous young beauty queen and the awkward, withdrawn woman she is now.

She hesitates. 'It was all I ever wanted. Then. Of course, now it's different.'

'What do you want now?'

'Now – you know what I want now?' I shake my head. I literally have no idea. 'I want a nice house, near the ocean. A good guy, a couple of kids, a normal life. And I want to stay working for you so I don't leave that world behind, because I love it. That's really all.' My expression must be incredulous, as she laughs and says, 'I like working for you, Sophie. You're doing so well but you're easy to get along with – you're talented, and you're not crazy. You need someone to look out for you. And forgive me, but you're kind of naive about some stuff in this town.'

This is completely fascinating. 'What stuff?'

But before she can answer, a husky voice calls from around a corner.

'Hey, doll.'

We both jump as a thin shadow falls on the ground, advancing towards us.

'All right, Tina. Hi. Sophie. Wow. The gang's all here, yeah?'

I blink, sunspots dancing in front of my eyes.

'Hi, Deena.' I kiss her, inhaling the familiar scent of cigarettes, sweat and Giorgio Beverly Hills. 'You got everything you need over there?'

'Yeah. Nice painting in the bedroom. Is it new?'

'Yes,' I say shortly.

'Cool. Cool. I like its vibe. It's all good. Listen, kiddo. Just wanted to say thanks, OK? Thanks for having me. Damn air con. It broke and then the water tank went and the whole house was flooded.'

'I thought it was—' I begin, then stop. *What happened to the roaches?* Tina glances at me, and looks at the floor. 'Hey. No problem. Stay as long as you want.'

Damn. As soon as the words are said I wish I could reach out and cram them back in my mouth. 'Hey, nice one, kiddo,' says Deena. 'We gotta look out for each other, haven't we?' She tips the imaginary brim of a hat to me. 'Listen, there's no kettle in the guest house.'

'Kettle?' Tina frowns.

'You guys don't do kettles. It's fine. Just wondering if you could put one in there for me.'

Bloody cheek. I sigh and look at Tina. 'Er . . .'

'I'll talk to Carmen on my way out.' Tina nods at me. 'So – I'm off now. I'll see you tomorrow. You have everything you need?'

I nod, trying to meet her gaze, but she's already halfway down the drive. 'See you tomorrow. Thanks again.'

'Odd gal,' Deena says, after Tina's vanished. 'So how's tricks? You're on fire, *en fuego*, at the moment, huh? Everything lining up for little Sophie Sykes!' She gives me a big wink. 'Hey, sorry! Sophie *Leigh*.'

She says this like she's revealing a massive secret about me, like I was born and raised as a boy, when in fact you can see my name's Sophie Sykes if you go on IMDb. It's not even an interesting story: Mum made me change it when I was sixteen because she said Sykes was too common, much to my poor dad's resigned amusement.

I'm trying to think of the right answer to this when Carmen appears at the French doors. 'Sophie. I got your dinner here. You want it outside?' She looks at Deena. 'Ma'am, can I get you anything?'

Deena runs a finger thoughtfully over her teeth. 'Hm. I don't know. What you got?'

'Anything,' says Carmen. 'What you want?'

'You got some ham?'

Carmen folds her arms. Her brows lower into one bristling black line. 'Sure. I got some ham.'

'Can I get a ham sandwich? With . . . some chips on the side. And some guacamole. Can I get that?'

Carmen says briskly, 'Sure. No problem.'

She's just retreating inside when Deena adds hopefully, 'And a beer?'

71

'You want Peroni, Budvar, Tiger? We got—'

'That's fine, just bring her anything,' I say. 'And thank you, Carmen. Listen to me, Deena.' I move inside through the French doors, motioning her to follow me. 'It's fine for you to stay. But I might be having someone from the UK over in a couple of weeks, so . . .' I scratch my head, searching for a name, any name. 'My friend . . . Donna? My friend Donna's coming to stay, yeah, probably in July? Just so you know.'

Deena takes a Zippo lighter out from a pocket in her impossibly tight jeans and starts flicking it on and off. 'Listen, kiddo, I don't wanna outstay my welcome. I said two weeks, I meant two weeks. I'm busy, you know. I've got a lot of stuff on. It's just while they're . . .' She falters, and I feel like a total bitch. 'While they're fixing the drains.'

'Of course.'

She moves a little closer. She's always looked the same, Marlboro Man's girlfriend: jeans, silk shirts, tasselled suede jackets. I see the flecks of brown in her hazel irises, the shadows under her eyes as her gaze meets mine, but then she swallows and says, 'Yeah, like I say, I'm busy. Got a TV pilot I'm auditioning for next week, did your ma tell you?'

'I haven't spoken to her in a while.'

'Hm, I know, she said.' Deena's still flicking the lighter. 'She calls me when she can't get through to you, you know that? You should call her.'

I change the subject back. 'That's cool, what's the pilot?'

'Oh, it's about this chick who lives down in New Mexico and . . . has a lot of fun.' She smiles enigmatically. 'And I'm working with a European director on a couple of projects. Made an advert for German TV a few months ago. It's all good.'

I would love to follow Deena one day. Just see what she gets up to, how she makes a living. Whether she's totally feral when no one's watching, living out on the hills and heading into the city to feed off scraps from restaurant bins. Her last entry on IMDb is 2004, some straight-to-DVD thriller. But she always tells Mum she's shooting a new pilot, or working with a European director. I am sure 'European director' is code for something.

Carmen brings in my tray of food. I make a vague gesture to Deena but she shakes her head. 'No, thanks. I'm gonna grab my sandwich and go. Got to see a guy about a fido, you know?' She slings her battered old leather satchel over her shoulder. 'See you later, kiddo. Thanks again.'

'No problem.'

She's halfway out the door when she hesitates, turns round and adds, 'Hey. We should talk while I'm here. I've got a few ideas I wanted to run past you. Really good ideas. Maybe you could get me a meeting with . . . with some people.'

Everyone wants something off you, that's the deal. I realised it when a camera boom hit me in the face while I was filming *Sweet Caroline* and the triage nurse at Cedars-Sinai gave me her head shot while blood was pouring from my scalp. It's money. All to do with money, whether they're aware of it or not. So I nod and I say, 'Sure. We'll talk soon. Bye, Deena,' and wave politely, as she strolls out of the room.

Carmen is setting up the tray as I settle back into the La-Z-Boy recliner. There are fresh copies of *Us Weekly* and *People* on the coffee table – I reach for the former, then put it back with a sigh, knowing it's for the best: it annoys me when I'm not in it, and it annoys me when I am. There was a time when I used to Google myself. I even had my own sign-in on a forum devoted to 'Sophie Leigh Rocks!' But I had to stop. Even the ones who like you still say things like:

> *I think Sophie's hair needs extensions or filling out, it's really thin/rank lol*

> *Why isn't she on Twitter? Why does she think she's better than us? Won't she give back to her fans who <3 her n made her what she is?*

> *I fucking hate her. Liked the 1st film and now it's like oh my fucking god how many times can one person play a dumb bitch. That cutesy act makes me want to barf.*

And this particular highlight from a 'fan site':

> *Who does she think she is? She acts all smiley and perky and she's NOTHING. Mate of mine knew mate of hers on South Street and said she was a fat slag who reckoned herself, had no talent and f*cked her way to Hollywood. Apparently she gave head to anyone who'd ask. Also her breath stank because of how much head she was giving. Gross.*

Nice, isn't it!

I switch on the TV. TMZ is on. They're standing around talking about Patrick Drew. He was filmed coming out of a club in West Hollywood, his arm around some girl. She's supporting him. He sticks his finger up at the paps, and then he's pushed into a car by some entourage member. He is beautiful, it's true.

'Car crash,' says Harvey, the TMZ head guy, who's always behind the desk leading the stories. 'That's a night out with Patrick Drew.'

'What about Sophie Leigh?' one of the acolytes says. 'He's filming with her next. Maybe that'll do him good.'

'Sophie Leigh?' Harvey says. 'She's too stupid even for Patrick Drew.' They laugh. 'How snoozefest is that movie gonna be? Him crashing into walls on his skateboard, her smiling from under her bangs in some titty top, following him round, saying, "I LOST MY RING!"' They all join in and collapse with laughter. '"Oh, here it is, Patrick!"' Harvey mimes a ring down an imaginary cleavage. '"Oh, it's here, here are my tits, look at my tits!" Then an argument with a mom or a wedding planner, yadda yadda yadda. GET ANOTHER HAIRCUT, LADY! BOR-ING.'

'I liked one of her movies,' says a girl behind another desk, taking a sip of her coffee. 'The one in LA. What was it called?'

'You're a moron,' says Harvey cheerfully. 'Seriously, these people. Patrick Drew doesn't give a damn so at least you give him props for that. But Sophie Leigh – oh, man, I hate that girl! She's so fucking fake and smiley and you know she's going through the motions for the cash. "Hey, honey. Put this tight top on so the guys can stare at your tits. Now smile, now say this pile of shit dialogue and put on a wedding dress the girls like, repeat every year till your tits reach your knees and everyone's died of total boredom . . ." ' He looks up. 'She's probably watching this now. Hey, Sophie! Your films suck! Message from me to you: I LOST MY WILL TO LIVE!!'

His voice is deadpan. The others are laughing hysterically. I switch the TV off and lean back in the chair, pretending to smile though no one's watching. My heart's beating. My BlackBerry buzzes.

Sorry babe, have to rain check tonight. Keep your tight ass on standby. I'll need u soon. Hard for u when I think about u. G

Oh. Well. It's very quiet in here. In my head I list the things I love about my life. I think about the house, my white bedroom with the closet filled with lovely clothes, Carmen's ceviche, my firm smooth body that the best director in town says he wants, the cache of Mulberry bags I haven't even looked at yet. I have to count like this; otherwise I'd go mad, and sometimes I wonder if I'm not going a bit mad, and it's just that everyone else here is too so I haven't noticed. I wish I had someone to talk to about it, someone I could ring up now and say, 'Hey, could you come over?' But there's no one. Somehow. And that's my fault.

I shiver, and switch over to TNT. *Lanterns Over Mandalay* is on. Eve Noel is a nun in the Second World War and she falls in love with an army captain, played by Conrad Joyce, while they're fleeing the Japanese occupation of the city. Something tragic happened to Conrad Joyce, too, I forget now. He was killed? He died young anyway, then he totally fell off the radar. Hardly anyone remembers him now, but he was just divine. I gaze admiringly at his firm jaw, his sleek form in uniform which is immaculate despite the fact that they've just crawled through several miles of mud and barbed wire.

'*Damn it, do you know what you're getting yourself into?*' Captain Hawkins demands angrily. '*Diana, you're a fool if you try to take these people out of here. We can manage it alone, but to attempt the rest – it's suicide!*'

I pull the rug over me, snuggling down so I'm as comfy as I can be and as hidden away as I can make myself. The black-and-white figures on the screen seem to glow in the darkening room. A world I can lose myself in where everything is, like the line says, fine and noble. I stare hard at the screen, sharp tears pricking my eyes.

'*I know, Captain. But I won't leave them here to die. I simply won't.*' I'm mouthing along with her, watching her perfect rosebud mouth, the dark, intelligent eyes that hint at something but never quite tell you what their owner is thinking. '*I'm standing up for something I believe in. I'm trying to do something fine and noble in this awful mess. I'm trying to do something wonderful.*'

Where is she? I look around our house, wondering how she came to lose her life here. How maybe I have mislaid mine.

I'll be around
Hollywood, 1958

EVERYONE WENT TO Romanoff's. It had started life as a
small bistro on the Sunset Strip, run by His Imperial Highness
Prince Michael Alexandrovich Dimitri Obolensky 'Mike'
Romanoff (otherwise known as Harry Gerguson, a small-time
crook from Brooklyn). I never did find out where he acquired
his knowledge of Russian aristocracy or English country houses
– he was able to describe the guest bedrooms at Blenheim Palace
in detail to me. Perhaps the library at Sing Sing was particularly
well stocked. But despite the fact that he was a crook, and the
food was middling to fair at best, everyone went there. When
I say *everyone*, of course I mean stars. By the time I was first
taken there, it was well established in Rodeo Drive. Almost two
years had elapsed since I came to Hollywood but it was still
the place to go and be seen.

One fresh evening in March, Gilbert and I drove there for
supper. We were both feeling extremely happy, on top of the
world, in fact. We had just that day completed the purchase
of a house just off Mulholland Drive called Casa Benita: a
sprawling white clapboard bungalow high in the Hollywood
Hills, complete with tennis court, swimming pool and suitably
impressive views. We had looked at places in Beverly Hills,

but I wanted to be able to see the city, not be right in the thick of it.

You were part of the club if Mike waved you into Romanoff's without a reservation. I had seen him turn away millionaire oil barons, nouveau riche Valley residents, and New York society matrons by the dozen. Aspiring producers, new punk actors, hotshot directors – all were shown the door. Yet Gilbert and Mike were old pals, and at some point Gilbert had obviously helped His Imperial Highness out. Whenever we turned up, there was no problem.

'Get a table for Mr Travers and Miss Noel. Snap to it, boys. Miss Noel, may I take your coat— Who, those sons of bitches? Fat fucks from Wyoming – get rid of them.'

Gilbert was always in a good mood at Mike's. His old cronies were there, the rest of the original Rat Pack that had hung around Bogie when he was alive. A lot of people had deserted Gilbert when he came back to Hollywood after the war. It was the way of these things: they called him a hero, but the truth was he'd been out of pictures for five years, was heavier and older and things had changed. The audience had moved on, and Gilbert Travers's brand of charming English gent wasn't what American teenagers were looking for. I winced whenever we passed a billboard for *Jailhouse Rock*. Gilbert hated Elvis, with a passion that was almost violent.

As we sat down at a discreet banquette, an executive from the studio with whom I'd dealt on my last film, *The Boy Next Door*, passed behind us. 'Great work on the *Life* magazine spread, Eve,' he said. 'Mr Baxter's delighted they chose to run the feature about you.'

'Two White Ladies.' Gilbert flicked his hand to the waiter. 'They're lucky to have her,' he told the executive. Then he gestured to one of the shots on the wall behind us, me arriving at Romanoff's after the premiere for *Helen of Troy* the previous year in my white Grecian goddess gown, gold sandals, gold jewellery, real gold thread in my hair from the Welsh Valleys and spun into a beautiful diadem especially for me, reflecting my mother's Welsh heritage. (Mummy was a vicar's daughter from Berkhamsted, but the publicity department never allowed the facts to obscure a good story.) On one side of me stood Cliff Montrose, my co-star, and on the other, his arm around me, Joe Baxter. 'Look at you, my dear,' Gilbert said. 'Many more such nights to come, I'm sure.'

His hand lightly pressed my arm, and I gazed up at him.

When the studio 'suggested' we go on a date together, I'd leapt for joy with excitement, but then demurred. It was well known in Hollywood that Gilbert Travers had a drinking problem. Margaret Heyer, his second wife, had left him and gone back to England three years ago; *Confidential* and *Photoplay* had still been full of it when I'd arrived here. He was a drunk; he beat her; she'd run out of the house naked, screaming, to be rescued by a zoologist who happened to be down on Wilshire Boulevard – which was a neat coincidence as Margaret Heyer's latest film was about a young wife who goes to the Congo and falls in love with a zoologist. (The publicity machine at work again; Hollywood wasn't ever that original in its ideas. Even I'd learned that, by then.)

But I thought about it some more and I felt sorry for him. I couldn't help it. Gilbert had enlisted the day Great Britain went to war with Germany, had seen his friends killed, had caught dysentery and nearly died, and had come back to Hollywood to find film stars who'd never fought a day in their lives playing war heroes and lapping up the adulation of an admiring public. He never talked about the war to me, and after a few cock-eyed attempts to find out more, which he rebuffed angrily, I never asked him again. I understood, at least I thought I did. We both had secrets, things we weren't to tell each other, and it was for the best.

The cocktails arrived and Gilbert lit our cigarettes. 'Well, my dear,' he said. 'This is quite a red-letter day. Our house, us together. Are you excited?'

I looked around nervously. If the wrong people found out we were going to be living in sin, even if only for four weeks, it would be the end of my career. I'd laugh, afterwards, at how hypocritical it all was: what actually went on in this city while the proprieties were so slavishly observed. The studio, and Mr Featherstone, had spent hundreds of hours and thousands of dollars on my image, the perfect English rose. If Louella or Hedda, or some other unfriendly source, should be close by and should overhear, all hell would break lose. 'Yes, of course, dear,' I replied. 'But – do keep your voice down.'

Gilbert clinked his glass against mine, his thin moustache twitching above his lip as he smiled. 'You're too concerned with appearances, Eve dear. We'll be married as soon as the shoot's over. And anyway, goddammit – you're a star. They can't touch you.' He gulped most of his drink down and put his huge hand on my thigh. 'Hm?'

'Miss Noel . . .' A photographer appeared, flanked by Mike and one of the doormen. 'Coupla shots, please?'

'Of course,' I said, smiling slightly. One had to be polite to the press, no matter how much the inconvenience. And the story of the quintessential English gentleman actor, once at the top of his game but mentally scarred by war, brought back into love and life again by a young English beauty, star of the highest-grossing picture of 1957 and heroine of every fan magazine, was proving to be addictive to the American public. They lapped us up, Gilbert and me. The studio, and Gilbert's new agent, fed the magazines and the radio shows a soapy romance about how I'd lured him out of his shell, taught him how to laugh again, and he had protected me, a young shy ingenue, from the bear pit that was Hollywood. It was a little ridiculous, sure, but I rather wanted it to be true, too. My old life – oh, it seemed as if someone else had lived it and then told me about it: a memory acquired elsewhere, not my own. My parents, the house by the river . . . Rose, her great fits of anger, her death, and my life without her – all solitary, sad, strange – and then my time in London, so much fun and so different again from this life here. Back in England, I had grown up feeling lost without Rose. I was working towards something unattainable. The reward was satisfaction of a job well done. Here, you just had to smile, and people told you how wonderful you were.

Gilbert put his arm around me. I moved against him, hoping

he wouldn't crush the black silk birds that perched on each shoulder of the heavy cream silk dress. We paused for the photograph, holding our cocktail glasses high, heads touching, smiles wide. All of Gilbert's teeth had been replaced by a zealous MGM in the thirties. Five of mine had been capped, but that was the least of what they'd done to me since I'd been here.

'Anything to say about the rumours that you guys are headed for the altar?' The photographer licked a pencil and took out a pad.

'We couldn't possibly comment,' Gilbert said. 'However, Miss Noel and I greatly enjoy each other's company.'

'Gilbert, how does it feel, stepping out with Hollywood's biggest new star?'

'She's just Eve to me,' Gilbert said. 'You have to understand, Sid. When we're together, such considerations aren't relevant.' He signalled for another drink.

'Eve, Eve – what's next for you?'

I paused, and blinked several times, smiling sweetly as if flattered by the attention; humble. 'I'm making a wonderful picture, Sid, with Conrad Joyce, which I very much hope the movie-going public will enjoy. *Lanterns Over Mandalay*. It's about a nun during the war, and it's a most powerful story.'

'She's going to be absolutely wonderful in it,' Gilbert said warmly. 'Just wonderful. Aren't you, darling?'

'And Eve, you and white roses – are they still your favourite flower? You're famous for it!'

My throat tightened; I felt hot, trapped behind the table, fixed to the floor. 'I—' I began.

'No, Sid,' the doorman said firmly. 'Three questions. We told ya.' He grabbed the photojournalist by the scruff of the neck and steered him past the tables and out through the door.

I breathed out. 'Gosh,' I said, taking another sip of my cocktail.

Gilbert said nothing, but stubbed a cigarette out viciously into the wide crystal ashtray, then immediately lit another.

'Darling, what would you like to eat?' I asked.

No answer.

'Gilbert—'

'You could have mentioned *Dynasty of Fools*,' Gilbert said. He sucked on his cigarette tartly, his nostrils flaring. 'I backed you up. You should have done the same for me.'

'Oh,' I said, appalled. 'I'm sorry – darling, I didn't think.' I shook my head and tried to slide out of the banquette. 'I'll go and tell him how good you are, everyone's saying so—'

'Forget it.' His hand was heavy on my shoulder, pushing me back down. 'Forget it. You couldn't be bothered to remember then so what's the point now?' There was a ripping sound. 'Oh, this damned fool dress.'

I looked in agony at the little black silk bird on my shoulder, torn and dangling, its beak almost in my armpit. 'It's fine,' I said, though he hadn't said anything. 'Perhaps I should just—'

Gilbert tutted in impatience. 'Here.' He wound the thread around my shoulder, tugging it tight, pulling the bird back into position again. 'Damn it, I'm sorry, Eve. Shouldn't have lost my rag like that, darling. Forgive?'

I smiled at him; he looked flustered and annoyed. 'Of course, forgive,' I said.

'You're a wonderful girl, you know that.' He kissed me lightly on the shoulder.

We were unnoticed at the back of the room. I kissed him back on the lips. 'You are a wonderful, wonderful man,' I told him softly, relief flooding through me. 'I can't quite believe my luck.'

And I couldn't, really. One part of me knew it was a good idea, this cooked-up romance with Gilbert Travers. Everyone benefited. The other part, the part I hadn't told anyone at the studio about, was the twelve-year-old me, swooning over Gilbert Travers at the Picturehouse in Stratford, watching his films week after week in the lean years after the war where they showed old thirties fare again and again. He was a schoolgirl fantasy to me. The only crime I had ever committed in my short, boring life was that once I had sneaked into the library and cut a picture of Gilbert Travers arriving at Quaglino's out of the *Illustrated London News*. And he was here, by my side – he was mine, and that was worth a hell of a lot of ripped birds, I supposed.

'I don't know how you put up with me,' he said, shifting in his seat, still slightly red. 'I'm a brute.' His mouth drooped, his eyes were filmy. 'A foul-mouthed, boozy, moody, selfish brute. You'd be happier if I let you go and find someone else. I'm more than twice your age, for God's sake.'

'You're forty-eight, and I'm a grown woman, darling,' I told him. 'I know what I'm doing.'

In truth, I did dread his moods, which came without warning, throwing a black cloak over a perfectly nice evening. He could sit there and say nothing for hours, with me darting around him like a sparrow – *Would you like another drink? Here's the paper, darling, I thought you'd like to see this. Oh, by the way, I ran into Vivian at the studio today, and he says you're marvellous in* Dynasty. *Everyone's talking about it* – working harder and harder to bring him back into the room. I was too afraid to call his bluff. I didn't know what happened if you did, in any situation.

I wish I'd learned then that when you call someone's bluff you usually win: it's simply not what they're expecting. And swimming along in the slipstream of another person's current is no way to live.

It was then that I looked up and saw someone, staring at me from the other side of the room. What would have happened if I hadn't? What if I'd never seen Don Matthews again? Would Gilbert and I have continued our evening and would it have been lovely? Would everything have worked out differently?

'Excuse me, darling,' I said. 'Let me go and fix my dress. I'll be straight back.' I squeezed his hand and stood up, and as I walked out towards the terrace Don turned and saw me. He whispered something to his companion and left the bar.

'Well, well. Miss Avocado 1956,' he said, shaking my hand.

'Don,' I said, clasping his fingers in mine, tilting my head to meet his dark, warm gaze. 'It's good to see you. How are you?'

'I'm the same, but you're much better,' he said, looking me up and down. 'Congratulations. You were – well, I thought you wouldn't make it. I thought you'd crack and go back home to Mum and Dad.' He said this in a terrible English accent.

I had the most curious feeling we'd last met only days before, not nearly two years ago. 'I don't give up,' I said. 'I wanted to be a star. I told you.'

'Yes,' he said. 'Yes, you did. But you were different back then.' He stared at me. 'Gosh. What did they do to you?'

I stared at him. 'Oh,' I said, after a moment. 'It's probably my hair. Electrolysis. They thought I should have a widow's peak for Helen. It was painful, but I suppose they were right.'

'No,' he said. 'Not that.'

'Or the teeth?' I said, opening my mouth. 'Five caps – it's made a world of difference.' He shook his head. 'I lost a stone, too, which was terribly hard, but I needed to.'

'No, you didn't.' He gave that sweet, lopsided grin I'd forgotten about. 'Forget it. I'm looking for something that's not there, I guess. You're all grown-up, Rose.'

I'd forgotten he'd called me that. *Rose.* I started and he smiled again.

'I know all your dirty little secrets, remember,' he said. I must have looked as worried as I felt, because he added, 'It's a joke. Hey, don't worry. I'm not one of those guys.'

'I know you're not,' I said, and I knew it was true. 'Anyway,' I said brightly. 'How are you? What are you working on at the moment?'

'Something special,' he said. 'I'm polishing it up right now. About a girl from a small town who moves to the big city and gets lost. In fact, I had you in mind for it. I always have done, Rose.'

His eyes never left my face but I avoided his gaze. 'How exciting. What's the title?'

He paused. 'Wait and see.'

'That's a great title.'

'No,' he said. 'I mean, Rose, just wait and see. In fact, I'd like to be the one to tell you. Soon.'

'Really?' I said. I was embarrassed and I didn't know why.

'Yes,' he said. 'It's for Monumental, and I think they're talking about putting you in it after *Mandalay*'s done shooting. I'll get you a copy.'

Typical that everyone else would know except me what I'd be doing next. My life wasn't my own to plan; it was the studio's, Moss Fisher's in particular, and I knew it and was grateful to them. 'That's – great,' I said. 'Listen, Don—'

Gilbert appeared at that moment. 'Darling, what are you doing?' He stared at Don in that curiously hostile way that upper-class English people have. 'Oh. Good evening.'

'Mr Travers, a real pleasure to meet you. Don Matthews.' Don held out his hand.

'Don's a screenwriter, darling,' I said. 'He wrote *Too Many Stars*.'

'Ah.' Gilbert could barely conceal his apathy. 'Darling, I see Jack over there. I rather thought I might say hello to him. Excuse me, won't you.' He nodded at Don and strode off.

'I don't follow the fan magazines, I'm afraid,' Don said. 'That's the guy they've set you up with? Gilbert Travers? He's a little old for you, don't you think?'

He tapped a cigarette on the side of a worn silver case. I watched him, rubbing my bare arms in the sudden chill of the restaurant. 'He's wonderful,' I said. 'We—'

'You going to marry him?' He rapped out the question, his voice harsh.

A commotion at the other end of the room forestalled my answer; a flurry of white floor-length ermine and flashing diamonds. I looked over to see Benita Medici, my rival at the studio, arriving on the arm of a suave, rake-thin man whom I knew to be Danny Paige, the biggest, wildest bandleader of the moment. 'Oh, my goodness, Danny Paige!' I said. 'I just love him.'

'I'm more of a Sinatra guy,' Don said. 'I like to listen at home. Too old to jive.'

'Slippers and pipe and a paper by the fire, while your wife soothes your brow and fixes you a drink?' I said. *You don't know anything about him. Why would you care if he's married or not?*

'Something like that,' he said, and he smiled again. 'Only it's hard for her to fix me a drink these days.'

'Oh,' I said. 'Why?'

'Vegas is a long way away,' he said. 'Too far to commute.'

'What does she do in Vegas?'

He waved his hand. 'Doesn't matter. She doesn't do it with me, that's the main thing. I'm not a great guy to live with. And I was a lousy husband. She made the right decision.' He tapped the side of his glass. 'I like to drink alone, so it worked out fine.'

I didn't know what to say. 'That's so sad.'

'Why?' He smiled again. 'Marriages fail all the time.'

'But they shouldn't,' I said.

'God, you're young,' he said. He jangled some change in his pocket. 'You know, I worry about you, Rose. You're such a baby. You shouldn't be here, you know it? You should be back in England fluffing up an Elizabethan ruff and getting ready to go out on stage, not living this – life, like a gilded bird in a cage.' His eyes scanned me, looking at the beautiful silk birds on my dress, the crooked one on my shoulder.

I laughed. 'Don't let's disagree. Not when it's so lovely to see you again.' I looked over to where Gilbert was standing at the bar, a greyish-blue plume of cigar smoke rising straight above his head, like a signal.

'Fine. Change the subject.'

'What's your favourite Sinatra album?' I asked him.

Don whistled. 'Gee. That's hard. You like him too?'

'Oh, yes, I love him too. More, in fact. He's my biggest discovery since I came here. I'd never heard him before.'

'You never heard Sinatra?' Don's face was a picture. 'Rose, c'mon.'

'We didn't have jazz and . . . music like that, when I was growing up.' My home was a quiet, forbidding house, full to me of the sound of echoing silence and my guilt which filled up the empty rooms, where once there had been shouts of joy, and more often screams of fury, thundering steps on hard tiles. When Rose was around there'd been no need for music.

'Well, in London . . . of course. In the coffee bars, and at dances. Not before then.' I shook my head, trying to remove the image of Rose singing, shouting, along to some song on the radio, her mouth wide open, eyes full of joy, with that intensity that sometimes scared me. She would have loved Sinatra. She loved music. I pushed the image away, closing my eyes briefly, then opening them. *There. Gone.* 'I'm dying to meet him. Imagine if I did. Mr Baxter says he'll fix it. We were in here once and he and Ava Gardner came in – I nearly died. I must have listened to *Songs for Swingin' Lovers* around a thousand times. The record is worn thin. Dilly's my dresser, and she says she's going to confiscate it if she has to listen to it again.'

'Well. *In the Wee Small Hours* is my favourite, since you ask. "I'll Be Around".'

'Oh.' I was disappointed. 'But it's so depressing. All those sad songs.'

'I like sad songs,' Don said. He looked over at Gilbert, then back at me.

My shoes were tight, and I rubbed my eyes, suddenly tired. It had been a long day, filming a gruelling scene in which Diana the nun hides out in a villager's hut as the Japanese kill scores of people and retreat, setting fire to the village. My back ached from crouching for hours in the same position, and the tips of my fingers were raw and bloody from scrabbling at the gravelly, sandy earth (Burbank's finest, shipped in from the edge of the Mojave Desert). 'You OK?' Don asked.

'Just tired,' I answered.

'I'll let you go. Just one thing, though. That white roses thing – why don't you like them? I was watching you earlier. I saw your face when that reporter asked you about them.'

I stiffened. 'What do you mean?'

'The publicity guys made it up, didn't they?'

'Don't let the fans hear you say that,' I said, keeping my voice light. 'I get about fifty a day.' Mr Baxter's publicity department put it out that Eve Noel the English rose missed her rose bush at home in England so much that she insisted on having white roses flown in from England for her dressing room, since when every day, to my home, to the Beverly Hills Hotel where I stayed on and off, to the studio, white roses arrived by the dozen. It was a sign I'd arrived, they kept telling me, as Dilly put armfuls in the trash or handed them out to girls on the set.

But I hated the things. Loathed them. They would always be linked for me with Mr Baxter in his car, hurting me, puffing over me, the feeling of his vile hands on me. The cloying sweet scent and the surrender I made that night; it was all linked. I tried never to think about that night, never. I assigned it a colour, cream, and if I ever was forced to think about it, like the time Mr Baxter tried it again, in my dressing room on set, or the time he and I rode in the same car after the premiere of *Helen of Troy*, I just thought about the colour cream all the way. I knew I'd done the right thing. I'd passed his test, and mine too, hadn't I? Wasn't I a star, wasn't I adored and feted by millions around the world? So what if the sight of a few roses made me want to throw up.

Unfortunately for me, like all good publicity, sooner or later even those responsible for the myth in the first place started to believe it. Gilbert hated it too, because people were always trying to give me white roses, at premieres, at parties, wherever we went. Hostesses at dinners would thoughtfully always put white roses on the table and laugh a tinkling laugh when I murmured my thanks: '*Oh, we know how you love them, dear!*'

I shook my head, and said 'Cream' softly to myself. Don Matthews watched me.

'Whose idea was it? The rose thing?'

I answered honestly, 'Joe Baxter's. I actually don't like them.'

'I thought so,' he said. 'He did the same with another girl he was trying to launch. Dana something.'

'Really?'

'Oh, yes,' said Don. 'He was obsessed with her. ' His voice was casual, as if he were giving me a piece of gossip from the studio, but something, something made the hairs on the back of my neck stand up.

'What happened to her?' I asked, my heart beating at the base of my throat.

'Oh, she was Southern, and he put it out that she missed the camellias from home. But camellias only last a day or two and they're a real pain in the ass to get out here. And then the big picture he'd put her in flopped – do you remember *Sir Lancelot*?' I shook my head. 'Exactly. She was poison after that. They put her on suspension for something, then she made B-movies when her contract expired, then she disappeared. Last I heard she was addicted to the pills and making ends meet in titty movies out in San Fernando. Poor kid.'

I knew all about suspension. People kept saying the studios were on their last legs, but the truth was my contract with them was still rigid tight. They owned me. I'd heard about the actors and actresses who stopped being favourites. Too old, too expensive, too demanding. They'd be sent scripts that the studio knew they'd never agree to do – playing a camp comedy part, or an eighty-year-old aunt. When they turned them down, the studio put them on suspension, which meant they couldn't work for anyone. And they could only watch as someone cheaper and younger, with better teeth and smoother skin, took their parts from under them.

I swallowed, as the noise of the bar and my own fatigue hit me in another wave. Don said softly, 'Hey, kid, it's OK. I'm just warning you. Don't become another Dana. You're on top of the world now, but they'll still spit you out if you get to be too much trouble.'

I nodded.

'Don't let them make you do anything you don't want to do. You promise me, Rose?' And again he looked over at Gilbert.

'I promise,' I said, not really sure what he was talking about, but knowing he was telling me the truth. His lean body moved closer to mine; I watched the grazing of nut-brown shadowing his jaw, the tight expression in his eyes. 'I'm OK, really.'

'I know you are.' He squeezed my arm. 'We'll talk about my script. I'll come find you at the studio,' he said, and I wanted to say 'When?' But Gilbert approached, with his arm round one of his friends, his third or fourth cocktail in hand. Danny Paige was tapping a rhythm out on the bar, someone was singing, the moon was shining outside and inside, tiny shafts of light spun from the crystal chandelier above us. The bird was still dangling from my arm, untended, unloved. I excused myself from Gilbert and went to the powder room. Alone in front of the mirror, I stared at my reflection for a long time, to try and see how Don thought I'd changed. I didn't know why it mattered to me so much that he thought I had.

CHAPTER SEVEN

IF YOU WANT to see how much of a blood sport Hollywood really is, go to an awards ceremony. You have no idea how the entertainment business really works until you've seen some doddery old children's actor pushed out of the way because Selena Gomez is coming through and her manager and publicist are screaming at the E! producer to get her in front of Seacrest, *now*. If Marilyn Monroe was suddenly reincarnated with Jesus and Elvis on each arm on a red carpet somewhere at the same time as the arrival of a cast member from *Twilight*, I'm telling you, the three of them would all be asked to move along.

I've only ever gone to these things when I've been famous, and so you'd think I'd enjoy them. And at first, I did. Hollywood loves to think it's a friendly community, so you wave at people you recognise and hug that girl from the sitcom who spent three months with you in Louisiana shooting a picture and who was your best friend for all that time but then you never saw again. You exclaim at how beautiful they look and examine their dresses so there's a friendly shot in the magazines of you with some other star both looking like nice people.

But it's business, like everything else here. You're promoting the brand of you and your newest film. You're like a mannequin with ten pre-recorded sentences, there to be studied and commented upon, while behind you a crazy woman with an earpiece and a clipboard shouts at your neck, 'This is NBC. This is CBS. This is E!' You say things like:

'Hi, everyone! Thanks for voting for me! I'm really nervous!'

'Oh, your dress is so cute too!'

Or the deep-breath one, which you have to rehearse beforehand with your stylist and manager, because God forbid you get someone's name wrong:

'Oh, thank you! I love this dress too, she [insert name of dress designer] is such a total genius, and my shoes are from [insert name of shoe designer], my bag is from [insert name of bag designer] and these cute earrings are from [insert name of jeweller].'

The other thing you don't see is the queue. The UP! Kidz Challenge Awards is at the Dorothy Chandler Pavilion in downtown LA, and a line of black limos or SUVs, all blacked-out windows and silver fenders, drivers in suits and shades, snakes down four faceless blocks. Inside each one is a star, waiting for his or her special moment on the carpet.

It's humid tonight and the air con in the SUV is on max to keep me cool, which is making me sweat even more. A huge screaming cheer goes up from the crowd in the bleachers ahead of me and I peer out of the blackened windows, trying to see where we are in the queue. I hate this bit. At first, when I was over here promoting *I Do I Do*, I used to love imagining who was in the car in front of me. It could be Brad Pitt! Or Julia Roberts! These days I know it's as likely to be some reality star with fake boobs who has 2 million Twitter followers and probably makes more money than most film stars. As the screams get louder I barely even look up from my phone. I'm waiting to hear from George, as ever. I don't know where he is.

'Did you meet Patrick Drew yet?'

I shake my head, fanning myself. 'No.'

Opposite me sits my manager Tommy Wiley, frantically chewing gum, sunglasses on.

'I haven't seen you for weeks,' he's complaining. 'This is how I communicate with you, these days? I ride with you to an awards ceremony? I'm like your security guy now?'

'I've been . . . busy.'

'Busy my ass.' Tommy shakes his head. 'Artie told me. You won't commit to a new project, you won't return his calls. What you been up to, for fuck's sake, Sophie? He's tearing his hair out trying to get something lined up for you.' Tommy smiles. He likes it when Artie's annoyed. 'Poor guy.'

Under Californian law managers can't negotiate contracts and agents can't be producers on films. So Artie finds the scripts and the talent, inks the deal, talks to my lawyers, has the lunches to scout out the next hot project, and Tommy – well, he's everything else. He has fewer clients, and I'm his priority at all times – I can call him day or night. He reads all my scripts and has a say in everything I do, but he also brings me business outside of the films. He takes care of the stylists and the journalists and the studios who want three extra days' publicity off me, the airline that wants a fee in cash to stop me being papped on the way out of the plane, and the gay star who has his staff audition girlfriends for a million-dollar fee. Oh, yes, those stories are true.

I look out of the window and shiver involuntarily. The air con is on max; it's freezing in here, and yet I'm still sweating in my pink silk dress.

'I want to do that Shakespeare movie,' I say. He growls.

'Not this again. I'm telling ya, Artie's right. For once! The guy is right. It ain't for you.'

I take a deep breath. 'Look, they reworked the script pretty quickly. We had the wrong version anyway. I met with Tammy Gutenberg, the writer. She only put in the crappy romp-through-history bit with Jane Austen and Nelson because the studio she was attached to made her. The new draft is great. Really great.'

One of the reasons why I don't want to commit to anything yet is because of Tammy's sending me this new draft. I read it and loved it. I loved how smart and funny and moving it was, how it deals with Shakespeare in an interesting way without making you feel dumb, how the modern story about Annie, the girl who works at the museum who is also young

Anne Hathaway when she goes back to the past, is interesting and sparky, how it pokes fun at tourists without being mean. And the stuff after she bangs her head and wakes up in Shakespeare's time . . . it shouldn't work, but she pulls it off. It's done totally confidently, so you buy it without knowing whether it's real or not. Anne Hathaway and Shakespeare are a really lovely couple, and the scenes with the older, solitary, Anne Hathaway musing on their relationship and her life after her husband's death are beautiful. A plum part for an older actress. And there's a delicious bit at the end in the present day and Annie's just woken up and is struggling to answer some punctilious question from an American tourist and Alec Mitford playing a modern-day bloke walks through the door of the museum and says, 'Hello, I'm the new manager,' and their eyes meet and he smiles like he knows he's met her before . . .

I'm not questioning how two hot people come to be working at a tiny museum in the depths of the English countryside. When I mentioned it to Tammy, over lunch at Chateau Marmont, she laughed and said, 'You need some suspension of disbelief in a film. Come on, Sophie. You ever seen *ET*? Exactly.'

I adored Tammy; she bowled me over, in fact. I'd forgotten there are people like this who work in movies. Lots of people probably, but you get past a point where you ever meet them. One, she remembered everything about our time back in Venice Beach – I was obsessed with frappe lattes (I know – so 2005). Two, she was really funny about all the guys we hung out with – I slept with way more of them than I should have, including Sara's ex, Bryan the hairdresser guy, but she also reminded me about Jules the performance artist who lived on the beach and played the banjo, and Troy who was basically a high-school frat boy who thought he wanted to be an actor because he was, in the words of Zoolander, really, really ridiculously good-looking but basically had meat for brains.

'Whatever happened to him?' I'd asked Tammy.

'He went to work at Goldman.' She'd rolled her eyes, stuck her tongue in her cheek, and that's when I realised I loved her.

The other thing I loved about her was that she ate her food. She ordered chicken and lentils and had a pudding. Didn't talk about it, just ate it. And had a glass of wine.

'I don't understand why you can't commit to this,' she'd said. 'It's not a big deal. It's not Ingmar Bergman. It's just a romcom – it's what you do.'

Afterwards I left and drove home, and I didn't know the answer. It was so simple. This is the kind of movie I'm good at; why am I not doing it? Because other people have vested interests in me and the money I can make them, that's why.

'You *met a writer*?'

'It's not that big a deal, Tommy.' I pat my hot face.

'It is for you. You don't like that stuff. Let me deal with the producers and the writers.' Tommy's jaw works even faster. 'Who the fuck is she anyway?'

'I knew her back in the day,' I say. 'Listen, Tommy, I want to do this movie. I'm serious. You and Artie'll just have to find a way to fit it in after *The Bachelorette Party*.'

'I looked into it, you know I did. The timings don't work. It's being filmed in England. This summer. You—'

'The schedule is fluid while they wait for the last piece of funding to fall into place,' I interrupt him. 'And—' I'm saving the best for last. 'Alec Mitford is confirmed as Shakespeare. So there.'

Alec Mitford is box office gold at the moment. His last film, with Meryl Streep and Judi Dench, was number one for five weeks, knocked some comic book off the top. He's a professional Englishman who plays smooth cool posh guys, although I happen to know he grew up in Swindon not far from me.

Oh, Alec. Actually . . . I knew him back in London, the summer I moved down when I got the job on *South Street People*. We had a . . . thing. He still makes me blush.

Tommy can't help but look impressed. 'OK then. Well, that's something. Alec Mitford, huh? So that's what you've been working on, these last few weeks.'

'Sure.' I shrug, like that's the explanation for it all, and I look into the mirror next to me, pretending to fiddle with one of the (loaned) diamond drop earrings that flash and dazzle even in the dim inside light. I don't tell him about the emails I've been sending about Eve Noel. Tina has found her UK agent, a tiny agency that barely has a website. They won't confirm anything about her. They just say they represent her. I've written them three emails now. I'll wear them down, I know I will. But Tommy does not need to know that, nor Artie; this is not part of their plan for me. Besides, I like the secrecy in my life at the moment. I don't tell Tommy about George, either, the fact that I sneak over to his house every other night, and what we've been doing. I'm not sure I like thinking about it too much during the daytime, but for these last few weeks of hiatus while all I've had on my mind is my weight, and who's been sending me these white roses, it's good to forget all about it at night.

Two more white roses have arrived, you see. Both taped to the gate. Each one a week apart, after the first one. The CCTV didn't cover the actual gate, just the path down to it. It's been changed but we can't see who put them there. I'm trying to play it down. I've told myself it's just an over-enthusiastic fan. Someone a little bit too keen.

It's strange though, I know it's more than that. I just do.

There's a loud banging and I jump. Someone knocking on the window, a guy in black with an earpiece. I wriggle in my pink dress, putting my fingers in my armpits. Tommy looks at me suspiciously. 'You get them Botoxed?' he says. 'We don't want slime.'

'Relax,' I say.

'Sophie,' says T.J., his voice a robotic static through the speaker. 'I have a message from Ashley. Patrick Drew's car is just ahead of ours. She says he'll escort you up the carpet.'

'I'll see you the other side,' Tommy says, putting down his

BlackBerry and staring at me intently. 'We'll talk about this. All of this.' He waggles his fingers at me, then reaches into his pocket for another piece of gum. 'Get out there and make nice. Enjoy Patrick. He's cute.'

I pull at my fringe, nod, and turn to Tommy. 'Don't worry, it'll all be fine,' I say.

The rushing sound is louder; the door is opened, and I step out onto the pavement, one glittering, designer-clad foot at a time, from the cool AC into the swampy evening air. It's really muggy. I think there's a storm coming. The roaring gets louder; I look up towards the bleachers full of 'fans' lining the carpet, as if I'm totally surprised, and smile my most engaging smile, waving enthusiastically. They scream back. It's two types, it always is. Middle-aged, large women with tight perms and T-shirts that proclaim their devotion to various film stars or God; and teenage girls, all braces, hysteria and long, flicky hair. They scream when you smile, but just occasionally, there'll be one who doesn't respond, a blank glaring face watching you with open dislike, and you can't show that you've seen them, that you want to go over to the bleachers and point at them, ask them, *'What's wrong? Do you hate me? Why?'*

I think about the roses; the white perfection of them, the fact that someone's hand put them there, laid the first one on the bed, taped the others to the metal gates. Is it one of these faces in the crowd? I shiver in the heat. There must be around a hundred cameras cocked like guns, firing in my face. People scream my name.

'Hey!' Someone pushes me from behind. 'Hey, girl!'

I jump, then look round. 'Hi, Patrick,' I say, smiling mechanically and kissing him on the cheek. 'It's good to meet you.'

Patrick Drew grins, takes off his baseball cap and nods enthusiastically. His long shaggy hair bobs in front of his eyes. He is wearing jeans and a T-shirt. Sure, the T-shirt isn't crumpled but . . . that's it. We were sent twenty-eight dresses, I had seven different meetings with DeShantay, and today I spent four hours getting ready.

'You look pretty,' he says. 'Wow, that dress must be hot.'

The pink dress with the cap sleeves is indeed hot. I stare at him, hating him.

'OK then,' he says. 'Are you ready?'

'Ready as I'll ever be,' I say.

'Let's do it!' As he kisses me, the people in the crowd nearest us roar their approval, like they're witnessing our romance. *Oh, fuck off*, I want to snarl at them. *This guy is an idiot.* Then I feel guilty: we're doing this for them, so they'll go see a film that hasn't even started shooting. I put my arm round him, like we've known each other for years.

'See you later, P,' someone says.

'J-Man! See you. Dudehead, Billy – catch you afterwards, yeah?'

'Yeah, man,' they call out. I don't know when it became obligatory to have an entourage if you're a male star, but these days there have to be at least three dufusy-guys with you at all times, otherwise you're nothing in Hollywood.

'Bye, fellas!' Patrick shouts happily. 'Cool! Good guys, crazy guys. What a trip!'

How can you be this up all the time? I wonder. Is he on something? Perhaps he's a Scientologist. I bet he is.

The crowd roars as we move and the photographers scuttle along beside us, crab-like at our feet. I remind myself of what Mum used to say to me as she pushed me into an audition. *This is your dream, isn't it? You like this. Enjoy the moment.*

'Sophie!' I spin around; stupid of me to turn and look when someone calls my name but I'm rattled, I don't know why – this is full on.

'You OK?' Patrick says. I smile brightly at him.

'I'm totally fine!' I tell him.

Perspiration starts to build on my back, on my neck. I keep my armpits closely wedged by my side.

'Man, you totally are beautiful, you know?' He shakes his head. 'Everyone says it, I mean, I know it, I've seen you in pictures, obviously. But wow . . . yeah, you really are.'

I think it's a line, but he says it like it's a fact, not as a compliment, nodding his head.

'Well, I'm really looking forward to working with you,' I say inanely.

'Me too. You're the queen of this kind of shit!' he says, with a kind of goofy smile. It's gonna be great. You know George, right?'

'Yes,' I say. 'I know George.'

Behind us, Ashley shouts, 'Guys, this is Cally Colherne, E! news.'

'Hi, Cally!' I say. 'It's so great to see you!'

Cally bares her white, white teeth at us and sticks a bright green mike under our noses. 'Hi, guys! Now, I hear you guys are just starting shooting a film together. That's so cool!'

Patrick answers. 'Yeah, Cally. It's . . .'

Smile plastered on my face, I let my mind drift as I go onto autopilot. I wonder where George is.

We move on, stopping at each reporter, answering questions about the movie, about working with each other, and we don't say, *'We just met two minutes ago, I've no idea what his favourite ice-cream is,'* we say, 'Hey, you love cookies and cream, I know you do!' like we're old friends in this big, shiny community of stars.

After about ten minutes I steal a glance at Patrick, as the intensity of the screams coming from the other end of the carpet indicate someone much bigger than us has arrived. He's kind of cute, I have to admit it. He has big brown eyes, a huge sweet smile and this funny floppy hair and gangly limbs that almost seem to take him by surprise. He turns and catches me looking at him, and I feel myself blush with embarrassment. Maybe Tommy was right – I should have taken Botox armpit action.

Patrick talks incessantly, when we're not being interviewed. How he just got a new dog. How he met Dennis Hopper before he died which was so cool because *Easy Rider* is his favourite film. How there's this great new restaurant out on the highway next to the ocean that does unreal shrimp. He keeps asking me questions, but I answer in monosyllables, barely listening. I just want to get inside. As we're reaching the end of the queue, he stops in front of a dinner-jacketed security guard, who nods and wave us through. 'I think we could go further with the script and what we guys do,' he says. And he looks across at me and smiles. 'You've never done anything like that, neither have I.'

I am instantly wary, as that always, always means the girl has to go naked, probably full-frontal. Or do something disgusting. Going further, pushing boundaries, mixing it up – it's all bullshit shorthand for: more girl nudity and if the girl complains, she's a humourless bitch who doesn't get comedy.

I know some cameras are still trained on us, so I keep my hands by my sides and say carefully, pretending to smile, 'Have you spoken to George about it? What does he think?'

'George is totally up for it.' Patrick claps his hands and rubs them together happily. 'It's going to be so cool! You're so talented. You'll love it. I'm convinced you'll get it.'

I know he's trying to butter me up to do something disgusting on film and I'm not doing it. I feel flustered, cross that Patrick and George have already discussed this.

'That's kind,' I say, buying time.

Patrick Drew nods enthusiastically, his broad grin even wider. 'It's not kind, Soph! You rock! You can really act, you know? I saw it and I was like— Hey, dude! You fucking rock, man! That beard is for real! It suits you longer! How are you!'

'Er—' I begin, then I turn around. George is standing behind us. The cameras click again; George is famous, the kind of director you might recognise on the street. Mainly that's because he was married to Billie Gorky the year she won an Oscar, but also because he looks like an important person.

His hand is on my bare skin, where the dress is cut out at the back. 'Hey, guys,' he says, kissing us both. His brown, tanned arms, thick with black hairs, envelop us both. His cool grey eyes, flinty under the beetling black brows, meet mine. 'Look!' he says, in his rich, husky voice, to the reporters and the crowd behind them. 'The stars of *The Bachelorette Party*! We're going to have so much fun making this picture. Summer 2013, OK?'

And I am so flustered – from seeing him, from the heat, from the whole damn thing – that I raise my arm and wave. The camera shutters click madly, like a swarm of crickets chattering together. As I'm doing it, I realise it's a mistake, and then I make a second one.

I look down.

Sure enough, the armpit is dark rose pink, and that's the picture that changes everything. Not a photo of me stepping out of the car in my beautiful borrowed diamond earrings and hair that took an hour to style. Not me and Patrick with our arms round each other, laughing like we're old friends or young lovers. No, the picture that runs on the front of *Us Weekly*, as the headline in TMZ, E! and every gossip website in the States, back home in the UK, on the front of *Heat* the following week, that's re-Tweeted by everyone, is of me looking down in horror at the sweat stain under my arm, my face contorted into a twist of panic. *SOPHIE'S STINKY SURPRISE!* screams a tabloid the next day, like I've lost control of my bowels in front of the Queen, not just got a bit sweaty in the 90-degree heat of a muggy LA. You're not allowed to sweat if you're a star. It was only me who did, not those other stars gliding by, untouchable, beautiful, perfect, glittering in the golden evening light.

CHAPTER EIGHT

A WEEK AFTER Armpitgate, tired of the uncertainty, annoyed by everything else, I ask George to stay over, and he says yes. I can hardly believe it. I think he's being nice to me because I want him more and more at the moment, I can't stop myself, and of course – duh – he loves that. Like every time we fuck it pushes everything further away. He's also being nice to me because he wants me to do something for him. I'm not stupid, though I think he thinks I am. But mainly I think he's being nice to me because Armpitgate is bigger than anyone could have realised. In fact, it's a total disaster.

But it's a mistake, having him in my pretty white house. He's like John Huston; I should have killed a bear and had it mounted on the wall to make him feel at home. He's too big and hairy and . . . *there*, in my space. He arrives late, after dinner with some old buddies (I'm never asked, and I don't want to go anyway), and he stinks of cigars and meat grease: I can smell it on his skin. I lie there watching him take his black silk shirt off and suddenly I wish he wasn't here. I don't know why.

So we don't have sex and I can tell he's pissed about it. He paws at me a few times and kisses my neck, says, 'C'mon baby, c'mon.' But I yawn, tell him I'm tired, I have an early start. I keep seeing the video camera by the side of the bed. I notice it more than I do in his room. It looks out of place.

'That's a shame,' he says eventually. He lies in the white bed, naked, playing with himself. I think he's going to go next door and jerk off in a minute.

I watch him, my arms crossed. 'George, Patrick said something at the awards about a nude scene. Did you discuss it with him?'

The hand under the sheet stops moving. 'What? No.'

'Don't lie to me.'

'I'm not lying to you, Sophie. I wouldn't discuss stuff like that with Patrick Drew. He's a pansy. He'd never agree. I thought you'd be totally into it though.'

'So you do want a sex scene.' I pull the sheet over myself, yanking it away from his body. He clenches his jaw and sits up. 'Why didn't you ask me? I'm not doing it, I can tell you that straight off.'

'Why are you being so uptight?' George is looking impatient. 'It's not that big of a deal. I thought you liked your body. You certainly act like you do when I'm filming you.' He reaches out and tweaks one of my nipples. It hardens instantly. 'Come on, honey. You're acting crazy.'

I hug my arms tightly to me. I wish I wasn't naked. 'George, I'm not—'

'It's a shame, that's all,' George interrupts. 'I know you don't do full-frontal, and I wouldn't ask you to. I respect you, you know that.' He leans in towards me and lowers his voice, even though we're alone. He strokes my ear and neck with his fingers, lightly dusting my skin, and I sigh a little, half-closing my eyes. 'Baby, I just want you to think about it. It's only your tits. You've done it before.'

'I feel funny about it. I want to move on. Not start doing this kind of stuff. And I'm – I'm nearly thirty.' *Yeah, right.*

'Listen, think about it. I don't want you to do anything you don't want. It's that I think it could be really great. Provocative. If we can get the mask right, it'll be like he doesn't know it's his fiancée showing him her tits – he thinks you're just some stripper. *You're* in control. That's why you take your clothes off. You see? I think the audience would totally get that.'

They're always saying that, I've noticed lately. Because of course we all know women who are in control are notable for the way they *always* take their clothes off.

Then he adds, 'You're hot, baby.' He kneels on the bed and rubs my arms. His cock starts to harden. 'You've had a crappy week, that's all. Been hiding away here too long. You haven't seen enough people. You need . . . some release. Mmm?'

I push him away and lie down, turning my back to him. 'Sorry. No. No to all of it.'

As he gets up and stalks into the bathroom, slamming the door behind him, I turn the light off and stare into the dark. He's right, I am hiding away. Festering. I've been to George's, been to Tommy's office, been to the Malibu Country Mart wearing my sunglasses and cap, but I haven't put my face on and got out there. I am still a bit mortified – I know it's stupid. I'm sure you'll agree that, in the great scheme of things, it's not really that big a deal, is it?

Yet all around me, people are treating Armpitgate as if it's something terrible. I've had emails of sympathy from other celebrities. *The worst kind of humiliation*, one of them, an Oscar-winner who played my sister four films ago, wrote. More humiliating than, say, losing all your money and having to beg on the street? I don't think so. I got a text from my co-star on *Defence: Reload*, an action star who is so far back in the closet he's practically out the other side in Narnia. *I really feel for you with what happened. Stay strong, Sophie.* I keep getting messages of support from the public. I even got a card from Sara Cain, a picture of a fifties lady in a pink dress, her hands in the air and the caption in white ticker-tape strip above it: *Sometimes Muriel wondered if it would just be easier to walk around in a sack.* Inside she'd written, *It was really nice to see you the other day. I'm sorry you're having a crappy time. You don't deserve any of this.* Which was actually really nice and made me smile.

Even Tommy said we should reschedule our original meeting and instead have a crisis meeting about Armpitgate, and when I told Artie, assuming he'd tell me Tommy was a madman, he said, 'Maybe we need to discuss it. It's going on too long. This thing has a tail.'

Perhaps he's right. It's been a week and this one image, with my terrible expression and my body twisted into a crazy shape and that dark raspberry stain, has become a sort of meme for the current celebrity culture. The hidden message of it all is: *Hah – see how stupid they look when it all goes wrong,* and I'm the one getting a kicking. There's a Tumblr page of Armpitgate mock-ups: me on the moon, me transposed over some aide in the Situation Room with Obama and Hillary waiting for news about bin Laden, me and Ryan Gosling and he's saying, *'Girl . . . I'd never let you go out without checking for sweaty pits.'* Ashley, my publicist, is on the phone fifteen times a day and her voice gets higher every time we talk. 'Laugh it off. Laugh like you're a sweet klutz and it could happen to anyone. OK? Don't be annoyed, or irritated, or comment in any way. You come off like a prima donna. OK?? Laugh it off. It'll go away.' Pause. 'It has to. OK????'

But a week later it hasn't gone away. Up on Hollywood Boulevard over the stars on the Walk of Fame they're selling T-shirts and mugs emblazoned with that photo and the slogan, *'I'VE LOST MY DEODORANT!'* I saw them today, on the news. Yes, it's on the news, a news story about how Armpitgate is still in the news. The world is going mad and I think I might be going mad too, because I don't understand it any more.

At three, I wake and know I'm not going to get back to sleep. I gaze up at the ceiling, thoughts tumbling through my weary brain. And the honesty of half-conscious thought tells me this feels wrong. My life feels wrong, somehow. I can't complain, I know that, but something's not right. I've taken a wrong turn somewhere. These things keep happening and I feel like there's a pattern and I'm too tired, too hungry, too self-obsessed to see it. The roses. The scripts. Armpits, journalists, girls in lobbies with tight, sad faces, Deena's brown fingers criss-crossed with suntan, grimy with years of cigarettes.

George lies beside me, sleeping like the dead, his huge naked brown body sprawled in a tangle amongst the white sheets. I get up and creep through the empty house, out to the pool, where the lights of the city twinkle below. The sky is purply blue, smoggy even in the depths of night. I sit on the damp lawn and dial.

'Hi, Mum.'

'Sophie? Is that you? Let me turn the radio off.'

I can picture the scene completely: the kitchen done up in best country-cottage style, the flat-screen TV in the corner, the Portmeirion china on the pine dresser. It's morning there and it's nearly summer. Even in the dingy little town I grew up in, the trees are greener, the fields and hedges nearby full of life.

I pick at the grass under my feet. 'Sorry we haven't spoken.'

'It must be two, three a.m. What on earth are you doing calling at this hour?'

'I knew it'd be a good time to get you . . .' I trail off. 'I couldn't sleep.'

'Well, Sophie. I wanted to tell you before but I can't trust the email. You must get better advice about what to wear, dear. That dress, there's pictures everywhere, of you with a sweaty armpit! It's terribly embarrassing.'

There's a pause. I pick furiously at some more grass. 'Yes, I know, Mum.'

'I mean, there's some tops I don't even look at now. The turquoise silk one with the gold buckle that I wore to the London premiere of *Wedding of the Year* – I'm afraid that's in the back of the wardrobe. I won't sell it, because I don't want people to have something I've worn in that way, but really, they should think of these things. You need to tell them! It really shouldn't happen again, Sophie. Everyone's talking about it.'

'Oh, for God's sake, I know,' I say, barely able to control my irritation. 'Don't go on about it. I was just ringing to see how you are.'

Mum's voice rises. 'Oh, well! Don't shout at me! I'm your mother. I'm just trying to help.'

'I'm sorry,' I say. The last thing I want to do is get her wound up; then we'll be here till the sun rises. I stretch out on the grass, the grey-black sky above me and the city glittering below. It's just me alone out here. I feel very small. I keep my voice light. 'So, how's the new bathroom? What's been going on? How's Dads?'

'Well, I'm fine, dear. I'm fine. I went to Cribbs Causeway John Lewis last week, with Mary. Her eyes are very bad. George has to have a knee replacement.'

'George – oh, that George. Oh, dear,' I say.

'And I meant to tell you this – you see, there's a couple of things I wanted to tell you, now. You'll never guess who I bumped into.'

I don't realise she wants me to guess till she says, 'Well, go on. Who?'

'Don't know.'

'I saw Jane Yardley.'

The houses below me are in darkness except for one, a way away, that's glowing with white light and the pool beside it is lit up, a beautiful turquoise against the black hills. The cicadas croak softly nearby and there's the faintest, faintest roar from down below.

'Who?'

Mum says in a rush, 'Oh, Sophie, you remember, the one who was always so stuck up with me around the village. Jane Yardley. Well, her daughter – you remember Rachel, with the terrible teeth? She's moving to LA to be a set designer and anyway Jane sidled up to me yesterday in Gloucester Quays M&S and asked can Rachel get in touch with you when she's out there! I took great pleasure explaining why that wouldn't be appropriate, as you can imagine! The nerve!' Mum laughs.

'I'm pretty lonely at the moment,' I say, feeling quite mad. 'It'd be nice to see Rachel again. Tell her to email me.'

'Very funny! Lonely.'

'I'm serious,' I say.

Mum ignores this. 'Now, dear. I want to know how you are.

107

You're not actually upset about all this armpit hoopla, are you?'

I stare down at the blue pool, then close my eyes. I can still see it, glowing inside my lids. 'No, God no. It's all stupid, anyway, isn't it?'

Mum sounds confused. 'What is?'

'The whole thing. I mean, it'll blow over soon. I don't understand why it's such a big deal.'

'That's because you've never done anything wrong before, dear.' I can hear her moving around the kitchen. 'You've not been caught falling out of nightclubs with no knickers on and going out with the wrong sort of boy. People love you! Because you're a nicely brought-up girl who makes nice films for everyone to enjoy, you see. And stuff like this – well, it's not . . .' She hums, looking for the word. 'Well, again, it's not nice. That's all.'

'Right,' I say, closing my eyes, and rolling back onto the grass. I wish I'd never called her. I remember now: I have to be a bit drunk when I do it. I don't have anything to say to her and it terrifies me.

Yet I owe her so much. I owe her my career. When I was eleven and I played Miss Hardbroom in the *Worst Witch* at school, the father of one of my classmates who happened to be a producer at BBC Bristol told Mum he thought I had potential. Well, that was when the cork came out of the bottle. I must have said I wanted to do it, I suppose. I loved acting. I still do, despite everything. I remind myself as I listen to Mum telling me about what's wrong with various actresses in various soap operas, how hard she worked, how she totally believed in me. How she drove me everywhere, waited, held my hand when I came out crying. How she believed I could do it when I didn't – I think because she wanted it, maybe more than I did. Mum propelled me here, no doubt about it, but the thing is, she doesn't get it. Even though she's been to stay loads of times, and even though Deena's her best friend, she doesn't get it.

'How's Dads?' I say.

'Dads? Oh, he's fine. Chugging along, you know your father.

He doesn't change, does he?' She gives a little snort. 'Actually, the manager of the garage over at Cirencester has just resigned, so he's been spending quite a bit of time over there. He's always covered in oil when he gets back – it's horrible.' She laughs. 'But don't worry, I won't tell anyone he's getting his hands dirty if they ask!'

Mum is slightly ashamed that Dad runs a garage business, even though he's got five and he's had a good living out of it. It's one of the things she doesn't get. Having a dad who's a mechanic, who's made something of himself, who I can talk about in interviews, helped me escape that Posh English Girl label in Hollywood. I didn't ever want to be someone who just does costume dramas. You get typecast as English and they don't know what to do with you, and the press in the UK gets obsessed with you and your weight, your boyfriends, your every move. The newspapers weren't ever that interested in me till I became a star out here and now they're constantly running stories about me when the truth is I don't feel English any more. I don't sound English – I haven't lost the accent but my speech is totally American. I say 'cell' and 'have him call me' and 'raisin', instead of 'mobile' and 'tell him to give me a call' and 'sultana'. I don't know where I'm from, really. But Mum is Middle England through and through. She was the one who suggested I change my surname to Leigh. 'Leigh . . . Like Vivien Leigh. Ladylike,' she'd said approvingly.

Honestly though, I have no idea what my dad thinks about it. He's never there. I can't remember now if he wasn't there before the drama classes and the tap and the ballet started, but as Mum and I turned into a mini production company, her ferrying me around to practices and auditions, he retreated further and further into work or his garage at home. He's probably there right now, not in Cirencester, hidden behind the *Mail*, with a bottle of whisky, some McVitie's Cheddars and a box of spark plugs, waiting for Mum to go out.

A pang of longing for home hits me. I rub my eyes. I'm just tired. 'Give Dads my love, won't you?'

'Well, yes,' Mum says. 'Yes, I will. When I see him.'

She's saying something and I try to listen, again, but there's a faint noise near me and I'm distracted.

'So, Deena's getting on well in the guest house. She loves being there – it's great for her,' she's saying. 'Have you seen much of her? She says you've been out a lot . . .'

Suddenly, there's that prickly, watery feeling of fear, that taste of something metallic in my mouth. *There's someone else here.* I know it in that instinctive way one has, who knows why.

It's deadly quiet. I look over at Deena's guest house. The lights are off. They're off all over the main house too.

'Hold on, Mum,' I whisper. 'Give me a second.'

I hold the phone down on the grass to muffle the sound, and I listen.

There's the noise again. It's coming from below me. Down on the narrow, winding road below the house. Someone's shouting something. I can hear the crunch of gravel and dry, parched earth, in the still of the night, and a car revving up nearby. Someone shouting something across the valley.

My shoulders slump. It's nothing to do with me, I realise. Some couple having an argument, or some lonely nutter – you get a lot of them in this town. I smile at my own preoccupation, self-absorption, and pick up the phone again.

'What happened to you?' Mum says, almost squawking with indignation.

'Sorry,' I say, biting my nail. 'I think it's fine. Someone outside down on the road.'

'Good, well, I was explaining to you that Marcy . . .'

I am suddenly tired, very tired. A cold, mean little streak of nastiness runs through me, the knowledge that I am powerful and I can do what I want, and she likes it that I'm like that.

'Look, I'd better go, Mum,' I say. 'I have a ton of things to do tomorrow and my lawyer's calling me first thing to go through some contracts.'

'Ooh, right,' she says. I hate that note of impressedness in her voice and I hate that I engineered it. 'By the way, what's the next project?'

'Something different.' I sit up. 'Actually, Mum, what do you remember about Eve Noel? Didn't she come from near us?'

'Not far away, over more towards Moreton-in-Marsh,' Mum says. 'I saw her round here once.'

I stop chewing my nail. 'What? When?'

'Ooh. About . . . five years ago?' she says. 'On the high street.'

'You saw Eve Noel? On Shamley high street?' I laugh. 'Mum – no, you didn't. No one knows where she is. She disappeared off the face of the earth like forty years ago.'

'Well, maybe it wasn't her,' says my mother slightly defensively. 'But it looked like her. Older, you know. Small, too. It's not out of the realms of possibility.'

'Eve Noel! You don't find Fred Astaire wandering round even in LA just doing his shopping,' I say.

Mum sounds prickly. 'Fred Astaire's been dead for years, Sophie. She has to buy food, you know. She came from near here, you know that. You of all people, you loved her. She must have some family still here, or something. Maybe she's got a sister.'

'Her sister drowned when Eve was six,' I say automatically.

'Oh, I'd forgotten how obsessed you were with her,' Mum says. 'Of course. Well, it probably wasn't her, was it.' She pauses. 'But Sophie dear, it comes to us all, doesn't it? Look at Deena. I mean, I know it's not in the same class, but . . . Deena used to star in the biggest soap on TV, and now look at her. She used to get hundreds of letters each week. Free dresses, holidays, the lot. And now who cares about Deena Grayson any more? No one. She's invisible.'

She sounds so pleased with herself, glad about Deena's failure. I wish she wasn't like this, and I wish it didn't grate with me so much. I stand up. 'Look, Mum, I have to go.'

'But, dear—'

'Sorry, Mum. We'll catch up soon. I have to go now. Bye.'

I end the call, feeling guilty. As I go back to the house I see a security guard shuffling around the edge of the pool. It's Denis, he's covering the night shift tonight. 'All OK?' I say. 'I heard you down there. I couldn't sleep.'

Denis chuckles and shoves his hands in his pockets. 'Some weird-ass shooting their mouth off, some crap about how someone should leave. Homeless, I bet you. They left this behind.' He holds up a tattered old rug, an ancient UCLA hooded top, torn and stained, and a plastic water bottle. Each of them looks like it's spent many nights out in the open air.

I'm astonished how many homeless people there are in Los Angeles walking along freeways, on the beach. They hitchhike to California from all over because it's warmer all year round, and when I told Tommy I'd donated to a shelter a few months ago and asked what else we could do for them, he didn't look up from his BlackBerry, but just said, 'Uhuh. Homelessness isn't the right area for you. We'll hook you up with that philanthropy advisor and work something out.'

I meant to ask him what would be the right area. I say bye to Denis, pad back through the empty house, and crawl into bed again, next to the snoring, warm, bulk of George. I sleep then, a heavy sleep, full of strange dreams.

CHAPTER NINE

IT'S HARD, WRITING a proper email that you want someone to take seriously. I'm normally on my BlackBerry just writing *Yes* or *Ask Tommy* or *Thanks guys!* or usually *Tina can you deal thx*. But I want to get this one right. It's like homework.

> Dear Melanie,
> I am Sophie Leigh, the film star.

No. What a jackassy thing to write.

> You probably know who I am. Hi!

Wow, I sound like a tool. I bite my finger.

> I wanted to write to you because I am a person who is interested in Eve Noel and I have studied her career for a long time and would like her contact details.

I press delete. Why can't I write a simple bloody email? What kind of idiot have I turned into? I want to yell for Tina to come sort it out, but it's 7.30 in the morning and she's not here yet, plus George is still sleeping down the hall, and I don't want to wake him. I sigh, and look up at Bette Davis, and then at the photo of Eve Noel in *The Boy Next Door* that's on the wall by the window. This used to be her dressing room. I stare at her. She's smiling just slightly, her back straight, her

113

dark hair swept back from her face in a low bun and as ever that smile in her eyes.

Where are you, Eve?

Dear Melanie,

My assistant emailed you last month without much success, but I thought I might try you myself to see if you can be persuaded to reply. I know this is a long shot, but I'm making a picture in the UK about Shakespeare's wife. We're looking for an actress for the part of the older Anne Hathaway and would love to talk to Miss Noel. Can you let me know if she ever considers parts any more, and if not, whether there is any opportunity of talking to her and discussing this film with her? I am a huge, HUGE fan of her work and would love the opportunity to work with her in whatever way she finds easiest. Please contact my agent Artie Morgan at WAM Associates or my manager Tommy Wiley at Focus Entertainment if you would like any of this verified.

Yours,

Sophie Leigh

There's about fifteen too many 'opportunities' and 'works' and I'm sure it could be a better piece of writing, but I don't know how else to put it. It's also a lie as I'm not actually 'making a picture in the UK about Shakespeare's wife'. Tommy and Artie are still clearly hoping it'll go away, *Bachelorette* starts shooting in about ten days' time, and I know from my almost daily emails with Tammy that Cara Hamilton is attached to play the older Anne. But she's a bitch. I met her once when I was auditioning for a bonnet film and she was playing Jane Austen's mother, or something, and she was kind of awful, looked down her nose at me and said loudly, 'You need to learn to speak more clearly, dear,' as though I was an untrained amateur with a pushy mum who got lucky. I mean, she's right, but it was bloody rude. So I wouldn't feel bad about replacing HER, that's for sure. I pull at my fringe and press send, and as the computer burps to let me know the message has gone I smile. I'm not sure why I'm doing this any more. It's like an idle video game, playing in this alternate universe where I'm a producer who gets things done, hustles scriptwriters, negotiates with agents, casts films.

'Hey, kiddo,' says a husky voice as I emerge into the bright morning light on the terrace. 'Look who the fuck I bumped into.' It's Deena, standing by the breakfast table, eyeing up the platter of food. I glare at her and see George, next to her; he's smiling politely but I know he's not happy. This sleepover is not going well.

'Oh,' I say apologetically, going over to him. 'I thought you were still asleep—'

'I woke up,' he smiles, scratching his chest. He's showered and shaved, and he looks ten years younger than he is in his jeans and black shirt, but still there's always that untouchable aura of power that shimmers around him like heat rising from a fire. He leans forward and jabs a thumb at Deena. 'I haven't seen this gal since . . . wow, how long's it been?' He grins mechanically. 'A long time.' She grins too. 'Wow. Deena Grayson. How do you know this little thing here?'

Deena throws her leather jacket onto a dining chair. 'I've known Sophie since she was a baby. She had this scabby rash over her head and she used to puke all the time.' She slides her fingers slowly through her hair and catches her bottom lip in her teeth. 'Her mother and I are old, old friends. Bit like you and me, George.'

'You know it,' George says, with his hearty laugh.

I watch them with amazement, and slight disgust. *She's my godmother, George.* But of course George would know Deena. They're around the same age; in her day she was pretty hot. Add to that the natural air of feline sexuality that hangs about her like flies around Pig Pen from *Peanuts* and it's a dead cert they'd have banged at some drug-fuelled seventies Margot Kidder–Robert Evans house party. What's interesting is that he remembers her name. I'm sometimes not sure he knows mine.

Deena sits down, with a hacking smoker's cough. George is watching her. I touch his arm and point towards the breakfast table, laid with croissants, fruit and a pot of coffee and fresh orange juice. 'Help yourself,' I tell him.

He flashes me that smile again. 'Honey, that'd be great, but I have to go. Last night was fun.' He grabs his keys from the table. 'They brought the car up already. So yeah, I'll see you soon, OK?'

'Sure. Cool.' I follow him through the French doors. I promised myself I'd never ask him for anything, or whine to keep him here. Indeed, part of me is glad he's going . . . but not like this. We've been sleeping together for four months, and he's still a total stranger.

I keep my voice steady. 'So – how do you know Deena?'

We're in the hall, and George starts patting his flak jacket, checking his bags. He produces some Chapstick and applies it liberally to his lips. I watch him, in distaste, as he says, 'Oh, you know. She was hot for a while. God, it was years ago. She's old now.' He screws up his face. 'Wonder how tight it is down there still. That was her thing, you know? Famous for it. All the guys wanted to try her – she had the tightest—' He stops, realising where he is, and chuckles. 'Man. Deena Grayson. That is – ugh. Crazy.' His voice is reproachful, as if it's disgusting that he, George, had to talk to a woman over the age of thirty-five.

I can sense this is a test, and I'm not going to fail. 'Well, it was good to see you.' I examine my nails casually. 'Have a great day!'

'Thanks.' He picks up his holdall, then turns to me. 'When's your coffee with Patrick?'

'Later this morning.'

He nods. 'Patrick's a good guy. I want you two to get along. So have a great time.'

'Yeah. So – see you around,' I say, as cool as I can, because I know, somehow, this is the last time we're going to hook up like this. Something's changed and it's not going back to the way it was. We stare at each other for a second and I

116

realise I hate the expression in his cold eyes. And then he picks up the other bag on the floor.

Slowly, slowly he pats the video camera, snug in its case. 'It's a shame we didn't get any of our own little project filmed last night,' he says.

'Right.' I smile politely.

'I'm telling you, it's hot stuff. I wish more people could see it. Right?' He mimics me.

'It's not going to happen,' I say.

'It might do if I uploaded it, though, mightn't it?'

I flinch as though he's hit me. 'You wouldn't do that.'

'Of course I wouldn't. That's so tacky. I do have friends who'd love it, though . . . some industry guys I know who'd wanna see how good you are, how hot you are . . . how much you want it . . . Prim cute Sophie Leigh, being fucked every which way and begging for more. Ha.'

He kind of shrugs.

The door is open and the morning sun is hurting my eyes but I don't move. I am trapped. I can see him now, in his library with his producer, financier, agent friends, smoking fat cigars and drinking expensive whisky, playing God and watching the prizes of their culling, like hunters. I've heard this goes on. I've been so, so stupid.

I grit my teeth. 'I hope you don't do that,' is all I say.

'Maybe I'll call you,' George says, and then he pats the video camera, snug inside its bag with its secrets. His voice is totally calm. Like he's sure I'll be waiting for his call, because I have to, because he's got me where he wants me. He opens the car door.

'Whatever,' I say, trying not to show how I really feel. A crazy hot rage is surging through me. Like I want to smash the camera into tiny pieces, throw rocks at his dickish Lamborghini as it passes through the gates, send him spinning off the road down into a canyon so he can't pull anything like this any more.

It's already baking hot. I stand in the doorway, aimlessly looking at the empty driveway.

CHAPTER TEN

DEENA WAVES A banana at me as I return to the terrace. 'Hey. Sit down, kiddo.'

'OK.' I realise I'm shaking. I stare at her, wondering why she's here, my rage at and fear of George blocking out everything else.

'So listen—' she says, taking another croissant and tearing it in half. She shoves one wedge into her mouth, as though she's afraid it'll be snatched away. 'Can we have that talk now? I wanted to ask you—'

'Hey, Sophie.' Carmen returns, bearing more coffee. She drops something onto the table. 'Is a package. It just arrived.'

'Who's it from?' I ask.

'Well, I don't know!' Carmen says in surprise. 'I'm not on the gate, I'm not watching the road. I'm in the kitchen, making your food. OK? It was on the table, in the hall. That's all I know.'

'I brought that up,' Deena says suddenly. 'Someone at the gate asked me to give it to you when I came back from . . . this morning.' She cackles, then coughs.

I don't want to know where she's been. I glance down at the label on the package. *Private and confidential* in a scrawling hand, underlined several times.

'Did you see who it was?' There's an edge to my voice.

'Some messenger guy.' She sighs. 'I don't know, OK? They

were ringing the bell. It wasn't a nutter carrying a knife, if that's what you mean.'

'I call Denis,' Carmen says.

'Denis saw the whole thing. It's fine.'

Three roses have somehow arrived and the other guards haven't seen anything. I know he's too old. I know I should have done something about it. I stare at the package again; the handwriting is familiar. 'I'm just going to read this. Excuse me, won't you?'

I rip open the cardboard package, hands still shaking. But it's just a letter.

Dear Sophie,

How are you? I think I can guess. I know you're beautiful as ever, from the posters I see of you all round town. I know too that you're flourishing, getting the adulation you deserve, and I hope you revel in it. That gruesome bedsit of yours in Shepherd's Bush must seem a long way away now. It does to me, though I remember that summer extremely fondly.

Forgive this handwritten, slightly eccentric missive. I wanted to contact you myself. I know you've read the second draft of My Second-Best Bed and you've met with Tammy. I am passionate about this film and about playing Shakespeare. T.T. Tohens is now attached, do you know him? He's a crazy guy but an amazing director. He is as keen as I am to make sure it's not too parochial and twee, and to focus on the love story between Shakespeare and Anne. We need two incredible actresses to play Anne. We have Cara Hamilton almost confirmed as the older Anne. But we've been searching for bloody ages for the right younger Anne/Annie and she's never quite materialised.

I really want that person to be you, Sophie. You are such a talented actress, I don't think you realise it. You're scratching the surface in terms of what you can achieve. I'm convinced this script is the one to break you through. I think this is your moment.

So I'm writing to urge you to consider meeting with me, T.T. and Canyon Pictures. We have tried going via Artie and he is not particularly welcoming, hence this approach. I'll be honest: the funding is extremely dicey. I am waiving my fee for a profits deal and there's a

119

marvellous head of production for Canyon Pictures in the UK, Tony Lees-Miller. You'd love him. He actually knows how to make a good movie, unlike a lot of people in this business. We were due to start shooting in early July, just in time for the English summer. You and I know that means continuous rain for two months, but I haven't told our US colleagues that . . . (And you know what? Lately, I have been longing for the soft rain of an English summer, and the heavy green of the trees, the smell of mown grass and rooms musty with heat, instead of sunshine and air con all day, every day.)

But it all depends on funding. You could help secure that last vital piece and make this film happen. We are flexible on timings. Please, will you think about having a meeting?

I think of you often and with such affection.
Alec Mitford x

Like a heroine in a period drama, I'm ashamed to say that after I finish reading I press the letter to my chest. Alec . . . Oh, Alec, you gorgeous, charming, funny, mysterious man. How does he know that's exactly what I've been thinking? How does he know that's what I miss most about home too, the velvety fall of rain on thick green country lanes?

'What are you smiling about?' Deena says. 'Love letter?'

'No. Business.' I stuff the letter in my back pocket, trying not to smile. I know what it is with Alec: he's a total flirt. I may be as big a star as him, bigger, in fact, but I'm no different to all the other girls, mothers, grandmothers, who love him for the twinkle in his dark blue eyes, his chiselled jawline with the beautiful plump lips, his firm, light voice.

I think back to that time in London. He had a flat in Notting Hill, on Westbourne Grove, near a rock star and the Paul Smith shop. It suited him perfectly; I've never really seen him as someone who'll stay in LA for ever. He should be outside a white stucco house somewhere, or standing in a field wearing jodhpurs. I only ever let him come to the Shepherd's Bush grot-hole I was living in once, when we were very drunk, and I can't believe he remembers it. He left for LA and his first US film while we were still having our summer fling, and I was kind of devastated, when I think about it, but then

I met that scuzzball Dave and that was that. I haven't seen him for a long while now, but there's something about Alec, some mystery about him that makes him especially attractive – it's always there.

I stick my lower lip out and blow upwards, fanning my fringe. 'Penny for them,' Deena says.

'Nothing.' I look at my phone. 'I need to get ready.'

'Right.' She chews on another pastry. 'So, you're fucking George, right?'

I stare at her, not knowing how to answer this.

'Give you a piece of advice?' Her hazel eyes lock with mine. We stare at each other for a moment. I scan her thin, tanned face, trying to read her expression. It takes me a moment to realise it is fear. I've never seen Deena look afraid.

'Go on then,' I say.

'He's trouble, that guy. He probably told you he knew me way back when. All I'm saying is watch out what you do for him.' Then she gives a short laugh and her face changes. She tears off another piece of croissant, flakes going everywhere. 'Why am I saying this to you? You know how to take care of yourself, don't you, kiddo.'

'Yes, of course I do.'

'Remember that drink we had when you first came to town?' Deena grins up at me and I see the gap in her front teeth. Her hair falls in front of her face. 'You met that guy, in the bar? And you just went home with him?' She nods, like we're old friends. 'I knew you'd be OK.'

'I was a different person then,' I say. I sound so uptight, and then I relent. It was, actually, a fun night, the two of us at the bar, her telling me old stories about her time in Hollywood, me still slightly in awe because even though I had my own movie opening and things were looking good, Deena Grayson was still such a legend to me, Mum's best friend, my godmother who made it big. We got hammered, and I went back to the Venice Beach apartment with some waiter. It's the only time in my life I have ever gone home with a total stranger. I felt crappy the next day, really embarrassed too, and it kind of ended that period of being pretty slutty in my life, but Deena always loves to bring it up, like it levels us again.

'I can't be like that any more.'

'Sure,' she says, grinning again, her eyes rolling. 'Yeah, of course. You're a reformed character. No more naughty behaviour, eh?'

The thought that I've basically been whoring myself out to George these last few months, but that it seems OK because it's more discreet, is laughable now, I realise. There was something totally honest about my time in Venice Beach, sleeping with different guys and picking up that waiter – Bernardo! That was his name. We were all basically kind to each other. We were responsible about our irresponsibility, if that makes sense.

'I think it's a bit sad to still be doing that after a while.' I'm a hypocrite. 'Anyway, I can't. It's different now.'

She's quiet for a moment, then she flicks her hazel-green eyes up at me and says, 'It's not so different. We're not so different, you know, Sophie. I'm just saying. Be careful.'

I'll take lectures from a lot of people but not from her. The two of us? Similar? I rub my eyes, not knowing what to say, but thankfully my phone rings and it's Daniel my lawyer wanting to talk about some point concerning *The Bachelorette Party*. I raise one finger in apology to Deena and turn away, hoping she doesn't see my expression.

CHAPTER ELEVEN

I HATE PAP shots, especially after Armpitgate. I apply one last slick of lipgloss, jam my sunglasses firmly on and get out of the SUV. As some lone guy appears in the parking lot, appropriately from behind a dumpster, I smile brightly. He starts snapping.

'Hey, Sophie, lift up your arm!'

I go into robot mode. You have to totally ignore them and keep reminding yourself that the readers of the magazines can't hear what the paps say to you and they'll say anything, anything at all, to get you to react.

'*Us* magazine has a poll asking if you're past it and eighty per cent of people said yes – how does that make you feel?'

I turn and smile. 'Great!' I say. 'Thanks, guys!' Two girls – they look like office workers – stand behind him, whispering to each other. I include them in my beam. 'Hi!' I say breezily.

The too-cool-for-school barista ignores me so studiously when I walk in that I know she's recognised me. Patrick Drew's already waiting up on the mezzanine level of the cafe, which is all exposed oak beams and untreated brown MDF, with today's coffees written in chalk on a board behind us, laminated menus in coffee shops today being rarer than a female romantic lead over the age of forty.

He's scribbling intently in a lined exercise book. I shake my head, gearing myself up for this stupid scenario I've signed on for, and go upstairs to meet him.

'Hey,' I say, touching him lightly on the arm. Patrick looks up and smiles and I can hear the shutter on the camera lens outside clicking as he stands up and hugs me.

'Hey,' he replies. 'It's great to see you. This is a cool place. I've never been here before.'

'Me neither.' Ashley picked it out for us.

Patrick sits down, then leaps up again, almost like he's nervous. 'Man, I'm sorry, Sophie, do you want a coffee?'

'That'd be great,' I say. 'I'll just get a double espresso, thanks.'

I say this nonchalantly. *Yeah, I don't order iced coffee, I'm actually a serious person?* He gives a kind of grin and nods, then stands up to go downstairs, but a waiter appears. 'Guys, what can I get you?' he says perkily, then does the triple: looks up and recognises us, does a massive double-take, then tries to style it out. 'Yeah, we got some great coffees today, there's a fantastic . . .'

He's so clearly an out-of-work actor, the old cliché. He starts on a list of about fifteen different types, blends and beans: 'OK guys, our dark roast is really exciting today. I can't wait to tell you about it – it's . . .'

I stare at Patrick Drew, glad the waiter is blocking the view of the photographer outside on the ground. I'm used to beautiful people, but he is extraordinarily good-looking, there's no doubt about it, the kind of pretty the camera loves and I almost feel sorry for the waiter, standing next to him. Patrick looks like a Renaissance prince in a miniseries. He could be James Bond, if he wasn't dressed like a beach bum and didn't always sound like he's in the stage right before deep sleep.

Order placed, the waiter retreats, throwing us a cheesy smile. 'That's great, guys! Coming right up, thank you!'

We're alone on the mezzanine, and there's an awkward silence after he's gone. The chatter of West Hollywood hipsters with their MacBooks and Brooklyn accents is a reproachful burr below us. I clear my throat.

'No entourage here today?' I say. Patrick looks blank.

'Oh, the guys at the Up! awards thing, you mean? No, my cousin and his buddies were in town. We were surfing all day, I didn't even have a chance to get changed!' I smile, remembering my annoyance at his T-shirt and jeans. 'It was a good day. Sorry you didn't have a better time. Artie told me what happened to you with the photos and shit. That sucks.'

'Thanks,' I say. 'You didn't see them?'

'No. I didn't even notice it happening, dude! I'm sorry, I shoulda pulled your arm down, maybe.' I shrug, 'I don't read papers or watch TV. Used to, but it messed with my mind too much. You know?'

'Uh-huh,' I say, disbelieving. There are many stars who claim not to read reviews or Google themselves, and they're the craziest ones of all, because they're doing it all the time in secret. 'I'd like to say I don't, but I do. It's too hard not to.'

'Just do something else!' he says. 'Go for a walk, or get on your bike, or . . . you know. Something.'

I try not to roll my eyes. *Yep, sure. I'll just hop on that bicycle I keep in the garage and pedal up the coast, shall I?* 'Right.'

There's another silence. I sense he's wondering how long before he can go. This is a farce. I hope the photographer isn't snapping this, then I realise of course he's not, it's too boring. Thankfully, the coffees arrive. Patrick Drew smiles awkwardly, and clinks his mug against my tiny cup like we're drinking tankards of German ale.

'So, I wanted to talk to you about the movie,' he says. 'You know we never really discussed it properly. I mentioned I had a few extra ideas.'

'I've talked to George,' I say. 'I'm not showing my tits. End of.' At that exact moment some guy in a suit walks past, obviously listening in.

Patrick Drew raises his eyebrows just a fraction as the guy backs away, looking amazed. 'OK . . .' he says. 'Uh – I just meant, my idea about changing the location of the road trip they take, from Vegas.' He takes a gulp of his coffee. I do the same.

'Oh. I didn't hear about that.' I look down at my now-empty thimble-sized cup. 'I thought you meant . . . well, nudity.' I sound like a nun.

125

'Of course you're not doing nudity, why would you?' He pours some of his coffee into my cup. 'Just think it'd be good to take it out of the usual road-trip clichés, you know. I'm bored of the whole let's-party-in-Vegas thing, aren't you?'

'Yes, very,' I say. 'I hate Vegas.'

Patrick leans forward. 'Me too. I took my cousin there last year and he was so into it, but it was way too hot and full of crazy people and it sucked! Plus, I really wanted to see Celine Dion? But she was out of town. I was totally bummed.'

I can't help it; I start laughing. 'Celine Dion? No way, Patrick.'

He laughs too. 'Come on, Sophie, it's Vegas, baby! You gotta see something totally camp. She's leaving soon, and she's got a voice on her, that girl. Those pipes . . . Phew.'

I nod, trying to agree, smiling. 'Sure. If you say so.'

He's nodding too, smiling at me. 'Trust me.'

I tell Patrick about my last trip to Vegas, when I took Dave the ex. We were on the rocks and I was trying to keep him sweet really, as he'd mentioned a couple of times that some of the papers had offered him money for photos of me. We had the biggest suite at Caesar's Palace and I gave him $5,000 worth of chips so he could go gambling while I got an early night. He never came back, and when I turned on the TV next morning there he was all over E! with a stripper. That's how I found out. I suppose it was a good thing, really, because we broke up. I still don't know how he got out of Vegas. He never carried cash on him, because I paid for everything.

Patrick winces, pushing his dark messy hair out of his face. 'So that's why I read the magazines and look at the Internet,' I say after a pause. 'I try not to, but sometimes I can't help it. I'm always afraid I'm missing something.'

'It's tough,' he says. 'That sucks, that he was threatening to release photos of you. It's hard for women.'

My eyes flick up to his, suspiciously, but his expression is only of concern. I take a sip of the tiny coffee cup. 'Well, yeah,' I say. 'That's completely true. Finding a guy is hard. Who do you trust and all of that. That's why I'm single most of the time.'

I have no idea why I've said this and all of a sudden I feel embarrassed.

'Hey, girls are just as bad,' he says, and two lines appear between his perfect eyebrows. 'You never know if they're after you for your money or your fame.'

I can't help laughing. 'Well, duh. I think you have to assume they're after both.'

He nods, but a flush of red grows on his cheeks. 'Of course. I'm pretty stupid.'

I gaze into his beautiful brown eyes, feeling like I've stamped on a puppy. 'No, you're not,' I say. 'I think I'm the stupid one.'

'You're not stupid.' Patrick drains his coffee. 'You're too smart to be standing in front of a camera saying stuff you don't care about for the next however many years. 'Cause I've been wondering about all of that, lately. Is this what you want to do, the rest of your life?'

The question floors me for a moment.

'I love films, so yes. I don't want to be on the stage or anything.'

'Do you love it? I don't know if I do.'

'Yes, I do. I love being someone else. And I love the idea you're making something . . . good.' I trail off. 'Something people will watch in thirty years' time.'

But that's not what I do any more. And I don't believe in myself any more.

Patrick is watching me, and I take a deep breath. 'In fact – I've never said this to anyone before—'

'Shoot,' he says. 'I have a terrible memory. I'll forget it tomorrow.'

I laugh. 'I'd like to make films, too. Produce them. Maybe direct too, one day. Find projects, put them together.'

'You should do it,' he says. 'That'd be so cool. No one else is going to do it for you.'

'Have you heard of Eve Noel?' I ask.

'Course,' he says. '*Lanterns Over Mandalay* was just on, a couple weeks ago. Awesome film.'

My hand shoots out across the table and I touch his knuckles. 'Really?' I pull my fingers back into a fist, embarrassed at myself. But he doesn't seem to notice.

'Sure. And I love *A Girl Named Rose*. It's my mom's favourite film. You know something? They shot a whole big section of it where I grew up.'

'Really? Where are you from?'

He smiles proudly. 'Along the coast. Big Sur. You know it?'

I smile. 'No, I've never been. I keep meaning to, it sounds so beautiful—'

He looks horrified. 'You've lived here how long?'

'Seven years.'

'And you've never been up to Big Sur? Wow, that's crazy. I miss it every moment I'm gone. At night, you can see more stars than anywhere else in the country, you know that? There's nothing else there, but sea and hills and sky. My mom and dad, they run a tiny inn up there, right on the edge of the forest. Been in the family for three generations.' He looks at his watch. 'If we leave now and drive non-stop, we'll be there for sunset. The wild flowers are out everywhere now, it's not really summer up there.'

I laugh. 'Let's go, then.'

'We should.'

We stare at each other for a moment. I look into his face. Why does he look familiar? Why do I feel I know him so well already?

He looks pleased. 'Seriously, you should come up for Thanksgiving. If you love Eve Noel. She stayed just along from my folks while they were making the movie. My grandpa remembers it. He used to go up and watch them filming. He said he'd never seen anyone so beautiful. She was so happy, he said, she used to sing all day.'

My throat is dry. 'Really? Was her husband there?'

Patrick shakes his head. 'I don't think so. I could ask my mom. She was born and raised there, like me. It's in her soul. She misses it when she goes away, says she feels like she's lost a limb if she can't hear the sea crashing against the rocks. I tell you, there's nothing like it. I miss them down here, some-times.' He looks around the cafe. 'All seems . . . kinda stupid.'

'You're a close family, aren't you.'

Patrick rolls my cup around the tiny metal table. 'Sure. My dad was sick last year but he's better. But it's cool – I can drive or fly up to see them all the time. My sister lives in San Francisco, so I can see her too. And we all go back to the inn, for holidays. Serve up a few breakfasts. Go swimming. Hiking. Sitting round the fire, waiting for the storm to pass.' He shakes his head. 'It's corny, isn't it, but if I had to give it all up tomorrow and go back there, that'd be totally OK.'

'I love the idea of you bringing out French toast to some tourists,' I say. 'Don't they go mad and lose it?'

'Not really. I mean, they're having a good time anyway. They haven't come to see a movie star. They've come to relax.'

I rub my arms. 'I can't believe your grandpa saw Eve Noel making *A Girl Named Rose*.'

'No, I love that you've heard of it. Most people my age have no idea.'

I shrug. 'I like old movies.'

'You know *Rebecca* was shot up in Big Sur? The stuff by the sea.'

'No way,' I say. 'I didn't know that. I love that film.'

'Well, it's a beautiful place – you really have to come up there some time. I'll take you.'

He stares intently at me for a moment and I meet his gaze. I can feel my cheeks flushing. This is so strange. But I remember to hold myself in check. Sure, he seems nice. But this is Patrick Drew, who is basically notorious for his bar-crawling, bed-hopping, car-crashing bad-boy behaviour. He's charming me, I realise it now.

I clear my throat and check my BlackBerry. Tina has been calling me and she's sent me a text.

Phone Artie when you get this.

Patrick looks at his watch, then at my coffee cup. 'Do you want another coffee? Are we done, do you think?'

I realise I've forgotten all about the photographer over the last few minutes. I look down and there's three of them now, one taking pictures, the other two smoking and chatting behind him, waiting for us to touch each other or even better, kiss.

'Do you have some place you need to be?' I say.

'No,' he says. 'This is fun.'

'I'll get myself a mug, if that's OK. You want anything?'

'Uh . . . I'll take a drip coffee.'

A drip coffee. I have no idea what that is. I was just getting into flat whites, and now there's something else I have to be into? Is it wrong that I still want to order an iced latte? I know the answer.

Patrick looks round for a waiter but I stand up. 'No, it's fine. I have to make a phone call.'

He's better than expected. He's . . . nice. I didn't ever consider he'd be *nice*. Like I'd feel as though we'd known each other for a while. As though . . . Oh, good grief, I tell myself, going carefully down the stairs. He's trying to charm you, Sophie, come on.

But I'm still thinking about him when I join the queue. First rule of celebrity in public: act like the most humble person in the world, much more so than you would if you were a normal person. Queue like your life depends on it, never ask for special favours. I can hear the shutters clicking outside and I stand up straight and try to look unconcerned, my default face. I call Artie, wanting to iron out this nudity thing, but I realise it's not a good idea to have a conversation about it in a crowded coffeeshop and I'm relieved when it goes to voicemail.

'Hey,' says a voice behind me, a girl's. I ignore them and keep my position. It's either a pap trying to get my attention or girls who are just being bitchy, who want you to sign something and then call you a bitch if you won't.

But this girl taps me on the shoulder. 'Hey – hi.' She steps to the side, out of line so she's facing me. I stiffen instinctively and glance at her with a small smile. Who is this psycho?

Then I recognise her, with a wash of relief. 'Sara!' I say. 'Hey, great to see you.'

'I was going to hit you in the boob so you'd remember me,' she says, laughing. 'What a crazy coincidence, seeing you here. It's been like five six years then what, twice in a month?'

Her ponytail is as perky as ever. She's wearing no make-up, and she looks great. I remember suddenly what she said back in the lobby at WAM, about her last audition and how they told her she was an uglier Sophie Leigh, and feel a prickle of shame.

'Thanks for your card, by the way,' I say. I lean in, so I can't be overheard by the fat guy in sweats behind us breathing heavily and the shark in the black suit ahead of us who's counting out the change for his iced coffee in cents on the counter. 'After the armpit thing. It was really sweet of you.'

'It's no big deal. It must have been tough. I just wanted to reach out to you and say I was thinking of you. I won't interrupt your coffee – I saw who you're with.'

I smile. 'It's just a photo-op thing. He's actually a pretty nice guy. Do you wanna come by and say hello?'

She gives a tight smile. 'It's OK, thanks.' I wonder if I sounded patronising.

'I just meant—'

'No, I have to go. It was great to run into you again, Sophie.'

'Sure,' I say. I don't want to sound desperate. 'Well – maybe I'll see you at WAM some time when I'm in the office.'

'If I'm still there. That'd be great.'

'Who's next, please?' the barista asks impatiently, as the suit departs with his coffee. She's the other extreme from our waiter: she wants to let you know she's recognised you and she's not impressed. She's wearing a badge: *Hi, I'm Maiko, and I want to make you your perfect coffee beverage. Just tell me how!*

Sara nudges me. 'You're up next. See you soon.'

'What do you mean, if you're still there?' I ask her.

'Oh, I think I'm gonna have to leave pretty soon,' Sara says. 'But – hey—'

'What can I get you!' Maiko says, more loudly.

'Well, two drip coffees, one with milk,' I say. 'Sara, you want anything?'

131

'Oh, wow. Thank you. Just an iced latte, please. Thank you!'

I give a small laugh, then turn back to Maiko, flashing her my biggest megawatt star smile. 'Thank you so much!' She gives me a death stare and turns to the huge espresso machine behind her.

I turn back to Sara. 'Sorry about that. You're leaving WAM?'

She rubs her nose. 'Oh, my gosh, I don't mean anything by it. Just that I've been with Lynn for a while now, and it might be time for a change. She's so successful, you know, but she has another assistant already and I'm only ever going to be the second person there.' She raises her finger. 'Might take another job for the summer, then find something else to do, retrain, you know? I should have told you. Do you remember Eric, from Jimmy Samba's?'

I rack my brains.

'Oh. I think I—' I begin and then stop, feeling uncomfortable. I remember Bryan. He was her boyfriend and I slept with him . . . But do I remember Eric? 'Wow, it's strange because I've been thinking about it all a lot, lately. That summer, how much fun we all had, just hanging out.'

'That's crazy, so have I,' Sara says, opening her eyes. 'Great minds think alike. Eric – yeah, you must remember him. Tall, red-headed kid, kind of arrogant?'

'Oh yeah.' I remember him – hm, in fact I think I made out with him.

'The night you got the part in *The Bride and Groom* and we all went out and did shots,' she says. I stare at her.

'Your memory is amazing,' I say. 'I'd totally forgotten that.' She blushes.

'I know. It's kind of freaky. It means I'm a good assistant. But it comes off a little intense, and I don't mean it to. Anyway, he's financing a start-up, and he wants me to come work for him, answer phones and fetch coffee.' She raises her eyebrows and smiles, as Maiko slides the coffees across the counter. 'It's a site where actors can upload their audition videos. I think it's a great idea. So I'll probably do that.' She smiles her perky smile.

'Thank you!' I tell Maiko, like she's just rescued me from a burning building. I look down at the drip coffees. They're just normal coffees. Right then.

Sara takes her latte with one hand, then says, 'Anyway! Thanks so much for this, Sophie. Have a good afternoon, and—'

'Hey,' I say impulsively. 'This might be a bit weird. My assistant's going on leave for a couple of months and I need a cover. If you're looking for a summer job . . .' I screw up my face – *is* this a bit weird? Sara is pulling her backpack on and I can't see her expression. 'Look, maybe I shouldn't have asked you – think about it,' I say. *For Christ's sake, she doesn't have to take it.* 'But it could be fun.'

Sara looks down, then up at me, biting her lip. 'Yeah,' she says. 'That could be . . . a lot of fun.'

'It's just for the summer. You can work out what you want to do after that, give yourself some breathing space . . . you know. It's kind of interesting, there's travel, we'd hang out . . .' I say. 'Hot guys, all that. Hey, maybe we could even get you to meet some people. You should act again.'

'Really?' She stares at me, her blue eyes sceptical.

'Well, I definitely think so,' I say. 'Anyway, just consider it.'

'Sure, I will. And thanks, Sophie. Should I talk to Kerry?'

'Yes,' I say. 'That'd be great! Good to see you.'

'Great to see you, Sophie,' she says. 'I'm so glad I ran into you again.' I nod, pleased. 'I'll call Kerry this afternoon.' And with a wave she turns to go, striding out of the shop, small and neat and indistinguishable from all those other thousands, millions of beautifully turned-out, perfectly manicured, polite American girls you don't get in England.

'Who was that?' Patrick says as I sit back down with our coffees and look outside again. Sara walks fast, head down, watching her feet on the sidewalk. I can't see her car.

'She works at WAM,' I say. 'She bashed into my boob in the lobby a couple of weeks ago. We used to hang out when I lived in Venice Beach. She's cute.'

He looks up, like a reflex, I'm sure it is, on the word 'boob'. 'She did what?'

'Like barged into me, out of nowhere. It was crazy. It hurt.'
I grab my left breast, in memory, and then I hear the shutters
go again, and flush with shame. Patrick glances down.

'Jesus!' he says, standing up. 'There are photographers
outside! Christ, how did they know? How – what the fuck?
No way, man. No way.'

He bashes his hand on the table, eyes burning, a red spot
on each cheek, and strides downstairs. I stare after him, realising that once again the studio – or is it our agents, or our
managers? – has played us off each other well. The photos
they'll use are of us touching hands, then Patrick standing up
and striding angrily downstairs, and it'll be yet another 'Patrick
Drew is a Wild and Crazy Guy' story, which is actually great
for his brand, you see: it means people think he's real, not
manufactured. It's such bullshit.

In fact that afternoon on its website *In Touch* goes with
PATRICK AND CAFFEINE – NOT A GOOD COMBINATION and
E! news has me clutching my boob and us smiling at each
other. I look about forty-five and puffy, but at least they don't
mention the armpit, which is a start. Perhaps things are getting
back to normal. I need to start working again, keep my head
down and concentrate on *The Bachelorette Party*. Patrick's a
good guy. It might even be . . . OK to work with him. In fact,
it might be more than OK. After that, the future's mine. I can
do the Shakespeare film, or do my best to persuade them.
And then I'm going to make the Eve Noel thing happen. It's
going to be the best thing I've ever done.

a brown paper parcel tied up in grey ribbon

THE FIRST TIME I met him, I didn't see Don Matthews again for almost two years. After our second meeting, I found myself wondering if it'd be as long again. I hoped not. In fact, it was three weeks later that he showed up on set, just as he'd promised.

The studio lot was in Burbank, the other side of the hills from the city. I liked the drive there in the early morning, before most people were awake, the cool fragrance of jasmine and fresh dew hanging in the air before the California sun rose too high. My call was for 6.30 a.m. which meant getting up around 4.30. But I was lucky this time – for *Helen of Troy* they'd had me in at 5 a.m. every day for the whole shoot, messing around with wigs and blue eyeshadow, my scalp red-raw from burns with curling irons for months afterwards.

It was always quiet first thing in the morning with the executives and producers absent and I liked it. I could sip on coffee in my tiny bungalow, just me and Dilly, my dresser, and Steve, the make-up artist. Later, the costume designer and on-set publicist would arrive, and then there was Moss Fisher, Monumental's head of publicity, whom I'd first met that awful evening in Beverly Hills, so long ago now. He was always turning up, no matter how far away in the vast studio lot you went, hovering around in the background with his sly, sidelong glances while all the time people dressed me in different clothes or cut my fringe, as the director and the director of photography came by, and they'd all stand back and stare at me as though I was a horse ready for market, or a painting on show. Moss often whispered something, or disappeared to make a telephone call, and the word always came back and was acted upon: 'Moss wants less cleavage.' 'Moss doesn't like the salmon colour.' 'Moss doesn't think the line will play well in the mid-West. Lose it.'

We were shooting on Stage 11, which was supposed to be lucky: it's where *Casablanca, Mildred Pierce* and *Now, Voyager* were filmed. I loved all of that, just as I loved to get Gilbert to tell me about the old days, before the war came, the studio heads, the parties, the old stars. So many of them were gone now, the women out to pasture once they turned thirty, the system itself crumbling because suddenly teenagers were everywhere, doing their own thing, listening to records at home, watching films about bobbysoxers, or sitting in front of the dreaded television. The solution, the studios had decided, was lavish. Go bigger than ever, give them 3-D, give them musicals, biblical epics, give them everything TV can't.

Lanterns Over Mandalay had none of that. It was merely a terrific premise and a good script and . . . two stars the public allegedly couldn't get enough of: me and the delicious, funny, handsome Conrad Joyce. *Helen of Troy* had been the highest-grossing picture of 1957. My next film, *The Boy Next Door*, was a smash, too. I was getting used to producers rubbing their hands at the sight of me, then touching my shoulder, as if I were a good-luck talisman. I was more and more nervous. I told myself Conrad Joyce was the real star, he was the one the public all wanted to see. But I knew the reality was different. I couldn't deny it. And I didn't like it. It felt as though too much was riding on me, and I wasn't sure I was up to it. What did I really know about the motion-picture industry, after all? This was my third film, and I wasn't even twenty-two. Louis Featherstone was still my agent but, increasingly daunted by the big guys around me from the studio, he was a silent, unhappy figure, his cowlick unkempt, his bossying, thuggish wife a diminished force. He'd never really been on my side, only his own, so I didn't particularly miss his counsel. But there was no one else, and I didn't know what I was doing when I wasn't acting.

It was quiet on the lot that day and Dilly and I were left in peace. At nearly 8.30, I was ready to go on set, without the usual agonising over whether my shoes were scuffed enough or whether my lipstick should be darker, when there was a knock from outside.

'Come?' Dilly said, and the door opened slowly.

'Good morning,' came a man's voice, and the door opened a little wider. I felt my heart leap, and I craned my neck, away from Dilly's hands.

'Hello? Who's that?'

It's strange. I remember how wild I felt, how desperate that it should be him.

'It's Don Matthews,' came the voice, and Don appeared, opening the door a little wider. 'How are we today?'

'May I help you?' Dilly said, at her most imperious.

'I just dropped by to see Miss Noel,' Don explained. 'I have something for her.' He dangled a package in front of me, brown paper tied up with a thin grey ribbon. Dilly tutted.

'It's fine, Dilly, he can come in,' I said, waving him in. 'Don, this is Dilly.' Dilly tutted again. 'It's good to see you, Don. How are you?'

'I'm well, thank you.' He came into the room. 'You look beautiful.'

I glanced in the three-part mirror. 'That's kind but it's not what we want you to say. I ought to look as though I've been hiding out in the inhospitable terrain of the Burmese jungle for two months, feeding myself and twenty orphans on roots and berries.'

He laughed. 'Well, clearly that kind of living suits you.'

'Sit down,' I said. 'Can Dilly get you a drink?'

Just then, a quiet voice spoke up from the open doorway.

'Good morning. Quite a little gathering we have here.'

Moss Fisher appeared on the threshold. I couldn't help smiling; I wondered who'd told him Don was here. Moss was like a snake; I never knew when he was going to slither, silently, into view. I hated him.

He advanced into the room. 'I just came to pay a visit to our star. I hear great things, Eve, you're setting the place alight. Hi there, Don,' he said, with all the warmth of an icicle.

Don stood up again; he was too tall for the tiny bungalow, and his lanky limbs seemed to fold awkwardly inside the space. 'I'll go,' he said. 'I wanted to talk to you about something. Another time.'

'What's that?' Moss asked, peering at Don. 'Eve, Refford wants to know—'

'No,' I interrupted. 'Walk with me a moment, Don. I'm going on set.' I shot Moss a look of annoyance. Damn them, so I couldn't have a visitor in my room? I could hear them. *What if it got out? What about Gilbert? He's a writer, for Christ's sakes, Eve, a writer.*

I called back to Moss. 'Moss dear, could you be an angel and help Dilly with my shoes? I can't carry them. I mustn't mess up my nun's habit.'

Since the habit was faithfully re-encrusted with pale orange dust every morning before I put it on, this was clearly a lie, but Moss couldn't say anything. He picked up the shoes and the make-up case as Don helped me out of the trailer, and as I left he gave me a look. I didn't like it.

The Stars and Stripes were fluttering in the breeze next to the water tower which had stood there since the Baxters opened the lot twenty years ago. A cart trundled past us carrying a vast, elaborate chandelier, as Don and I weaved our way through the lot. People stopped to wave at me, and I waved back.

'You were great yesterday, Eve!' one of the guys by the loading bay, a cameraman, called out. 'They loved it.'

'Oh, thank you!' I said, in my most English accent. 'I'm still terrified. That's very kind of you.'

Someone else clapped. I smiled as widely as possible. There was a murmur of approval. My head ached, the pins holding my hair in place pulling at my scalp, as the curls, rigid with hair lacquer, began to crack.

We skirted behind the loading bay. Don had his hands in his pockets and was whistling, though I could tell he was trying not to laugh.

'So,' I said, as we crossed a tiny road over towards the sound stages. 'I loved *Rose*. I absolutely loved it.'

'You read it?'

'Of course I read it,' I said. 'I asked for it after I saw you. They gave it to me a couple of weeks ago.'

He shrugged. 'Very kind of you.'

'Listen, Don.' I turned and looked at him. 'I've asked Mr Baxter. I've told him I have to do it. You're a genius, Don Matthews.'

He smiled and didn't say anything.

'How do you know?'

'How do I know what, Rose?'

'How do you know all those details?' I asked him. 'About women, how we think, what we're really like. I loved it. I can't stop thinking about it.'

'Listen, I've changed my mind,' he said simply. 'I don't think you're right for the part any more.'

I stopped in the middle of the road, holding the black sacking of my habit over one arm. 'What?'

'Sorry.' He carried on walking. 'I was wrong. I think someone else would be better in the part.'

'But it's me, this film,' I said, trying not to sound childish. I looked at him, trying to work out what was going on. 'Why have you changed your mind?'

'I haven't – just that I was wrong, as I say.' Don shoved his hands in his pockets and carried on walking.

A group of Red Indians – a squaw, a chief and some children – passed by with a cowboy in leather chaps that creaked as he walked. One of the children pointed at me and whispered something to the chief. I smiled perfunctorily at them as they turned the corner.

Then we were alone in the middle of the quiet, fake road,

the sun rising higher in the silver-flecked sky behind Don. He nodded towards the stage ahead of us. A lighting technician was carrying a huge arc lamp in through the open door. The beam of the rising sun behind us meant you couldn't see anything inside, just a black hole.

Suddenly I was angry. 'I don't understand this, Don. You told me when we met at Romanoff's—'

'I ran into someone from the publicity unit, an old friend. You're marrying him, aren't you, Rose?' he said. 'Why didn't you tell me, that night at Romanoff's?'

My mind was racing; it took me a moment to catch up with him. 'Gilbert? Yes, I am.'

He nodded. 'When?'

'Just under two weeks' time. At his house.'

'*His* house?'

'Our house – his – oh, does it matter who's paying for the house? What's that to do with it?'

'I – I don't know,' he said, almost angrily. 'It doesn't matter at all. You're right.'

'I love Gilbert. He loves me. We can't live together without being married – too much scandal. And – well, it's right for both of us.'

'You mean it's right for the studio,' Don said. 'It's not right for you. You can't love him.'

He said it quite matter-of-factly.

'Well, I do,' I said, struggling to keep calm. I thought about Gilbert and smiled. 'You have no idea. I think he's wonderful. I can't believe I'm going to be his wife.'

'A schoolgirl's fantasy, not real life.' Don shrugged. I faced him, square on, only inches separating us. Underneath the sacking cloth of my costume I could feel my heart, pounding in my chest, almost aching with some strange feeling I did not understand.

'Don't treat me like a child, Don. I know what I'm doing.'

He took my hands, and then enclosed them in his warm palms, his fingers tangling with mine. 'No, you don't,' he said calmly. 'You don't belong here, Rose. Go back home. Go back to England, be an actress there. You're running away from

140

something, I know you are, but whatever it is, you won't find what you're looking for here. Trust me.'

I looked down at my dusty habit, at my white hands enclosed in his, then up at the mammoth studio buildings curving away from me against the endless blue sky.

'This place is a nest of vipers, Rose. It'll destroy you. I know you. I know you and you don't even know yourself.' He faced me, his jaw rigid, and I almost flinched under the intensity of his gaze. 'Moss ruins people's lives with the stroke of a pen. And the Baxters, they don't care. You're fresh meat to them, goddammit, and when that beautiful face gets the hint of a wrinkle they'll spit you out.'

Joe Baxter's blubbering lips, his clammy hands on my body . . . I shuddered, completely involuntarily, at the memory, then closed my eyes, trying to block it out. Rose's face appeared, as it always did when I was trying to forget something, pushing something bad away.

'*Hello!*' she said, her hair a black tangle around her flushed face. '*Hello, Eve! Come and play with me!*'

And as always, before I could reach her, she got up from the grassy bank where she was sitting and ran away, her skinny white limbs flashing through the dappled green tunnel of memory . . . then the sounds I'd heard that haunted me – crying in the night, the screech of brakes – and the lights flashing . . .

I could hear her calling for me. The strange thing is, I heard it more and more these days. I kept having the same dream: the car that came in darkness, the sound of screaming filling the house, and then I always woke up, heart thumping, drenched in sweat, calling out her name.

'Miss Noel!' A voice calling out behind us. I jumped, recalled in an instant to the present. I wrenched my hands away from Don's and turned to see two ladies from the French court, slowly gliding towards us in vast powdered wigs and huge, bell-shaped crinolines. 'Miss Noel, I'm such a fan, oh, my goodness! May I—?'

'Hold on, please,' I said to them, for the first time in my life. I walked down the little alleyway in front of us, and Don followed me.

141

He said, 'Listen, it's none of my business, I suppose—'

'You're damned right it isn't.' The force of my anger surprised me; people were always telling me they knew best, and I didn't know why this upset me so much. 'Me, I'm the one they go to see. I'm the one they look at, I'm the girl on the poster. You write what they tell you to write, do what they say. Who the hell are you anyway? Nobody,' I said, flinging the words at him. 'You don't know anything about me.'

'I know you lost your sister and you blame yourself. I know you're homesick and you don't understand why, and you're worried you'll do something wrong. I know they've ripped out your teeth and plucked out your hair to make you look less like yourself and more like some ideal that doesn't exist, because they don't understand you, Rose, not the way I do. I know you like avocados, and Frank Sinatra, and butter, and sunshine, and I wrote that damn script for you, but I won't let you do it as you are now. You shouldn't be here—'

I reached up and slapped him, my fingers stinging as they hit his smooth chin. 'You pig. Leave me alone. You can't talk to me that way.'

'I know. I'll go.' His dark eyes were black. 'I just wanted to see you again. Tell you why I—'

He gave a growl of impatience and then pulled me towards him, his hands on my elbows. We stood there for a second, firm against each other, completely still. I think he was waiting to see if I'd pull away. But I didn't and so he kissed me swiftly, there on the street, his lips firm on mine. I could hear his breathing, rushed and erratic, as our bodies met briefly, and then I stepped back and pressed my hand to my mouth.

'How dare you,' I said, looking frantically around, praying Moss wasn't nearby, that no one had seen us. 'Don Matthews, I'll report you—'

'So report me,' he said. 'I wrote *Rose* for you, you know. Do it if you want, but if you do, do it as you, the girl you were. Stop letting them bend you whichever way they want. They're trying to make you perfect, Rose, but you were perfect before. You promised me the other week you weren't going to let them

142

push you around. So don't marry him. He's a pig. He'll break your heart.' He took my hand, squeezing it so tight it hurt. 'And Rose, I couldn't bear that, I couldn't. Goodbye.'

Someone was approaching behind us in a slow car; two of the crew stepped out from another stage, carrying ladders, a huge arc light on a trolley. Dilly appeared at the door of the sound stage. 'Miss Noel, what you doing out there?'

'I'm just coming,' I said. I turned and faced him. 'I'm making the movie,' I told Don. 'Don't come back here. Don't destroy me just because you want to destroy yourself, Mr Matthews.' I walked into the building, holding my habit, without looking back at him.

I had forgotten about the parcel. When I came back to my dressing room for lunch, four hours later, my head pounding from the huge arc lights, there it was on the table, the brown paper parcel tied up in grey ribbon. Written on it in a scrawling, huge fist, was the inscription:

For Rose from Don, in the hope she never needs it.

It was that Sinatra album, *In the Wee Small Hours*. On the inside of the brown paper he'd written:

I think about you when I hear this.

Just now and then
Drop a line, to say that you're feeling fine
And when things go wrong,
Perhaps you'll see, you're meant for me –
So I'll be around when he's gone.

CHAPTER TWELVE

'YOU'RE THE BEST! You can do it, Sophie! Three more! Two! One! Go! Feel the burn, reach it reach it reach it REACH IT! Yes! Fulfil your goal, do it now, on the floor, go go GO! One, two, three, that's the goal, yes! Yes!'

Laney, my trainer, comes over twice a week to work with me. She's mean and hardcore. We do squat thrusts, we do bench-pressing, we run on the spot, we stretch, we do sit-ups and more sit-ups, and all the time she's yelling at me, in her intense Californian way, 'You can do it! *You can do it!*'

I have a slight girl crush on her. She is a brilliant mixture of loony zen and Nora Ephron. She looks like she's been styled before she comes over, and as she gets here at 6.30 in the morning twice a week, I don't know how she does it. She has thick brown wavy hair in a Rachel-Zoe-without-being-super-evil-style centre parting. I have realised I'm getting sick of my bob. The studio won't like it but I might even start growing it out. In *My Second-Best Bed* Anne Hathaway has long hair, and the modern-day Annie a crop, so if I did the film I'd have to wear a wig anyway. *If.*

Laney's skin is flawless, glowing with the zeal that totally focused exercise-Nazis get, and her body is amazing, slim and toned and slightly tanned. I was born to be a bit podgy. Nothing much, just a bit. Being this thin doesn't sit well with me, I know it. Laney was born to it.

It's early on Saturday morning. We're outside, on the lawn doing sit-ups. At least I am – she's yelling at me. When I stop, Laney shoots water into my mouth like I'm a professional athlete, and as I lie panting on the ground she says, 'That was good, Sophie, but you can do better.'

'I don't want to do better,' I rasp. 'I want to die.'

'You're so funny.' Laney smiles, her teeth glinting in the morning sun. She's gone a shade too far with the whitening, I think, but the world of HDTV will teach her that, I'm sure. 'So I'm gonna take off, OK? I'm filming later.' Like all good personal trainers, Laney is on TV and has her own DVD empire. 'Stay focused on yourself. Remember the sunshine you bring to people.'

'OK,' I say, totally straight-faced. 'Thanks, Laney. Good session. See you soon.' I want to reach out and touch her hair, like Vicky Watkins's hair at school.

'I'll see you next week.' She nudges me lightly with the pristine white toe of her sneaker. 'Is this all for the Patrick Drew movie? Did you meet with him yet?'

'Sure,' I tell her. 'Last week. We had coffee.'

'What's he like? My girlfriends and I are obsessed with him. Is he really dumb as a plank? Or does he have a special aura?'

I think for a minute. 'He's not dumb.' I think about his smile, his stories about his parents, the Celine Dion Las Vegas conversation, and I grin. 'Actually, he's lovely.'

'Oh, my goodness, did you guys—' Laney's mouth opens and she claps her hands.

'No!' I say loudly, too loudly. 'Laney, no way!'

'You have a crush on him.'

'I do not. I met him, once. He's a big dufus.'

Laney ignores this. 'Did you call him?'

'We've . . . we've texted a couple times.' I pull my arm across my body with one hand, stretching my shoulder, pretending I'm focused on this and not on Patrick Drew.

Laney straddles the mat, pulling her hair into a ponytail. 'That is so lame. Texting is like nothing. You might as well be Facebook friends. Ask him out!'

'It doesn't work like that. Anyway, we have nothing in common.'

'That's for the birds, Sophie. You should ask him out.' I cross my arms and she changes tack, smiling. 'Makes shooting the movie more interesting, right?'

'It does make a difference, that's for sure.'

She claps her hands together. 'OK, well I'll see you next week! Even more reason to enjoy those extra sessions, am I right?'

'What?'

'Tommy called me. I'm coming by four times next week. Just to make sure you're in the best shape of your life before shooting starts.'

'Four?' I shake my head. 'I don't think so. Tommy asked for four sessions?'

She looks awkward, pulling her foot up behind her, each leg in turn. 'I don't think it came from Tommy, Sophie. Some request from the studio. He told Tina. The director asked that we move you up to four times a week prior to shooting.'

I get up slowly, turning away from her so she can't see my face.

Fucking George. It's him. I know it's him, trying to screw with my head now he's not screwing me. No contact since he stayed over that time – what, well over a week ago now? First the costume designer calls Tina and tells her I'm too big for the costumes and they're being remade; now this. This is his way of letting me know he's still in control. Tell her she's fat, tell her she's unfit, get to her so she's a crazy mess and I can do what I want with her on set and she'll end up taking her clothes off out of desperation to keep me happy. For what? For him, for the film? I don't know which yet.

Before we even started sleeping together I'd heard stories about him and what he does to actresses. He made one girl once do fifty-two takes of the same six-word line. *Fifty-two*. She's a big star, too – you'd know exactly who I mean. And she's good, a total professional, not a flake like some of

146

them. She was crying by the end, and he'd just stop every time and make them do her make-up, touch it up, wait till they could go again, then shout 'Cut!' and swear at her that she wasn't getting it right. Then, *then*, he went with the first take. He's a bastard.

Laney looks at me, a little concerned. 'Hey, Sophie, that's OK, right?'

I bend down, touch my toes, feeling the stretch in my back, my shoulder blades, my arms. 'That's absolutely fine. It'll be great to see you!'

'Well, totally,' she says, looking relieved. 'OK! I wasn't sure. It's such a blessing that we—' when the French doors open and Ashley, my publicist, appears.

'Hi! Hi, Sophie! Hi, Laney, how're you?'

'Hi, Ashley, how're you!'

'I'm good, I'm good. Sophie, we have to talk. Something happened.' Ashley's jaw is tight, her dead straight ginger hair is sticking out slightly, and her hazel eyes are bulging. She still has her phone headset on. 'You didn't see the papers yet?'

I laugh and gesture at Laney. 'Well – no, not so much.'

'Come with me,' says Ashley, grabbing my hand. 'We got a problem.'

Ashley's iPad is propped up in my study. She's got a British tabloid website on-screen, and I glance at it more out of curiosity than anything else. Then I start to read:

SOPHIE AND ME: MY TIME WITH BRITAIN'S NO.1 STAR

* Wild nights in LA sleeping with 'every man in town'
* 'Village of chavs' – her snobbery about home town
* 'I'm so fat' – paranoid star's insecurity about looks
* Armpitgate – DOES Brit lovely have hygiene problems?

DAVE OLDMAN, ex-boyfriend of Hollywood megastar Sophie Leigh, last night broke his silence on their four-year relationship, and insists – 'I DUMPED HER because I couldn't take her demands for sex and booze any more.'

The 29-year-old former child actor turned IT technician, and father of one, was with the West Country lovely after her career Stateside went global. In this EXCLUSIVE interview he tells us all about her insatiable appetite, her . . .

I scroll down frantically, and see yet another snap of me with the soggy armpit. There's a photo of Dave too and I zoom in and stare at him, at his thin face with the weak chin, patchy with sparse hairs. He wears a wounded expression and he's sitting on a sofa, holding a baby, with a short girl, so fake-tanned she looks like an Oompa-Loompa. Doting Dad Dave now prefers the quiet life at home with his fiancée Sherree and baby Armani, says the caption. I shake my head.

'Jesus, Ashley,' I say. 'Why the hell didn't you try and stop it?'

'They kept it totally hidden. The bastards didn't want it to go viral. They needed a splash for the Saturday edition – they're locked in a circ war with the British Sunday tabloids,' says Ashley robotically. Her jaw's so tight I'm surprised she can speak.

The air con is on full blast. The fresh sweat from my workout is like an icy chill on my body. I stare at the screen and a photo of me and Dave, arms round each other: I've got red streaks in my hair like I'm a Spice Girl, and we're laughing, sticking our tongues out. I remember that night. He was over staying for one of his periodic bouts of interest in me, when everything would be cool to start with and four days in I'd have realised it was all a big mistake. But I couldn't ever seem to get rid of him, tell him to fuck off back home. I don't know why, now. So naive. 'I thought he was so great when we got together,' I say. 'Couldn't believe he was interested in me. He was so sharp and cool . . .' I push the iPad away and stand up. 'What did I ever see in him? What a cliché! What a knob.'

'If I had a nickel . . .' Ashley says grimly. 'Honey, Tommy and Artie are on their way up. They wanna talk it over. What you do next.' I rub my eyes, my vision cloudy in the sudden dark of the room. 'Listen, we got caught sleeping on the armpit thing. We need to handle this, otherwise people aren't gonna get you any more, Sophie. They'd just forgotten about the action movie and the indie movie – now this stuff. We need to make you America's British sweetheart again, not someone dragged into the tabloids for all the wrong reasons.' I stare at her, nodding mutely. 'Don't panic, honey,' she says. 'We'll regroup.'

'Angelina Jolie's in the tabloids every fucking week.' I try to keep my voice level, and turn on my computer.

'She's crazy – she doesn't count. You're supposed to be a normal girl.' Ashley starts drumming on the table, her slim fingers beating a rhythm. 'Normal girls need to be in there trying on new nail polish, yukking it up with their friends over salads, playing with their babies in the park, going on dates. Normal girls aren't walking round with wet pits, rubbing their boobs in front of Patrick Drew—'

'I was showing him how Sara whacked into me!' I exclaim.

Ashley shrugs. 'Honey, they don't care. That's what they see. And now this – some scuzzball linking himself with you, and his white-trash girlfriend and their baby.' Her face is screwed into a picture of distaste as she looks at Dave. 'Look at them. You don't want the association. The US tabloids'll pick it up and run with it. It's already on TMZ and People.com. It's a disaster, honey. You're supposed to be sweet, cute, classy.' Her cell rings. 'Sure,' she says, after a few seconds. 'Sure, I got you.' She strides out of the room, holding her index finger up to me, mouthing, *One minute. One minute.*

Left alone, I sniff my armpits cautiously, and then catch my reflection in the glass doors. I want to laugh, a mixture of hysteria, fatigue and bewilderment. Because this is ridiculous, isn't it? Normal girls, Ashley says. None of this is normal, none of it. I stretch and then sit down at the computer and log into Twitter to see what people are saying. I know I shouldn't, but if you were on the front page of every tabloid in the UK with exclusive revelations from your ex in the *Sun* about how you're a nympho who drinks too much and has severe hygiene problems you'd kind of care, wouldn't you? Don't tell me you wouldn't.

It's the usual depressing kind of stuff. My eyes run up and down the columns, drearily reading it all: the worst, most inhumane corners of people's brains, the smegma they think it's OK to put out there, like there's no repercussions, no one is affected by it.

> @SophieLeigh smells – knew it already @SophieLeigh can clean her teeth on my dick @SophieLeigh stay in the US we hate you @SophieLeigh go back to England, USA USA #godblessamerica @SophieLeigh I love u yr amazing who care's if yr fat @SophieLeigh I HATED YOUR LAST FILM YOU SUCK HOPE YOU DIE @SophieLeigh Don't listen 2 haterz! @SophieLeigh You'll be getting another white rose from me soon. And then you're going to get what you deserve.

I feel my heart stop, then it starts to pound again, and then someone bangs on the glass door and I scream.

'Hey, kiddo.' Deena steps inside. 'Can I ask you—'

'Get out!' I shout. 'For fuck's sake, Deena, leave me alone, I'm—' I cover my face and turn back to the screen and she stares at me in astonishment. I hear her boots on the terrace as she walks away.

I peer again at the screen, my head throbbing and my heart thumping so loud I can hear it. I stare at the message.

> @SophieLeigh You'll be getting another white rose from me soon. And then you're going to get what you deserve.
>
> @SophieLeigh You'll be getting another white rose from me soon. And then you're going to get what you deserve.

The username is White_Roses and I click on their profile.

> White Roses
> @White_Roses

Location: Nearer Than You Think

Watching Sophie Leigh. Waiting for her next move. Wondering if this scares her. Hoping it does.

0 Followers

1 Friend

CHAPTER THIRTEEN

'IT'S SOME NUT-JOB,' Artie says. 'It's a crazy fucking nut-job and we should just ignore it.'

A crackling voice yells, 'It's a nut-job who might break in and stab her to death! Artie, you lost your mind? We need to get security doubled, OK? I've spoken to the guys already. I'm on this, Tina's on this, T.J. is on this. Sophie ain't going nowhere without a driver and a detail on her twenty-four seven. And . . .'

The voice goes dead. Ashley sighs, Artie looks at his fingers. I sit between them on the cream sofa that looks out over the pool, showered and changed and feeling like a pupil who's done something bad and been called to see the headmaster. I hadn't told them about the white roses and now they're furious. I told Denis. I thought that was enough. Well, I know it wasn't, deep down – he's an old guy and he's not quite up to it any more. I knew he wasn't. I just didn't want to deal with it, I don't know why. Maybe to avoid all of this. Tommy is on speakerphone; he's out on a yacht this weekend and can't get back but he's been patched through, like this is the Situation Room.

'Listen,' Ashley says. 'Now we know about it –' she glances at me – 'it's gonna be fine. We just have to make sure security is in place. I'll stay here. What are your plans for later?'

152

'I have Steve and Suzy's party tonight. But I don't know if I'll go, now.'

'You should go,' Artie grunts. 'Listen, Tommy – are you there?'

'I'm fucking there! Of course I'm there! Whose party?' The phone on the side is practically jumping with static and barely controlled rage. 'Whose party you going to?'

'Steve Levine,' I yell. 'It's Suzy's benefit for something. Suzy's his wife.'

'I know who fucking Suzy Levine's married to, OK? I know Steve Levine. Cock-sucker wouldn't return my calls when I started out – he can screw himself.' Tommy has an outsider's chip on his shoulder; he didn't come up through the agent system but worked in the music industry first and he's extremely sensitive about what he sees as 'old' Hollywood.

'Tommy, I got this.' Artie is eyeing up the cakes, sliding his finger inside his watch strap so the thick silver links rub over his knuckles. 'Let me take care of it.'

'No way, Artie. You said you had it before and we got ourselves into the armpit thing, OK? We shoulda caught the tabloid before they printed the story. Now we look like we were fucking sleeping our way through this thing, plus this – if she gets whacked by some psycho . . .' Tommy leaves the sentence hanging in mid-air.

'What the hell does that mean?' I say. 'Tommy, you're freaking me out.'

'I know, sweetie, but you don't need to worry. It's all gonna be OK. I got fucking Mossad and the fuckin' SAS coming out to look after you. And after that, you know what I think? We have you hospitalised for exhaustion. I know this place in Arizona . . .' He cuts out. 'Shit. I'm breaking up.'

Artie's grinning, wolflike. He knows he's winning this one.

'We get you to Arizona and you wait this thing out there. In the desert for two months. It's fine, we'll . . .'

There's another loud crackle, and after a few moment's silence Artie turns the phone off and slides it down the side of the couch.

'This will all work out OK,' he says. 'I promise you.' He picks a cupcake off the tray Carmen has left. 'Mm. So good.'

'"Work out OK?"' Ashley watches him incredulously, clutching her hands in her lap. 'How can you—'

'You can go, Ashley. I'll call you,' Artie says. 'I wanna talk to Sophie alone.'

'Oh.' Ashley looks at me for explanation. I can only shrug. She stands up, pulling her wrap dress over her thin tanned knees, and smiles mechanically. 'I'll call you guys later. I'm working on this.'

I watch her walk out of the sliding doors into the sunshine. In the distance, I see Deena pass by with her loping stride. She is clutching the keys to her truck, and smoking a roll-up. She doesn't look in, just keeps on walking. Guilt washes over me; I shouldn't have yelled at her. And I remember the message again:

> @SophieLeigh You'll be getting another white rose from me soon. And then you're going to get what you deserve.

It's just me and Artie. He dusts the cake crumbs from his trousers, gives a little laugh and then says, 'We need to get serious, Sophie. OK? You listening to me?'

I nod.

'We got two problems, the way I see it.' Artie holds his palm face out towards me, pulling his index finger down towards the floor. '*Numero uno*. The armpit thing, the boyfriend talking about boozing and that crap – your image is no good. Out of nowhere, I don't know why either.'

Because I'm being found out, at last. 'It's bad tim—' I start to say, but he interrupts.

'If we don't lock this thing down fast, you're in trouble. Trust me, I've been around. I don't like this pattern.' He pulls down the next finger. 'The other problem is some weirdo who's got into your house and left you roses. That, in my opinion, is distracting you from what the real issue is. Don't get me wrong, it's scary, but we deal with it. We get you better security, proper protection, and they don't do it any more. OK?'

I think about the roses. Each one, velvet-and-wax petals, barely unfurled. Someone brought them. Someone came into the house, put one on my bed, left the others at the gate. Someone created this Twitter account. Whoever it is is thinking about me right now. This person hates me and wants to kill me.

'But – they were in my *house*. Now they're sending me death threats, and—'

'Honey, I totally get that,' Artie breaks in abruptly. 'Try and see what I'm telling you. The truth is we get about ten letters a week from people who wanna kill you.' Artie slices the butter cream off another cupcake and inserts it into his mouth. 'Mm. That's good.'

'*Ten people?*' I say, trying not to sound hysterical.

'Yuh-huh.' He licks his finger, swallows. 'Hey, maybe not ten, but a lot. Every big star has someone who hates them. People are jealous of you, Sophie. Girls want to be you, boys want to do you. When you don't do what they say they get . . . kinda mad. Fame is a crazy business. But they're not *going* to do it because we eliminate the possibility of it happening, OK? You should have told us about it before. You're getting distracted by it and making it out to be something it's not when the fact is Denis and the current set-up you got needs to go and we need a proper security system up here and that's going to happen. I know you better than you think. Stop using it to get other ideas in your head.'

'I'm using it? Gee, thanks, Artie.' He shrugs. I've never seen him like this. So . . . kind of . . . *uninterested*. 'What ideas?'

'Like "I'm going off to England, UK, to make some crazy movie about Shakespeare."' His voice is girlish and high. 'Like "I don't wanna do comedy any more." Like "I'm too good for it all of a sudden."'

I lean forward so we're almost nose to nose. 'Hey. I never said that.'

'I know you didn't, but you think it. So here's where we're at.' He licks his sugary fingers. 'You gotta trust me. *The Bachelorette Party* is a great script, it's a great cast.' He throws away the cupcake casing. 'Sophie, I know you been screwing George and I know it's not working out and you're pissed at him. Stop acting like a baby. Grow up, turn up on set and don't let him get to you. He's just messing with you. You're a big star, you got people relying on you, you hear me?'

I sit back again and fold my arms. 'It's not like that.' I try to keep my voice steady. 'He's a bully.'

Artie sighs and turns his watch around his wrist again. 'He's a freaking director, Sophie. That's what he does.'

Maybe he's right. 'I don't trust him any more.'

'You don't have any choice. Do the movie and then we'll see.'

'What about *Love Me, Love My Pooch*?' I say. 'I'm not doing that film. I won't do it.'

He doesn't say anything for so long I wonder if he's heard me, but then he says, 'I can't force you to do it, so I won't. But you're making a mistake. It's the perfect vehicle for you. And if you're serious, we need to make a decision on what you commit to. Urgently.'

'But I've found what I want to do,' I say, trying not to sound impatient. 'I really want to make *My Second-Best Bed*.'

Artie rubs his nose and closes his eyes. 'I thought we were clear on that one. It's not for you.'

'I think it is,' I say. 'And the Eve Noel project after that. I want to do them both. Go to the UK to film the first one and research the second one while I'm there.' I clutch my hands, pushing them away from me, stretching my arms. 'You have to listen to *me*, Artie. Just because it's my idea doesn't mean it's wrong. I know what I'm talking about, and I know I'm right. In here.' I touch my heart. 'I'm not stupid. I'm going back to England, I'm going to do that film after *Bachelorette*'s finished shooting, and I'm going to find out about Eve Noel too. And you're just gonna have to trust me, OK?'

156

Artie stands up, slides his BlackBerry into his jacket pocket. 'I gotta go.'

My mouth falls open. 'Did you hear any of that?'

'Sure I did. But *My Second-Best Bed* went away.'

'Went away? What the hell do you mean?'

His eyes meet mine for the first time. 'We found the last piece of finance for them. They start shooting in a week's time. They got some girl off of *Downton Abbey* to play Anne Hathaway.' I slam my hand down on the table, but he smiles. 'So it's all worked out for them. They'd have loved to have had you . . .'

'You paid them off?'

'No,' Artie says. 'Listen to me, Sophie. I'm not the villain here. You got it right. It could be a great movie, and the agency wants a piece of it – we got a couple of clients involved, Tammy, Cara Hamilton, T.T. the director. We need to make sure it works out. OK? And it's looking good. They got Tony Lees-Miller from Canyon producing it – the guy knows what he's doing, for a Brit. And they got Alec Mitford. Plus the script is way better now. It's actually a good picture.'

'*I'm* the one who got the better script for them!' I yell. 'That was *me*!'

He's fumbling in his pockets. 'Sure, I know it was, and you were right. Listen, it's a fantastic project, for the right actress. But you're just not the right actress. You're a star!'

'What do you mean?' I'm facing him, so angry I could slap him, my teeth gritted.

'Listen, it's not a *bad* thing!' He laughs at my furious expression, this man who's controlling my career. 'OK? It's good! But you're . . . Honey, you're just a little too sweet and nice. Bland. Is that the word?' He thinks to himself for a moment. 'Maybe not, but you know what I mean.' He pats his stomach in a satisfied way. 'You do know what I mean. Tell Carmen those cupcakes were the business. I gotta go.'

CHAPTER FOURTEEN

I FLOAT ON my back, staring up at the blue nothing, then down at the gold hoops of my bikini glowing in the heat of the afternoon sun. I flip over, sliding down towards the bottom of the pool. You can't hear the rest of the world underwater. Just the womb-like sounds of the world outside. A plane or a car going by, a conversation inside the house, the whooshing, clear sound of my slippery body. I emerge into the light, blinking. My fingers are pale and wrinkly after too long in the water. Twenty minutes? An hour? I don't know. I lie back again and stay very still, like I'm listening for something. If you saw me you'd think I was dead, arms spread wide, just floating like a lily on the surface. It's peaceful.

Another tear slides from my eyes into the water. I'm being childish, I'm sure. But I don't like this. I don't like any of it.

I hear the buzz of the gate, behind me. There are footsteps on the patio. I turn around, and look up. A figure stands in front of me, blocking the sun.

'Kiddo, I'm off.'

I look up. 'Deena?'

Deena's standing beside the pool, ancient leather bag slung over one shoulder. She lowers her aviator sunglasses. 'Been great to stay with you. Stay gold, Ponyboy.'

I tread water and stare at her. 'You're going? Right now?'

'The condo people called. My place is clean again. Won't be troubling you no more.'

'I'm sorry about earlier. I was – I got some bad news.' I climb out and put my robe on. 'Listen, you can stay as long as you want—'

She interrupts, putting her hand on my shoulder. 'I'm in your way. Don't want to take up your space. I'll see you soon, OK? Maybe we'll have a drink. Or . . .' She trails off. 'If your mum comes to visit.'

'That's right,' I say, since there's no other way I'd see her and we both know it. I peer at her, my eyes dazzled by the setting sun. 'So – you're going home, yes?'

'Sure,' Deena says, but there's something odd about her tone, a cavalier ring to it, and I'm not sure. Because I know her condo wasn't ever being sprayed in the first place. I'm not sure she *has* a condo.

'Deena – where are you going?' I ask. 'Tell me the truth.'

She strokes her long, dry hair and gives me a smile. 'Gotta go where the work is, kiddo. And I know when I'm overstaying my welcome. So I'll see you around, OK? Thanks for the hospitality. It's been great, hanging out with you.'

I can feel the chlorine and sun tightening my face. I raise my hand. 'OK. Thanks . . .'

She walks towards the truck and I feel uneasy. Panic at letting her go suddenly hits me, I don't know why, except that maybe she's a link to my old life, someone who might look out for me. She's my godmother, after all, even if she is crazy and drives an orange pickup with three sets of manne-quin legs in the back.

'Deena—' I yell. 'Hey. Hey, Deena! Will you call me if you need anything? I mean, you know where I am.'

She doesn't stop walking, and I think she's just going to go. She climbs into the truck, and then there's silence, and the door opens again.

'Can I just say something?' She stands on the driveway.

'Yes, of course.' I ruffle my wet fringe with my fingers.

'You're better than you think, you know?'

'Um – thanks.'

Deena puts her bag down, and takes a Zippo from her jeans pocket. She flicks it open and lights it, then smartly snaps the lid shut, then lights it again, and I try not to laugh because every second-rate loser at school with a bomber jacket used to light and relight their Zippos. 'Kiddo, listen, I know you're doing really well. But I want to give you some advice.'

I chew on a tiny snag of my cuticle. 'OK.'

'So look. I know you don't like to hear it, but there was a time there when I was the same as you. Not quite the same –' Deena leans forward as if reluctantly acknowledging this point – 'but yeah, it was looking good for me. You know, I had the biggest comedy motion picture of '81?'

'You did?' I say, trying to conceal my disbelief. I pull the towelling robe closer around me, a little colder now.

She smiles. 'Sure. *Caring and Sharing*. Yeah?' I shake my head. 'Oh, OK. Load of balls, but it was massive.' She shrugs. 'Course, because it was a load of balls no one remembers it now. They don't show it on TNT, you know. It wasn't bad enough to be camp, either.'

'Was that before *Laurel Canyon*?'

'No, right after,' she says. 'I left because my agent kept telling me I should be making movies, I'd be huge. But they kept putting me in the same old crap. Not even terrible, just unmemorable, you know? And then I made my big mistake.'

She falls silent and shakes her head.

'What did you do?'

'I took my clothes off. Death after that. I was a titty actress, no going back.' She takes a deep breath. 'You know? No, you don't, because it's different now and you're a little princess. But still – yeah. If you're a woman and you take your clothes off – bam – you kinda can't put them back on again. Ever.'

We're silent, staring at each other. My robe falls open. I look over at Deena's long hair. It's blonde, but it's dry and looks as if it'd snap if you bent it. She's really thin: she always has been. But she's not young any more – she must be well over fifty-five – and years of drugs, extreme diets, starving herself (or bingeing and throwing up) have given her a stringy, washed-out, flappy look that means she looks a lot older. I glance down at my flat stomach, at my jutting hips, my sharp elbows, at the way all this makes me feel so in control. I've always loved the exhilaration you get from feeling thin. But lately, the thrill isn't the same. There will always be someone thinner than you. Someone younger than you, prettier than you, cheaper than you.

'I'm not going to do that,' I say. 'That's not – I'm not going that way.' I pull the robe around me again, a little tighter.

'You're a woman in Hollywood,' Deena says. 'Hate to break it to you but your days are numbered anyway. So get your back-up plan organised, you hear me? You're clever, but you're being stupid. There's stuff going on with you you don't even see. I see it and I'm just saying you ought to be worried.'

'What the hell does *that* mean?' I say. 'Have you been – do you know about the roses?'

She stares at me, blankly. 'What roses?'

'Someone's been leaving roses in the house.' I sound nuts, I can hear it in my voice. *And Princess Di and Jesus are sending me secret messages through my washing machine.* I backtrack. 'Don't worry. It's nothing. Nothing.'

'Kiddo, it's not about roses, OK? That's what I'm saying. It happens slowly. Real slowly. You're on top of the world and then you wake up one day and it's another beautiful blue day and – you're over. You've spent your life making trash, and trash don't hang around – it gets buried in the ground. For every Julia Roberts there's a hundred girls who used to open the biggest pictures, star opposite Tom Cruise, and then they disappear, because they turn thirty and that's it, then they're forty and they might as well be dead. You don't see them any more. Unless they marry some young guy and start getting really good work done, or they go totally nuts or totally upmarket. Those are your options.' I'm gaping at her. 'I've thought about it,' she says, smiling grimly. 'A lot.'

'That's rubbish, look at . . .' I rack my brains. 'Look at Kathleen Turner. OK. Meryl Streep.'

'Meryl Streep's Meryl Streep. That doesn't count and you know it. Kathleen Turner? Come on, she's exactly what I'm talking about. Used to be the hottest actress in town, and the last thing I remember her in was Chandler's fucking *dad* in *Friends*.'

'She's got other things to do—'

Deena's voice is sharp. 'I'm not having some long conversation about the highlights of Kathleen Turner's career, OK, Sophie? Give me a film. What's your favourite film?'

'*A Girl Named Rose*.'

She shrugs, stamps her foot a little. 'Something more recent. Not Eve Noel for once. Give me a film you love that's not got Eve bloody Noel in it.'

'I don't know . . . *Four Weddings and a Funeral*. I used to watch it every week on video when it first came out.'

'Fine, so that's what I'm talking about. Andie MacDowell, what the hell are you doing now? Advertising make-up with enough airbrushing to make a fucking plane fly, dude!' She cackles and then starts coughing. 'Where's Hugh Grant? I hate the guy, but he's still getting ten mil a movie. Hey? So listen to me.' Deena takes out a stick of gum, pops it in her mouth, chews it for a second. I stare at her, wondering if she's drunk, and she smiles at me. 'You think I'm a crazy lady.'

'No, but I just think you're exaggerating,' I say. 'I know it didn't work out for you, but things are different now. I'm in control, I've got plans for the future—' My own voice sounds weak as I say this. 'I'm fine, don't worry about me. And – don't go, Deena. Stay here.'

'I can't, OK?' She hoists the bag over her shoulder. 'I'm not crazy. I'm just not twenty-five any more, and you won't believe me but I was just like you once.' Her voice is thick, and I look at her. Is she crying? Deena doesn't cry. She pushes her sunglasses up the slim bridge of her nose. 'So now I'm leaving because I have to go have sex with some guy in a crappy motel out in Long Beach who wants me to wear my *Laurel Canyon* costumes and let him whip me, but he'll pay me a thousand dollars if I let him film us doing the do and that'll pay the rent and get me some food for a couple weeks.'

I move towards her but she starts backing away. She's grinning.

'I'm fine. I just want you to think about what I'm telling you. 'Cause you see, that's what it comes down to in the end – you're getting fucked by someone, doesn't matter whether they're actually giving it to you or not, it's all the same thing.' She wags her finger at me. 'Get a plan, kiddo, that's all I'm telling you. Get a plan.'

Then she turns and walks towards the pickup truck. The naked mannequin legs are still lying in the back, and as she thunders down the drive through the open gate I see them, rolling from side to side as she disappears down the hill.

CHAPTER FIFTEEN

I WISH I could just bail out of this party, which will be full of industry people and gossip, and stay home, but for the first time I can remember I want to get away from the house. I call Deena several times, but she doesn't pick up. Then I waste time deciding what to wear and it occurs to me as I'm pulling my dress on that I've regressed – I'm once again the twelve-year-old who used to wait for Mum to come in and flick her be-ringed fingers through my wardrobe, pulling out her choice and flinging it on the bed. 'That one, dear. With the blue shoes.' In the end I settle on a bright green-turquoise Diane von Furstenberg dress, with gold sandals, a little bronzer and some shimmer around my eyes, carefully low-key. You don't overdress in California. Your clothes have to be expensive, but you don't go all out in a taffeta dress unless it's the Oscars. It's not cool. It shows you don't get it, you don't belong. You have to look relaxed, like you don't care.

I'm just heading out of the door when Tina appears from the shadows, like she's been waiting for me to appear.

'Sophie—'

I clutch my hand to my chest. 'Tina, you scared me. I thought you'd gone home.'

'I was finishing up some stuff here.' She hugs the iPad, knitting her fingers together. 'And you were talking to Deena

– I didn't want to interrupt. So – uh, I don't know where to start. OK. Kerry called me today.'

'Right.' I can feel the heat on my skin, and I don't want my make-up to start melting, or God forbid to have a repeat of Armpitgate. I shift my weight from one leg to the other. 'What's up?'

Tina's eyes are huge. 'She said you hired that girl Sara? That she was coming here next week? She wants to start as soon as possible?'

'OK, so that's fine, you can go a bit earlier,' I say. I vaguely remember Sara asking if this was OK at the interview. 'What's the problem?'

Tina takes a deep breath. 'OK, Sophie. I wish that you had told me yourself, that's all. Because Sara just called me and was totally out of line and asked me all these questions about you, and – I didn't know what to say.' She slowly twirls a piece of hair around her finger.

'Oh, Tina, I should have told you, I'm sorry.'

'She was kinda off with me,' Tina says. 'Because I wouldn't tell her anything at first so . . .' Her voice rises. 'She said she had to know all this stuff, like your passport details and . . . and what tea you liked, because she had to get the job right and I was trying to obstruct her and why was I being so rude. She said she was gonna call you because you were old friends.'

T.J. appears with the jeep and gets out. I call out my thanks to him, trying to buy some time. Sara isn't like Tina; she doesn't have her undead beauty-queen vibe. She's just a bright, slightly intense gal who wants to get everything right.

'I don't know where she got my number from, or anything, and I . . . I wish you'd let me know you'd found someone so . . . so I could have been more prepared.' Tina rubs the side of each eye with one finger. 'Oh, Sophie. I'm sorry. I'm being a total basket case. It's only that I don't think she's a good fit for you and I do wish that you had worked with me on this one. I have to say this from the bottom of my heart.'

I can't stand girls getting emotional about girl-behaviour, and I shift my weight from one foot to another, trying not to feel annoyed – with myself, with Sara, or especially with Tina, because I thought this last month or so we were getting past the weird reserve we've always had with each other. My knowing a bit more about her has made her open up. I teased her last week that she had a cabinet of beauty-queen trophies and she laughed in a weird embarrassed way, but later that night she texted me a picture of them. A whole cabinet, five or six trophies and medals and those sashes you get to wear, with her name picked out in gold: Tina Kesheshian. She's almost a Kardashian. I wonder what it must be like for Tina, a trophyful of proof of your beauty, when every day the mirror is a reproach to that.

It feels like we're back to square one. Trying to keep my voice even, I face away from the car. 'Look, Tina, I don't know what's wrong. I'm happy for you you're taking some time off and I'm sorry I didn't tell you I'd found someone. Sara is an old friend of mine, yeah.' That's stretching the truth a bit. 'I bumped into her a couple of times recently and we got talking. I hope it'll work out, because I need someone as good as possible while you're away. And I really apologise if I've upset you.'

Tina's brown eyes flash a little. 'Yes,' she says uncertainly. 'OK, I'm sorry, Sophie, I just felt like – well, it was just she rang me and she was *totally* in my face and all. I mean, she was kind of strange, wanting to know all that stuff when—' She stops, and then laughs. 'Listen to me. I sound totally nuts. What's wrong with me.'

Who knows? I want to say. But instead I say, 'Oh, Tina, nothing's wrong with you. You'll have a great – er, trip and I'll have a great summer with Sara and it'll all be . . . great,' I say. 'Are we cool?'

'Sure.' She smiles again. 'I'm so sorry. Call me when you get back tonight. In case you need anything,' she says quickly. 'I'll be at home.'

I nod and slam on my sunglasses, closing the jeep door so

her face is peering in at me. Sheesh. I turn on the radio, remembering Deena's mannequins rolling in the back of her truck as I head out onto the road.

I'm late and irritated by the time I leave, so that I remember only when I'm driving that maybe I shouldn't be doing this alone. I'm supposed to be being accompanied by a phalanx of thickset men in black suits with radio mikes, but I want to talk to Denis in the morning about what's happening and how he'll be taking on some lighter duties, so they arrive tomorrow. Suddenly, though, I don't care. Maybe Artie was right, it's all in my mind. He's right about a lot of stuff, it's true.

I'm in my huge white Cherokee Jeep driving along Mulholland, looping up and around till we're up in the highest section of the Santa Monica Mountains, where the air is even cooler. The party is at a producer's house in Bel Air. I worked with Steve Levine on *A Cake-Shaped Mistake*. He's OK, and his wife Suzy is lovely. He has some experience, unlike a lot of producers who don't know what the hell they're doing and are only there because they're banging someone. The house has a winding driveway festooned with bougainvilleas and jasmine, and stone balustrades covered in lichen. There are steps down from the stone house to a pool beside which is this amazing ancient Greek statue Steve bought Suzy for their wedding anniversary. It's a woman in a draped dress with no arms. All this – Bel Air, the lichen, the ancient classical statue – is supposed to say one thing: we're the real deal. We're old-school.

This is the ideal place to exercise damage control: parties like this one are where the elite of Hollywood does business. All the rest of it is immaterial compared to this exclusive world, the world even Tommy Wiley doesn't get an invitation to. I get out and tug my dress down, but just a little, so the bright green-blue is snug against my taut breasts, lightly bronzed by the sun, and I hand the car keys to a waiting attendant.

The evening is golden, soft shimmering light covering the

hills. I stand and take in the scene for a moment; the shallow steps up to the beautiful house are thronged with people, and someone nearby is singing jazz standards. I recognise most of the faces here. All A-list. I hesitate, suddenly unsure: I don't want to join them. I could still get into the car and drive up the hill back home, curl up under a blanket and watch an Eve Noel film again. Then I think of an evening by myself trying not to go online and see what people are saying about me, what the latest bad-news story is, and I stiffen my resolve. *Come on. It's just a party.*

I hear footsteps behind me but I ignore them, hoping that I too will be ignored. But then a low, soft voice says, 'Hey. Sophie.'

I turn around. 'Patrick. Hi.' He is a friendly face; I realise now how pleased I am to see him. He looks almost smart, his scruffy hair is neat and he's shaved. I want to touch his smooth, still-dark jaw. 'I didn't know you'd be here.'

He takes my fingers, half handshake, half awkward. I look at him and smile.

'Well, I was hoping you'd be here, Sophie.' He clears his throat. 'You look beautiful.'

My heart is thumping, which is crazy. But like I say, that's not an original point of view. Not liking nuclear war, thinking kittens are cute, having a crush on Patrick Drew: all part of being human.

I cross my arms, then uncross them, then pull on my fringe. 'Well . . . I'm glad you're here too.' It's true. He always feels very safe, for all that he's one of the most famous men on the planet.

Patrick rubs his face like he's embarrassed. He has a little scar by his eye, a small white crescent like the moon. I wonder how he got it. I feel as though I know him so well it's strange to realise that really, I hardly know him at all. 'I wanted to talk to you about coffee the other week. I should have realised it was a set-up. I think Artie told me. I'm not good at listening sometimes. I get lost thinking about other stuff, you know?' He shakes his head. 'No, you don't know. Anyway, I wanted to apologise. And—'

'I do know,' I interrupt him and then shiver, I can't help it.

He looks at me. 'You OK?'

'Sure,' I say. 'Just had a long day. My own fault.'

The burr from the party below us sounds like a wasps' nest. 'What's happened?'

I laugh, shrug my shoulders. 'Don't know. Everything's a bit crazy at the moment. Do you ever have days with this job where . . . you don't know who you are any more?'

He frowns. 'Yeah. Kind of. Sophie, are you OK?'

'Not sure. Maybe I shouldn't be here,' I say. 'Patrick – do you want to—'

I look down at the crowd just at that moment, and I freeze. George is right in the centre, sucking on a cigar. As if he knows I'm watching him, he breaks off from his conversation, and turns to stare at me and Patrick. He makes an old-fashioned filming gesture, turning the reel with his hand. It seems so innocent. But I know what he means.

'Come say hi!' he calls.

Then I know this was a mistake. I'm not good at these parties at the best of times, but I usually get through them by acting cute and laughing a lot and there's always someone who wants to talk to you if you're famous. Suddenly they all seem like sharks, big black hulks swimming around me, waiting to take a bite. I can't do it any more. I can't go down those steps and laugh and pretend I don't care that someone's out to get me, maybe wants to hurt me. Or that every celebrity website today has Dave's kiss-and-tell about how I'm a bitch, even in some cases how I like it doggy-style, or that people will be watching my armpits for signs of sweat, or that George has probably told someone about the tapes he has of me, or that no one here is actually my friend, someone I like and can trust, except the man standing right in front of me, and he's one of the biggest stars on the planet, and therefore not someone to rely on.

'You know what?' I say to Patrick. 'I think I'm going to go. I'm not feeling great.'

'I'll take you home,' he says immediately.

169

I shake my head, numbly. He puts his arm around me.

'Jesus, Sophie, you're really cold.' He's right. It's a humid night. I lean against him, just for a moment.

'You're warm,' I say.

'I'm always warm. Growing up I was the warmest part of the house when there was a storm and the wind blew the spray into ice off the sea. My dogs used to come sleep on me in the winter. Listen, Sophie, I think you should go home. Maybe you need to rest. Let me get your car. I'll drive you.'

'No, it's fine.' I gesture to the valet guy to collect the jeep. 'This is crazy. I haven't even got here yet. I haven't been inside.'

'I'll tell George you're sick, you don't want to risk the shooting schedule. Hey, you sure you don't want me to take you home?' Patrick's voice is soft in my ear. Part of me wishes I could say yes. I'm so used to being this me that I don't think I remember what it was like to be half of a whole. I've never known what it was to feel that way.

Now is not the time. I stand away from him, embarrassed now, wishing I was gone already, hoping I don't burst into tears. 'I'm fine, honestly, Patrick. Thank you. It'll make a bigger thing of it if we leave together.'

'OK then. If you're sure,' he says.

'I'll be so fine. I'll get into bed, watch TV and get some sleep.' The valet appears with the Cherokee and I look round, and at the same time I see George again, watching us both, his wolfish smile still plastered on his sick, stupid face. Impotent rage bubbles up inside me. He's talking to Steve, the host, now, one of his old buddies. He looks up and sees me and smirks, and something in both their expressions makes my blood run cold. That tape of me . . . why the fuck did I let him film me. Maybe everyone's seen it. I have been so stupid. I clear my throat, trying to push the thoughts out of my mind. 'Go enjoy the party. I'll see you next week for the first run-through, OK?'

'Sure. And Sophie?'

'Yes?' I take the keys and give the valet a tip, my fingers fumbling with my purse.

'Maybe we could do that coffee again. Or have a drink. Or something.' Patrick takes my hand again and holds it. Just holds it like we're going to walk off somewhere together. His warm fingers squeeze mine. 'Anyway, I'll stop because you want to go. Just take care of yourself, Sophie, and I'll see you soon. Call me if you need anything, won't you.'

I nod, though I'm sure I won't. He watches me drive off. I know him. I know him so well and I've only met him three times, for a total of, what? Ninety minutes? Then I remember – of course, he's one of the most famous people on the planet. I tend to forget that. I know him because I've seen him on-screen a bunch of times, besides the fact that he's on the front of every magazine. That's why, nothing more. It's been a long day and I need to go home.

CHAPTER SIXTEEN

THERE'S NO ONE at the house tonight. Deena's left, Tina's gone, Carmen sleeps in the guest cottage by the gate and she's out at her cousin's wedding. There's the security guy who covers for Denis whose name I can never remember but who has a moustache, but he wouldn't pay any attention anyway. Is his name Moustache? The thought of locking the doors and screaming as loudly as I can is so enticing as I drive home, sitting up straight, trying not to cry.

It's monotonous, this route, one barred entrance after another off a dusty road. There's this gate I always like to see as it means I'm nearly at the top of the hill. It's tacky, pearlescent white wrought iron, and it always makes me think of the Pearly Gates. I accelerate past it towards my home. Someone has been having a paper trail, or a wedding: there's confetti, little scraps of white, strewn all over the road beneath the house. I turn into my own drive, itching to rip the gold sandals, which are pinching, off my feet, to change my clothes and do whatever I want. Cry, then eat too much, probably. I wonder what ice-cream there is in the freezer.

The gate is open, and that's strange . . . I drive up, wondering why. A light is on, at the top of the driveway by Deena's room, and there's something odd about it, but I can't work out what. Where's Moustache? Maybe the new guys are here already? I pull up and get out.

There's no one around. And it is really almost dark now, and the light's disappeared. I wonder where it was coming from. Suddenly something flashes at me again, and it's moving – it's a torch, or something, inside my house. Someone is inside.

A loud roar behind me, and I scream as a car swings up the drive and pulls over, fast. Red and blue flashes stripe along the whitewashed walls. I turn around, confused. It's the police. 'Miss Leigh?' someone says, flashing a badge. His face is hidden by his cap. 'We had a report of something—'

The light's still flickering on and off inside, and I stare at it, mesmerised, and then all of a sudden there's a loud scream, and a cracking sound, and someone from the road below shouts something, I can't hear it fully, but there's another cracking sound, and the cop pulls me to the ground.

The flashing light stops moving, and there's a figure framed in the front door of my house. It's the substitute security guard, Moustache. Manny? Manuel? I stare up at him from my position flat on the ground. My knees are grazed.

'Miss Leigh . . .' he says. 'Thank God you're OK. I'm so sorry, Miss Leigh . . .'

'Who's in there?' I ask, standing up and brushing myself off. I wince; my knee hurts.

'No one, but – someone was. Someone was there.'

He's shaking his head.

I push past him and run into the house, limping, a cop following behind me.

Someone has been there all right. The furniture's pushed over and slashed with something sharp. Pictures ripped, legs broken off chairs, like a poltergeist or the Incredible Hulk has swept through the room. Cups and plates and little stupid knick-knacks like the china bull I got in Barcelona when I was filming *Jack and Jenny*, smashed to bits. I go from room to room, in silence, my hand over my mouth. My study, my stupid office that I was so proud of, is almost the worst: the film posters pulled off the walls, cabinets and shelves broken, glass lying like sparkling snow an inch deep on the floor. The

173

Eve Noel framed pictures have been particularly viciously treated: the frames are smashed and the photos have been torn out and ripped into pieces. Paper is scattered over everything. The window is open, and I realise that what I thought was confetti is, in fact, the new version of *My Second-Best Bed* on my desk, torn into tiny pieces and thrown out onto the road.

I turn away, unable to look. I don't know what to do. The Moustache is behind me, wringing his hands. 'I was asleep – I don't know what happened, like someone drugged me. I didn't hear it, Miss Leigh, I'm so sorry . . .'

I walk towards the bedroom, but a female cop, who's already gone around ahead of me, puts her hand on my arm.

'Don't go in there.'

'Why?'

She says flatly, with no empathy, 'You just don't want to.'

I push past her into my room, my beautiful room . . . It is trashed, like the rest of the house, but worse. Someone's written all over the walls:

YOU'RE GOING TO DIE, SOPHIE. I'M GOING TO KILL YOU.
YOU'RE WORTHLESS. YOU'RE NOTHING.
THE BABY'S CRYING AND SHE'S CRYING AND CRYING
SOPHIE, YOU'RE GOING TO DIE

My silk nightgown, white with lace trim, has been slashed to ribbons, and laid carefully out on the bed. There's something else there, too. There must be about two hundred, three hundred white long-stemmed roses in there. Scattered over the bed, jammed into the drawers, inside the closet, trampled underfoot.

another beautiful blue day
Hollywood, April 1959

THERE WERE NO seasons in Los Angeles. Sure, it was colder in winter, and warmer in summer, but only by a few degrees. Some people – Gilbert, for example – loved the idea that we were cheating our English blood, living here amongst oranges and jasmine all year round.

I didn't. At first, the novelty stayed with me – it was delicious to wake up with sunshine pouring through the window, and to know it was November and that, were I still in London, I would probably have chilblains and a leaking hot water bottle. It had been worse back home in Gloucestershire, where the cold, biting wind whistled through the valleys and hills, slipping into my room at night, so that often I would wake and find icicles on the inside of the windows.

The first winter after Rose died I was seven. From my bedroom window you could quite clearly see the river, frozen into a thick sheet of grey. At night, it was as though the wind got caught inside the hollow trunk of the rotten willow tree beside the river and it would wail, literally weep.

Some nights, when I couldn't sleep and thought I heard her calling me, I'd carefully pile my books up and stand on them, leaning on the high sill cut into the ancient brick of the house.

175

I can still feel the cold stone wall against the fronts of my thighs. I'd stare at the tree, drooping branches trapped by the ice, my chin heavy in my hands, my elbows aching from the pressure of hanging on with my small, frozen body. Sometimes I was sure I saw her, peering through a tear-shaped gap in the empty trunk, her thin face pale in the moonlight that bounced off the frozen milky water. I never moved, nor waved to her, though I desperately wanted my sister back, and for the longest time I couldn't rid myself of the idea that she was outside, calling to me, that she wanted to come back inside. I would replace the pile of books carefully on the dark carved mahogany bookcase that Mother said I was lucky to have in my room, and climb back into bed, shivering even more, and I'd imagine her long arms tight around me, keeping me warm just as she used to when I couldn't sleep and she'd crawl into bed with me. But not any more.

No one else mentioned her. I wasn't allowed to ask Mother and Father about her. Mother grew more and more religious, spending most of her time alone cleaning the local church. When, after a year in Hollywood, I wrote to ask if I could visit them during a trip back for the premiere of *Helen of Troy*, my father replied that a visit from me would provide 'too much disruption'. What could I say? It was only afterwards I realised I didn't even know where they had buried Rose and I had the thought again, for the first time in a long while, that she wasn't dead, that it was all a plot.

I had never truly believed she was really gone, you see. She was calling me, calling me for help. She was alone somewhere and afraid. And I was alone in our bed without her because I had left her to die. And so I had become used to being cold and as I grew up and grew further apart from my parents it seemed normal to me, all of it. Only when I went away did I start to wonder what it all meant. And though I loved the Californian sun, I never felt it was real, that it was shining on me.

Up in Casa Benita Gilbert swam before breakfast, and most days, if I wasn't on set hideously early, we would eat in the sunny breakfast room overlooking the pool, drinking fresh orange juice and staring out at the view. Every morning, I'd remind myself how lucky I was to be able to live in this world. Like an athlete training for a race, I'd exercise the ungrateful muscles of my brain that led me into thinking dark, awful thoughts, rewinding myself to enjoy it. *Today is a great day. Everything is wonderful. You love Gilbert. You act for a living. You have a beautiful home. Why do you think everything is so bad?*

For the last few days Gilbert had been in a good mood. The Academy Awards, the previous week, had been a total disaster; the producer had been under dire imprecations of death and unemployment (death being better than unemployment in Hollywood) if the show overran, with the result that number after number was cut, in case proceedings should slow down. The telecast had ended twenty minutes too early, leaving us at home watching a blank screen on our beautiful television set with the walnut case, scratching our heads along with the rest of America before someone at NBC slotted in a rerun of an old football game. I'd been horrified, then mesmerised, that no one seemed to know what was going on. Even in the war, we'd always known what to do, what would happen, and had acted accordingly. But Gilbert had loved it. He'd slapped his thighs, chugging back drink after drink. 'Those damn fools! Damn bloody fools!' he'd said, over and over, tears of mirth coursing down his face.

And David Niven had won an Oscar. This pleased Gilbert because David Niven was his kind of actor, the sort who should be rewarded for being a dapper British gentleman, who didn't forget his obligations to his country, who was unashamedly of a type, rather old-fashioned perhaps, not in the first flush of youth, but all the more comforting for that. Gilbert loathed with a passion the Tony Curtises, the Brandos and the Montgomery Clifts, the young guns in town who showed scant regard for the way old Hollywood worked, who took no care to conceal their bad behaviour; in fact, seemed to revel in it. He had actually said to me once, of James Dean, 'Good riddance to bad rubbish.' I'd thought he was joking at first, but I should have realised; Gilbert rarely joked about anything.

He had been so pleased at the unspooling of the evening that he'd come to my room that night. We rarely had sex, and I was glad. At first I found him terrifying – he had been my idol. Then disappointing – he was old, and I was young and cruel, heedless of what he'd been through, of what he might be looking for. My fumbling nights with Richard, my ex-boyfriend from Central, squashed together onto the tiny single bed in the Hampstead flat, shushing each other amid giggles, while praying that Clarissa slept soundly next door, had been far more fun, more astonishing, more exciting than those nights I dreaded, then tried to remove myself from mentally. Gilbert was rough; he liked to tear my clothes off, like a hero from the swashbuckling films he used to make. He liked to feel strong, for me to feel defenceless. He never hurt me, not much really, and it never lasted long. Often it was over before I'd even realised he was inside me, and I'd know it wouldn't happen again for a good few weeks. I'd lie in the vast, curved, wooden bed with the silk sheets slipping away from me like water, watching us in the mirror of the grey French dressing table that a December issue of *Photoplay* breathlessly reported had been flown specially from Paris just for me. And I'd remove myself entirely from the situation. Back to Hampstead, or home again to Gloucestershire. Or the part I was playing at that moment. I was getting better and better at it, pretending to be someone else entirely.

More than anything, I wanted to love him, but I didn't know how to reach out to him. We were in this marriage together, yet I found I didn't know him at all. What was more terrifying was that I was discovering as time went on that I didn't know myself at all, either. I couldn't remember who I was, what I was supposed to be. I had a new name, new hair, new teeth; I played parts all day; I came home to a beautiful house where unseen hands changed the sheets and pressed the dresses in my closet and made my food, and to a husband who was the dream-boat idol of my teenage years – and none of it seemed to make sense to me. The *Photoplay* story had been a triumph of optimism.

Hollywood's Newest Sweethearts, at Home and at Play: us playing tennis, kissing at the net after I lost, Gilbert swimming in the pool, me brushing my hair at the dressing table, entertaining a group of friends to dinner, playing with our poodle puppy Maurice:

> Maurice, a gift from the couple's close friend Conrad Joyce, star of the new Mrs Travers's upcoming film, *A Girl Named Rose*. Mr Joyce gave the bride away at the couple's private wedding last year. 'It was so romantic,' Eve tells us. 'A bower of white roses, and I walked through them with Conrad, and there was Gilbert waiting for me. Conrad was rather angry; he said I was pulling at his arm, so eager was I to reach the groom!'

It was the usual pack of lies; however, I'd become used to it. I'd worked with Conrad on *Lanterns Over Mandalay* and loved him. We'd become firm friends; he was a darling, hilarious, vain, terribly catty, the best fun to be with, but kind and considerate too. One of the few people I felt I could be myself with, talk to just a little about where I'd come from, and how strange it was, these lives we were leading. But Gilbert couldn't stand him. Said he was a cissy.

We'd had white roses, but not at my behest. I hated them. Hated them. The sight of them at the top of the aisle, as I got ready to walk towards Gilbert, had nearly made me up and run away. The Baxters were there, that horrible fat man and his brother, smiling solemnly as I walked down the aisle, and I wished so much I was Rose, that I was brave enough to hold up his hand and shout 'Pervert!' as she had once done to Tom, the chemist's son who used to drop things and then look up ladies' skirts. And Moss Fisher, sunglasses on, his shiny grey suit oily in the sun. They sat in a row, like crows. I wished I hadn't had them to our house.

The rest of it was tosh, too. The poodle was hired for the day, we never played tennis, and we rarely had friends over. Gilbert had his bridge chums, and I was either working or sleeping.

* * *

It was a normal morning then, that April day, as I came out of my room humming to myself, and dropped a kiss onto Gilbert's head. He grunted, shifted away from me, and went back to reading his paper – *The Times*, which he had flown out every week and read religiously, even if the news was by then out of date. I'd set my head into place: *It's another beautiful day. You're filming your best part yet. Gilbert's been offered the role in that WW2 drama and he's going to take it. Maybe next year you'll have a baby.*

'What are you up to today, dear?' I asked him, reaching for a thin slice of toast, buttering it methodically, and then pouring some coffee for myself and him.

He shook his head. 'Going into the studio. See a few chaps. Do a few final tests.'

'What do they want you in for again?' I said. I'd spoken to Mr Baxter two days ago, and he'd told me they'd already drawn up contracts, that Gilbert was signed to the part. 'I thought it was all agreed.'

My husband looked up at me in annoyance. 'I don't know, do I? I'm sure if it was you, they'd be rushing to roll out the red carpet, scattering damn white roses as high as an elephant's bloody eye, but I'm awfully sorry, they're not. It's me, my dear, not you. No one gives a damn about me.'

I took a tentative sip of my coffee. 'I'm sure it's a formality. The part's definitely yours. They said so.'

'Who did?' His voice was low. He narrowed his eyes. 'Have you been interfering, Eve? Tell me.'

I shrugged, trying to stay calm. 'Of course not, darling. Mr Baxter mentioned it to me, and I said—'

Instantly he was on his feet – he still moved fast when he wanted to. He came over to my side of the table, in one step. 'Listen to me, Eve,' he said, breathing heavily. 'Don't interfere. Keep your damn skinny arse out of it. Otherwise—' He was almost growling in my ear; I could smell his anger, as fear rose inside me. 'Otherwise I'll damn well kill you. You understand? You understand?'

He wasn't touching me. He was inches away from me. I met his gaze as calmly as I could and nodded. I didn't say anything.

My heart was thumping. Gilbert came back to his side of the table and sat down.

'Good. Now. Did you say you were away, filming? When?'

'Well, I'm going today,' I said, trying to keep my voice steady, to not show how much he'd disturbed me. 'Darling, I did tell you—'

He shrugged. 'That's a shame. I'll miss you.' He still said these things, and I never knew what he meant.

'I'll miss you too,' I said. 'I – why don't you come up, join me one weekend? It's in Big Sur. We're staying in an old lodge off the highway. It's supposed to be beautiful. They'd love to have you.'

He laughed. 'I'm sure they wouldn't.'

I was warming to my theme. 'I'm sure they would, Gilbert! You could go fishing, do some hunting during the day, then we could have dinner. It's very remote, so beautiful. There's a darling little town not far, with a golf course on the sea, you'd love it.'

'The ocean, not the sea,' he corrected. 'I've been there, my dear. That's very kind, but I'll stay here and make my own amusement. If you don't mind.' He bowed his head, touched his lips to his fingers and blew me the tiniest of kisses, and I gave him a small, glad smile, before he disappeared behind the paper again, and chuckled about something else.

the cream kid gloves

THE JOURNEY TOOK longer than I'd thought. A section of the highway had fallen into the ocean, which frequently happened in spring after the stormy wet winters that lash the northern Californian coast. We had to take a detour through the rolling plains that stretch out towards agricultural Steinbeck country, the land of *East of Eden*, then up on crumbling, rocky roads through the misty hills, where eagles soared in and out of the clouds that seemed to sit right next to us, so high were we. I sat in the back of the car transfixed by the unfolding vistas, the occasional flash of cliff and blue ocean, sometimes opening my window to inhale the sea air, and thinking how glad I was to have left Los Angeles.

By the time we arrived, it was a beautiful evening, and the smell of pine floated in through the open windows of the car as we arrived. The lodge was an old wooden hotel with a series of chalets nestling into the hills. Birds sang overhead as I stepped out onto the soft earth and took a deep breath, glad to be out of the car, on firm ground again. Two men carried my bags in, the Revelation leather trunks and suitcases, hatboxes and vanity cases, navy leather and stamped with my initials. Half of what was packed I wouldn't need, I was sure.

'Hello, my dear.' Jerome Trumbo, the director, strode into the lobby, pressed his hand into mine. 'How wonderful that you're here.'

I took in his outfit – the tweed jacket and jodhpurs, the yellow turtleneck sweater, the boots – and clapped my hands together. 'Dear Jerry, you look terrific. D. W. Griffith would be intimidated by you. What a get-up.'

Jerry smoothed his hand over the rough tweed with some pride. 'Why thank you, dear Eve. Long journeys must suit you – you look even more beautiful than ever. I love that darling jacket, bouclé is it? Will you join me for a drink in the bar, after you've freshened up? I have a couple of things to talk over with you about tomorrow. Not changes, just suggestions.' He squeezed my shoulder lightly. 'Dear, this film is going to be wonderful.'

We were finally starting work on *A Girl Named Rose*. It was a spruced-up version of the script Don had written for me, but he had detached himself – or been detached – from the project long ago, and though it had been changed somewhat to fit the Baxter brothers' whims, it was, indeed, wonderful. I don't know whom Jerry had got in to rewrite it, but it worked just as well, maybe even better than before. *Lanterns Over Mandalay* had been a hit, but not quite enough of a hit. Musicals, historical epics, were still all the rage, so out went the black-and-white drama, in came the Technicolor fantasy. Rose was no longer a shy young girl from a small town who came to work at a bustling New York fashion magazine; she was a shy young girl who dreamed extraordinary, fantastical daydreams and who came to work in a lavishly oversized Manhattan. There were a lot of musical insertions, and some, I dare to say, rather fey routines involving me and special effects: a talking cat, on the roof of the apartment next to Rose's; and an all-singing, all-dancing set of mannequins in beautiful couture frocks in the window of Sak's Fifth Avenue that came to life and sang with me. We were in Big Sur to shoot some of the final home-town scenes, as well as most of the fantasy set-pieces, beginning with the picnic I have with my true love Pete (played by Conrad) where the wind sways the grasses in time to the beating of our hearts. I really wasn't sure if it would be a complete failure or a rather clever triumph, which just goes to show you, doesn't it? How funny to think that now. It was so unusual that one just couldn't tell, but luckily the rewrite was terrific, unusually for rewrites. And there was still enough of Don's original script to make me confident it could work. I loved saying his lines.

I hadn't seen him since we had kissed and had our terrible row on the studio lot, over a year ago. I'd heard he'd been fired from a couple of projects. Gilbert had even brought him up in conversation one evening, which was strange, although I should have known; Gilbert noticed everything, even if he pretended not to. 'That friend of yours has got himself into more trouble, I see,' he'd said, reading Louella's column in the *Los Angeles Examiner* one evening, not long after we were married.

Once Hollywood's favourite screenwriter, one of the few pinkos to have survived the McCarthy era unscathed, Don Matthews seems to be making more enemies every day. Spotted getting cosy at the Cocoanut Grove last night in a dark booth with a young starlet named Priscilla Jones, Matthews ran into an old buddy – ex-wife and Vegas top-liner Bella Brettner – and her newest buddy – her partner in their act, Carl von Kant. Words – and drinks – flew as the gentlemen did more than embrace . . . wrestling on the floor like brawling teenagers, till Matthews was forcibly ejected onto the sidewalk, nursing a bruised jaw – as well as ego. Third time this month alone our hero's been asked to leave this way. And we thought screenwriters were dull. Stay tuned, folks . . .

I'd heard several times that he'd been drinking too much, and I was worried for him. Hollywood had a crazy attitude to screenwriters. They were happy to let them drop like flies, send them to jail or lose them to TV, to alcoholism; they didn't understand that the very thing that made a success of their biggest pictures was the script. They analysed everything else to replicate it again: the stars, the composer, the costume maker, the title, the setting . . . everything but the person who wrote the story.

Moss Fisher was the architect of my relationship with Gilbert and had the most to lose if it went wrong, and of course he had passed all this bad news along. I always felt he had his suspicions about something happening that day and I did wonder once or twice if he'd seen us. But it was so very long ago now. I told myself this, whenever I thought about it, which I tried not to; it seemed like such an extraordinary thing to have done, kissed this man I barely knew, then felt such anger towards him. *No.* Don was simply a friendly face, part of those lost early days in Hollywood.

'Good evening, Miss Noel,' the receptionist said, smiling shyly, when I returned from my room having combed out my hair, smoothed down my skirt a little. 'We're so honoured to have you staying with us.'

'Thank you,' I said, smiling back at her, swallowing back the prickle of embarrassment I still always felt at moments like these.

She paused and took a deep breath. 'There are several members of the cast and crew in the bar having drinks, if you care to join them.' She pointed to her right.

'That's lovely,' I said. 'Thank you so much,' and made to leave.

'Oh – Miss Noel.' She made a sweet little gulping sound, like a frog. 'Please, forgive me. I just have to say, *Lanterns Over Mandalay* is my favourite film, and you're my favourite star,' she said, in a rush. 'I think you're a wonderfully talented actress.'

'Gosh,' I said. 'Thank you, that's awfully kind of you.'

'You coming here is the biggest event in my life. I'm so excited. I've been planning for days what I'd say to you, and now it's gone out of my head. Miss Noel,' she added, bright red.

I put my head on one side. She was so young, younger than me, I'd say about seventeen. 'What's your name?' I asked her.

'Katie,' she said. 'Katie Hyde.'

'Would you like a signed photograph of me, Katie? I can arrange to have one sent up here,' I said.

Katie's eyes filled with tears; she blushed, and took a gulp of air. 'Oh, thank you, Miss Noel.' She twisted her fingers together. 'All those dumb magazines – they say you're forgetting your fans now that you're married and so famous. I knew that it simply couldn't be true!'

I took the key from her, touching her fingers briefly. 'It's so very nice to meet you,' I said, and walked into the bar.

It was a long, low room with beams and a fire crackling merrily in the grate. The evening light, splintered into shafts by the trees, shone softly through the leaded windows. Moss Fisher was waiting by the door, along with Jerome and the others. 'Nice work, kid,' he said. 'Good job. Well remembered. I'll tell her she don't get the picture of you if she don't write the letter.'

I loved acting, but I loathed this part, more than ever. To be told a week before that the vile gossip magazines like *Confidential* have decided it's open season on you, that you could easily become box office poison; to be called to a meeting with the heads in the studio to decide on a strategy; to concoct these stupid, humiliating, false sessions with girls who genuinely like you. I had had Katie's name written down on a piece of paper for two days now. *'We'll start with the girl at the hotel. She's a huge fan. I've told her when you're arriving, she'll be on duty. This is what you say . . .'*

'Please, Moss,' I said quietly now, putting my coat down on the bench and slowly pulling off the cream kid gloves I always wore. 'I won't do that again. It feels so unnatural.'

He tapped a cigarette slowly out of its case, without looking at me. 'You mean you can't be bothered to make nice with your fans?' he asked quietly. 'You don't care what they say about you any more?'

I shook my head, smoothing my hand over my aching brow. 'It's not that and you know it. I'd happily send a photo to anyone who wants it. I'd have had that conversation with her anyway – you didn't need to set it up like that.' I paused. 'I've only ever said no to signing an autograph once. It's the . . . lie. The set-up. I hate it.'

'I see.' Moss nodded. 'Listen, Eve, Mr Baxter wouldn't

want you to be reminded there's plenty of girls coming up behind you who'll do anything for—'

I raised my hand in front of him. 'Go away, Moss, please.' I'd realised lately I wasn't frightened of him any more. He was a bully, Mr Baxter's enforcer. I hated him, but I didn't fear him.

'She's tired,' Jerry said soothingly. 'Honey, sit down, have a drink.' He patted my arm, then turned to the gentleman sitting next to him, whom I hadn't noticed in my anger. 'Hey, Matthews, what'll you have? Same again?'

I looked at his companion, and nearly slid off the bench. It was Don. Just there, two people away from me.

'H-hello!' I said.

'Hey, Rose,' he said softly, so the others didn't quite catch the name. He gave me one of his funny, one-sided smiles. 'Surprised to see me?'

'I – I am,' I said, simply staring at him. I knew him so well, yet I'd only really seen him three times in my whole life. He looked older, the lines round his mouth and eyes more pronounced, and he was thinner than ever. But the face was still kind, handsome, with its long jaw. The same dark, shining eyes. 'You got a haircut,' I said eventually.

'In twelve months? I should say I did, honey,' Don said, tapping a cigarette against a case. He moved over, as Jerry ordered the drinks. 'Sit down, why don't you. Let me look at you.'

'You guys know each other? That's great,' Jerry said. 'Why didn't you tell me, Eve? Don's an old buddy of mine.' He patted Don's thigh, rather defensively. 'Back on board to tighten a few scenes up.' He shot a glance at Don. 'Shh. This one up at the beach needs looking at. And when Rose is back in the office, and of course the final scene with her and Peter. I wanna really punch them up. This is gonna get us an Oscar, this picture, honey. One way or another.'

I nodded. I couldn't stop smiling. 'It's very good to see you,' I said, turning back to him. 'How've you been?'

'Me?' His head was nodding. His long, strong fingers were

splayed out on the table. He drummed them on the wood. *Clickety-clackety-clickety-clackety*. 'I'm great, Rose. Oh, I'm just great.'

I watched him curiously. 'I wondered—'

'Don'cha wonder about me, honey. Rose.' He nodded again. Then it struck me. *He's drunk*. Jerry didn't seem to notice, but then Jerry was a pretty hard drinker himself.

Moss was hovering behind us, and I knew why he was here, or at least wasn't leaving. He was checking up on me.

'Eve, come here and say hi!' I looked over to the next table where June Dexter and Conrad, my co-stars, were sitting. I went over, almost relieved, to greet them.

'When did you folks get here?' I said.

June nudged Conrad. 'We came up together this morning. Had little Miss Tiny Tears here crying his eyes out over some affair, so I thought I'd keep him company.'

She rolled her eyes as Conrad sat up straight, looked around and said, rather waspishly, 'What a crock, young lady. I only came early to help you shake off that oaf you call a boyfriend and you know it.' He smiled at me. 'Darling, how are you? Did you finish that crossword?'

When Conrad played Captain Hawkins in *Lanterns Over Mandalay* he'd kept a book of crosswords in his jacket and produced it at odd, hilarious times, which is when I'd first loved him. Since then we'd do crosswords together in our dressing rooms during any break from filming. I loved working with Conrad; he made everything a little better, brought a little more warmth and sparkle in the world. June I knew less well, but she was fun and full of incredible stories. She was an ex-child star who'd got rid of an overbearing mother and fought off a lecherous studio head attempting to deflower her on her fifteenth birthday. She was always perky, a wise head on young shoulders, a terrific comedy actress. She'd also slept with virtually everyone I knew.

'I'm fine,' I told Conrad. 'I made it up here. And now I need a drink.'

June drained her glass. 'I'm having Gimlets, Eve darlin'. Join me. They're out of this world. Never thought this goddamn place would have a bartender who knew how to make a decent cocktail.' She gestured to him. 'Another one for Eve here.'

Conrad smiled. 'Eve, don't fall in with her. She's a bad influence on a good girl like you. I've always told you that. Stick with me, honey.'

'Oh, I will,' I said solemnly, but something like joy gripped me, because it was all so carefree and funny.

'Goddammit!'

There was a splash and an oath from Don in the corner, and when I turned I saw he'd spilled his gin Martini over my gloves.

'Shoot,' he said, pressing them to his thigh, to blot the liquid with the wool of his suit. 'Look at that.' He pressed them again. 'Oh, darn it.' They were streaked with black, ash from his cigarette that he'd scattered over them somehow. He wasn't even focusing, just smiling a stupid juvenile smile and patting the gloves ineffectually.

'Give them to me,' I said. I was almost embarrassed, as though he were my responsibility. I snatched the gloves back from him, surprised at how upset I was.

Don sank the rest of his drink. 'No, no, no need for that, Rose,' he said. His head seemed to be detached from his shoulders; it was rolling around loosely, like a marble in a pinball machine. I stared again at him. It had only been just over a year, but what a change that time had wrought in him; I could see it now, when I looked at him properly. It wasn't just the lines on his face. He looked tired, too – so tired. He shrugged, defeated. 'No need. Don't want to cause you trouble.'

'You're not,' I said. 'Just – don't.'

'How's married life? How's it treating ya?' he said. He brought a floppy hand up to loosen his collar; even when he was drunk, his shirt was pristinely pressed, the lines of his suit sharp on his long, lean body.

'Very well, thank you,' I answered primly.

He stared at me. 'You're not so green any more, are you.'

There were so many things I wanted to say to him, and they all sounded far too intimate; after all, I really did barely know him even though I felt he knew me, better than most people. *Why have you been blacklisted? Who's your wife? Oh, Don, why are you drinking so much? What can I do to make it better? What can I do to make you grin again like you used to?*

But I couldn't ask, in front of everyone. There was an awkward silence. I smiled, pleasantly, my best polite Eve way.

Though he was also several drinks down, I could see Jerry knew Don was far gone. He patted him on the back. 'Hey, old chum,' he said. 'Why don't we go get some food? We'll go over what we need to, Eve, then give you the changes tomorrow. It won't affect the morning shoot, I promise you.'

He patted Don on the back, and he heaved himself to his feet. I stood up to let them pass, and Don's hand dragged across my shoulder. I touched it lightly, a farewell gesture. I remembered then how his hands felt as he clutched mine, that long-ago day, how his lips felt on mine, our bodies meeting like that.

I shook my head, and said out loud, to distract myself, 'Goodnight, boys.'

'Night,' Don muttered. He turned to look at me, but I pretended to be moving seats. I couldn't bear to see his face. June and Conrad watched politely. I don't think they knew how drunk Don was; more likely they were too absorbed in their own gay world to notice. I moved around to join them.

'Say, Eve,' June said, in a friendly way. 'Did Gilbert hear yet about that part?'

Katie from the reception desk appeared with a Gimlet, and I took a long sip, giving her a grateful smile. 'No, not yet. I'm so anxious he gets it. He's perfect for it. It'd be plain wrong if it went to someone else.'

They both smiled, and Conrad stubbed his cigarette out. 'Young love is a wonderful thing,' he said. 'Well, Gilbert's a lucky guy, and I'm not the first person to say it.' He smiled sweetly; Conrad was genuinely without an ego or a malicious bone in his body.

'I'm the lucky one,' I said, and in that moment I believed it. Gilbert had been so nice that morning after breakfast, kissing me goodbye, seeing me into the car, shutting the door solicitously, so much so that I had scolded myself for my bad behaviour towards him. Poor Gilbert, I'd told myself on the drive up. You fight for King and Country, you nearly die, and what awaits you when you return to your job? Indifference, then rejection. 'I'm very lucky indeed.' I smiled, glad to be thinking these thoughts. Behind me, Jerry shepherded Don out of the room as he muttered something to him. I heard my name, but I ignored it.

too good to last

WE BEGAN THE shoot on Pfeiffer Beach the next day. Shooting by the sea is not ideal in an industry that prizes the re-creation of reality above actual reality, with the result that people fuss around you, even more than usual. The sound of the sea and gales ruin take after take. The wind whips the hairdresser's most careful preparations into a mockery. Screams of surprise kept ruining the shots, as the freezing cold surf slid across unsuspecting feet or once, to everyone's amusement, when a tiny, translucent crab nipped at one of Jerry's toes as he was yelling out a direction to the cinematographer. Yet it was wonderful to be there. The beach is only accessible down a long, thin road that is gothically dark, with arching trees and greying vines, then suddenly opening up at the end onto a wide cove about three-quarters of a mile long. A vast, dramatic lump of rock, with an arch hollowed out by the waves, stands in the centre, foaming surf crashing around it. I wanted to paddle beside it in between takes, but they wouldn't let me. The current was too strong, they said.

For the first few days of the shoot Moss Fisher was everywhere. He came to the beach, watching all the while, sand flecking the pants of his suit, hands thrust into pockets, occasionally taking notes. He was there, he said, to report back on filming for *Photoplay* magazine, who wanted pictures and a story. I didn't believe him. He or one of his underlings were always watching what went on, and normally I was used to him – but now I found his presence especially unsettling, I don't know why. I think he would have had me attached to him with a string if he could. Moss's one concession to the beach was his tortoiseshell glasses. His tanned, deeply lined, impassive face gave nothing away. But he looked like a mobster, a joke, standing there watching the comings and goings of the crew with their shirtsleeves and trouser legs rolled up against the sea.

I didn't see Don after the first night. I think Jerry was protecting his old friend, keeping him out of the way. Jerry knew how good Don was. He also knew how much Moss and the executives disliked him. We shot on the beach for two days, then up on the hill, in an old cafe overlooking the sea. Through the windows the Californian coastline stretched out below us for miles and miles. I could see sea lions and otters playing in the water far below as the crew changed the lights, and adjusted my hair, June's make-up, Conrad's hairpiece.

It was hard work, tiring but joyous, and after a couple of days I had fallen in love with Big Sur. We all had. Perhaps it was the sea air, perhaps the magic of the place – Highway 1 the only way in and out, the people completely unlike Los Angeles people, or movie people. Every night we all of us ate together in the old wooden dining room, and a camaraderie sprung up, the like of which I'd never had on a film set before. I felt – we all did – that we were living in a lovely, gilded dream, like the memories of a summer childhood holiday, too good to last.

I have always loved the sea. Perhaps it was growing up far from water that did it, and thus the holiday I remember particularly is the summer before Rose died. In 1941 Daddy was a doctor at the army hospital in Keynsham, and he got four days' leave in July. We went to Dorset and swam in Lulworth Cove every day. Sand got into everything. Rose ate a handful of sand when Mother told her not to, and was immediately sick. She went limp, her eyes rolling back in her head, totally still. It was terrifying, but my father knew what to do. He called out to our fellow holidaymakers, 'She's allergic to the seawater. Don't worry. Nothing is wrong with her. ' I remember thinking then how lucky we were. If the sea was that dangerous for Rose it could render her totally limp and lifeless; though I loved it so much, best that we live far away from it, in the very middle of the country.

It was the last time we were all together for any long period of time as a family; my father was always at the hospital, and for the rest of the summer though I was always out in the garden or playing amongst the stones in the ruins of the house nearby, more and more my mother made Rose stay behind, for some breaking of the rules or another, some piece of silly behaviour or hysterical fit she was increasingly prone to having, when my parents tried to cross her.

And by the following summer Rose was dead, and I was playing alone amongst the stones, although she was always there with me, talking to me, telling me what to do, who should ride out next, and where I should hold the following night's feasts, just as it always had been, as though I was acting and she was directing me.

On the fourth night, dinner broke up earlier than usual. The party had begun to disperse anyway; there was an ungodly start the following day. I'd been sitting between Conrad and June, as ever, exchanging funny stories about our co-stars, swapping cigarettes, stealing sips from June's unending supply of Gimlets, when Katie appeared, holding a telegram.

'For you, Miss Noel,' she said, smiling shyly. 'Hope it's good news!'

I snatched it from her and she looked surprised. I read it, my heart racing; any communication from the outside world seemed sinister, threatening to me.

GILBERT HAS PART OF EARL SOMERS IN DARE TO WIN STOP WANTED ME TO LET YOU KNOW STOP FILMING BEGINS TWO WEEKS' TIME NEVADA STOP FEATHERSTONE

I smiled, and let the telegram drop to the floor. 'Oh, thank God,' I heard myself say. I turned to Conrad, who was whispering something in Jerry's ear. He sat upright.

'Everything all right, Eve dear?' he said.

'Gilbert got the part!' I said. 'Oh, it's such wonderful news!'

'That's great,' said June. 'Just great. He'll be terrific. He sure can act, your husband. And no one deserves it more'n he does. Hey, Rudy! Another over here, please, my friend.'

'What's the good news?' Jerry said, standing up to leave. I slid the telegram across to him and he peered down to read it. 'That's wonderful, Eve. You'll miss him though, I guess?'

'How so?' I said.

Jerry was patting his jodhpurs for his key. 'Three months' shooting in the Nevada desert – I don't envy him that, at least.'

'Three *months*?' I frowned; perhaps I'd got it wrong. 'It can't be for three months. He'll be – that's for ever.'

'Didn't he tell you?' He took my silence as the answer he needed. 'Sorry, kid. It's a real long shoot. They train 'em up almost to pilot-level standard, that's why. It's gonna be as realistic as any battle. That's the whole point of it.' He shrugged. 'I'd have loved to direct it, but Refford got there first, and I can't say I'm sorry now. Lot of macho egos and a lot of guns and bombs – not quite my thing. Not any more.'

I was barely listening. Three months. Why hadn't Gilbert said so? Perhaps he didn't know. It was such a long time to be apart. I didn't want it; these few weeks were long enough. I kept thinking, if we could spend more time together, living a quiet, cosy life, we'd find ways to bridge the gaps between us. Three months with Gilbert shooting a war movie in the desert wasn't going to bring us any closer, was it?

And then I cursed myself, for being so damned selfish. He'd hardly had work the past few years, let alone a part worthy of him, and Earl Somers – the young idealistic peer who gets caught up in the hell of war – was perfect for Gilbert. Although I couldn't help wondering, as I'd read the script, how they'd address the fact that Gilbert was nearer fifty than the twenty-four indicated on the list of characters.

'Any reply?' Katie said nervously.

'Oh, I'm so sorry, Katie.' I recovered myself. 'Here.' I scribbled my reply on the bottom of the form, and handed it back to her: *So pleased so proud give him all love his delighted wife.*

As I watched Katie trot back towards the hotel, I realised I meant it, too. I wanted to be a wife. I wanted to be consumed with love, to adore him the way he needed to be adored. I didn't want this . . . this polite, careful existence in which the two of us seemed to tread so carefully, all the damn time, until Gilbert snapped, like he had the morning I left. I wasn't this girl back in London; there I was messy and loud and I had a dreadful coral scarf knitted by Clarissa, with more holes in it than a fishing net. I had black hands from fingering the coal in the tiny flat, and I was thin and pale and ungainly and . . . full of something. Urgent, Miss Gauntly, my voice teacher had said. I didn't feel urgent in Los Angeles. I felt . . . slightly dead. Silly thing to say, you can't be slightly dead. But I did. As if little by little I were slowly shutting down.

'One more drink to celebrate, honey?' a voice said, and I looked up and saw June.

'Sure,' I nodded. Conrad got up to leave, putting a hand on each of our shoulders. 'See you tomorrow, girls,' he said, as June and I settled into our seats by the wide window ledge, staring out at the starry sky; the reflection of the fire in the leaded windows, the scent of summer blossoms floating in from outside.

'You must be relieved, yes?' June said. She gave me a quick, appraising stare.

'I am,' I said, closing my eyes briefly. 'It's wonderful. I'm going to miss him, though. It'll be awfully difficult.'

'I don't know,' she said. She stabbed at the quarter of lime in the bottom of her glass with a plastic cocktail stick. 'They're often better out of the way, you know. I mean, husbands.'

There was a little pause, and then she laughed, to show it was a joke, and I joined in with her, my laughter a little too loud.

*   *   *

We had a couple of drinks and talked about nothing, this and that. I walked back to my lodge under the almost-black sky, deep, deep blue pricked with thousands of stars.

As I fiddled with my key, I heard a sound in the bushes by the lodge ahead of mine, a groaning, then a rustling. I jumped, and tried not to scream, but a short, high gasp came out of my mouth. Two figures sprang up from the bench outside the door.

'Conrad! Hello!' I called, then stopped. 'Oh, I—'

Conrad and Jerry were standing next to me, guilt written larger than life on their faces. Jerry's hand was still on Conrad's hip; I looked down, then saw what state Conrad was in, and turned away, giving a short wave, my cheeks burning.

'Night,' I called softly, not wanting anyone else to hear. 'See – see you tomorrow.'

'I—' Conrad began, pulling away from Jerry and coming towards me. He looked horrified; Jerry hung his head, shaking it and muttering to himself. 'Eve—'

I smiled at them both, shook my head. I wanted to say, *It's fine, it's no problem, your business not mine*, so I winked at them, but then I thought that might look too salacious, so I nodded again. 'Bye, dears.'

Once inside I leaned against the door, smiling to myself. Jerry and Conrad! I wondered if this was an ongoing relationship, or whether I'd interrupted their first tryst, and ruined the start of something special. It made sense, the two of them together – why hadn't I thought of it before? Though immediately following that, it struck me there was no way it could ever come to anything, not in Hollywood, especially not for Conrad, kind sweet Conrad. Unhooking my dress, and slipping off my heels, I put my dressing gown on, shivering slightly; it was several degrees cooler up here than in Los Angeles, and always chilly at night. I could hear the rush of the river below us, the crackle of the fire the maid laid in my room every evening. And waiting for me I had a new Georgette Heyer, wrapped in brown paper and sent over last week from England by the publishers, no less.

I sat at the dressing table and ran my fingers over my set

of brushes, a wedding present from Gilbert: black ebony, my married initials – *E. N. T.* – inlaid with mother-of-pearl. I picked up the nearest brush and stared at my reflection in the three-way mirror as I started to brush my hair. My face stared back at me, three different angles. Eyes, tired blueish smudges underneath them. The eyebrows, perfectly shaped, the widow's peak just a fraction off (it had to be retouched with black eyeliner every time my make-up was refreshed: the price of perfection). I was thinner than I had been, older, more sophisticated I suppose, but I didn't know.

Then I looked away, because I hated having to look too long in mirrors. It made me wonder if I was looking at myself, or the wrong version of me. Sometimes Rose herself smiled back at me, and seemed about to speak. Sometimes I didn't know myself and it made me feel strange, odd.

Shaking the thoughts out of my head, I brushed my hair with such viciousness my scalp tingled. Then I realised I could hear something else above the fire and the river below. There was a noise, a quiet tapping, so soft and subtle it didn't make me jump, just eased gradually into my consciousness. I tightened the knot of my gown around my waist, and stood up. Which one of them would it be, come to beg my discretion? I opened the door with a ready smile.

A blast of sharp night air sent the flame in the grate shooting high, and sparks flew.

'Don,' I said, clutching onto the door.

I remember even now being utterly floored at the sight of him, his presence in front of me. He stood in the doorway, coat over his arm, suitcase in one hand. He raised his hat.

'I'm sorry for the hour,' he said. 'I – listen, Rose. I wanted to apologise. And say goodbye. I'm going back to LA tonight.'

'Now?' I said.

He nodded. His jaw was black with day-old stubble. 'Jerry loaned me his car. He's a good guy, Jerry.'

'He is,' I said.

I watched him carefully. The lines under his eyes were etched into his skin like river through land. He looked so tired. So

– beaten down. I knew he was sober. But I didn't know what to say, and I still didn't feel like making it easier on him.

'Where have you been, these last few days?' I said. 'I thought you'd disappeared.'

He cleared his throat. 'Cold turkey,' he said. 'Holed up in my room. Jerry threatened to throw the key away but it didn't come to that. Not a drop of liquor since that night. It's almost all gone.' That explained the worn, strung-out appearance. I wondered how hard it had been.

'Are you – all right?' I said.

'Jerry had them send me up food and leave it on the porch. I worked on a couple of new scenes. And when it got real bad, I'd pace around, and smoke, and howl at the moon, like the lone wolf I am.' He shook his head and smiled. 'So I'd like to think. No, Rose – I was an ass the other night,' he said. 'In fact, I'm an ass in general. I tried to write you, but it didn't come out how I wanted it to.' His smile was bitter. 'I can't say what I need to when I have to. You most of all. I'm a phoney. Anyway, I saw your light was on and I wanted to say sorry before I go.'

'It's fine,' I said inadequately. 'I just hate to see you like that, that's all. I don't know you.'

He gritted his teeth. 'They want me to fail, and sometimes it's easier to just give them what they want,' he said. 'But I'm not making excuses. It's my weakness. I have no one to blame but myself, and I swear to you, I won't ever touch another drop again.'

'Swear it to yourself, not to me,' I said.

Don ran his fingers over the felt of the hat in his hands. 'I have you in my head as this symbol, Rose. A symbol of what I don't deserve. And so seeing you is sometimes hard for me.' His voice was low, cracked. 'You have to understand this – I don't ever want to cause you any harm. Or embarrassment. Or damage. To your beautiful gloves.'

He produced a new pair out of his coat pocket. I tutted in annoyance, my hands still clinging to the half-open door.

'You didn't need to do that,' I said: ever a child of rationing, waste or duplication seemed so unnecessary to me. 'Where on earth did you get them, Don? There's nothing around here for miles.'

He smiled then, the edges of his eyes crinkling just a little. 'I wanted to. It's my penance. Goodbye, Rose. I have to go. It's a long drive.'

He waggled the gloves in front of me. I reached out one hand and took them. He lifted his hat again, and turned away, and I closed the door again.

I sat back down at the table, and picked up the brush. *E. N. T.* I stared at it, at myself, in the mirror, and then I carried on brushing. But then suddenly I stood up, plucked the key from its hook, and raced out into the night. The wind was fierce, but the sky was still clear, a huge April moon golden in the black sky among the stars. I ran towards the main building, my hair flying behind me. I didn't know what I would say. All I could hear, all I could feel, was the insistent *thud-thud-thud* of my heart beating.

He was climbing into the car, which was resting under a large, dark tree. I pulled him by the arm, and he closed the door. 'Don't go,' I said. I put my finger to his lips. 'Come back with me,' and I took him by the hand back to my lodge, and we closed the door behind us.

Perhaps it was the air, perhaps it was the full moon. Perhaps it was something amongst us all, seeing Conrad and Jerry kissing. Perhaps I felt the normal rules didn't apply. I don't know. I only knew I loved this man. I couldn't bear to see the hurt in his eyes; I had to hold him, be with him, make him smile. I didn't know then how great the grip of his addiction was, and I wanted to try and make things better.

The glow of the fire warmed us as I took off my dressing gown; it slithered to the floor, and then my underthings, and I stood before him, our shadows leaping against the old photos on the wall, his silhouette incongruous with its trilby and coat, next to my nudity. I removed his clothes, piece by piece. I smoothed my hands over his tired, sweet, handsome, sad face, and then we climbed onto the bed, together, and held each other, totally naked, just feeling our skin meet, touch, against the crisp white sheets. He held me in his arms, and he was so warm, and he didn't smell of anything but Don this time, just Don.

He held my head in his hands, staring at me, and then he kissed me, and as he did he gave a sigh, deep in his throat, like a moan. Then we kissed again, and started to touch each other, and I wanted to hold his hands, his body, every part of him. I felt I knew him so well already, yet hardly at all. I lay back against the pillows and he parted my legs, and touched me, kissing all of my body. I felt like crying; a wave of sadness that hit me, hard. He did too. We didn't say anything. When he entered me, it felt as though it was the first time. Honestly and truthfully, as if I had never had anyone before, and I held onto him, as if clutching on for dear life. I felt dizzy, alive, terrified – and happy. The hair on his arms, on his chest, was dark; his skin was tanned and smooth to the touch. He moved inside me, and I pushed up to meet him, to feel him, as deep as I could. And feeling was so wonderful. Feeling something at last, falling, falling, falling. Don. Don, my Don.

We slept afterwards, and I woke once and moved onto his chest, so he held me through the rest of the night. The embers were barely alight. One log glowed, in the corner of the grate.

not without you

WHEN THE LOCATION shoot was extended for another two weeks, as Jerry decided that it would be cheaper to get the shots of Rose in her small home town up here rather than in the agricultural towns east of San Francisco, no one demurred. I didn't believe for a moment this was unconnected with his relationship with Conrad, but I was in no position to judge. Indeed, I was gloriously happy for them.

Have you ever been unfaithful? It gives one a curious sensation. All through that short, blissful time, I was so happy with everything, glowing with love for everyone. I needed no sleep; I was as alive as I've ever felt. I didn't mind the wigs that pinched, the hot lights and long hours, the endless questions from Moss about where I was, what I was doing, who needed an autograph, who'd requested an interview. I wrote to Gilbert, recently arrived in Nevada, every day. I told him I loved him and wished him luck, and I meant it all, most fervently. Isn't it strange?

What seemed extraordinary to me was how commonplace it felt, Don and me, our falling in love. I think I had always loved him, since I'd first met him that night at the party. And he said the same. He was a new man during those days. I said it was the drying out, he said it was me. On set out in the hills above the sea, he'd stand behind Jerry, changing lines here and there, adding in brilliant suggestions, working with the actors, never intruding on our performances, merely giving us confidence. I had always liked slipping into someone else's shoes, and now I simply loved it. I loved this character, because it was written for me, by him. I felt as if, every time, I became Rose. I became myself, truly myself.

And at night, when the moon was waning but the bright stars were scattered like a million diamonds across the inky sky, Don would come to my room, unlock the door with the key I'd given him (I'd lied to sweet, lovely Katie and said I'd lost mine), and I'd be waiting for him, the fire crackling in the grate, the dark wooden panels glowing with the warmth of the room, the warmth of our love for each other, it seemed.

To hear the key in the lock as I lay in bed reading was the sweetest sensation; ever since then the sound of that movement has, for me, been the most beautiful in the world. To feel his arms around me, to smell him, hear the beating of his heart, and his low, kind voice, 'Hello, Rose – how've you been today?' in my ear. To know this was our world; no one else knew or could intrude. I will always remember it, but at the time it seemed normal. I knew I'd found what I was looking for. I knew the frightening moments I often experienced, when I had taught my brain to disconnect itself from my body and sometimes I couldn't quite get back to being me, when Rose haunted my dreams, laughed at me in mirrors, were over. I didn't need to pretend to be anyone else, anywhere else, when I was with Don.

What did we talk about? Everything. Poetry, books, films. Our respective childhoods, his in a small town in Oklahoma, mine in the English countryside. What we liked, what we didn't. I had a portable gramophone, and we played Sinatra constantly, especially 'I'll Be Around', though as Don said, we needed to pick a more cheerful song.

He knew every poem under the sun, it seemed, and I admired his schoolteacher father for the passion he'd inspired in him. He loved England, though he'd been only once. We discussed going back to Britain all the time, how he would look up a cousin he'd stayed with near Windsor, how we would walk

203

through Hampstead Heath, visit Keats's House, and sit in the pub Shakespeare sat in by Borough Market – though he'd promised me he was never drinking again.

'I won't start that up again, Rose. The studio knows me too well. They're done with me, think I'm too much trouble, a relic from another era, and they couldn't ever pin anything Un-American on me in the dark days but that doesn't mean they aren't going to try. They want me out of the way. So this is what they do: they send some guy to meet me in a bar, to discuss future projects. I say no, I don't care for a Martini. He insists. I say no. I ask what work they've got coming up for me. He says nothing. He orders one drink, then another. I eye it like a dying man in the desert. He offers me a job writing something new. I leap at the chance. He says, come on, let's toast this. Just one Martini, what's wrong with one? And I, like the dumb schmuck I am, accept. But I can't ever just have one. Three days later, I'm still drinking.'

He was lying on the bed, naked and tangled in the sheets, his head in my lap, one hand reaching up to stroke my breasts from time to time. I smoothed his hair away from his forehead with both my hands, and kissed it. 'How did you get back on this picture, then?'

'It's Jerry,' Don said. 'He's a true friend, that guy. He brought me in to do the whole rewrite, paid me out of his own pocket, then when the Baxters were pleased with the new draft he told them the truth, that it was me and I should carry on.'

'He loves you.'

'He's the best. I've told him I owe him now. Whatever he wants, I'll do it. No matter how big or small. He brought me to you, didn't he?' He kissed me. 'Jerry got me back on the project. Told 'em I was cheap and available and knew the script – well, I wrote the damn thing, of course I know it.' His face was angry. I stroked his chest, his shoulders, feeling his heart pounding under his skin. 'But they'll get me in the end. They wrecked things with Bella, you know. Moss told her I was cheating on her before anyone else did. That's why she ran off to Vegas, got herself a rich new playboy.'

'Were you, though?'

'No,' he said, smiling. 'I wasn't. That's the irony. Hell,' he said, sitting up. 'She was better off without me, though. I was drinking too much. I was unhappy.' He caught my hands in his. 'Rose, you realise what you're taking on with me, don't you? You'll be a pariah. Moss, Lenny, those guys at the studio. You think they're going to make it hard for you to leave Gilbert – well, wait till they hear who you're leaving him for.'

I shook my head, smiling. 'I don't care,' I said.

'Your film career will be over.'

'I don't care,' I said again. 'Honestly. I don't like it that much. I never did. I'll act somewhere else. I just want to be with you.'

I pulled him against my breasts, tracing his dark hairline, the scroll of his ear, his jaw, with one finger. He stroked my back, and I hugged him tighter with the other arm. 'We'll move to London,' I said. 'We can rent a place in Hampstead – it's cheap there. At least it was. I'll easily get work there, on the stage, in television, maybe even in films. And they'll love you, darling. You'll be rolling in offers. We'll be so happy. We will.' I looked around the small, warm room. 'Even if it doesn't work out, we have everything we need, right here,' I told him. 'We don't need anything else.'

On our last night in Big Sur, Jerry took over the whole restaurant for cast and crew. He sat next to Conrad, and whispered in his ear all night, and though Conrad seemed more embarrassed than he by it, I wondered if perhaps, perhaps, something might change. I wished I could talk to Conrad, confide in him myself. Tell him I knew what I'd seen and I didn't care. We'd never discussed it once. I wanted him to know he wasn't alone. But it would be such a scandal if it came out, and it was their secret to keep, not mine.

I wish now, more than any other of the many regrets I have in my life, that I'd spoken to Conrad. Pulled him aside and talked to him like the friend I thought I was. He left after dinner, drove straight back home to Los Angeles. Or at least I thought he did. If only he had.

Before he left Jerry made a speech. 'We are making a very special film,' he said. 'And this has been a very special time.' He looked at Conrad, then at me, then briefly at Don, and I knew he knew, and I smiled at him.

That night, after the meal, Don and I made love for the last time in our little room. It was fast, furious, passionate, as if we wanted it over, wanted the next stage of our lives to begin. I remember the weight of him on top of me as we lay afterwards. Like a shield, covering me. We had a plan; we discussed it every night, went over every stage so both of us were clear. He was going straight from LA to Vegas to see Bella, to set in motion the quickest possible divorce. I would meet him back in Los Angeles. Gilbert had a week off from shooting, and was due back at our house. I'd tell him I was moving out, and check into the Beverly Hills Hotel, where I'd first stayed all those years ago. I would finish filming *A Girl Named Rose*, then Don and I would leave for Europe. Hollywood was currently scandalised by Elizabeth Taylor's upcoming marriage to Eddie Fisher. And it was not so long ago that Ingrid Bergman had returned from Europe in triumph, years after being cast out for running off with Roberto Rossellini. No one would care two hoots about my marriage breaking up, I told myself. It was nearly 1960. Times were changing, and Gilbert didn't love me; I knew he didn't. If I could find a way to minimise the shame he'd feel, that would go a long way to smoothing things over. I owed him that much.

The morning we left, my car arrived early. Katie sent a message through to say it was here. I stood just inside our lodge, and kissed Don lightly on the lips. We were dressed for the outside world once again, he in his tweeds and sharp slacks, I in my little Yves Saint Laurent travelling suit, and I felt curiously shy with him. He took my hand.

'I love you, Rose.' He pushed a lock of my hair away from my face.

'I love you too,' I said.

'Will you marry me?' His expression was deadly serious.

'Yes,' I whispered, putting my head on his chest one last time. 'Yes, of course I will.'

They knocked on the door again. 'Then go,' he said, kissing my hair. 'I'll see you in three, four days. Soon, so soon, we'll be together. And the past, it won't matter any more. It's the future. I can face the future, but not without you.'

'Not without you,' I repeated, and we stared at each other.

When I opened the door, morning light flooded the dark room, and I blinked as I came out onto the porch.

Jerry was standing just outside, waiting for us. He smiled at me, but I noticed his face was pale.

'Don, I need a word.' He touched his friend on the shoulder.

'Anything for you, Jerry,' Don said cheerfully, putting his arm around him. 'You know that.'

Jerry smiled mechanically, then kissed me. I wondered if he was all right. 'Goodbye, my dear,' he said. 'See you tomorrow, the day after, for ever. Back in the real world.'

That's not the real world, I wanted to say. This is, this right here, standing with Don, so close I can reach out and touch him, knowing in these last few seconds that he is mine, that we love each other, that everything is clear and simple.

They stood together and Don waved as the car drove slowly down the drive. We turned onto the highway and he disappeared out of sight.

I never saw him again.

PART TWO

CHAPTER SEVENTEEN

THE YELLOWING OLD clock radio alarm wakes me with a start at 6 a.m.

I sit upright, as I do every morning, my heart racing, and turn it off. Then I blink at the heavy patterned chintz curtains, the old green silk upholstered chair, the wooden beams. *Where the hell am I?* I look through the gap in the moth-eaten curtains at the rain drumming on the windows, hear the faint *thud-thud-thud* of ancient hot-water pipes. I see my battered old Eve Noel biography, a jumper and my trainers, a script, smell the faint old smell of cleaning fluid and dust, mingling together. Yes. I'm here. And it's still raining.

It's July, and I've been in England for three weeks. Everyone around me made it clear I was risking everything to come here and make this movie. And they were right. We actually started shooting *My Second-Best Bed* a fortnight ago, and it's about to fall apart. The last piece of funding that means we can actually finish the film hasn't appeared, the weather keeps holding us up and T.T. the director is crazy. Plus last night, we found out that Cara Hamilton, the actress playing the older Anne Hathaway, is quite seriously ill and might have to drop out, in which case we are probably screwed. There's three good things, though. One, Sara is here, and it's a lot of fun having her around. She's the kind of person you can look at and know she's thinking the same thing as you. Two, this film could be so, *so great*. The script is fantastic, the set is happy and fun, and the people are brilliant. I have to keep reminding myself of this when I'm standing outside in the rain for two hours on the stretch. What was the other good thing? Oh, yeah! I'm not in LA any more, waiting for some psycho to murder me while I'm asleep or something. Which of the three is probably the biggest plus, wouldn't you say?

I close my eyes for a second, and I'm back in my bedroom that night, looking at the torn curtains, the ripped clothes, the stuff this psycho had scribbled all over the walls. In those first few minutes, I wasn't scared. I wasn't upset. That came later, not then. I was completely calm, knowing something would change, and it was up to me to make it something good. I wasn't going to make *The Bachelorette Party*. I was going to listen to myself for once, and do what the hell I wanted. The next day I called up Alec Mitford and asked to have a meeting with him and the director, T.T. Tohens. Then I told Artie what was happening.

Turns out Artie hadn't been quite honest with me, anyway. There *was* an actress from *Downton Abbey* lined up to play Anne, but at the same time, the package – the fact that Alec Mitford was attached and that the revised script was so great – meant the project was getting heat and a couple of big-name stars had shown interest. Emily Blunt had even met with Alec and T.T. The movie had a buzz. You can't buy buzz. So once it was confirmed the insurers would pay out for my exit from *The Bachelorette Party* (security reasons; the LAPD agreed with me it was best I left LA for a while), Artie changed his tune. But I know he thinks it's the wrong direction for me, and it makes me nervous: the guy knows how to put together a hit, for all that we don't always agree. I am still annoyed with him, though I need to get my head down, prove to him he can take me seriously.

As for what happened at the house and who's doing it, and how they got in, I don't know.

They said they knew what I was thinking. They said I was going to die. That handwriting haunts my sleep: huge crazy words scrawled on the white walls in black marker pen. I keep seeing it, when I shut my eyes. *Someone stood there and wrote that.* How did he or she look, scribbling that they wanted me to die? Were they laughing? And the white roses, too: I kept telling the police about the ones before, left in my room, outside the house, but the strange thing is I don't know if they believe me or not. I'm not making it up. I'm not crazy. I have to remind myself of that almost daily at the moment.

I didn't sleep there again. I moved into a hotel and nearly two weeks later, I was on a plane to the UK. Denis is pensioned off, he'll come back twice a week to supervise the garage and the repairs. My security detail became insane: four massive men walking with me at all times, so I couldn't see anything from between their big black blazers, couldn't hear anything behind the constant crackle of their earpieces.

Here there's a revolving team of people who are with me most of the time and I have two personal guards now, Angie and Gavin. Angie is by my side almost twenty-four/seven but Gavin, her boss, covers for her in the afternoon. She's six foot four, ex-army, and she sleeps in the next room connected by a door we leave unlocked at night. This is a bit of a blow to my love life, as there's an extremely hot cameraman called Rick who Alec Mitford keeps teasing me has a thing for me. He looks like Patrick, even his name sounds like Patrick. He has lovely dark hair that falls in his face when he's embarrassed about something and he's quiet and shy. Maybe it's the itch I need to scratch, or maybe it's just more hassle than it's worth. You're not supposed to hook up with random guys if you're a famous actress. Fine for the boys – it's a big slap on the back if they turn up in some small town and bang everything that's going – but not me. It's just . . . it would be nice to feel the warmth of another body at night, to know someone is next to me.

I keep thinking about Patrick; he's in my mind more often than I care to admit, a proper old-fashioned crush which I know is ridiculous. I rang him a couple of times before I left, to apologise about bailing out on the film. He never returned my calls. He's probably mad at me now, and I don't blame him. I had no choice. I wish I could tell him that.

And though the film might be falling apart I feel safe here. I don't say this, though, as whenever I rail against the amount of people around me to Gavin, the head security guy, he stares at me and tells me I'm crazy.

'Do you want me to be ringing your mother to tell her you're dead? Huh?'

'No, obviously not. But you could ring her anyway, get her off my back for me.' I sound more British since I got here, more piss-takey. It's creeping back into my language and my voice, over the years of LA gushing and industry slang.

The LA cops interviewed me a bunch of times and they've combed the Internet too. They've actually gone to Ohio, to question some girl who posted threats to me on Twitter. *Come on, guys*, I want to say. It isn't some thirteen-year-old from Toledo with a grudge against me.

Or is it? The truth is, I have no idea. I don't have any control over it, either. I did get Gavin to reduce the constant guard that surrounded me wherever I walked from four huge men down to two, which felt like a victory. I'm scared – of course I'm fucking scared. But four guards make it far scarier somehow. Realistically, what's going to happen in this *Fawlty Towers*-style old hotel in the middle of nowhere when everyone's either in the bar till 4 a.m., getting up at 5 a.m., and knows each other's business? We are in the middle of nowhere on the edge of an ancient wood: forty-five minutes' drive from Anne Hathaway's house, fifteen minutes from the ancient Cotswold thatched cottage we're using for extra scenes, and only half an hour's drive from where I grew up. This is my life now. It's kind of strange. But I like it.

I'm rubbing my face, trying to wake myself up, when there's a sharp tap from outside. 'Sophie, are you OK?'

'Sure.' I jump out of bed. 'Sara, is that you?'

'Yes. Well, good morning! Another nice British day. I have your breakfast.'

I open the door, on a chain like Gavin taught me, to verify

that it is in fact Sara. I don't know why the cops think someone would try to kill me by so accurately impersonating my assistant's voice that I let down my guard and allow myself to be stabbed by a breakfast knife, but I'll take what precautions he gives me.

'I'm so glad I brought my bikini,' Sara says, putting the tray down on the bed and patting my arm, in a gesture of hello. She stares out the window. 'Wow, England. How did you cope growing up here? Do you have webbed feet?'

'No. Alec does. Ask him to show them to you,' I say. She laughs.

'OK, so I have your schedule here. I checked with Marie. They're setting up for the modern-day shot inside the house, but if it stops raining they'll try and get the first scene in the garden. I left the script for that scene on your bed last night . . . did you see it?'

'Yes, thank you,' I say. Sara is extremely efficient. Dare I say it, even more so than Tina. She double-checks everything, I never have to make a decision because she knows what I want, by some strange ESP. And she's also a free gossip service: she loves being first with information. 'Anything else?'

Sara nods. 'It's bad news. Cara's got pneumonia for sure and she has to stay in the hospital another couple of days. The drugs aren't working.'

'Poor Cara. Maybe I should go see her? This evening?'

'No visitors in case of infection.' Sara shakes her head. 'But I sent a bouquet and a muffin basket from you. The message read—' She whips out her BlackBerry and intones: ' "Dearest Cara, Get well soon, we need our Anne Hathaway back on set! We are all praying for you and a speedy recovery. With all my love, Sophie." ' She slides the BlackBerry back into her pocket.

'Oh, that's great,' I say, though in fact I'm not sure a bouquet and muffin basket is what you do in the UK. Plus Cara Hamilton, the much-feted and adored actress playing Anne Hathaway, is an old boot and has made it clear she loathes me, T.T., and most of the US crew. She communicates only with Alec, whom she considers to be at her level. She keeps

215

going on about 'the *first* time I was at Stratford, doing the Henrys with Peggy and John'.

I shouldn't be horrible about Cara. She's old, and not well, and I know everyone's worried about her. It's just she's one of those people who makes you feel like shit. I'd forgotten what it's like, being back in the UK. When we met this time (I didn't remind her I'd auditioned opposite her once) she said, 'How nice to meet you,' in that way English people do when they mean totally the opposite. 'I haven't seen your work, I'm afraid, but I know you don't need people like me to watch your films when you're so . . . *popular.*'

'Can I get you anything else?' Sara asks. She's standing there at the end of the bed, all bright-eyed and keen, her ponytail bouncing.

'No,' I say. 'That's all. Thank you so much, Sara. Why don't you take a day to yourself. I'll call you if I need you.'

Her face falls. 'Oh. You sure? You don't want me to bring your other shoes over later? In case it stops raining?'

'Go on,' I say. 'Go to Stratford or something. You'd love it.'

'You really don't need me to do anything else for you?' She pats the bed. 'Hey. It doesn't feel right, just feeding through your calls and hanging out all day. You never need me. It sucks.' Then her face freezes. 'I don't mean I don't like being here,' she says intently. 'Listen, I'm not trying to be dramatic. I don't mean that at all, Sophie.'

I pull at my face in the mirror, grimacing at its reflection in the dim room. 'Oh, my goodness, I know that. I just feel bad, dragging you all the way over to the UK and leaving you hanging around all the time.' I stop again, feeling my way. It's sometimes awkward: we know each other, we were young together. Always at the back of my mind with Sara is the line that director said to her. *'This girl's just an uglier Sophie Leigh. Next, please.'* Guilt makes me feel responsible.

'I'm so glad you're here. I just don't want you to feel you're missing out on anything back in LA. Any . . . opportunities.'

Sara pulls back the curtains. 'I have plenty to do!' She smiles. 'Now we got Wi-Fi we got all we need, am I right? Hey, did you check Deadline this morning? The script William Morris were touting that someone bid ten million dollars for? *Starlight*?'

I miss the sunshine in LA. I miss my beautiful house, the ocean, the markets, the food trucks, the beach, the people. And I miss California, the dream of a golden land that I fell in love with the moment I arrived. But I don't miss Hollywood. I've totally stopped paying any attention to the business since I got here.

'No. Is it good?'

Sara nods, biting her lip. 'It's *amazing* apparently. Fox bought it and it's going straight into production – every actress in town is going nuts for it.'

'Oh,' I say. 'What kind of thing?'

'Very dramatic, really meaty.' She pauses. 'Should I ask Artie to—'

'Yes,' I say without any conviction. We both know I'm not getting that part. 'Can you get me the script?'

'He wants to talk to you. He called again last night.'

'Tell him I'm shooting all day.'

'No problem,' says Sara. She types furiously on her BlackBerry, looking pleased to have something to do. 'Will you let me know if there's anything else?' She looks up. 'I think you're feeling kinda uneasy about us knowing each other from before, Sophie. It's not a problem for me. I promise you. I'll do anything, anything at all. I'll clean up your toenail clippings if you want.' I laugh. 'Gimme something.'

I tie my hair into a stubby ponytail and pin back the famous fringe, which I'm growing out now, so I'm all ready for my make-up and the wig that makes me look dramatically unlike Sophie Leigh. When Tommy saw the early head shots he rang me in a raging panic. 'No one will recognise you! What's the point of this film at all?'

'Just give Artie the message. And have a nice day. Read something, go visit something,' I say, ushering her towards the door. 'Shall we have dinner later?' She looks delighted. 'Alec lost the bet. He's buying drinks, so we have to go to the bar tonight.'

'How come?'

'Some bet about pulling Eloise.'

'You're joking me. That crazy set-designer lady?' Sara laughs. 'She's intense. Way intense. She told me she's looking to get married by the end of the year.'

My eyes widen. 'Oh, my goodness. Poor Alec.'

'Hm,' says Sara. 'This should be fun. OK, I'll see you later! And – thanks, Sophie!'

I wave and as I'm shutting the door I see Angie outside in the corridor. I wave to her too. She raises her hand. She doesn't smile. She never does.

I jump in the shower and get dressed quickly. I sip some tea, skimming the script just one more time. I feel suddenly nervous as I reread what we're filming today; Alec and I have a couple of big scenes. I'm usually well prepared, but this movie is testing me. I want to say Tammy's lines like they make sense. I want to be good, to make a film you'll want to watch in fifty years' time. I *have* to be good.

When I get downstairs it's still only 6.30, so hardly anyone's about, though to be honest the other patrons at the Oak Hotel and Carvery never recognise me anyway. I pretend to be relieved about this but am secretly annoyed. Wouldn't you be? They always recognise Alec. He's costume drama central. When I made *Jack and Jenny*, in a tiny town 5 miles from the middle of nowhere in Wyoming, I couldn't leave the hotel without ten people waiting outside to get my autograph, and at the diner we all ate in most nights people would smile and come over, shake my hand – Americans are much politer than Brits. 'It's a real honour to have you here in Dead Dog Ridge,' they'd say. 'Old Tom here, he wants to shake you by the hand.' And some grizzled old war veteran would stump into view and stiffly have his picture taken with you and then stump off into the night with a hearty farewell. Here: blank, annoyed incomprehension, and some subtle social signals I can't interpret. I've been away too long.

'Morning, Sophie. I hear Alec's buying tonight,' Bill

Claremont, the cinematographer, calls from the alcove where he's working his way through a hearty breakfast. Bill is a living legend, nominated for an Academy Award, actually worked with David Lean and Alfred Hitchcock. I don't know how we got him for this film, to be honest, but people say Tony Lees-Miller, the famous producer of this whole thing, whom I've yet to meet, pulled him out of his bag of tricks. They've been doing it for years, this band of mild-looking British guys, and they have Ealing, Rank and Gainsborough in their blood. Bill can drink Alec under the table, which is pretty easy, but he can drink me under the table too, which is not bad going – as I told him after a night at the bar when I woke up the next morning fully clothed hanging off a corner of the bed and immediately fell off it, causing Angie to rush in from the adjoining room with a chair above her head ready to knock out any assailant, like we're in an old Ealing comedy. In fact the whole thing, now I come to think of it, is a little like an Ealing comedy.

'Morning, Bill,' I say. 'You off now?'

'Just finishing my breakfast. I don't need the make-up you do. I'm all natural.' He slaps his jaw and smiles. 'Big day today. You ready?'

I nod, chewing the inside of my mouth. 'Sure!'

The car's outside. Jimmy, the driver, is having a cigarette, sheltering under the porch.

'Morning, Soph,' he says, stamping the cigarette on the ground. 'You ready?' He nods at Angie, who climbs in the car

'Sure,' I say again. He comes round and opens the door for me.

'Ready to make some more magic today?' he says as we drive away, down the long verdant drive, out towards the cottage where Shakespeare's wife grew up, through the yellow fields and green hedgerows. A swift darts out in front of us, under and up into the trees, and I sink back into the leather seats and smile, because he says this every day, and it's sweet.

'Ready as I'll ever be, Jimmy.'

CHAPTER EIGHTEEN

ACTUALLY, IT TURNS out it's a bad day on set today. You have them, sometimes – nothing goes right. When the budget's $80 million you can afford a few upsets. But if you're shooting on a shoestring and you've only paid the crew for eight weeks, a bad day is a disaster. They're only short scenes, right at the end of the movie, but they are crucial. I am Annie, back working in Anne Hathaway's cottage after the whole knock-on-head-wake-up-in-dream-world scenario, wondering if it was all in my imagination. I see a guy walking through the gardens with his mother, out for a nice day trip. He comes into the house, smiles at her and tells her he's the new manager, and you realise it's Shakespeare, in the modern day, and the elderly lady who's his mother is the same actress who's played Anne Hathaway in the later scenes. After the first couple of takes I'm sure it's not as good as it could have been. I'm not bringing the warmth to Annie that I want and I've fluffed my lines, nerves I think. And now filming has totally stopped.

Halfway through the morning we get the message that Cara is definitely out of the picture. She'll be in hospital for at least another week and then recovering, and the insurance company is saying we have to find someone else. There's an idiot producer from LA, Carl, who's just arrived and who knows nothing; he's yelling into his phone and slicking his hair back. T.T.'s jumping up and down, waving his arms and screaming. He can't cope in a crisis. 'Where's Tony?' he keeps screaming. 'Where's fucking Tony? What are we gonna do? I can't take this any more! I can't!' Carl stares at him and looks even more panicked, and the assistant director, Paula, keeps wiping her brow in stress, and pushing her baseball cap so far back on her head it slides to the ground, so she picks it up and then hits her head on a piece of equipment. It's turning into a farce.

I sit there, watching this all unfold. I know what I'd do if they asked me for my advice. Find Eve Noel. Re-jig the schedule so we shoot the scenes without Cara that don't mention her in any way so we can reshape the script if we have to go ahead using Cara's already-filmed stuff and a swift rewrite if we can't get anyone. Luckily her scenes are mostly ones that lift right out of the action. She's almost like the narrator of the story. I know that script backwards, I could do it in my sleep. But it's not my position to jump in, some star giving her opinion is the last thing you want here. And I wrote to Eve already anyway, and got the briefest brush-off from her UK agent, Melanie something. *'Miss Noel is not contactable'* was the line I loved best. What does that even mean? I emailed back asking for more information, but she never replied, not to me or Tina, or to Sara either.

When I can't hack the cold any longer, I stand up and stretch, then climb the steps to the long, low thatched house – it's not a bloody cottage, that Anne Hathaway must have been minted – and slip inside.

'Do you know where these beams came from?' comes a voice from the next room, an old lady's voice.

'No,' comes the reply, that voice that always used to send a shiver up my spine all those years ago. 'Ships? Do tell me. They're beautiful.'

'The Forest of Arden,' says the old lady. I can see her now, a stern figure just inside the door, staring beadily up at someone. 'And do you want to know something very interesting about the Forest of Arden?'

'Oh, absolutely I do,' says the silken voice, and she makes a gruff, pleased sort of grunt.

I gently open the door. 'Hello, Alec,' I say.

Alec Mitford eases himself away from the old window-seat. He's in modern dress for this scene: chinos, a navy polo shirt, a casual jacket. His black hair is close-cropped; usually it flops a bit. His eyes are dark blue too, and his mouth pouts, just a little, when it's in repose. The summer we were sleeping together, his beautiful Notting Hill flat was on the corner of two main roads and the traffic would wake me up. I'd lie there, one arm propped up on its elbow, and watch him sleep, then snuggle against him, trying to get him to have sex again, and make him think it was his idea. He wasn't ever as keen as I was, especially on the sex part. Thankfully I realised, before I was told, that it wasn't going to last.

'Ah, Soph,' he says. 'Escaping the sturm und drang outside, are you? Great minds.' He kisses me on the cheek. 'Margaret, this is Sophie Leigh. She's the star of the film. Soph, Margaret helps out at the house.'

'Nice to meet you.' Margaret glances at me, then goes back to staring up at Alec.

People like Margaret are like the patrons of the Oak. They have no idea who I am. Unless Margaret's seen *Wedding of the Year*, which I doubt. 'Don't let me disturb you,' I say.

'Just telling Alec about the Forest of Arden,' Margaret says.

'Yes, how interesting. Where is it now, what's left of it?' Alec says.

'All gone,' Margaret tells him, slapping her thighs in pleasure at being able to impart this information. 'None of it left, not a single tree.'

'Why?' Alec says. 'What happened to it?'

'Humans,' Margaret tells him grimly. 'Most beautiful forest in all of England for thousands of years. Beech, rosewood, oak. Taller and thicker they are, the better, see? Then we start cutting it down, for houses like this.' She pats one of the ancient beams. 'And for the navy. The Hundred Years War, the Armada. You know, most of the ships built to fight the

Armada came from the Forest of Arden. The *Mary Rose*, she was too. By the eighteenth century – *phut*. All bloody gone.'

It's moments like this I start to feel very far from home. Alec is shaking his head. 'That's awful. Just awful,' he murmurs. 'And now they want to privatise our woodlands. What next.'

Margaret rolls her eyes at him. 'Well, I know. Sometimes I think, you know, running this place here, it's the last piece of really old England we've got left?'

Alec puts a fist to his solar plexus, and intones quietly, ' "This blessed plot, this earth, this realm, *this England*." '

'Aah,' Margaret says, gruffly thrilled. 'Marvellous stuff.'

I hide a smile and turn away, looking out of the window at the rain, my mind wandering. Alec will always be in work. He's like one of those actors in *Upstairs, Downstairs* or *The Jewel in the Crown*; there will always be an Alan Ayckbourn or a Noël Coward revival in Bath or Richmond that'll be glad to have him. His female co-stars, however, won't be so lucky. When I try to think about what parts I'll have in five, ten years' time, I can't see it at all. I've got no successful template, unless you count Jennifer Aniston, and I'm not sure I want to be like that, to be honest. All that yoga must be exhausting and the tan – her skin'll be worse than Deena's when she's older.

I wonder how Deena is, with a start. I keep thinking about her, and our last meeting, her face as she held the car keys in her hand, ready to drive off and have sex in costume with some disgusting guy in a motel. Does she feel like this, when she comes back to England? Not fitting in. Does Mum know how she's making a living, these days? I smile though it's not funny. Of course Mum doesn't know.

It occurs to me then that Deena might want to stay in the house. That place is like Fort Knox now plus I don't fancy anyone else's chances against my godmother. I take out my BlackBerry and email Sara:

Hi. Can you find Deena Grayson please and ask her if she wants to stay at my house while I'm in the UK?

Tell her I'd really like her to if she wants. Check with the cops and the security guys that's ok.

Then, as an afterthought:

In fact, find out what the situation is overall with the cops. Ask them not Artie. Have they found who it is yet?

I know the answer to that one. But it doesn't hurt to ask. And then, because I tell myself I want to give her something to do:

Can you also contact Patrick Drew's office and send him over a Celine Dion Live in Las Vegas DVD and a note from me: Hope to take that trip to Vegas one day. If not to Big Sur. Thanks again for understanding about the movie. Sophie

It's just my way of apologising again, I tell myself. My heart thumps as I do it. I reason with myself that I'm only trying to make sure he doesn't bad-mouth me all round town, though I've taken no similar action with George. Rather, I hope to slide out of George's life as easily as I came into it. Anyway, Sara told me yesterday the project was back on. They found some actress from *90210* to take my part. Good luck to all of them. Patrick can take her to Big Sur for Thanksgiving.

I'm behaving like a Taylor Swift song. I shake my head and put the phone away. Alec is nodding sympathetically at Margaret. 'Listen, Margaret, will you excuse us? I need to talk to Sophie.' He pulls me by the elbow. 'OK if we go upstairs?'

'Of course.' Margaret clenches her jaw and looks straight at him, then nods. 'Jolly good to talk to you,' she says. 'Think you're – damn good news. Anything I can do, let me know. Hm?'

'How kind you are.' Alec smiles graciously and almost bows at Margaret, while I try not to be sick. He leads me up the oak stairs, varnished into blackness over the centuries, and into a large room, the roof sloping up on both sides. 'Is this Anne Hathaway's room?' I ask. 'Did Shakespeare . . . sleep here?'

'Fuck knows,' says Alec, looking around cautiously. 'Thank God, we're alone.' He stares at me. 'You all right? You look tired.'

'Oh, I was rubbish this morning,' I say.

'It's nerves. You're doing damn well, especially considering you were parachuted in at the last minute.'

'But I want to be brilliant,' I say. 'And it's really hard.'

'Brilliant?' He laughs. 'Don't we all. Look, you know better than me how to make this script work. You're the one who pummelled Tammy into revealing she'd even done the rewrites. And you're the queen of being likeable. You can do this standing on your head.'

'I don't think I can.' I try to make it sound like this is a casual conversation, not my darkest fears given an airing. 'I'm not feeling it. Every line I say comes out dull and . . . *bleurgh*. I don't believe the situation. I don't believe in me. It's easy in LA. Everyone . . .'

Everyone tells you you're great even if it's a lie. And here I don't know what I'm doing.

Alec sighs. 'God, Sophie, what do you want me to do, read you out some Eckhart fucking Tolle? Listen. Just because you're used to being surrounded by people telling you how *amazing* you are every time you fart on set doesn't mean your acting's any better. Trust me. I know what they're like. Those guys like to make you think they're essential so they keep themselves in a job. And it's crap.'

'Maybe you're right.'

'Maybe?' He rubs his forehead. 'They've made you think these things are important and they're not. You're a great, natural comedian. And a bloody good actress. Grow up and get over yourself.'

I blink at him. 'Wow. Thanks for going easy on me.'

'You know what I mean. I yell because I care, sugar tits. Take responsibility for your own happiness and all that. I got rid of everyone and moved back to the UK last year and it's been so much better ever since.'

'I hate the way people assume the UK is morally right and LA is automatically some cauldron of evilosity,' I say crossly. 'Like Mordor.'

'Well, it is.'

'It's not. Just a lot of people there are.'

'So don't let them tell you how to have your hair, or what you're doing next, or all of that. And definitely don't let them put you in pink dresses with sleeves.' He raises a wicked eyebrow. 'Apart from the pit stains, darling, pink is so not your colour.'

'You bitch.' I jab him in the arm, laughing, because it's true, though no one says that to me any more. 'I'll flounce off set and then you really will be screwed.'

'You wouldn't dare and you know it.' He kisses me on the head, then something catches his eye and his expression changes. 'Oh, fuck. Listen, Soph. Can you do me a favour? Look out the window.' I peer out of the old wooden casement. He stands behind me.

'Yes,' I say. 'What do you want?'

'Er – um. Is Eloise out there?'

I can see a group of people from the crew standing by the willow cabin, in massive kagoules and padded jackets. They're pissed off, if their crossed arms and tight expressions are anything to go by. At the edge of the group are two women.

'I think I see her,' I say. 'She's got some large garden shears in her hand. The thin, beautiful one with straggly split-endy hair?'

'Yes.' Alec shudders, and moves a little closer, so he's just slightly leaning against me. 'She's a nutter, Soph. What am I going to do?'

I try not to laugh. 'Alec, you make your bed, you know, darling.'

As I turn around he grabs my arm. 'She was waiting outside my door this morning. She writes me notes. I gave her my mobile—' He smacks his forehead. 'Why the fuck did I do it? She rings me, texts me, all the freaking time.'

'Hold on, when did you – er, actually sleep with her?'

'About a week ago.'

'And then you shagged Helen.' Helen is the runner, a bright, bouncy twenty-year-old with enormous tits. 'And now Eloise has gone mad. She's French, Alec, they don't like that sort of thing. She's not some English slapper you can bonk and leave.'

'You weren't a slapper, don't do yourself down,' he says.

'Har-di-har-di-har,' I say. 'Well, she's the one who's about to get us kicked out. All. Because. Of. You.' I jab him on the chest.

'Oh, God. Why?' Alec's thin face grows pale.

'She went mad with some shears after lunch and over-trimmed the willow cabin. It's ruined.'

Alec looks pale. 'Oh, shit. Oh, shit.' He stops. 'What's a willow cabin, when it's at home?'

'Make me a willow cabin at your gate,' I say. *'And call upon my soul within the house.* Come on, Alec! If I know that, you must do. You were the one quoting Shakespeare downstairs to that old biddy.'

'Margaret. Don't be rude. Anyway, I only knew it because it used to be a Tetley advert. Where's the willow cabin from?'

'Twelfth Night,' I say, pleased with myself. 'Olivia. I listened at school, you see.'

'You were a no-mates at school,' Alec says acidly. 'Shit. What am I going to do?' He clears his throat and then looks mournful. 'You know, I don't want to, but I think I'd better skive off the bar tonight, just to be safe.'

I laugh in outrage. 'If this is some crap ruse to get out of buying the drinks, don't even try it.'

He turns out the pockets of his trousers. 'Look. I've got no money.'

Alec is notoriously tight. Though it's very generous of him to introduce me to Margaret as the star of the film, he must be earning more than anyone else on this picture. He's the one that'll pack them in in the leafy suburbs, not me. I know that. I may have secured the vital piece of US funding, but everyone here knows I'm the risk on a project like this that's so much about word of mouth and repeat visits. We're all on small fees and big profit shares, but I know for a fact Alec got $15 million for his last movie. Yet he is so super stingy he actually claimed a packet of tissues he bought from a petrol station back from the film company last week. It cost 65p.

'You're buying the drinks,' I say firmly. 'You made the bet with Bill. I saw it. About ten people were witnesses. If you slept with Eloise, you pay for drinks one evening.'

'Oh, I loathe you,' he says grumpily.

'Don't be rude, Alec. Come on. Splash the cash around. We all have. It's your fault, anyway. You shouldn't be such a slapper.'

Alec turns back, an evil grin on his face. 'How's it going with Slick Rick, anyway?' Rick is the cute cameraman. 'Have you pulled him yet?'

I shake my head. Rick reminds me too much of Patrick, I've realised.

'Come on, Soph. Lure him to your Sophie Security Bunker, where that silent Germanic-looking prison warder watches over the two of you all night to make sure he's not a psycho killer.'

'Shut up. It's not funny.' I look out of the window, trying not to look flustered. 'Who'd have thought filming this would be a rerun of my holidays on the Isle of Wight,' I say, changing the subject. 'Peering out the window every two minutes, saying, "Ooh, I'm sure it's getting brighter."'

Alec touches my arm. 'Hey, sorry, Soph. Don't mean to joke about it. Well, I did, but it's not funny. Sorry.' His voice is low; I can feel his breath, tickling my ear.

'It's fine,' I say. 'I'm being stupid. Just – don't like thinking about it.' I turn back so I'm facing him, sitting on the edge of the window ledge. 'You haven't told anyone, have you?'

He moves closer, so he's between my legs, and we're millimetres apart. 'Of course I haven't, darling,' he says. He kisses my cheek, holding my chin in his hand. 'I really am sorry. It must be awful.'

I can smell him, he's so close. There's something so comforting about him, so familiar. He reminds me of home, if I knew what home was. But he's always, always picking out the next face in the crowd to shag. Like it's a game, and love doesn't come into it. I just want a hug, someone to hug me. I wonder if Sara would hug me, if I asked her, as part of the job? How weird would that sound? Well, *very* weird. Knowing her though, she'd probably do it to be helpful, and the thought makes me smile.

I look up at him. 'I'm fine, Alec.' There's a scream from the garden, and we turn round to see an elegant figure breaking away from a knot of people and striding towards one of the Winnebagos, clutching some shears. Alec shrinks away from the window. I jump off.

'I'm going down,' I say gleefully. 'You'd better stay here. See you in the bar. Mine's a glass of Cristal, by the way. Start saving.'

CHAPTER NINETEEN

THERE'S NO MORE filming today. An air of unease hangs over the set, and back at the hotel. Sara and I eat dinner in the restaurant, just the two of us, with Angie and Gavin at the next table. They never acknowledge us; at one point the waiter drops a pepper mill on the floor and Angie's eyes swivel round, her hand shoots out almost simultaneously and she snatches it up before it's even reached the ground, then hands it back to him, expressionless, and goes back to carb-loading in silence. I watch her, open-mouthed. I have so many questions I want to ask her and Gavin. Where did you train? Have you saved someone's life? Can you do the running up buildings and flying like in *Crouching Tiger, Hidden Dragon*? Could you really save me, if someone tried to kill me? But she won't tell you anything about herself. Not even where she's from. It really is like getting Alec to buy a round of drinks.

It's still raining and the restaurant is pretty empty. The crisis meeting in the residents' lounge along the corridor has been taking place for the past hour. Tony Lees-Miller, the famous producer everyone keeps talking about whom I haven't met, has even come down for it. It does make me smile sometimes, the contrast between here and Hollywood: this is one of those times. A prep meeting for a film would be a four-day affair in a Ritz-Carlton in downtown LA with PowerPoint presentations, scripts, and each department head from the studio, endless men called Ryan or Jerry and no decisions taken without recourse to studios in Culver City or suites in Beverly Hills.

Well, there was no prep meeting for this film, and the crisis meeting to save it is taking place in a room with an orange-and-brown five-piece suite and a coffee table with old copies of *Reader's Digest* fanned out across it, metallic-flavoured tea and rattling window casements, but it is no less important. Top of the agenda must be Cara's replacement, who they can afford, and whether they're properly insured to replace her with someone people have heard of. Second: money. Third: the willow cabin that Eloise desecrated has now led to the Anne Hathaway house people officially saying they don't want us there any more and they don't care if we sue them. Presumably they know that if we sued them the film would collapse.

'How was your day?' I ask Sara, picking at my salmon and trying not to stare up every time someone appears in the doorway. 'Did you do anything fun, or did the rain get in the way?'

Sara looks up and smiles. 'Oh, yes, thank you! I had such a great time. I got in the car, and I drove to Bristol. It was beautiful!'

'Wow,' I say. 'Didn't you want to go to Stratford?'

She looks momentarily confused. 'Oh. Well, I wanted to – I didn't want to run into you guys. Thought it'd be interesting to visit someplace totally different.'

'Did you like it?'

'It was so great but it was raining a lot so I didn't hang out there too long. But I saw the big tower, and the shops, and the docks, and everything. Yeah, my grandpa always said we came over on a ship from Bristol like, hundreds of years ago.'

'I didn't know that, how cool,' I say. 'You should send him a postcard.'

'He's dead.'

'Oh. I'm sorry. I know you were really close to him,' I say, embarrassed.

'That's my other grandpa,' Sara says. She smiles. 'It's OK though, thanks for even remembering!'

There's an awkward pause. Sara chews furiously, swallows a tiny morsel of salmon, then looks up with relief. 'I didn't tell you a bunch of stuff, either. I heard back from Deena about house-sitting. She said thanks for the offer and she'll move in tomorrow. She said she appreciates it.'

'Great,' I say. That's fulsome, coming from Deena.

'She's funny,' Sara says, laughing a little. 'A character.'

'You can say that again,' I say grimly. 'She's a—'

I stop myself. What's really that odd about Deena, after all? If she were a chain-smoking tanned leather-wearing middle-aged man with a penchant for video sex, people'd say she was a good guy, one of the lads. She'd be George, in fact. What's she done wrong, other than grow old? I start to get indignant, then I remember the missing Chanel earrings and the silver fountain pen I never found again and I don't feel quite so indignant, then I fall silent again, chewing my nails.

'So,' Sara begins brightly. 'They cast a bunch of people in *Starlight*.' I look blank. 'You know, the script that went for millions of bucks? I'm getting it for you. The whole town is talking about the writer apparently. I spoke to someone at WAM – the word is it'll never work because it's so big already?' As she carries on talking I can feel myself starting to sweat. I don't care about this stuff like I should, and it's probably a big mistake to have taken myself out of LA, out of the game. Like when I go back they'll say, *'Sophie Leigh, huh? Used to be hot, then she went off to England to do that crazy movie about Shakespeare going back in time and she put on ten pounds and came back ugly, and she's what? Thirty now? She's totally like box office poison. Alec Mitford? Oh, sure. Didn't he just win an Oscar for something, that amazing Shakespeare film?'*

Sara's still talking, and I try to look interested.

'. . . stopped at a lovely pub! In this village called Shamley, down towards like somewhere called Swindon?'

She pronounces it Swin Don. I'm about to put a forkful of

spinach in my mouth but when I hear her I drop the fork. 'Shamley? You didn't,' I say. 'But that's where I grew up.'

'No,' she says. 'No way. You? Grew up there?'

'Yeah. I'm sure I mentioned it? It's in my—'

I stop. *It's in my biog* is a dickish thing to say. Why would she remember?

She looks upset. 'Sorry, Sophie – would you rather I hadn't gone there? I didn't . . .'

I pour myself the rest of the wine. 'God, no. Just weird, knowing you were there. I haven't been back for – well, ages.' I glug the wine.

'Really?'

'They named the new gym after me,' I said. 'I went back then. It was kind of strange. I was like, twenty-seven, and . . .' I trail off.

'You didn't know what you were doing there and all your old teachers stared at you like they wanted to kill you?' she asks, then mimics a grouchy old guy: ' "Her? That girl? We're naming the new gymnasium after that girl?" '

She's so spot on, the way she suddenly becomes this old British man, the accent, shoulders back, jaw protruding, eyebrows wrinkled, that I laugh. 'Exactly! That's totally it.'

Sara shrugs and smiles. 'So what about your parents?' She spears some broccoli. 'Don't you go see them?'

'They usually visit me in LA.' I shift in my seat. 'My mum came for a month last year. Or we meet when I'm in London or somewhere else in Europe – they stay with me.' I sound like I'm making it up. 'They'd rather come and see me some-where nice, I suppose. Shamley's not all that nice.'

'It didn't seem so bad.' Sara puts her arms on the table. 'Where did you live then?'

'About five minutes' walk from the school. Near the garage before you get back onto the main road,' I tell her. 'Mum and Dad are still there.' And I still haven't been to see them.

'OK. I ate at a pub around the corner from there? Something crazy like the Hand and Racquet, the Hand and Bracket?'

'I remember the Hand and Racquet,' I laugh. 'It's on the

same road as my parents'. Wow, Sara, that's so random. What was it like?'

'It was great, very atmospheric,' Sara says politely, though that can't be true. The Hand and Racquet used to be totally rank. You'd get blokes pissing up the wall behind before they went home.

I push my food aside. 'You grew up in LA, didn't you? Did you ever live anywhere else?'

She shakes her head. 'No, ma'am. Lived there all my life. Pacific Palisades.'

'Gosh, I didn't realise that,' I say. 'This must be a bit of a comedown from the Palisades.'

Sara shakes her head. 'No way. It's all so fake. That's why I wanted to be an actress.' She catches herself and gives a twisted half-smile. 'That didn't work out either. This job is great, Sophie, honestly. I get to see the world. It won't seem like much to you but if you've been in LA most of your freaking life –' she stops, and her face is flushed – 'you think nothing else matters, nothing but fame and all that.'

'Do you miss it? Acting, I mean?'

She touches a little mole on her forearm with one slim finger, not looking at me. 'Sure. Sometimes I miss it a lot. It was my life. I grew up watching movies, I'd beg my mom and dad to take me to New York every year in the school holidays, and I'd just go from play to play, so happy?' She rolls a coil of silky hair around one finger. 'Daddy's surgery was next to our house. I'd see these totally famous actresses going into his office, so beautiful already and they didn't know how lucky they were and they'd come out of hospital a month later looking like stuffed dolls. You know? I mean, I was proud of my dad, he did some great work with people, burn victims, and this woman who had her face blown off by some dick boyfriend. He stitched her back together again, made her look good as new, better even. But it's the stupid movie people who made him a millionaire. When I grew up and I realised I wasn't beautiful enough . . . it hurt.' She takes one long, ragged breath in.

'You're a really talented actress,' I say. 'It's true. I don't know if that's helpful or not, but you are. And you're beautiful too.'

She opens her mouth to say something, then shuts it.

'Go on,' I prompt her, intrigued.

'Thank you. But – I mean, I studied at UCLA for four years. I auditioned for every fucking part going. I knew I was better than so many people, and one day Daddy stops me on my way out and asks me if I don't think a nose job wouldn't help just a little with my career.'

'No way.'

Sara's blue eyes are fixed on me. I think again, fleetingly, how alike we are.

'Yeah,' she says. 'Fucked-up, isn't it?'

'He probably thought he was helping.' I search her face, still a little worried. 'Listen, Sara—'

There's a tap on my shoulder and I yelp. Angie and Gavin immediately stand up, facing me.

'My goodness, I'm sorry,' says someone politely. I turn round to see T.T., Paula the assistant director and Carl, one of the executive producers, and with them a man who looks like an advert for an English gent.

'Sophie,' says T.T., pulling at his hair with both hands. 'Meet Tony. The British guy, the producer. He's gonna sort it all out. He has to. Because I'm telling you I cannot do this shit any longer. I can't do it! It's doing my fucking head in! The weather! These people, the money, this stupid hotel . . .' He shrugs, and rolls his eyes, and I think he might start crying.

'Oh, my goodness,' says Sara, concerned. I ignore him. T.T. is like this every day.

Carl, who is totally useless, and only on the picture as a producer because I think he is the boyfriend of the VP's daughter, says, 'Dame Judi Dench. I keep telling the guy, let's get Dame Judi Dench!'

'Good evening, Sophie.' Tony Lees-Miller leans forward, ignoring the others, and shakes my hand. 'It's a pleasure to meet you. I'm a great fan of yours, you know.'

I want to laugh. 'Really?'

He nods. 'Of course. *The Bride and Groom* is one of my favourite films. *A Cake-Shaped Mistake*, too. The bit with the waterskis, it makes me absolutely roar with laughter, every time.'

Is he joking? I assume he must be.

Carl jabs him in the arm. 'You seen *The Girlfriend*? Opening weekend of twenty-three million dollars, this girl. She's gold! We got Sophie Leigh!' He shouts this around the room, and shame prickles across my skin.

Tony fiddles with his watch. 'Yes. I'm afraid I didn't much care for *The Girlfriend*, if you'll forgive me. Not your best work.'

There's a short silence. Carl looks at Tony like he's just grown three heads. He puffs out his chest. 'Listen, mister—'

'Why not?' I say.

Tony has his hands in his pockets. He says, semi-earnestly, 'I didn't like the lead chap. Rob something? And I don't like it when they make you act so terribly daffy.' He takes out a handkerchief and wipes his face, scrubbing the linen roughly across his skin like he's a little boy being cleaned up by a nanny. 'I have a theory about you, you see. You're chronically underused. And you could be one of the best comedic actresses since Diane Keaton. Plus you've got soul. And of course this is obvious and everyone knows it, but you really are very beautiful.'

He says it complacently, as if I'll be so sure of this. And I, who am so used to hearing compliments, I who know how to accept them gracefully, with a smile and a word of thanks, I blush, and bite my finger, to stop myself smiling with pleasure, because for once I desperately want to believe he's telling me the truth. 'Well, that's really kind of you.' I touch his arm, almost shyly. 'How was the meeting? Have you found a solution to the Cara problem yet?'

'No, alas,' Tony says. 'But Paula, T.T. and I have just re-jigged the shooting schedule.'

'I thought we didn't have the money to shoot the later scenes.'

He waves this away as if it's a minor problem. 'I encouraged the financiers to release it to us.'

'Really?' I'm impressed.

'I'm a very persuasive person,' Tony says, smiling. 'We'll just shoot around Cara's scenes for as long as possible. I've spoken to Bill Claremont about it – he thinks he can sort something out.'

'Dame Judi Dench,' Carl hisses, at his elbow.

'What an excellent idea. Alas, I suspect it is more than likely Judi is not free at such short notice, but I will certainly check,' Tony says, unruffled. 'I think we need something, or someone, more unexpected than that.'

Carl looks angry and runs his hands through his slicked, thick hair. I ignore him – he has no idea what he's talking about. I turn to Tony, trying not to smile.

'I'm sure you know this but maybe we should be shooting all the scenes inside Anne Hathaway's house first. Cara's not in any of them, and—'

'I'm afraid,' he interrupts me politely, 'the Anne Hathaway house people are saying they don't want us back there. This is another problem for which, as yet, I have no solution.'

'I think we can win them round again, if we tread carefully, you know,' I say. 'The lady who runs the inside of the house, not the garden, is a big, big fan of Alec's. She specifically said today to ask her if he needed anything. If we can use her to get them on our side and agree to let us finish the filming there we'll have all that in the can by the end of the week.' I think back to Margaret's face of grim adoration as she watched Alec. 'Yes, I'm sure she will. And then shoot around Cara's character so that if we absolutely can't find anyone else Tammy can rewrite it, so we use what we've got of Cara as the older Anne but cut her character right back. It'll be a blow, because she's kind of the heart of the film, but I don't see another option. If we do it cleverly it should only mean one, two new scenes.'

Tony's nodding. 'Thank you, Miss Leigh,' he says. He opens both his hands, then shuts them. And he gives me a funny look. 'I was right about you.'

'Were you?' I grin at him. 'Let me know if there's anything else I can do.'

'I will,' he says. 'Very good to meet you.' He holds my hand for a second, and then his phone rings and he looks at it. 'I have to take this, I'm afraid.' He moves out, Carl and T.T. following in his wake.

I watch him go, mulling over what he's said. *Something, or someone, more unexpected than that.* Beside me, Sara checks her watch and stands up again. 'It's nearly lunchtime in LA. I have to speak to Tommy,' she says. 'Something about the publicity for the DVD of *Blue and Gold Dress*.'

'OK, great. By the way,' I say suddenly. 'You never did get any news from Eve Noel, did you? Her agent never replied to you, right?'

Sara gets that rabbit-in-the-headlights look she so often has when I ask her something, like she's terrified she won't know the answer. She shakes her head. 'Um, no. Why?'

'Nothing,' I say. I'm about to add something, but I stop. 'Listen, thanks for everything today.'

'Really?'

'Of course! I'm so glad you're here.'

'I'm glad too,' she says. 'I'm really enjoying this experience with you. I'm so happy Tina had to take the time off.' Her eyes widen. 'That sounds terrible. Please, I don't mean it like that.'

I sometimes wonder if Sara has a touch of Asperger's. Or something like that. She is so efficient and organised, so up all the time, almost robotically so, that I find her kind of scary and then she'll say something completely off the wall and I realise she is bonkers. She picks up her iPad, muttering something to herself. I smile at her.

'Hey, no problem. Are you coming for a drink?'

She frowns. 'No. I'd better not. I – I'm going to get some sleep. Unless you need me?'

'No. See you tomorrow.' I watch her go and then head through to the bar, Angie and Gavin following behind.

The huge old hearth has a fire crackling away. I sit on the

oak settle and tuck my feet under me, it's really quite cold. This summer is a total washout. I gaze at the flames leaping in front of my eyes. I feel strange today. Tired, uneasy.

A line from *A Girl Named Rose* pops into my head. Oh, it's such a sad film. Rose is saying goodbye to her boyfriend Peter from the small town; he's marrying someone else because she's gone to the big city and he thinks she's dumped him. It's Conrad Joyce, whom I love, playing Peter and he's on his way to the church when he sees her in the window of her parents' house and realises she's come back, and it's too late, he has to marry drippy Samantha.

'You'll be fine, Rose. You're always fine. Just think of me occasionally, will ya?'

And he leaves and walks off, and Rose watches him go and she says, *'My thoughts are yours already, Peter darling. You know that. I'll never love anyone else. Never.'* And then it says 'THE END' and the music starts.

Oh, man. It makes me cry every time. Eve Noel, when she says it, she just looks so totally, totally heartbroken. She's staring into the distance, not at him, and her eyes have tears in them, but she never actually cries. It feels so real. She should have won the Oscar that year, every moment she's on-screen you can't see anyone else. She is mesmerising. She glows with something – love, happiness, urgency, I don't know what it is. She had her first breakdown a year or so after it came out. I know it's because of that film. I don't know why, I just know it is. It scares me too, because I'm afraid of what would happen if you poured yourself into a part like that. It seems to consume her: she's acting, but it's more than acting. It's her life.

Someone taps my arm, and I uncurl, shaking myself out of my reverie.

'You look like a heroine in a film, Sophie,' Bill Claremont says, sitting down, a pint in his hand. 'Mind if we join you?'

'Course not,' I say, moving over. The camera crew – all identical-looking men with close–cropped hair, paunches hidden by heavy flak jackets, jeans and trainers, and variable only by age – sit down. They are always together, and apart from Bill, their leader, and Rick, the one I fancy, I haven't quite got a grip on all their names. I know only that one of them is called Wally. So I'll say 'Wally' vaguely from time to time and look round at them all and that seems to cover it.

Someone puts a vodka, lime and soda down on the table for me. That's 'my' drink here at the Oak. We know what everyone's tipple is now. I like being in a gang again.

'Ta,' I say.

'Got sick of waiting for Alec to appear and buy the drinks, eh? Don't worry, we're here.' Bill smiles, but I don't smile back. 'Hey,' he says. 'Penny for your thoughts?'

'Oh . . . nothing. Just thinking.' I look round. 'Hi, guys . . . Wally. Er . . . Hi, Rick.'

Rick raises a hand in greeting. I stare at him hopefully. But he doesn't look like Patrick, I realise. He's good-looking, in fact his face is more chiselled than Patrick's. But there's something missing. I close my eyes to see his face again, dark eyes melting as he asks me if I'm OK and I sigh, annoyed with myself. *This Patrick thing is ridiculous. You don't even know him. Of course he's gorgeous, he's a film star. Of course you fancy him. He's a player, right? Remember the photos of the girls, the TMZ footage of him drunk, the crappy movies, the idiotic behaviour . . . ? just get over it, Sophie, get him out of your head.*

Bill takes a sip of his pint. 'What are they going to do about Cara, have you heard?'

'No idea,' I say. 'I did think maybe—' Then I shrug. 'Forget it. I'm sure Tony'll know what to do.'

'Good guy, Tony,' says Bill. 'Been around. Knows his onions. We worked together on David Lean's last film. Clever old boy.'

'You worked on *A Passage to India*?' I ask.

Laconic Bill moves his pint across the table. 'Ah. Yes. You're good, Sophie. You know your stuff, don't you.'

'I like films. Maybe it's being back here. I'm remembering a lot of things I'd forgotten.'

But as I sit in this dark, wooden English corner, the thick greenery of the summer lashing against the old lead windows, I wonder, again, for the fiftieth time, where Eve is. How great it would be if she joined the film, if I could just somehow find her. If only she'd let us know she is all right. Because now I'm back, only miles away from her old home and my home, I get the strangest feeling she's nearby. That she wants to be found.

I will lift up mine eyes unto the hills

YOU SEE, AT first I thought Don was coming. I was stupid, I suppose. I should have learned by then that nothing is as simple, as good, as nice as that. And I'd stopped being the Eve who had a fire inside her so long ago now that even those few blissful weeks I had with him in Big Sur weren't enough to turn me back to my former self. The eighteen-year-old Eve Sallis who berated the lounging, bequiffed Teddy boys at the bus stop for not giving up their seats to the old gentlemen beside them, who complained that the girls weren't given the same quality of parts as the boys at Central, who demanded that Clarissa do her share of the laundry and the dishes: she was nothing more than a distant memory, like Rose. She had left me, a long time ago.

I was driven back to Los Angeles, the day I left Don and Big Sur behind. We didn't arrive at the long white house on Mulholland Drive until after midnight. Being back at home roused in me no emotion; and I realised then how I had been skating along pretending to feel these things, when the only thing that was real was how I felt for Don. I didn't need anything but him, not the pool, the closet full of clothes, the jewellery.

Gilbert's bedroom door was closed and I stole noiselessly into my room, crawled between the sheets and lay awake, listening to the call of a hoarse, lonely crow high in the hills behind me as the enormity of what I would do the next day sat upon my chest, like a physical weight.

In the morning, I got up early and swam in the pool until my skin was wrinkled and my lips were blue, till there was no trace anywhere on me of Don, every last touch of his washed away. The early sun had not reached the terrace, and it was cold. I floated on my back, watching the hydrangea leaves the gardener hadn't cleared from the pool. They lay on the tension of the water, moving slowly against the bright blue, tiny waves lapping gently over my shoulders.

Victoria brought me my breakfast. 'Good morning, Miss Eve,' she said, wiping her hands on the yellow apron she wore every day before lunch. All these things about home that I'd forgotten. 'Welcome back.'

'Thank you.' I climbed out of the pool and wrapped myself in a towelling robe. 'How are you, Victoria? How is your foot?'

'Ah, my foot, you don't want to know,' Victoria said. 'Have some corn bread, dear.' She peered at me. 'You look wonderful, you know? The trip was good?'

'The trip was fantastic,' I said, smiling, then I adjusted myself. I sat down. 'It all went very well, thank you. Where's Mr Travers?'

She shook her head. 'He didn't tell you? He's back tomorrow, maybe Monday. He got held up. Something overran.'

'What?' I said, raising my hand to my head in dismay, and in the process knocking over the coffee cup. 'Oh – oh, God.' I dabbed at the rapidly browning linen. 'Oh, good grief.'

'Stop it. I'll do it later.' Victoria gently brushed my hand out of the way. Again she said, 'He didn't tell you?'

'No, no,' I said. I closed my eyes. One extra day to go. One more day. I couldn't bear it. Don and I had said we wouldn't contact each other until he had been to Las Vegas and asked his wife for a divorce, until I had told Gilbert, and until he was back in LA. I wondered where he was now, if he had arrived in Vegas. He was driving back to LA and then heading straight on to Vegas, he meant to get there by late Friday night. Perhaps he'd cross Gilbert, on his way back from somewhere in Nevada.

I clutched my napkin. Victoria looked at me. She was Gilbert's old maid and I had never really trusted her; I don't know why. I felt she was on his side.

'You miss him, it's too bad,' she said tenderly. 'Ah, dear.' She reached out a hand. 'You poor girl.'

Tears came to my eyes; inside my head, the old voices started, jabbing at me, telling me how rotten I was. 'I do,' I said. 'I do miss him.'

I spent the day at home. I unpacked, I read a little of my book, I watched the television, but I couldn't find anything I liked, anything to latch onto. Mostly, I sat in the sitting room, looking out towards the west of the city, over the hills. A psalm Rose and I had been taught to sing at school kept coming into my head. *I will lift up mine eyes unto the hills, from whence cometh my help*. It was hot, humid, and there was no wind. I felt terribly alone, though Victoria sang all day in the kitchen. June telephoned, wanting to know if we cared to join her for dinner, her voice lightening noticeably when I said Gilbert was away. We spoke fondly for a while about the wonderful time we'd had up in Big Sur, and I wondered if maybe it wouldn't be fun to meet up with her.

'No point in moping around after Gilbert, dearest,' June said. 'Come out with me. I'm trying to get hold of Conrad. We'll wow the town, show them all we're back. It'll be a riot, darling.'

But I said no, though I missed June and especially Conrad, his funny jokes, his witty repartee, his shy, kind heart, already. I simply felt I couldn't leave the house and live a lie when I hadn't told Gilbert, when Don hadn't arrived yet. *But Gilbert won't come until at least Monday, you know he won't. There's no way he'll be here tonight*. No matter how many times I told myself this, I couldn't bear to leave the house, just in case.

I was a prey to my own fears, when in Big Sur everything had seemed so simple, so wonderful. Gilbert, what would he do? Where would he go? What would people say?

It was an interminable day, but I almost welcomed it. I felt as though I should have to live through this, to have the happiness I thought was almost with me.

And then it was Sunday.

'Where are you, Eve?'

It was mid-morning, and I'd been reading in bed. At the sound of his voice, I jumped up immediately.

'Eve?'

'Here, dear. I'm here,' I said, standing up by the bed, as if I'd been doing something illicit.

Gilbert came striding into the room. He looked around, as if he thought someone were here. 'Ah,' he said. He nodded, looking me up and down.

'You seem well,' he said. 'Had a good time, then?'

There was something about his tone I couldn't quite make out. 'Yes,' I said. 'Hard work, but it's a wonderful place.'

Gilbert glanced at himself in the mirror. I saw the twitch of his mouth, the bristle of his neat moustache. 'Hm. Sounds like it.'

'How do you know?' I asked him.

'Just – oh. From what you've said. Your letters.' He turned towards me. 'I've missed you, my dear.'

He came around to my side of the bed, gripped my shoulders, and kissed me, hard. 'Mm,' he said, with a grunt. 'You seem different, somehow. Why are you different?' He slid his hands down my back and clutched my bottom, grasping it painfully, so that he drew me against him. I pulled away.

'I'm not different,' I said. I scratched my cheek and coughed, as a diversion, backing away from him towards the dressing table and pouring myself some water. 'I'm the same. You look wonderful. The desert air obviously suits you, darling.'

It was true, he did. He was leaner, more agile, virile. He seemed younger, somehow. How funny, that our being apart should be so obviously good for us both.

'It's a living. A bloody ridiculous one, but it's good to tell a story people damn well ought to know about,' Gilbert said. 'So, you were back on Friday?'

245

'Yes,' I said. 'I thought you'd be here the whole weekend.'

'Mm, well, I couldn't in the end. Something came up.'

He turned towards the mirror and adjusted his collar; he was in a denim shirt, it didn't need adjusting.

As I watched him, I realised he knew. I didn't know if he knew it was Don, but he knew something was up. There was something about him that I hadn't seen before. A confidence, an ease. He had always been handsome, agile, strong – but before it had been defensive, as if he had something to prove. Now he moved like a warrior, someone who knew how to get his own way.

Suddenly I was scared of him.

'Come here,' he said softly. 'Come here and give me a proper welcome back. You're my wife, aren't you?'

I hate the word 'wife', I always have done. I did before, I think, but as I submitted to him in the bedroom, I couldn't think how to act with him. I'd forgotten what it was like to tolerate someone's hold over you, to lie and be dutiful. Gilbert was different, yes, and I wondered who had been keeping him company in the desert.

His chest was brown, the hairs bleached blond with the sun.

'Come on, my dear.' First he pulled my loose silk pants down. 'You could at least pretend you've missed me.'

'I have—'

He tugged my pyjama top over my head, hurriedly, silencing me, and pulling my hair over my ears. The static sent sparks cracking off my head. He laughed. I felt like a schoolboy, or a village idiot, standing in front of him with my trousers about my ankles, head bowed, naked. He undid his trousers, slid his belt out of its loops, pushed me onto the bed so I sat facing him, my legs dangling off the side; then he hoisted me against him, then pushed me back so he was standing between my thighs, thrusting inside me as I lay looking up at him, not sure how to react, how he wanted it, what would make this moment pass. And I locked myself out of my mind again, for the first time in weeks. It should have saddened me, how easy it was to bring it back, the blank feeling of something else. I looked into his eyes and saw nothing there, so I thought about Rose, about the funny-shaped stones in the old monastery where we used to play, about how one day, I would show them to Don if I ever went back there.

Gilbert was looking down at my breasts, then up at the wall, as he rocked backwards and forwards. He didn't look at my face. I realised he didn't care it was me. He was thinking about something else.

What could I say? And what could I do? He finished, heaving into me with a strangling, grunting end. Then he buttoned his trousers, and patted my knee in what I thought was a show of affection.

'I say. Move it,' he said.

I looked down. My leg was clamped against the bed frame, trapping his belt. 'Oh,' I said. 'Sorry.'

He left then, leaving me lying on the end of the bed. I looked out, up towards the hills, as the midday sun rose higher in the sky.

So then it became rather like a farce, for the next twenty-four hours. I didn't know that it would end, or how, of course. And I came to realise, when I thought about it, that Gilbert had misplayed his hand. He couldn't admit that he knew I was leaving him, he wasn't that kind of man. It would be weak. He wanted me to tell him. But he didn't want me to tell him, either. He couldn't be seen to be the kind of man whose wife left him for someone else, not after this, not when – as he told me in detail that evening – Refford and the studio were praising his performance to the sky, and *Life* had covered his 'big screen comeback' in a special on-set feature, and when only a few weeks into the shoot people were already – raised eyebrow – talking about what would happen come Oscar time.

Yet by pushing me into this corner he made himself complicit in what I was withholding from him. As the day wore on into evening, as we dressed for dinner and sat at opposite ends of the lovely long table shipped over from Heal's in London especially for us, as Victoria served the chicken salad and roast lamb and fruit salad she'd made for Mr Travers's return, it felt more and more as though we were in a film. As though what was reality and what was fantasy were changing places. At times I couldn't remember what was true and what wasn't. Was Don and Big Sur all a dream? Had he lied to me? Had I misunderstood him, when he kissed me at the door and whispered, 'I love you, Rose'?

I knew I hadn't. If it wasn't a dream, where was he?

After dinner, I said I had a headache. 'It must be the heat,' Gilbert said. 'Very humid. A storm's coming, tonight, tomorrow.' I shot a look at him, suspiciously, but he was all solicitude, very caring, calling Victoria to bring lavender water to bathe my temples, as though I were a Victorian heroine. I said I would go to bed and have an early night.

'I might step out to Ciro's,' he said. 'If that's all right with you, my dear. I won't disturb you when I come back. Promise.' He blew me a kiss.

'Thank you, dear,' I said. My head did ache. My body ached, blood seemed to be thudding in my ears, like the sound of waves on the shore. I was desperate for rest but unable to sleep. Yet I went to bed, and locked the door, though I knew he wouldn't come in now. He'd had me to show his strength, not because he wanted me, and I lay looking out towards the window, waiting for a sign. I knew something was coming. I prayed it was Don.

the facts and the names

I DIDN'T HAVE long to wait.

The very next morning I came into the breakfast room to find the *Los Angeles Times* and the *Examiner* waiting there as usual, but there was also a new issue of *Confidential*, the lowest rag of them all, lying on top of them.

And I stared, and then laughed.

Confidential: tells the facts and names the names!
HOLLYWOOD'S DIRTY LITTLE SECRET
TOO MANY STARS SCREENWRITER ARRESTED
FOR PUBLIC DISORDER
'DIRTY DON' STOLE DIRECTOR'S CAR; FAVOURITE
SONG SHOULD BE
'MAD ABOUT THE BOY'

Apparently, they said, Don had stolen a well-known director's car, driven to a local beauty spot outside of LA, near Malibu, and attempted to pick up a young man. The young man, who had been there with his girlfriend, had rung the police, 'in disgust', given them the licence-plate of the car, and they'd tracked him down.

249

The vehicle belonged to the Academy Award-winning director Jerome Trumbo, who is an old friend of Mr Matthews. Mr Trumbo has posted bail for Mr Matthews. There is no suggestion that Jerry Trumbo knew of the incident or of his friend's homosexual proclivities. He was dining at Chasen's at the time in question and was seen by several witnesses. Mr Matthews, once one of Hollywood's most favoured screenwriters, has fallen from grace over the last few years. He is well known to have a drinking problem. Sources on the set of his latest movie, A Girl Named Rose, report that he was replaced by another writer, due to poor standard of work and questionable attitude. Mr Matthews remains in the LA County Jail. The real question is: This is the third such arrest in as many months. Senator McCarthy's long work in this area has stamped out the stain of the Left. The art of screenwriting is manipulation. Is another new wave of screenwriters inserting amoral, disgusting messages inside our films, besmirching a whole new generation? When will someone act?

My eyes flicked over the page, again and again, but no matter how often I read it, the words stayed the same.

Victoria came in with a pot of coffee. 'Morning, Miss Eve,' she said. 'Mr Travers went out early today.' She jabbed a finger at the magazine. 'Someone delivered that for you this morning. He said to make sure you saw it. He'll be back later. He said to tell you there's a dinner at Harry DiMarco's tonight and the boys are all taking their wives, and for you to be ready at six.' She added, 'If that suits you.'

I nodded, my head still bent over the magazine to hide my face from her. 'Yes, Victoria. Thank you.'

'You all right, Miss Eve?' Victoria said.

'I'm not all right, no,' I said. She stared at me. 'Go away, please. I need to think. I can't think,' I said, and I could hear a wild, strange strain in my voice.

* * *

I started to forget things around then. Everything started to mix together in my mind. I never heard from Jerry again. Or Conrad. They had both disappeared off the face of the earth, though I tried to reach them many times. I went to both their houses, I drove myself, I am sure. But neither of them was in. And neither of them returned my calls. No one else could help me. No one cared about Don. He was only a writer, after all, a writer with a drinking problem.

Moss Fisher was everywhere in those days. Every time I went to the studio he was there, watching me. When I rang Mr Baxter, the studio head, one afternoon from my dressing room, wanting to know where Jerry was, it was Moss who answered, as if the line in my bungalow was connected directly to his phone.

'He's resting before his next picture. We need to make sure he's looked after, Miss Noel.'

I'd been silent, taking in the implicit message of what he was choosing to tell me.

'Why are you doing this?' I'd asked him. 'You know it wasn't Don.'

'Don who?' Moss gave a tiny inhalation. 'Don Matthews? Oh, right. The fag they just arrested who used poor Jerry's car to go off and get himself into a whole heap of trouble? Jerry has an alibi, Miss Noel, you know he does. He was in Chasen's that night. A hundred witnesses.'

'It must have been someone else, then—' I began, but he interrupted.

'Listen, my dear girl. We really must stop ourselves jumping to conclusions. I, more than anyone, want to see Don cleared. Of course. Until then, we have to hope justice prevails.' And the phone went dead.

They even took his name off the credits of his latest film. *A Girl Named Rose* was released at the box office just over six months later and though the increasingly remote from reality and desperate studio was out of love with it themselves, the film became the biggest hit of 1960. The very same day it was released, Don was sent to prison. Two years, in the LA County

Jail. For moral turpitude, attempted sodomy and intercourse with a minor.

I wrote to him at his home address, offering to help. I didn't know who'd be reading his letters so I wrote in several different guises, but he never replied. I feigned illness on the set of my new picture one day, and slipped away to the County Jail when I knew it was visiting time. He wouldn't see me. Finally, on the day he was sentenced, I drove to the LA Superior Court on Hollywood Boulevard, waited in my car around the corner from the courthouse. I just wanted to see him, one more time.

I kept thinking of the *Confidential* byline: *Tells the facts and names the names!*

I didn't know why they were going after him, why he was the fall guy, where Jerry had gone, what had happened. But I knew he'd do anything to help a friend. And he owed Jerry, he felt he owed him everything. Oh, Don. Suddenly, I remembered what he'd said up in Big Sur and it terrified me.

'I've told him I owe him a favour. . . . No matter how big or small. He brought me back to you, didn't he?'

I began to understand. And I was helpless. I only knew I had to keep letting him know I loved him, I was looking for him, and I always would.

Then it was time. They came down the steps like a swarm – reporters, photographers, cops, campaigners with placards screaming at the cops, who pushed them out of the way.

'You goddamn filthy faggot! I hope you burn in hell!' a man waving a placard screamed at the group descending the steps, his face a dreadful rictus of hate. I saw a flash of a dark grey suit, the glint of sunlight bouncing off a car window as a door was slammed and he was driven away, to jail. I watched him go, and then I sat in my car for a long time, not knowing what to do, where to go, how to get anywhere. I could feel my brain unravelling, the thoughts in my head whirring round like a spinning top. I looked in the rear-view mirror, trying to tell myself to calm down.

My eyes danced in front of me, my face rippled, my hair seemed to be on fire. Voices clashed – me, Don, Rose, Gilbert,

Moss – voices telling me what to do . . . 'Stand here, Eve.' 'Turn this way.' 'Tilt your chin.' I was alone, in my madness, but I knew there were two people inside my head, so I wasn't really alone, was I? 'It's just you, now,' I said, to my reflection. 'You and me. Come on, we'll go home.'

I didn't know what else to do.

CHAPTER TWENTY

'WELL, LIKE I say, your father's not here, as per, I'm afraid. Yes, he's off in Swindon, seeing some dealers. Stayed there last night and I don't know when he'll be back. He never tells *me* anything.' Mum pushes a teapot towards me. 'Have another cup of tea. Or maybe water? I always keep Perrier these days. I don't trust the local tap water.'

'Tap's fine, honest, Mum. Thanks. It's my fault – it's such short notice. I've got another week or so here. I'll come back and see him.'

I've been at the house for one hour and twenty-five minutes, hoping Dad will walk through the door, but no sign. He always was the Invisible Man.

'Well, I wondered when you'd call, because like I say, I knew you were here. And it's funny because, well, we've fallen out now, but Dawn from next door said she'd been at lunch at the Oak for her dad's eightieth and they had the cast and crew from some film staying there, quite a to-do, she said. Well, I know you've got some security thingy so of course I didn't mention you. Don't worry, I haven't said a word to anyone.' She mimes buttoning her lip. 'Funny if she'd seen you, though I suppose you wouldn't remember *her*.'

'I remember Dawn.' I'm lying. 'How is she?'

'She's not so good. Mark isn't very well, and the kids – well, I don't usually like to interfere, *love thy neighbour* as they say,

254

but that little girl is so fat. I had to say something. She's just like a barrel. I only mentioned it to Dawn and she flew off the handle at me. Went completely berserk. I said, "Dawn, I'm just trying to be honest with you."' Mum runs a complacent hand across the immaculate kitchen surfaces. 'Because that's what it says you should do, in my confrontations chapter. "It's for your own good, you have to understand. I'm telling you, Shannon is OBESE."'

She shouts violently in the direction of the kitchen window and I turn, almost expecting to watch these last three words float outside and into the garden next door. Then she stands up, smoothes down her trousers, fluffs out her hair. The same set of gestures, always the same. I watch her curiously.

'What you staring at?' she says.

'Nothing, it's just nice to see you,' I tell her.

'Right.' I don't think she believes me. 'Anyway, so much to catch up on! Still! How's the film going? Are you happy? Are they treating you well?' She screws up her face. 'I must say, it's very strange you don't have a trailer or anything like that.'

'It's not that kind of film.'

'Well, but Sophie, I was always fond of the phrase, *If it ain't broke, don't fix it.*' Mum gives me a tight smile. 'You're doing so well. We're all so proud of you. Do you know, last week I had lunch with Julie, you know, my old friend from drama college. She and Deena and I lived together in – oh, right grotty little flat it was, in Hither Green. How times change! We laugh about it, I can tell you. She's done all right for herself, few parts here and there, she was in *The Bill*, you know, the usual. Nothing like Deena's success, of course. Well, obviously she wanted to hear all about you and I told her everything. She said you'd done very well. Very well indeed. Yes, she's an interesting woman . . . Julie.' Mum fluffs her hair again, then moves the cups onto the draining board and wipes the table down, a grim expression on her face. 'She was always a bit funny with me, you know, after I got the part in *No Sex Please, We're British* and she didn't, but I suppose she had the career after and I didn't – I gave it up for you.

Poor Julie, she never got married and I think it's been a real sadness to her. No kids.'

The phone rings.

'Oh, Deborah! Hello! Listen, Deborah, can't chat. Sophie's here. Yes, Sophie! Yes, I know! Oh, I know. You saw it? My word! I haven't seen an actual copy yet! I hate that photo of me! No! It's dreadful . . . Oh.' She turns to me and then back to the phone, speaking quickly. 'Listen, we're just having a cuppa, catching up, girls' chat, so I mustn't be long. Yes. Yes, of course I will. Yes. Bye, Deborah! Bye!'

Mum's eyes are sparkling as she puts the phone down. 'That's taught her to call at teatime. Hah! Who she thinks she is I have no idea. She knew you were back, I'm sure. Must have seen the car outside.'

'I shouldn't keep Jimmy,' I say. I look at my watch: it's only five. I thought it was later. Jimmy has gone to the Hand and Racquet while Mum and I have tea. He'll read the paper and find someone to have a chat with – Jimmy knows everyone round here.

'Your driver? Gosh, you are funny, love. He's a driver – he can wait, can't he? Sophie, you're too much of a pushover.'

'I'm not really. Like I say, it's not that kind of film.'

She looks at me blankly, and I match her gaze for a second, both of us completely still in the immaculate kitchen. She had it done up last year in best chintzy style; it was my birthday present to her, though they rarely take money off me. I wish they would, but I don't know why. Makes me feel less guilty about never coming home, I suppose.

I break the gaze first and look around me. The kitchen looks exactly the same after the makeover as it did ten, twenty years ago. I stare at the Portmeirion china lined up on the dresser, the boxed sets of *Poldark, Dallas* and *Laurel Canyon* on the windowsill. *The Microwave Hostess Cookbook*, my mum's cookery bible, is stashed neatly in the cubbyhole next to the microwave. The apron featuring a Roman statue's naked body hangs off the pine hooks, and there's even the same magnets on the fridge: I close my eyes – three Forever Friends bears, one holding a shopping list pad, one saying '*A bear is a friend for life*' and one wearing a T-shirt that says '*Hug Me*'. I used to think they were the cutest things ever.

This is the house I grew up in. This is where I'm from. But I feel absolutely nothing, and a kind of cold panic grips me. I don't belong here.

'So, I'll have to be the one to mention it first, I suppose.' Mum rubs her hands together. I look at her, worried.

She can't know about the stalker and the attack on the house. I haven't told her, Deena doesn't know. I explained the bodyguards away as 'extra security insurance' and she bought it, of course. I say cautiously, 'What's that?'

'Oh, come on, Sophie. Like we wouldn't talk about it! Everyone's asking me!'

'Asking you what?'

'You are coy. But I can tell, even by looking at you, that you're in love. You just look different. Oh, it's exciting. I think he's *gorgeous*!' Her voice rises.

'Mum, what are you talking about?'

My mother's eyes sparkle as she pushes the plate of French fancies towards me. 'Oh, come on, dear! Patrick? Your new boyfriend? *Closer* said you were going to marry him. Is that true? Of course you'd tell me, I just – is it?'

'Patrick?' My mind is blank. Then I say, 'Patrick *Drew*?'

'I know who he is, silly! I saw those photos of you two.'

'I don't know what you're talking about, Mum,' I say. 'I'm not going out with him.'

'You're blushing!' She points at me, delighted. 'You can tell me, come on.'

I put my hand up to my cheek; it's burning red. I say, annoyed, 'It's hot in here. I'm not going out with him, Mum, I promise you.'

'It's in all the magazines, Sophie.'

'Oh, well, that must mean it's true.'

'They're saying you're serious. Now I didn't want to ask you till I saw you. I'm very happy for you, love, he's absolutely gorgeous!'

'That's . . . rubbish,' I say, wishing my face wasn't so hot. 'Mum, I've met him two, three times in my whole life.'

'But they had those photos of you two, kissing, touching each other . . .'

I frown, then remember. 'Oh, good grief. No! That was a coffee we had for the film I was going to do, the one that got cancelled. I was showing him something and the photographers got me.'

She smiles, disbelieving. 'Oh, really?'

'Really, Mum,' I say. I don't know why I'm so annoyed. The more cartoonish photos from that coffee were everywhere immediately afterwards: Patrick losing it with the photographers outside, me clutching my breasts. They never got round to using the ones of us simply talking, looking intimate, till now presumably, when they need to give the story some more oxygen. I'd forgotten the photographers were there most of the time. I was enjoying myself. I wonder how he is, where he is. 'We met to talk about the film, that's it, I promise. He's lovely.' I bite my lip. 'But there's nothing going on.'

'Silly girl! What you talking about!' Mum refuses to give up on it. She slaps my wrist playfully. 'I know you, you can't hide it from your mother! It looks like he's halfway to proposing to you! Think of it, oh, my goodness, what a beautiful wedding. And the coverage! You'd be in *Hello!* for absolute certain.'

'It's rubbish, honestly. Promise.' I don't think Mum has spoken all day, other than to herself. I take a last sip of water from the glass and stand up. 'Mum, I'm sorry it's so short, but I do have to get back. I promised the producer and Alec I'd have a meeting with them tonight about the schedule—'

Mum frowns. 'You're off already?'

'I'm sorry, Mum.'

'I thought you'd want to give Donna a call, see if she's around for a cuppa.'

'Oh.' I shrug. 'I'd love to have seen her . . . I just can't, sorry.'

'You sure you don't want to pop in and see Mrs Bates,

stretch your legs? All that sitting around in a car can't be good for you.'

She doesn't care about Donna; she wants to walk down the high street with me, I know it. I don't think Angie would have much to say about that. 'I can't, Mum, I'm sorry.' I sound like a stuck record.

Her pearly-pink lipsticked mouth is turned downwards, a comical moue of spoilt disappointment. 'I wish you could stay longer. You've been here hardly any time.'

Nearly two hours, Mum, and you've mainly talked about yourself, Patrick Drew, and how big my trailer should be, I want to say, but I don't. I pick up my bag. 'Come to the set. I'll get Sara to call you and fix up a good time. You'd like to meet Alec, wouldn't you?'

My mother almost bridles. 'Oh, wouldn't I? Go on then. Maybe, maybe you should suggest me for the part of Anne Hathaway, the older version!' She touches me lightly on the arm with one almond-shaped coral nail, and gives a little laugh. 'Be a bit of a story, your mum doing the part! Might steal the show from you!' I look into her eyes and realise a part of her is deadly, 100 per cent serious, and I don't know what to say.

'I'd never do that to you, you're my mother,' I say, and I give her a kiss. 'Thank you for having me. It's lovely to be back.' I look round the kitchen one last time.

The back door opens suddenly with a loud pop and I jump. Mum stares at me. 'Afternoon, Marilyn,' says a middle-aged man. 'Early copy of the paper for you, thought I'd drop it round before it goes out tomorrow.'

'Oh, thank you, Steve! How kind!' My mother scurries over to the door and practically snatches it out of his hand. 'Bye then, see you soon.'

Steve turns to acknowledge me. 'Bye then,' he says, then he recognises me, stops and stares. 'So she's here right now! Well, I never. This is . . . blow me down.' He wipes his hand on his trousers, then holds it out. 'Didn't realise it. I'm Steve Jobs.'

'Steve Jobs?'

'Yes, Steve Jobs,' Mum says. 'Thanks, Steve.'

'Your name is Steve Jobs?' I ask him.

He looks pleased. 'Name ring a bell? I'm on the Jubilee committee as well as editor of the local paper, and we do cover all the villages over towards Stroud. But not Stroud itself, obviously. It has its own paper.' He rubs his shining pate. 'I can't believe I'm in the kitchen with Sophie Leigh! Can't believe it. Big fan of yours, Soph. Big fan. So pleased! Well, so here it is!'

He opens the paper with a crackling flourish. Mum is strangely quiet as I read over her shoulder.

FILM STAR'S COMING HOME . . . 'I OWE IT ALL TO MUM'

International screen superstar Sophie Leigh, 28, is coming back to the place she loves best – home. The worldwide star of *The Girlfriend, The Bride and Groom* and many others is staying at the Oak Hotel in Farley and filming down the road for another raunchy comedy! She's told her mother Marilyn she can't wait to come home for some of Mum's home cooking! Marilyn Sykes, 50, gave the *Shamley Examiner* an exclusive interview about Gloucestershire's most famous daughter. Marilyn, herself a famous actress in her day, says Sophie inherited her talent – and she doesn't mind that she's a star while she, Marilyn, is a housewife! 'It's not the life for me,' Marilyn told me over tea in her beautiful kitchen on Dawes Road. 'I never liked films. I preferred TV or the stage.'

'Mum . . .' I say weakly. 'No one's supposed to know where I'm staying . . . You shouldn't have done that.'

'Yes. Well, I forgot, didn't I.' Mum gives a little laugh. 'I remember now. Don't worry though, dear. Who's going to see it?'

'No, Mum,' I tell her. 'I'm serious. Someone's after me.' She cocks her head on one side, looking at me. 'You shouldn't have given this interview.'

'Someone's after you?'

'It's probably nothing, but – that's why I've got all these people all the time.'

She laughs again. 'Silly Mums. But . . .' I'm blinking, wondering how serious it is, and she suddenly says sharply, 'Oh, really, Sophie. It's not like you're . . . Barack Obama. Who's going to read the *Shamley – Charlton Lacey – Ambleside Gazette*?'

Steve Jobs looks hurt.

'Anyone who has a specific Google alert looking for me,' I say, trying not to shout. 'Everything's online now, even some crappy local newspaper.'

'Hey,' Steve Jobs says, but Mum holds out her hand.

'Shh, please, Steve. Look, Sophie. I've got a life as well, you know. It's about me too, you know. They wanted to know about me.'

I breathe out heavily, and just stare at her. I don't know what to say. I am a horrible person.

'Who's this?' I look up at the voice in the doorway. It's Angie. She says to Steve Jobs, 'Sir, can I help you?'

Steve Jobs looks utterly confused.

Mum says crossly, 'This is my friend Steve. Do you mind?' She looks annoyed, whether at me, at Angie, or at her interview I don't know.

I turn to Angie. 'It's fine, honestly. Let's go.' I look back at Mum, but she's looking at the photo of herself in the paper. 'Mum, please don't do that again. I'll call you.'

She doesn't answer. I don't know if it's because she's cross with me, or because she's absorbed in the photo of herself. But she turns back to the newspaper as I leave. One coral nail traces her grey-inked face on the paper.

I climb into the car. It's raining again, a thick, heavy, silent sort of rain. I stare out of the window, trying not to cry, as we drive through the outskirts of Shamley. It's grim here. No one could miss it. No one could want to stay here, or belong here. I sniff and shake myself. We go past Dad's first garage, where I used to sit on the stool by the entrance, reading comics and eating sweets with him, when I was really small, and people would walk past and smile. That Chris Sykes with his new garage and his sweet little girl, he must be worth a go, they'd think. He called me his lucky mascot. Maybe he lied to Mum, maybe he's here. I crane my neck to see him, but there's no sign, and we carry on. The a Co-op, a charity shop, the bus stop the cool girls used to hang out at, and there's –

'Oh, my God.' Angie jumps and Jimmy swerves, just a little, at the harshness of my voice.

'Sophie? What do you see?'

'What's wrong, love?'

I jab my finger against the wet, steamed glass. 'Donna. It's Donna! Jimmy, can you pull over? Donna, my best friend from school, she's over there—'

Angie says, 'Sophie, we need to clear this if you're going to get out.'

Jimmy pulls over. The rain is even heavier now. 'Donna!' I wind down the window and call her name. 'Donna!'

A woman pauses at the entrance to the Co-op and turns around. My wet fingers fumble to open the door. She stares at me. It's definitely Donna. She looks totally different, her semi-Afro hair scraped up into a messy ponytail, her face drawn and uneasy.

I yell again, my heart beating so fast. 'Donna, it's me! Sophie!'

An old man stares at me from the bus shelter. Donna glances at me from under her umbrella, her face immobile, then at the car. The automatic doors of the Co-op suddenly glide open as a clock somewhere starts to chime, and she turns and walks through the doors, not looking back.

There's a silence in the car.

'Maybe it wasn't her,' Jimmy says gently, after a few seconds.

'Sure,' I say. 'Probably. Let's just get out of here.'

We drive through the deserted streets, running grey-black with walls of rain, and soon we're out on the main road again, and it might never have happened. I rub my eyes.

'Miss Leigh,' says Angie from the front of the car. 'I'm

talking to Gavin as soon as we get back. We can't have you staying in the hotel if it's been published in a newspaper. That's a specific risk to your security. We'll have to move you.'

'Oh, Angie.' I lean between the seats. 'Seriously? Come on, it'd be easy enough to find out where I am if you wanted to. It's only my mother spouting off in some local newspaper. It's only just come out today, anyway.'

'My job is to protect you, Miss Leigh,' Angie says. 'I'm not doing that if I don't warn you about stuff like this. We'll have to get you some options, that's what we need,' and she turns and speaks, softly and fluently, into the phone. I sit back, watching the town I grew up in recede into countryside again.

The next day I'm doing exterior shots in a rare break from the rain. It's that stage in the shooting schedule when you seem to have been shooting for months and be no nearer completion. In a couple of weeks we are supposed to be moving on to Leavesden, to film the more technical and bluescreen scenes.

When I get back to the hotel Sara's waiting in the bar, holding her BlackBerry aloft. As I raise a hand at Nicola, the hotel manager, and a couple of guys from the crew, she bustles towards me. On her face is a curious mixture of excitement and something else, I don't know what it is. Fear?

'She wants to meet you,' she says. 'She's changed her mind. I – I don't understand it.'

'Who?' I say stupidly, fiddling with the kirby grips in my hair, pulling them out and into my coat pocket. Sara hands me the BlackBerry.

'I don't understand it,' she says again. It's an email addressed to me, sent to my account. I read it aloud, and as I get to the end a big grin is sliced across my face.

Dear Miss Leigh,
Most unusually, I have received a phone message from Eve Noel. She would like to meet with you. She apologises for not replying to your previous requests

263

but she has been prevented from doing so by circumstances beyond her control. She has been trying to contact you herself but has not found it possible to reach you. She has considered your proposal and would be interested in discussing the part of Anne Hathaway. To that end she would like you to visit her for tea next Monday. The address is Heartsake House, Charlton Lacey, Gloucestershire. She requests you arrive at 4.30.

I cannot emphasise how unusual this is.

Yours

Melanie Hexham

CHAPTER TWENTY-ONE

THE FOLLOWING MONDAY Tony Lees-Miller comes with me. Jimmy drives us. Mike, Angie's afternoon stand-in, is there too of course.

I'm nervous like I haven't been since I was auditioning for *South Street People*. Three failed auditions beforehand (an Ovaltine ad, a British period film about the Raj, and an ITV drama about runaway prostitutes which I was pretty glad not to get, if I'm honest) meant Mum and I were both extremely tense, as she drove me to London. Mum managed to make it clear that *everything* – all the money she'd spent on classes and private tuition and clothes and the rest of it – boiled down to this moment, that if I didn't get the part, it would be a big deal. I chewed half my cuticle off, I was so nervous, and it spotted my new Oasis dress with red dots of blood: we had to stop at a Little Chef and sponge it off. Maybe the drama took my mind off the other drama, because I knew as I was acting that I was nailing it. I was in London, at last, out of Shamley, and I was good, too. I could start to see what Mum had been pushing for all those years.

I feel this drive is similarly important. They talk about 'Act Three' in scripts – the point at which everything has changed and you can't go back to the way things were. I feel like we're getting to Act Three. We're going to see Eve Noel. I'm nervous, but I'm also uneasy, and I don't know why. I don't know what to expect.

We're crawling through Charlton Lacey, a beautiful Cotswold village dozing in the rare afternoon sun. There's a thin river, almost a stream, cutting along the edge of the last crop of buildings, and an overgrown field, with a dilapidated old building standing in the middle of it, the remains of a garden sloping down to the river.

'Village doctor used to live there, back in the day,' Jimmy says. 'Shame, it's a beautiful house. Been boarded up for years.'

The river runs through lush, low fields, a golden bridge arching over it, incongruous in the middle of nowhere. It winds near us, then away again, a grey-blue ribbon through the land. We drive a mile or so longer in silence, until the car swings round a corner and up a narrow path.

'This is it,' says Jimmy. Tony and I peer ahead. The drive is only about 20 metres long, but it's impossible to see what's at the end. There are yew trees on either side, so thick and black and unkempt the car almost gets stuck pushing through them.

It occurs to me that we are the first visitors for a while.

'Do you want to get out here, sir?' Jimmy says.

'Maybe, maybe,' Tony says. 'Thanks, Jimmy. Wait here.'

Mike opens his door but I stop him. 'It's fine, Mike. I'll call you when we get inside.' He frowns but sits back again.

Jimmy hands Tony a bouquet wrapped in paper, and we walk up the drive. It must have had gravel on it once, but it's dry and mealy now, thronged with chick weed.

A long, low house sits at the end of the thicket of yew. It must have been whitewashed once, but the surface is grubby, mildewed with years of neglect. There is ivy everywhere, creeping up the side of the house, curling into a lead window, around a chimney pot. There's a smell of something too – oil? Gas? I peer through the window, but I can't see anything at all. Then I realise I'm looking at cardboard boxes piled high, blocking out the light from the outside. Beside the front door, it says *Heartsake House*, or at least I think it was supposed to.

The black pointed letters are decaying, swinging on red rusted nails, and the 't' and 'u' are missing.

Tony stands up very straight and holds out the bouquet, like a child being inspected. He rings the plastic bell that just clings to the wall with one bent wire. I look down.

'Why did you bring her those?' I say sharply.

He glances down. 'White roses? They're her favourite flowers. She's famous for it.'

I feel slightly dizzy. A sweet, strange taste comes into the back of my mouth as I stare at the flowers, peering out from the paper. I know this is a mistake, I just don't know why.

There's no sound inside the house or out, only the whispering of the breeze in the yew. I wonder if we should press the bell again. But if we don't, we could just go . . . back away from this dark, unhappy place.

I don't know Tony, I realise. I stare at the mildewy wall, then at the white roses. It's white roses, I tell myself. It's got nothing to do with you. Everyone likes them. It's a coincidence.

'Perhaps we—' I begin, and then I intake my breath. There's a soft, soft rustling sound, scratching, and something scrabbling at the other side of the door.

'Miss Noel?' Tony says clearly. 'Good afternoon, Miss Noel? It's Tony Lees-Miller. From the studio. We agreed—'

The door opens, very slowly. A piece of ivy, caught in the hinge, springs out towards us and I jump, then look ahead.

A woman is standing there. She is rail thin, her skin papery, but she is beautiful. Her eyes are dark, black as night, but vacant, clouded with some sort of film. She smells musty, or perhaps it's the house behind her.

She shakes her head at the two of us, blankly, her hands clutching onto the door. 'Good afternoon. How may I help you?'

'We were looking for Eve Noel,' says Tony politely. 'We were told she lived here.'

He holds out the white roses and she looks down, then breathes in sharply, a terrified little hiss.

'She's not here.' She shakes her head. 'Go away.'

'Miss Noel,' I say. She turns to me, her eyes huge.

'Go away. They shouldn't have sent you. I'm Rose. Eve's been dead for fifty years.'

For a brief second the film clears and the liquid black eyes flash silvery fire, and she stares right at me, and it's her, I could swear it is. Then the cloud descends again and she turns. I catch a glimpse inside, of boxes stacked high against the walls and a black-and-white cat running down a corridor behind her, and then the door is closed in our faces.

a huge bite of the apple
April 1961

'LUCILLE HERE WAS just saying it's in the bag for you, honey.'
Dilly smiled up at me and pinned the last section of hem into
place.

I smiled politely. 'That's wonderful.'

'Aren't you excited?' Lucille, the seamstress beside her, asked
curiously.

'I'm tired,' I said truthfully. 'I'm honestly thrilled just to be
nominated. It's a wonderful year for the movies.'

'Well,' said Dilly, my dresser, her mouth full of pins,
kneeling beside Lucille. 'If you want my opinion, it'll be
incredible if you don't win. Just incredible. That movie, I
don't know what it is about that movie but it's . . . special.'
She clasped her hands together, pushing her large bosoms up
between her elbows as she did. 'Oh, my. I've seen it seven times.
Seven times, and I still cry like a baby at that ending. My
husband won't let me go no more. When are they gonna show
it on the TV, Miss Noel? I read it someplace, they'll be showing
movies on TV soon.'

'I don't know,' I said, and I couldn't help but smile at her
dreamy expression, the thrill in her voice.

' "*You'll be fine, Rose,*" ' Dilly recited, looking up to the ceiling,

269

her voice tremulous. '"*You're always fine. Just think of me occasionally, will ya?*"'

'Oh, my,' said Lucille, her curly hair bobbing around her face. '"*My thoughts are yours already, Peter darling,*"' she told Dilly, gazing at her intensely. '"*You know that. I'll never love anyone else. Never.*"'

Lucille sniffed, and they turned to face me as if expecting applause. I clapped feebly, a couple of times. It didn't hurt me to hear them any more. Every woman in America, it seemed, had seen that film by then, every woman wanted to recite those lines to me.

'Stand up and walk around,' said Dilly suddenly, switching focus. 'Let's see the length.'

As I crossed the floor there was an admiring gasp from the ladies, and from Walter, the costume designer, and his shy assistant Janet, both watching from the doorway. An Academy Award dress was like a bridal gown according to the modern-day myth: every woman dreamed of stepping into one.

'You're still so tiny,' Dilly said. 'Six months gone. You'd hardly notice there was a baby in there.'

'You look wonderful, dear,' Lucille told me, darting forward to adjust a fold. 'What a dress. Though I say it myself! It's just darn beautiful. Take that, Elizabeth!'

I shivered and she said, 'What's wrong? I'm sorry. You like Elizabeth Taylor?'

'Yes, yes, of course I do,' I said. 'It's nothing. The baby's kicking.' I looked at my reflection, ignoring the thoughts in my head as I touched my stomach. 'It's a gorgeous dress. You're very clever. I love it.'

Sometimes I wonder what happened to that dress. It *was* beautiful: turquoise, draped heavy fabric, decorated all over with golden stitching and metallic patterning.

Walter pushed himself off the door frame and came towards me. 'Divine, darling,' he said. 'Darnell will do the finishing touches with the hair, and you'll look like a queen.'

My hair was long now, and pregnancy had made it glossy and heavy. Darnell, an amber-eyed beauty with a lean body and a shy smile, was the studio's top stylist. He was coming to the house tomorrow afternoon especially for me, just to pile it up into ringlets, then cover it with diamond-studded gold pins. This alone, they'd told me, was evidence of my high standing at Monumental. I had to believe them, though everything else lately had been to the contrary – my last film, out a couple of months ago, *Triumph and Tragedy*, had been a big disappointment, and I hadn't worked since finishing the picture. I wouldn't accept any of the scripts they sent over. They were terrible, and I knew it was their punishment. I'd get so desperate that I'd do what they wanted, that was how they worked. And after *Triumph and Tragedy*, they seemed to care less and less. Ironically now, were it not for *Rose,* I'd be sent packing, whereas Gilbert's star climbed higher and higher every day. 'Thanks, Walter,' I said politely. 'You're very kind.'

'It's a great movie, and you deserve to win, darling, and I don't usually think that,' he said. He glanced at Darnell, then winked at me. 'Darnell and I have seen it five times, you know.'

'Oh, gosh,' I said. 'That's just terrific to hear.'

Yes, there was an awful lot riding on me and this picture, that year. This movie had bucked the trend, you see. The studios were on the way out, actors and directors and producers were making their own films now – even Gilbert was putting together his latest project, another World War Two action movie, and he was producing it too, for a slice of the profits. He could do what he wanted these days. After the success of *Dare To Win*, who'd turn down a Gilbert Travers picture? He'd be fifty-two next year, but like Cary Grant, Jimmy Stewart, John Wayne, age was no impediment if you were a man. I was only twenty-five, and already people assumed I was old. An aged relic. Rose and I had overheard Cook saying that about our grandmother once, and we used to whisper it to one another over and over again, the strange words singing on our tongues.

Rose. They'd written to me about Rose, after my parents died. Father first, a heart attack, then Mother a few months later, the influenza, one after the other. The letter told me where to find her, but it didn't make sense because I was Rose now, wasn't I. I'd put the letter in the hiding place in my wardrobe, where I kept secrets, for this was a secret, one I didn't understand, and I couldn't ask anyone about it, because they'd either find out I was mad, or they'd tell me I was making it up. I didn't know if it was a trick, you see. I'd never seen where she was buried. Perhaps they'd buried her again.

I knew something was wrong, but I couldn't think about it. I had to keep pretending. See me in the costume department, laughing and having fun, and I seem fine, don't I? No one knew what I knew, which is that my head buzzed all day with thoughts that made me exhausted, with voices that taunted me to the edge of madness. That since Don had gone to prison, the thread that kept me tightly bound to the outside world had been cut, and I had retreated into – well, I don't know what it was. My parents were dead, and the news had not even made me cry.

The letter about Rose – that was why I needed to get well again, to be strong and brave. One day, I told myself, I will go back home, with my baby. One day soon. We will visit our old home, then we will walk towards Rose's grave, and I will put wild flowers on the stones, her favourites, forget-me-nots and daisies. No roses for Rose. Then it will make sense. Then it will.

I lunched in the studio canteen that day, as part of the publicity build-up. I hadn't eaten there for years; I wasn't hungry, I felt sick a lot of the time. Pregnancy didn't agree with me; I wanted it over, to hold him or her in my arms, to see the face of my child, to see what they'd be like. The baby moved a lot, twisting inside me, kicking my ribs. They told me I'd feel better, and I didn't. They gave me pills to calm me down, but I still didn't sleep. I felt heavier, more tired, with every passing day, and even smiling for some photographs was a physical effort.

And things were starting to be different too, and it scared me. Every time I looked in a mirror, I saw Rose, not me. Inside my head, thoughts multiplied and split into tiny fragments, buzzing around in my brain sometimes so loudly I couldn't hear what people said to me.

While I ate my burger and chips, or pretended to eat them,

the photographers snapped away: I smiled and talked to a couple of young secretaries from the accounts department at the studio, who had loved the film and just had to say hello. I wanted to believe they, at least, were real, but I felt so nauseous I thought I might vomit and had to simply concentrate on them. 'Great stuff,' said one of the photographers, as he replaced his lens cap. 'Run this tomorrow, in the *Examiner*. Thanks, fellas. Thank you, Miss Noel.'

'Thank you,' I said.

'I'll send you a copy, with some white roses, when you win tomorrow night, miss!' one of them called out.

I raised my hand, trying to smile, and as I looked around me to see if I could make my escape and take myself home there was a light clearing of the throat, and someone slid into the seat beside me.

'Very well done, Eve,' said Moss Fisher. He was eating a half-finished apple. 'Wonderful. Now you should go home and get some rest. You have a big day tomorrow.'

I knew Moss was behind it all. I knew he'd sacrificed Don on the altar of his damn studio. And I knew he'd told Gilbert what was going on. Moss was one of those people who operated on a purely strategic, not human, level. He saw a problem, identified a solution, and then put it into action, no matter what the cost. I'd heard a rumour that he'd been first on the scene when Clark Gable had killed a pedestrian driving while drunk, and that he'd gone to the house before the police when Jean Harlow died.

Moss took a huge bite of the apple, right into the core. I watched him, trying to suppress my nausea, then I looked around at the almost-empty canteen. There were a couple of maids chattering and banging dishes in the kitchen behind us but otherwise it was very quiet. My head started to hum with its own noises again. I knew I had to take my chance then.

'How is he?' I said quickly, desperately. 'How's Don?'

Moss didn't react. He bit on the apple and crunched loudly. 'That fag? He's fine. Prison suits him, so I hear. There's a load of other pansies in there for him to pal around with.'

'He's not a – a fag,' I said. 'You know he's not.'

'You ought to forget about him,' he said. 'Concentrate on your marriage. You're a lucky girl. There's millions of women who'd kill to be where you are right now.'

I started to laugh. I couldn't stop myself. It came bubbling out of me, hysteria mixed with anger. Moss didn't react at first, then after a while he looked around, annoyed, put his hand on my wrist. 'Stop that, Eve. You sound mad. You don't want them to think you're mad, do you?'

That shut me up.

'I'm not mad,' I said. I could hear my voice, far away, above the babbling voices that talked only to me. 'I'm not.'

He nodded, his face twisted into an expression of concern. 'Of course you're not, Eve. But it's an important time for you. And Gilbert. He needs your support. And you need his, of course.' I looked at him suspiciously. He slid the apple core across the table, leaving a wet trail. 'I did wonder if you should get away from Hollywood for a while. A vacation. Maybe go to Miami for a couple of months until the baby's born. How would you like that?'

I gave a small laugh again, but this time I was in control. 'That is terribly amusing, Moss.' His brow puckered; he didn't understand. 'That you think I'm so easily pushed around,' I said, but I bit my lip: I *had* been easy to push around, been gullible and naive and docile. Not any more. Not while this baby grew inside me. I didn't care any more. 'I know you want me out of the way.'

He shook his head. 'You couldn't be more wrong.'

'I know the studio's furious at how well *Rose* has done, when you tried to shut it down.' My mailbag still ran into hundreds every week, letters saying, *That was me* and *I've seen this film so many times and cried every time* and, most often of all, *What were you thinking, when you said goodbye to Peter at the end? Were you thinking about someone yourself?* 'You've had it in for Don for years because he wouldn't dance to your tune, and you're terrified of anyone dismantling your precious system. And Jerry, too.' Moss flinched, and looked around. I hissed in his ear, 'Have you heard from him lately, by the way?'

He looked impatient. 'Jerry's fine. It was his decision to go to Europe. There's a lot of interesting work going on there.'

'Jerry's not fine – he hasn't worked for two years, no one's heard from him. Don's still in jail – he's not fine,' I said. I felt so tired, I almost didn't feel like fighting any more, but I had to. I hugged my stomach, the warm, hard mound a comforting buffer between me and the rest of the world. The baby moved, softly – a hand, the head, a knee? I couldn't tell what. I rubbed the side of my bump, and Moss looked alarmed. 'You hounded Jerry out of town.' My voice was low. 'You're an evil man, Moss, you do know that, don't you?' I shivered, because it was a terrible thing to say. 'You think I don't have anywhere to go. You think I have to stay with Gilbert, because of the baby. You think you can hold the scripts over me, control my career. Well, you can't. I'm going to win tomorrow night. You know I am. I'll thank Don, I'll tell them all what's going on, what you've done, and I'll say how disgusting it is that in this day and age people can't be free to sit where they want in a diner or on a bus, love who they want, no matter who they are, without being sent to prison.'

The buzzing in my head was very loud, but just above it I could hear Moss, breathing rapidly, as he picked some apple out of his back teeth. Then he stared at me, surmising. 'OK. What do you want?' he said.

This was the moment, the chink of light for which I had been searching, stumbling through the darkness, these endless months. I balled my hands into fists under the table, feeling the stretched roundness of my stomach.

'Tell me the truth,' I said quietly. 'I want to know what happened. Why did Don take the fall for Jerry?'

He opened his mouth and then closed it again, and ground his teeth. The muscles in his cheeks moved. He nodded. 'OK. Jerry's pretty boy, he's the one responsible.'

'What?' I didn't understand.

'That fag Conrad Joyce. Your little friend. You thought he

was your friend, didn't ya?' He was smiling. 'So, that last night in Big Sur, remember?' I nodded. Of course I remembered. 'Conrad leaves that night, takes Jerry's car. On the way back, gets horny, drives to some queer spot to get some action, but the cops, they're staking the place out and he's caught with his cock in some guy's mouth. He panics and manages to drive off, but the cops get his licence-plate, see? They track him down to Jerry's.'

Two pairs of legs went by in the window above us: fawn strapped heels, clicking rapidly to keep up with a striding man's grey-checked suit. My eyes flicked over them, then back to Moss, and I nodded, without saying anything; I wanted him to keep talking.

'Jerry gets hold of me and Don in a panic, asks what he should do.' Moss licked his lips. *He's enjoying this,* I thought, trying to focus. 'He doesn't tell Don what Conrad's really been up to, see? Just tells him he's taken the car, got into some trouble and the press can't find out, it'd ruin his career. And he asks Don to take the fall for him. Gives him the real sob story. Begs him, says it's his only chance at happiness, that he loves Conrad, that he's helped Don out over the years, Don promised him a favour.'

'But why the hell—' I started to say, but I knew the answer.

Moss Fisher looked up at me, surprised. 'Why would Don agree to help him? He owes Jerry everything, you know it, Eve. He brought him to Hollywood out of New York, all those years ago, he's given him all his biggest jobs, he'd be nothing without him. Jerry's poured him into more taxis than anyone, paid off people, all 'cause he believed in the guy. And now it's time for Don to pay him back. It's true,' Moss said. 'Don Matthews has hit the bottom more times than the hammer bell at the fairground. And Jerry was always there to pick him up.

'So it's the middle of the night and Jerry's screaming, crying down the line, and Don agrees to say it was him. Help him out. I don't know what he thought. I think he thought he'd take the hit for a speeding ticket. Or something.' Moss fingered his tie. 'He calls me, and I call up Mr Baxter, get him out of bed, we talk it over. We know Don's going to self-destruct in the next coupla years, why not get rid of the guy now? We got a lot of money invested in Conrad, and times are hard, we need all the bankable stars we can get. We need to keep the system intact.' He adjusted his tie and smiled. 'So – yeah. I didn't tell Jerry how bad the fallout could be. Didn't want him changing his mind about asking Don to help out. We needed to have this whole thing sorted by breakfast. It's usually the case that business done at night ain't for talking about during the daytime.'

'What did you do?' I asked him slowly.

'I got friends in the force. Tipped them off about who they needed to talk to, they go round to our friend Mr Matthews, catch him at home before he's setting out for – Las Vegas, was it? Some trip he had planned. He said he'd come willingly. It was the best solution. We didn't tell Don how serious it was. Don't think he'd've agreed to go through with it all if he'd known. We said it was a little local difficulty. How am I supposed to know it's jail, the works? Sure, he was angry but . . . He knows he owes Jerry, and by then it was too late.'

Moss's eyes were black as night. He wiped his hand across his comb-over and nodded. I remember very clearly watching him, thinking, *He believes he's right.*

'Listen to me, Eve. He was trouble, that guy. He's out of the picture now. So much the better. We got our three stars. Conrad's OK, you're OK, Gilbert's OK. Some dipso writer goes to jail for being a homo – who cares?'

'You're – you're a monster,' I said. 'You can't mess with people's lives like that.'

He leaned forward, across the scratched Formica surface, his flat face immobile, his lips moving only slightly, and he hissed, 'It's for the good of the studio, Eve. Millions of people spend their hard-earned dollars with us Friday night at the movies. It's our job to give them the stars they want, the pictures they want. We have a responsibility. To the American public. You don't get that, you don't get anything.'

'The studios are dying. They're over, Moss,' I hissed back at him. 'You're playing God.'

'No, Eve. Some filthy homo decided to try and ruin his own life by getting sucked off by another guy in some dust-bowl clearing in the woods. I'm just saving him from himself.'

'He wasn't doing anything wrong!' I thumped my fist on the table, and Moss's hand shot out and grabbed me by the wrist, an iron grip that burnt my skin.

'Shut up, goddammit,' he said. 'Shut your fat stupid mouth.'

I could see Don's face as he waved me goodbye that morning in September, as I turned around on my seat for one last glimpse of him as we drove away. His dear, kind face, his crooked smile, his dark, passionate eyes, hand waving furiously as he followed the disappearing car intently. *Not without you.*

I stood up, unable to bear another second with Moss. 'I have to go,' I said, and I walked away.

'It was the right thing to do,' he called after me. And then, 'Think about Miami. It's best for you. And the baby.'

Of course, movie stars don't just storm out of places. I walked so fast out of the canteen I was almost running, in my black kitten heels, feet aching, back aching. There was a long row of buildings just outside, with parking spaces neatly labelled: *Mr Joseph Baxter, Head of Studio*; *Mr Leonard Baxter, Head of Production*; *Mr Moss Fisher, Head of Publicity*. The Rolls-Royce Mr Baxter and I had ridden in that fateful night had long since, like me, been traded in for a younger model: exactly the same, just newer, fresher. I stood and stared. Five years, five years.

'Miss Noel?' Gary, my driver, was leaning against the car parked in front of the sign: *Miss Eve Noel*. I had been there for a long time now. I had my own space. I looked around me, at the water tower, at the outside sets in the near distance, the ones the Baxters had built twenty years ago, exact replicas of New York tenements, with fire hydrants on the sidewalks and cracks made by a heavy's hammer. Main Street, USA, complete with diner, sheriff's office, grocery store and gentlemen's outfitters. And beyond them the sound stages, twenty or so, each one the size of a small cathedral, black and scuffed when empty, bursting with colour, people, lights, when the cameras were rolling. I had spent so long on this lot it never occurred to me that I might not come back here again. But I wouldn't, I knew that then. The studios were dead. The Baxters and Moss and their henchmen were still clinging to the old system, the one that had worked for them for so many years. They'd ignored television, the rise of the superstar, of pop idols and teen dreams, but it'd all catch up with them soon, it had to, and I wasn't a green girl any more either. I'd grown up.

Gary was standing by the car, waiting for me to tell him what happened next. 'Take me to Bel Air, please,' I told him, and he nodded and opened the door. I climbed in, not looking back.

once I had a secret love

I KNEW WHERE Conrad lived: a modern condo, high up in Bel Air. I'd been there, in happier times, to a New Year's Eve party he'd had a few years ago. Three – was it four? I wasn't with Gilbert then. It was a young Hollywood gang I'd run with for a while; Conrad was always in that group and it was always fun, girls in pedal pushers and with heavy fringes, boys in shirts without ties, playing Sinatra and Brubeck, someone passing round a joint, highballs and eggnog. Funny, that scene, I enjoyed it. I liked them all; it could have been back in London again, like we weren't all famous, beautiful, adored by millions around the world – we were just young kids, enjoying ourselves.

My fingers were knitting themselves together, plucking at the tight skirt; I wished I could loosen the waistband as I worked out what I was going to say. 'Won't be long now,' I whispered to my bump as we turned into the drive, and the baby moved cautiously, sleepily, inside me. 'Nearly there, and then we'll go, go away from here.'

'Did you say something, Miss Noel?' Gary called to me.

'Nothing.' I climbed out of the car. 'Wait here. I won't be long.'

Conrad's maid answered the door. It was strange to be there in the middle of the day, unannounced: you didn't do that in

Hollywood. The surprise showed on her face. 'Good afternoon, Miss Noel,' she said. 'Are you looking for Mr Joyce?'

'Yes. I want to talk to him.'

She hesitated. 'He's – sure . . .' she said doubtfully. 'I don't know if he's working or not. Wait here, please.'

I waited alone in the lobby, looking at the parquet floors, the tartan wallpaper on one huge wall, festooned with kitsch: antlers, photos, awards on a shelf. I could hear music playing faintly in the distance. The front wall of the lobby was glass, looking right out over the canyon and onto Sunset and the rest of the city.

'Well, hi! Miss Noel!' Conrad's voice came floating towards me from the direction of the music. I turned and he had his arms open. 'This is a lovely surprise, darling. What can I do for you?'

'I wanted to see you.' Despite my anger, I couldn't help smiling a little at the sight of him. We had been so close. He'd picked me up when I was blue, he was always on the end of a phone. We'd laugh for hours together, on sets, in restaurant booths, out on the town, in a way I never did with Gilbert. And when I think of Conrad now, it is with a smile, despite my sadness, because he never meant to hurt anyone.

'How fine for me, darling.' He licked his lips. 'Want something to eat? A Martini?'

'I'd like a Martini, thanks,' I said. 'I want to talk to you.'

'Uh-huh, uh-huh. Come this way.' He led me through to the den, which opened with glass sliding doors onto a terrace, complete with drinks cabinet, table and chairs. The music was Doris Day, I recognised it now. 'We'll sit here by the window, not outside – it's too hot, darling. I'll make your drink. See, I've got everything we need. Olive or a twist?'

'Olive, please,' I said.

'Sit yourself down. Cigarette?'

'No—' I pushed my hand away. 'I'm off them. I'm having a baby, did you know?'

'Yes, yes, I heard,' he said, glancing briefly at my stomach. 'That's so wonderful, darling, what a great mommy you'll be. I'll make you something safe, something sweet, you'll love it, darling.' He was chattering manically. There were two empty glasses already on the table, and an ashtray filled with butts. I could smell them, and there was a grey worm of ash hanging off one, as though the cigarette had burnt out. I wished that they weren't there, that the table was wiped clean and sparkling again. Lately, anything messy disturbed me. I cleaned the house obsessively, waiting till Victoria was gone to polish and scrub and wipe.

'What did they say at the studio? What does Mr Baxter think? Great publicity. I'll bet Moss is pleased.'

'I don't really care,' I said. 'I don't want a relationship with them any more.'

He swivelled round and the sun caught his face and I stared at him, as if seeing him properly. I hadn't seen him in so long, not since the premiere of *Rose*. He'd never returned my calls, replied to my postcards, and now I knew why.

He had become terribly thin, too. His legs in their hip-hugging nylon pants were skeletal, his cheeks sunken. 'Oh, Eve. Always the renegade. You're about to win an Oscar for them, you shamelessly stole the picture from the rest of us, and you're finished with them? I don't know that they'll let you, darling.' He laughed and lit a cigarette, then jumped up to mix a drink. 'I certainly wouldn't. June and I are still furious at you for the way you're the best thing in every scene. Unforgivable.'

The worm of ash from the dead cigarette fell onto the table, scattering into grey flakes, some mixing with the condensation from the glasses. I stared at it, itching to take my handkerchief out, wipe it down. He smiled, and jabbed his cigarette out, though it had barely been smoked, then handed me my drink. It had a little pink plastic stirrer in it, a tiny pineapple on the end, so incongruous, so sharp and pretty and silly. 'To tomorrow, darling,' he said, too loudly. 'Good luck, not that you'll need it. It was a great picture, wasn't it.'

'Yes, it was,' I said. 'Because of Don.'

'Sure, sure,' Conrad said. 'Oh, I'm about to start working on something in two weeks. It's a comedy. European. Should be a lot of fun.'

Something rang a bell in my head. I looked at him over my Martini glass. 'You're going to Europe?'

'Sure, sure,' he repeated, his eyes ranging around the room, out to the terrace, where a little sparrow landed on the cream-grey flagstones just beyond us. 'It's a silly thing, but Jerry's finally brought it all together. We'll have a blast.'

'With Jerry? You're making the film with Jerry?'

'Yes,' he said. 'Jerry's the director. Good old Jerry, hey?' He sank the rest of his drink.

'Conrad,' I said slowly. 'Don's in jail because of you. Don't you realise that?'

He clamped his mouth shut. After a few seconds his pointed pink tongue shot out between his lips. He nodded nervously. 'Sure I do,' he said. 'Don's a great guy.'

'That's all you've got to say?' I shook my head slowly, staring at him. 'He's in jail, his career's over, his reputation, everything. For you.'

'How do you know?'

'How do I know? Because no one'll employ him now!' I was almost laughing. 'You know what his track record was. He'll never work in this town again. He—'

'No – ' Conrad interrupted. 'How do you know about Don . . . about all of this?'

'Moss,' I say. 'He just told me. I came straight here. I've never really understood it, you see. Not till now.'

He gave a nervous half-giggle. 'We have to keep it secret, you see. If it got out that I'd done it . . .' He trailed off.

I got up slowly. 'Goodbye, Conrad. I hope you enjoy Europe.' I turned and looked at him. 'I hope you realise how lucky you are.'

'Hey,' Conrad said, reaching out for my hand, pulling me back firmly but gently towards my chair. His voice was sharp. 'Listen. I'm not lucky. I'm unlucky. I wish I wasn't like this . . . I am. OK?'

He rattled his cocktail stick loudly against his own glass.

'What?' I said. 'A liar?'

'No,' he said. 'A queer.'

'It's not so bad,' I said. 'There's nothing wrong with it. You're not in prison—'

283

He laughed. A big belly laugh, like we were watching a Laurel and Hardy film. Like I'd just said something hilariously funny. It echoed around us, bouncing off the great glass walls, rolling down the hill, and I shivered as I watched him.

'You have no idea, honey, no idea at all.' He waved my hand away. 'And I wish I wasn't, Eve. I don't want to be like this. I've tried so hard not to be like this. It's just like my mama said it was, it's a disease. I could cure myself if I let it happen, and I keep trying and trying and nothing . . . nothing. I'm sick.' His beautiful mouth was turned down like a Pierrot's, an almost cartoonish expression. His eyes bored into mine. They were hunted, dark, huge, so sad.

'You're not – you're not sick,' I said. 'Conrad, you're not.'

He gave a choked laugh. 'Oh, yeah? I'll just tell them then, shall I, tell the girls who cream themselves waiting outside the studio, the women running after me in the street, I'll tell them I prefer screwing boys, shall I? See how they like that. What I am is illegal. There are people who want to castrate me. You know that?'

'You could just—' I began, but I didn't know what to say next.

'I can't, Eve,' he said. He began to laugh. 'You know how often I wished I could be in love with you, ask you to marry me? That would have solved so many of my problems, you know? And I couldn't do it. To me, or to you.'

Gilbert's baby moved inside me again, and I wondered what life would have been like with Conrad. How I loved him more than my own husband, in so many ways, and yet how I hated him, now.

'I'm supposed to be every housewife's dream. And they have no idea what it's like, to be lying all the time. That whenever you talk to someone, smile at someone, you're hiding a part of yourself. The part that matters most, who you love, how you love. It's all that matters, and it's all a lie.'

'Why can't you just be honest, though?' I said. 'Tell the truth, let them set Don free. You'd feel better. I'm sure you would.'

'You say that to me?' He laughed. 'I gave you away at your

wedding, honey, your sham of a marriage, and you've got the nerve to come up here and lecture me about telling the truth so I go to jail and you can walk out of your marriage with your lover? Come on, Eve.'

How had we come to this? This gentle kind man whom I had liked so much, and I, heavy, pregnant and desperate, both trapped by our fame.

'It's different.'

'It's not, Eve, and you know it.' His eyes narrowed. 'I – I can't.' His breathing was shallow and quick. 'You think I'm a coward. Well, I am, then. I don't have the strength to do it.'

We sat in silence, listening to the opening shimmering strings of 'Secret Love', and Conrad gave a small, wan smile.

'I know Don wanted to help Jerry,' he said. 'I know he felt he owed him a huge debt, that he had to right that debt. He's Irish, you know what they're like.' He shrugged, as though that was the answer, but he wouldn't meet my eye. 'I just – I didn't realise, when Moss suggested it, how it would . . . snowball, become this thing way out of my control . . . That we'd have to can *A Girl Named Rose*, all the crew would lose their jobs . . . all these things, I don't know . . .' He covered his face with his hands and carried on talking, his voice soft, the words fluent. 'I've been so stupid. I hate myself. I can't – I wish . . . When I think what would have happened, if I'd just kept on driving, but I couldn't, I just couldn't. I'd been there before, I knew there were always cute boys from the town who'd turn a trick for a few bucks, I was horny as hell, I had to . . . Jerry didn't mind, he said I had to get it out of my system . . . But if I'd just carried on driving back to LA, none of this would have happened.'

I nodded. I couldn't speak. 'No.' My white-hot anger had dampened down. I didn't know what else to say. Pointless to think about what might have happened, what could have been, where Don and I would be now. The compulsion to move the ashtray out of sight was almost overwhelming; I felt dizzy with the force of something mad, crazy, driving me. I put my hand to my stomach. I couldn't think like that now, for his or her sake.

285

'He's a great man,' Conrad said. 'I'm not.'

'No,' I said. 'You're not. I wish it wasn't like this for you, but you shouldn't have done it.' I bit my lip; I mustn't cry, I mustn't.

He looked at me, his kind face so thin, pale in the blazing sun.

'Goodbye, Conrad.' I touched my hand to his shoulder, lightly. 'I'm going now. Hope Europe works out for you.'

'Yes,' Conrad said. He stood up and squinted into the sun. 'I'm sorry, Eve.'

'You should be,' I told him.

He flinched, as though I had slapped him.

'Don't say that,' he said quietly.

I knew I had been too unkind. I left him, tears of impotent anger blurring my vision, and as we drove home I looked out at the houses perched on the hills around me. *More Stars Than There Are in Heaven* is what it said on the gate above the entrance to MGM. I wondered what they were all doing, this huge cluster of stars, in a 5-mile radius around me. Playing tennis? Listening to the radio, having a drink, laughing with their families, their friends? Did they ever feel the way I did, as though their mind were splitting into two, one side totally rational, able to answer questions and sign autographs and remember lines, the other side . . . oh, like a crazy, terrible jumble, a kaleidoscope of sounds and images and words that kept turning faster and faster until you wished you could drill into your head, release the whirling demon inside your skull, so that you could have some peace, even if only for a few hours? I knew it wasn't like that for Gilbert: he drank when he was thirsty, ate when hungry, slept when tired, assumed he was the star and took his due, didn't worry about anything else. Not me.

The trouble is I didn't know who I was any more. *I will lift up mine eyes unto the hills, from whence cometh my help.*

I breathed in steadily. Keep breathing, just keep breathing, I told myself. I looked at my watch and realised it was nearly six. This time tomorrow, I'd be arriving at the Santa Monica auditorium for the biggest night of my life in my turquoise dress, the jewels glinting in my hair, my hand tightly clasping Gilbert's, as hundreds of people – fans, press, friends – called our names. Our picture would appear in the newspapers and magazines the next day, and girls from New York City and Boston to Dayton and Dallas would sigh over my photo, wishing they had my husband, my clothes, my job. My wonderful life.

'your sister, Rose Sallis'

After my visit to Conrad, I couldn't sleep. Rose's face was always there when I closed my eyes. And there were other things, too. I wasn't sure who I was, sometimes. I thought that perhaps it was the pregnancy, but I was becoming more and more sure it couldn't be. When people called my name, I didn't hear them. If they called me Rose, I did. Except no one called me Rose any more. I tried to look for the letter they wrote to me about her. But I was too afraid to look for it. I don't know why. I think I saw it was all too late now.

I was Eve Noel, I was a creation of the studio; my hair, my teeth, my name all Mr Baxter's, from the night he pulled up my skirt, planted his hairy big hands on me. I'd been passed from the Baxters to Gilbert Travers, and I was his now. I was carrying his child, I was bound to him in every way and all of a sudden, since I'd found out about Conrad cheating Don, I didn't have anywhere to run. What would I do? Where would I go? Now I would have done everything differently, of course. But it's too late, now.

Other things had changed, too. I thought about sex constantly. I fantasised about it, I rubbed my hands over my smooth, taut body, I even demanded it from Gilbert, who formerly had repulsed me. He, of course, was delighted, as an extension of his ego I believe, not because he wanted me to feel satisfied. I liked feeling him deep, deep inside me, fucking me, hurting me, when I hated him and myself. I liked thinking about rude, disgusting things while he did it. I became obsessed with cleanliness, having everything just so. After I'd left his dressing room, I'd stay up all night, prowling quietly around the house, looking out of the windows towards the hills, picking up things, rearranging them so they were perfectly in place for the next day.

Outwardly I was the same. I think what scared me the most was that I knew I wouldn't ever ask for help. I knew that I couldn't break down and reach out to anyone, admit my weakness, that I felt I was losing a grip on myself, that I didn't know if it was me, if I was mad, or the baby, that this baby was eating away at me, sucking something out of me. Or that people around me were doing it deliberately, planting things in my way, trying to control me. I was more and more convinced that was the case.

The strangest thing was, when I got home, there was another letter addressed to me like the first one. From England. I hadn't had any post for a long time, but Victoria was out, and there it was, on the floor, on the champagne-coloured carpet, just sticking out by the bureau, so maybe it had been kicked under there or maybe it had only just arrived. I don't know, because the date kept changing.

And I read it and reread it, but I didn't understand it. It didn't make any sense. '*Your sister, Rose Sallis*' it said – but I was Rose, wasn't I? A girl named Rose. I didn't understand why they were writing to me – Rose was dead, my parents were dead, and I was all alone. Don was gone and I had to help myself, and my brain hurt so very much all the time, I knew I wouldn't be able to. The letter stayed in my hand, but after that I put it in the back of my wardrobe, in the secret place where I put my valuable things, the possessions I wanted to keep safe. The first letter was in there too; maybe I knew that all along. I don't know. I put all these secret things away for a time when I could think about them.

the winner is . . .

THE NEXT DAY I sat in the auditorium in my beautiful dress on an uncomfortable shiny leather chair, and twisted my head to watch the rest of the audience arrive, trying to look as if I knew where I was and what I was doing. But it seemed to be getting harder for me to block out the noises, to stop seeing people when they weren't there, to try and go back to normal. They had put me and Gilbert on the end of a row at the front. 'Must mean something,' Gilbert had whispered, nostrils flaring with barely concealed nerves. I stared at them all. All the men looked like Mr Baxter. Old. White. Black horn-rimmed spectacles. Greying hair, perfectly pressed dinner jackets and immaculate cuffs. Nearly all the women old too, in evening furs, silk boleros, dripping with jewellery. The stars stood out a mile. They were young and good-looking.

Despite my bravado, my claims that I'd tell everyone the truth, denounce Conrad, praise Don, when I was up on the stage, I knew I wouldn't win. And I wasn't surprised when I didn't. I don't even think the studio's best attempts to scupper my chances made much difference either. Elizabeth Taylor had nearly died three months before, what chance did I stand against that? She was dressed all in white – a silk dress with a tulip-shaped skirt, long white gloves – a fairy queen come to life. I watched her walk up to the stage. I watched Bob Hope gurning, the old men clapping and cheering. Next to me, Gilbert put a hand on my thigh, grinning for a film camera, the husband of the gracious loser. I stared at him while he smiled. He had a gap between his front teeth. I'd never really noticed it before. I smiled into the camera, at the people on the other side of the aisle, up at the stage, and then I felt the most curious sensation, as if I were there still, but not there. I flew up high to the ceiling instead, watched the whole thing from the furthest corner of the vast auditorium. I could see me, sitting down below, trying not to touch my head, to stop the noises. Do you know what I mean? No. No, of course not. There were other people up there with me, and we could see the whole room spread out above us, and one of them looked like Conrad, and he nudged me and pointed down to where I was sitting. 'That's you,' he said.

All the time I clapped and clapped. 'Bad luck, dear,' said Gilbert, smiling again at the camera. 'Bad luck.' Bad luck.

'The winner is . . .' When they called Gilbert's name out, I was still daydreaming, I didn't quite understand at first. He jumped up, his big hands clasping the armrests of his chair and lifting himself bodily out, as if he might swing up to the stage in one movement, like an ape in the jungle. He strode up the aisle, shaking hands and smiling at the old men. Many of them were those who'd ignored him when he came back from the war. The beautiful people were watching him and clapping, for they were pleased; they liked Gilbert. He was them, in ten, twenty years' time. He'd made it back and they could afford to be generous, for one night.

They handed him the statue. Gilbert put his hands on the lectern, leaning forward, scanning the crowd. I felt myself float up again, all the way to the ceiling. Everyone was craned forwards, waiting to hear what he'd say. Everyone was silent.

'This is for all the good old chaps who've had a rotten time of it,' Gilbert said. 'For freedom amongst lands, friendship between nations.'

There was a light ripple of applause.

'I accept this award with deep humility. I should like to thank the men of Forty-fourth Battalion Lancers, who inspired this story. The cast and crew on this wonderful picture. *Dare to Win,* we bloody did. And I'd like to thank Colin Cowdrey and Fred Trueman of the English cricket team, something you don't have over here, along with rain and a decent cup of tea.'

They roared with delight – Americans love a gentle ribbing, though not as much as they love an English stereotype. Gilbert was giving them both.

He grinned again, acknowledging the applause. I looked up at him, at the matinee idol, at his hand gripping the golden statuette, at the beautifully cut new dinner jacket I had watched him shrug himself into not three hours ago.

'Finally I'd like to thank my beautiful wife, Eve. As many of you will know, we are looking forward to the future with great excitement. We have an exciting year ahead of us. She has asked me to tell you all something. As of today she is retiring from the motion picture industry. She will concentrate on being a wife and mother instead. In this day and age, I can only step back and admire her even more than I do, for she is going against the tide of modern opinion somewhat.' He gave a delicate cough. Then he stared at me. Not at me, but at me. I can't explain it. 'But it's good to know that some people do still hold onto the old traditions.'

The old men were nodding and clapping, the old women whispering and smiling at me. I sat alone in my hard seat, no one either side of me. I could hear him talking, saying these things. I nodded, because I knew it was right what he was saying. I honestly believed it was right, you see. I thought I shouldn't be around here any more. I started humming to myself, as the applause grew louder.

I'll be around
No matter how you treat me now
I'll be around when he's gone

One of the ladies in the row in front of me turned in her seat. She had horn-rimmed spectacles on, long gloves, a bright ginger stole. Emeralds glittered in her ears, on her neck, on the stole itself, so huge and plentiful I thought of the lair of the Great Wizard of Oz – green stalactites flashing every-where. 'Well done, dear,' she said. 'Good for you. What a wonderful thing to do.' I hummed some more, nodding furiously at her.

'Eve, dear, this is for you, for us,' Gilbert called out, with a flourish, and the applause was louder than ever. Someone stood up. They all stood up. I couldn't. I was afraid I might fly away if I did. There were faces staring at me, standing up, turning around and staring. I saw the Baxters, whispering to each other: Joe adjusting his cufflinks and smiling at me, nodding indul-gently; Lenny, chewing gum, nodding at his brother. Next to Joe Baxter's corseted, respectable wife stood Moss Fisher. He clapped and clapped, smiling his crocodile smile.

There were white roses all over the house when we arrived home. Gilbert clutched his statuette as though it might fly away like I wanted to. It was ten o'clock, not late, but Gilbert wanted to change his shirt before we went out to celebrate at the Cocoanut Grove.

'Congratulations, Mr Travers!' Victoria said, almost shyly. 'You deserve that statue, everyone says so. May I hold it?' Gilbert handed it to her, indulgently, his lips making a moue of enjoy-ment. She held it, her hands sagging slightly under its unexpected heft, then curtseyed to each of us. 'Thank you, Jesus! Thank you, Mamma! I wanna say—' Her eyes swept over me. 'Oh, you look tired, Miss Eve. Do you want a glass of milk? I'll get you a glass of milk.'

I sank into an armchair. Gilbert stayed standing, pacing up and down. I saw him look at his reflection in the dark window.

'You'll stay here, then,' he said flatly. 'You must be tired.'

'I—' I didn't know what I was. I didn't want to be alone, I knew that. But to be with other people seemed unbearable, too. To smile and make chit-chat, be congratulated and admired, this farce, this stupid farce. I shivered, I was very cold. 'Maybe I'll come for a little while.'

'Eve.' Gilbert came over towards me. He crouched on his

haunches, his hands on either side of the chair, so I was trapped. He smiled, one black brow raised. He was so alive, so virile, so bursting with confidence and vigour. 'Eve, you need to consider your future now, dear.'

'You've considered it for me,' I said, fighting to get the words out.

He leaned forward so our faces were almost touching. I could smell stale cigarettes and whisky on his breath. One stray eyebrow hair curled out onto his shiny, tanned, porous forehead. It was grey, the others were black. 'I'm doing what's best. You don't know what you're doing.'

'I do,' I said. 'I've just been tired. Things are . . . hard.'

'Mmm.' He grunted, and adjusted his position so he was kneeling. 'I'm worried about you. The studio is, too. Your friends, your family. We know you're not yourself at the moment. So you need someone to take care of it for you.'

I tried to keep my breathing steady. I faced him down, staring into his black eyes. 'Take care of what? Of me?'

His lips twitched. 'Of it all, the whole damn thing. Now, my dear. You've had your time in the sun, but now you're going to be a mother. I can provide everything we need. You don't need to act any more. You don't like the studio, do you?' I shook my head. He was right. Maybe he was right. 'So you don't go there. You stay at home and bring up our son.' He said softly, 'It's my time now. Got that?'

Victoria came bustling back into the room. 'Nice glass of milk and I found you some cookies, here we are, Miss Eve—'

He flung one arm out behind him. 'Go away, please, Victoria.' His voice was calm, cold. 'Leave us be. Mrs Travers isn't feeling well. Go.'

'Victoria—' I called out.

'Shut up. Just go,' Gilbert said again, more loudly.

And Victoria bowed her head so I couldn't catch her eye. She turned slowly and left, shutting the door behind us, and I knew then that help was gone. Gilbert put his hands on my neck, gripping me firmly, so my head wobbled above his wrists, as if totally separate from my body. 'You are sick. Your mind is confused.

You've done some things that I've never asked you about. And I won't. But you have to understand, my wife must be like Caesar's: above reproach. My dear, I think it's best if you remove yourself a little. You're – well, you're a danger to yourself.'

Then he took one of the white roses that stood in a vase on the sideboard beside us. He pulled it across my chest, so the thorns caught on my skin, snagging and tearing, beading blood. I pushed his hand away, and he gripped my fingers around the stem of the rose, so the scent caught my nose, as the thorns pressed into the pads of my fingers, and I screamed.

'No!' I said, pushing away from him. He wrapped his fingers around my neck again, his grip like iron, and I knew I couldn't break free.

'Oh, you are. You're mad,' he said, hissing at me. 'Well, let's be polite and call it unstable, darling, everyone knows it.'

'I'm not,' I said, struggling to breathe. 'Just – I can't see things clearly. I want to—' His hands tightened around my throat and I cried out. 'Stop it, Gilbert! Please . . . please stop.'

'I won't hurt you, Eve,' Gilbert said. He loosened his hands, slid them onto my shoulders, shook me slightly, chuckling as if it was all a joke. 'Don't be ridiculous, dear. I only want to help you. We're seeing a doctor on Monday, you and I. And he'll help you.'

'I don't need a doctor,' I said. But I knew I did. I knew I needed rescuing in some way, just not by Gilbert.

'Well, I think you do.' Gilbert looked down at his nails. 'The studio does. Your friends do. People are starting to talk. He's a very good doctor. You'll start to see everything clearly again, afterwards.'

'I'm not going to a doctor,' I said, sitting upright and struggling out of my chair. 'I want my life back, I can decide what I—'

He pushed me back dismissively, as if I were a cardboard cut-out, and I fell heavily into the low-sprung seat with a howl of weary, impotent rage.

'Shut up,' Gilbert said. 'Shut the hell up. Now I'm going to change my shirt, and I'm going out tonight, and you know, Eve, dear? I'm going to be the most popular person in the room, for once, *for once*, and you won't be there. Who knows what my reward will be?' He looked down at me with an ugly expression. 'Not a pregnant bag of bones with a lopsided hairline who's like a feral cat in heat. You're disgusting, my darling. Only a blind man would want you now, do you realise that? And one more thing.' He snapped off his cufflinks, started unbuttoning his shirt, as he walked towards the door. 'I'm afraid there's bad news about that fag Conrad Joyce. Another of your fag friends, got himself into trouble.'

My blood ran cold. I rubbed my bruised neck and then said, quietly, 'What do you mean?'

'Moss told me as we arrived this evening. He shot himself. Last night.'

I breathed in, gasping for air, as if I'd just jumped into an icy sea. 'Conrad? He's dead?'

'Oh, he's dead all right.' Gilbert gave a little whistle. 'Shot clean through the head. He left a note, but it's the saddest thing, it's gone missing. Something about how he couldn't stand being a queer any longer and it was the best thing for him.' He cleared his throat. 'Well, I agree. I'm sure you don't, but then you love fags, you filthy whore. You're my wife full-time now, no more Eve Noel the star, so perhaps now you'll realise what decorous behaviour is and isn't.' His hand was on the door. He was drumming his fingers on the brass fingerplate, leaving smears. I would have to wipe those smears off. 'Goodnight, dear,' he said, his voice like honey. 'Get some rest. I'll see you tomorrow. Everything will be different, tomorrow.'

CHAPTER TWENTY-TWO

SUMMER HAS FINALLY come, almost too late, to the water-logged, lush fields around us. Suddenly it is beautifully warm, and we bask like cats in the unaccustomed heat. Since Tony arrived on set two weeks ago, the shoot has been transformed. Things are on time; people know what they should be doing. T.T. still stands around looking confused and pulling his hair out, but now it feels like part of the creative process rather than something costing us all thousands of dollars. I honestly believe Tony had a hand in that as well. And here in this green, lush valley, it feels like there really is nowhere lovelier.

In a short space of time Tony has turned the film around. We have a sense of purpose and I think we might just pull this off. I might be good. I don't think I ever realised it till now. We live in a bubble, I haven't seen the news or read a magazine in ages. I get up, go to work, say my lines, come home. I haven't weighed myself in days, or got undressed and stared, despairingly, at my fat arse, for weeks. I haven't 'accidentally' logged onto some site to see what a few teenage girls are saying about me, or checked out TMZ to make sure another schmuck is taking up the paparazzi's attention. I think Sara thinks I've gone mad.

As for the white roses and everything – it's like another world. The LAPD don't seem to be any closer to finding out who it was. Every time I ask them, or Sara does, for an update they give a 'we're following several different lines of inquiry' brush-off which Sara has to read out to me with a straight face. Anyway, I feel safe here. I've persuaded Angie's boss Gavin to let me stay on in the Oak. She agrees with me – it's no big secret we're here, and there's security in the hotel twenty-four/seven.

To be honest I don't think about it too much at the moment. We are working hard, there's no time for delays now. I'm in the zone: I understand the production, what's missing, what needs fixing. I know what the budget is, where we're over-spending. I know when T.T. needs hand-holding and when the light's not right or how to cheer up a pissed-off cameraman. I can see the schedule in my head, what's missing, what's on track. I grew up with a dad who felt more at home with the challenge of starting a business than the challenge of family life. Maybe I'm my father's daughter, not my mother's. Instead of fixating on the bad stuff and what might happen, I'm just getting on with it. And at the end of every day I fall into bed completely knackered, but happy.

A week or so after our strange trip to see Eve, I'm sitting outside on a warm, starry night watching the second AD round up everyone for the next shot. It's a night shoot, at an old timbered cottage a few miles away that's standing in for Shakespeare's house. Annie the modern heroine has just landed back in the past and met the Bard for the first time. He's sitting in the garden, musing, and she surprises him. He jumps and breaks the quill he's holding, which makes him furious, and then he stares at her and thinks she's a spirit from another dimension because of her appearance.

It's a bit chilly, and I'm wrapped in a big cardigan. Alec and Paula are standing next to the monitors, talking intently. I watch Alec, admiring his legs in his Shakespearian costume. He totally pulls it off, because there should be something ridiculous about a man in a leather blouson shirt and knick-erbocker-style breeches having an intense discussion with a woman in jeans but he looks . . . right, somehow. He's always totally at ease, wherever he is.

I can hear him now. 'Well, when will you know, Paula?'

Paula sighs sharply. 'I have no idea. Ask T.T. Ask Tony. There's no one available.'

They're talking about old Anne, the part they were hoping Eve Noel would play. They've been on the phone to agents again all day, seeing who's available. They want it to be a Name and they've had no luck so far.

Alec is cross. I can hear the thin reedy tone his voice gets when he's peeved floating across to me in the chill night air. 'It's getting bloody ridiculous, Paula darling. I can't react off Doug.'

'You're going to have to, I'm afraid.' Paula is extremely calm. 'We'll know later this morning.' She looks tiredly at her watch; it's nearly two a.m.

'What happened with Eve Noel?' Bill Claremont asks, looking through his director's viewfinder at me, then at Alec. 'Thought we were going to try her.'

'Didn't you hear?' Alec shoots me a look. 'Tony and Sophie went to see her, but some old bag answered the door and said she was dead.'

'That's not quite right.' I raise my voice so they can hear me from where I'm sitting on the ground. 'I think it was her. I'm just not sure. And she wasn't . . . an old bag.'

'That's not much help to us, is it, dearest.' Alec is sarcastic. 'Anyway, if she is dead, when did she die? Wouldn't it have been on the news? She was a huge star.'

Bill steps behind a camera. 'Not necessarily. The story I always heard was she had a breakdown and came back to England. Don't know if it's true but it was fifty years ago, you know. That's a long time. People forget about you. They watch your films on bank holidays but they don't wonder where you are.'

'But that's extraordinary, when you think about it,' Alec says. 'She just – what? Vanished? Hid herself away? What on earth happened to her to make her do that?' He turns to me, almost accusatory. 'You were always obsessed with her. Isn't there some biography or something?'

'*Eve Noel and the Myth of Hollywood*,' I say. 'I've read it more than any other book I've ever read.'

'So you've read it more than *Fifty Shades of Grey*. Big deal.' Alec doubles up with hilarity. 'Ah, sometimes I make myself laugh so much it hurts.'

I ignore him. 'It only goes up to 1961. After Conrad Joyce killed himself she went away for a few months, no one knows where. The biographer interviewed this driver at the studio who says he took her for a drive some time in June but he wouldn't tell him where he dropped her. It's weird. What happened to her afterwards, no one knows.'

'Didn't she have any family?' Alec asks, interested despite himself.

'Her parents were dead by then, within a couple of months of each other. She wasn't close to them, they were cold fishes. She had a sister . . . but she died. Drowned when she was eight and Eve was six. Her roommate at drama school says she blamed herself.'

Paula is peering into the camera next to her chair. 'Well, she was an actress. It's easy to make yourself invisible, if you want to walk down the street and don't want to be noticed.'

'How extraordinary. I *always* want to be noticed,' Alec says.

'I know what you mean,' I tell Paula, ignoring Alec. 'You don't have to have twenty photographers waiting outside some bar for you. But you have to be clever about it. If you adjust the way you walk, don't act suspicious, keep yourself to yourself – people don't see you.'

'Exactly,' says Paula. 'I'm telling you, no one goes looking for you unless you want people to know you're hiding.'

I pull awkwardly on the long sleeves of my granny cardigan. 'What I don't understand is that she told her agent she'd see us. She sent her an email. Why would she do that if she was just going to deny all knowledge of us and say she was someone called Rose when we turn up at the door?' I don't like talking about it; the memory is still unsettling, upsetting. Those blank, sad eyes. Whoever that woman was, she needed help.

'Rose?' Paula says. 'You never said that.'

'Yeah.' I pull the cardigan round me tightly. '*A Girl Named Rose* – weird, eh?'

'I love that movie,' Paula sighs.

'But that doesn't prove anything, either way,' Alec says. 'If she was Eve, she might say she was called Rose, if she's off her rocker. And she might say she was Rose if she was trying to be Eve. It's the part she's best known for. Everyone knows that film.'

'There's something that doesn't make sense.' I shake my head. 'If it is her, why did she tell her agent she'd see us and then freak out when we turn up? What's she been doing all these years? By herself, in that creepy house.'

Bill looks thoughtful.

'Maybe she's not by herself,' he says. 'Maybe she's got someone with her. Or maybe she's dead and someone else is . . . I don't know. Beyond me.' He shrugs.

We're all silent for a moment. 'No, it was her, I'm sure it was her,' I say obstinately. 'I'm not mad.' I rub my eyes. 'I know what I saw.'

I sound too emphatic. There's an uncomfortable silence, broken only by the thud of a sound man hitting something with a boom and cursing.

Alec breaks the tension. 'Well, you say that, but you did go out with that pranny Dave Oldman,' he says. 'For four years. What you see and what others see isn't quite the same thing if I'm honest, darling.'

I can't help smiling, and he pats my arm. 'You were just jealous,' I say.

'You bet I was. He was cute, for all he was an idiot.' His eyes glint.

'Oh, go away and check your make-up again.' I sit back down on the damp grass.

At that moment my phone rings and Sara, who is sitting

next to me, glances up from her laptop. 'Want me to get it?'

'It's fine.' I look down at the flashing screen, and see a photo of a face I haven't seen for a while. I think for a second, and then I pick up the phone and say, 'Hey, Tina!' Sara looks up quickly.

'Hey, Sophie. How – how are you? How is everything?' I'd forgotten how timid she sounds, with that low, slightly lisping tone. I'm pleased to hear from her; but I don't know what to say. *Do your lips still look like that?* 'Good, thanks. How – how was Vegas? How are you?'

'Great. Thank you. The procedure went really well.'

'I'm so glad!'

'Thanks. Yes, this whole process has been . . . very, er, helpful. Made me see a lot of things more clearly.' Tina gives a little laugh, which I find disconcerting. 'I'm sorry, I just realised what a strange time it is to call, but I had to speak to you, Sophie. Did you get my message?'

'What message?'

'I called you last week about coming back early – I was going to fly to London. I'm kind of going mad, hanging round here. I'd love to start with you again as soon as is convenient. I'll pay for the flight—'

I interrupt. 'When did you call me?'

'A few days ago. I left a message. I emailed you too. I know you've been busy—'

Tina's voice is really faint but it's still weird, hearing her after six, seven weeks. It takes me straight back to Hollywood. 'That's odd, I never got it.' I look round for Sara, but I can't see her. 'Look, there's no need for you to come over. Things are working out really well,' I say, then regret my choice of words. 'I mean, Sara's here and it's all fine so why don't you just take some more time for yourself and I'll see you back in LA.'

There's silence. 'Tina?' I ask tentatively, after a few seconds.

'I wanted to come back and help you right away,' Tina bleats, suddenly loud in the murmuring static. 'You need me.'

It's such a curious thing to say I can't reply immediately.

302

'Stay in Vegas for a while and I'll let you know what's going on.' I realise that doesn't sound good so I add, 'I'll need you soon, that's for sure! Sara's great, but she's not you.'

I realise someone's at my elbow and I turn to see Sara standing next to me, slightly out of breath, her eyes enormous as she watches me intently. I give a little start, and then roll my eyes and silently mouth, *Tina* at her, in a co-conspiratorial way that makes me feel shitty.

Sara says in a loud voice, 'Sophie, I have Artie on the line for you, it's urgent. About the police case.'

I stare at her. 'Hey, Tina,' I say into the phone. 'I have to go. Please don't worry. Enjoy your time and I'll see you in a month.'

'But—' Tina says. 'But Sophie, are you sure? Are you OK?'

'I'm good. I'll see you soon.' I say goodbye and end the call, turning to Sara.

'Is that Artie?'

'What?' She smiles. 'Oh, no, he's not there. I just figured you could do with a little help.' Then she says, 'I mean, not to – Tina is great, I just thought maybe—' She passes her hand over her forehead, like she's tired. I've noticed it lately, she seems less perky. 'I'm jealous of her, I guess! I like working for you.'

'Sara, I—' I look around, as there's some sort of commotion on set and I think they'll need me soon. 'What are you going to do next, after this job?'

'Is Tina coming here?' she asks immediately.

'No, no, of course not.' I choose my words carefully. 'I mean, it's just – it's a three-month contract and it's halfway through now and this has been great, but – don't you wonder what you'll do afterwards?'

'Sure,' she says. 'It's OK. I've got a plan.'

'Cool. What is it?'

She taps the side of her nose. 'Can't tell you. But you're going to love it.'

'Are you going back into acting?' I say suddenly.

She gives me a strange look. 'No. Why would you say that?'

'No reason,' I backtrack. 'Just think it's a shame you don't do it any more. You were really good.'

'I think I've found something else to be good at,' she says. 'And it's all thanks to you.' She touches my arm and points over to where T.T. is standing. 'They need you, Sophie.'

My mind is racing as Alec comes towards me and takes my hands. 'Do you mind standing in to play an old lady?' he says. 'Mm, I see a little touch of loose skin around the upper arms. Yes, you'll do perfectly.'

He smiles and I roll my eyes. His fingers are warm in my clasp, and the night is chilly. 'Who was that on the phone?'

'Oh, my old assistant. My assistant, sorry.'

'The one with the crazy face?' I bat him lightly on the arm. 'Where'd she go?'

'She went to Vegas to get her crazy face fixed,' I say, watching Sara walking away. 'At least I think she did. I'm not sure any more.'

CHAPTER TWENTY-THREE

NIGHT SHOOTS TOTALLY mess me up. By the time we've finished, a rosy dawn is creeping out behind the black trees around the cottage. Kim, a new on-set security guard, drives me and Alec back to the hotel. I look at my watch and it's almost five o'clock. I'm numb with tiredness, that slightly fizzing feeling you get after a red-eye flight. Thank God we don't have to work today.

I'm still in the loose cotton Elizabethan dress Annie changes into during the scene; they said I could wear it home. I stare out at the sunny yellow wheat fields. The sky is now bright, candy pink.

'Red sky in the morning, shepherd's warning,' Alec says, beside me. 'What does it mean? I've never known a red sky in the morning mean a storm's on the way.'

'I don't know.' I think about it. 'You don't really get dawn in LA. Not in the same way.'

'Get some lovely ones in London,' Alec says. 'Rising up over the rooftops. I often see it if I'm on my way home from somewhere.'

'I bet you do,' I say. 'How's Eloise, by the way?'

He frowns. 'Who? Oh, her. She's – I think she's fine, isn't she?'

'Alec!' I say, shaking my head.

'I'm not the total slag you think I am, you know,' he replies.

'Of course you are.'

He clicks his tongue almost impatiently, and purses his lips. 'You don't understand. I'm not really like that.'

I put my hand on his knee. 'It's fine by me,' I say. 'Honestly, I don't care. You never messed me around. I don't have any hard feelings.'

The car purrs along, and otherwise there's silence. There's a dewy mist rising just above the contours of the fields, gentle curves like bodies. Across the horizon towards the south, a bird rises up above the yellow corn. I watch it circling, higher and higher.

'Sophie, there's something I want to tell you—' Alec opens his mouth to say something, and then suddenly clamps it shut.

I rub my eyes. 'Go on then.'

We swerve around a corner and I loll against him.

'Never mind,' he says, after a pause. 'Doesn't matter. I'm talking rubbish.' He kisses my hand swiftly, and it's so abrupt that I feel my heart jolt. I hold his hand in mine.

'Alec—' I say. 'You think you have to change for me. You don't. I love you just the way you are.'

'I loathe the way you misquote romcoms and try and pass them off as your own off-the-cuff remarks,' he says, and then he leans forward and kisses me. 'Darling Sophie.'

He slides his hand around my neck, his tongue into my mouth, and I hear him sigh, deeply, somewhere in the back of his throat. I am surprised, but I move towards him, sliding my hand up and around his smooth neck. I'm not *that* surprised, after all. It's Alec. Haven't I been wanting this to happen, since the day I first discovered he was on this film? The answer is yes.

I need to give Kim the new guard the slip, so as we walk through the deserted lobby I say, 'Give us a minute, will you, Kim?' I wink at her. 'Angie's in the next room, it's fine. You can leave me here. I just want to say goodnight to Alec. See you tomorrow.'

She nods shyly. We creep up the stairs, tiptoeing hand in

306

hand and trying to avoid the creaking floorboards. We walk past my room, down the corridor and around the corner, up some stairs, to Alec's room. When we get inside, he shuts the door and pushes me against it, cupping my breasts in his hands and burying his head between them.

'My Elizabethan wench,' he murmurs. 'Aren't you?'

He kisses the top of each breast in turn, running his lips over my skin, then fumbles with his leather breeches.

'I love you in costume.' I pull his cotton shirt out, take off the leather top. It makes a creaking, rubbing sound against my skin. 'I love the leather.'

'Me too,' says Alec. He gives me a smile. 'I really didn't think this'd happen. Aren't you seeing that chap?'

'Who?' I pause for a second, thinking of George.

'Patrick Drew. The surfer dude with the idiot hair. I thought you were banging him. Said so in *Heat* last week.'

'No, absolutely not.' I don't want to be annoyed, or get distracted, not by Patrick's kind face, his intense gaze, his warm hands. I shake my head. 'He's not an idiot—' I stop. 'It's all made up, you should know that. I'm totally footloose and fancy free.' I run my hands over his shoulders, his smooth, pale skin like marble.

'I am so glad to hear that.' He tugs my knickers off. I'm not wearing a bra. I'm naked underneath the loose cotton shift and corset, my hair free from its wig, tousled and longer than it has been for ages, my shoulders bare. He puts his hands round my waist, staring at me in delight. 'What an unexpected treat this is going to be,' he says, as we climb onto the bed. I laugh. 'I'm going to enjoy every inch of you, Sophie, and I hope you return the favour.' He pulls my hand down to his crotch, and rocks his erection against me. I kiss his neck, smiling into his skin, because it just feels lovely to have someone again, and it's him, it's Alec, it's – just great.

It's nearly seven by the time we fall asleep curling together, my head on his chest, his arms around me, and then half an hour or so later I'm woken as he pushes me aside and rolls to the other side of the bed, where he lies on his back, his hands clasped together on his breast bone, like a prince on a medieval tomb. I stare blearily at him, and then drift off again and sleep like the dead, until a noise wakes us and we're up again.

I'd forgotten, when we were together that summer so long ago, that I'd roll against him so hopefully, and he'd always leap out of bed in the mornings. He never wanted sex then, though I always did. The one thing George had in his favour was that he wanted sex. Most of the time. In fact, that's – yes, that's the one thing we had in common.

'Come back to bed,' I say, holding the duvet open.

'No fear, you'll just clamp your woman muscles around me and I'll never get free,' he says, leaning over and kissing me. 'Besides, look at the time. It's nearly eleven.'

I lie back grumpily. 'But we didn't go to sleep till seven. It's fine. They're letting us sleep in. Sara isn't coming to wake me till midday.'

Alec is tying his dressing gown, a blue silk affair with a nice purple weave to it, tightly around him. 'Well – but we don't want to lose the rhythm of the day.'

He wants to get rid of me. Of course. I have to get out of here before he thinks I'm begging him to let me stay. Poor Alec – I sneak a look at him. He's rattled. He's worried I'm going to start crying and telling him I want his babies, because all women fall for him: Eloise the poised French epitome of elegance; Helen the bouncy unguarded runner; even Margaret the pensioner tour guide at Anne Hathaway's cottage – they all fall for him, because they know he's bad news in some way, but he's curiously comforting at the same time, unthreatening. Why? I'm dangerously close to being that person too, I realise.

I sit up and ruffle my hair in what I hope is a cool, unbothered fashion. 'Actually, darling, I need to speak to Artie anyway,' I say, ignoring the fact that it's three a.m. in LA. 'Can you do me a favour?' I stretch and yawn. 'I'd better get back, but I don't want to do the walk of shame in this.' I hold up the Elizabethan shift. 'Would you mind slipping along to my room and grabbing some clothes? Jeans and a T-shirt, they're both in that cupboard on the left as you go in.'

Alec is torn between laziness and relief. 'Sure,' he says, relief getting the better of him. 'Let me just put my dressing gown on. Give me the key.'

After he's gone I lie back again, rubbing myself luxuriantly against the sheets. It's lovely being here with him, it's lovely feeling someone else's skin on mine, someone inside me, someone I love as much as Alec. In fact, it's a lovely day. Everything is good. I reach over to my bag and take out my BlackBerry, turn it on, scroll through my emails on the achingly slow Wi-Fi.

Then the phone messages start loading, and buzzing as I hold the phone in my hand. One after the other.

'Sophie, where are you? It's been two hours now since the last one . . . call me, this is Artie.'

'Sophie dear, it's Tony. Would you call us? We'd love to know that you're all right. I'm sure you are – just be good to have it confirmed! Ah – if you could. Just call. Please. I don't know if you've been back to your room yet, but please don't – it's a maniac. I'm sure you can't have been.'

I jump out of bed, pull on the white towelling robe that hangs on the back of the door, and race down the corridor, around the corner. There's a crowd of people, a policeman looking like an outrider in a fluorescent tabard and black jacket, a rumbling walkie-talkie attached to his shoulder. 'She's here,' he says briefly, as he sees me approach. I run into my bedroom.

The ancient wallpaper has been ripped and torn off. The curtains are slashed, and there's stuff all over the floor, ground into the carpet: make-up, jewellery, everything. I found out later that's so it didn't make any noise. They used the fire extinguisher to crush it all, like a tarmac roller. No one heard anything. The old, old walls of the Oak helped them, whoever they were.

Alec is sitting on my bed, looking dazed. Angie and Sara are talking to the policeman, Tony next to them, then Nicola the hotel manager rubbing her hands together, and when I burst in they all look up in relief.

'Oh, my God,' says Tony. 'Thank goodness.' He puts his hand on his heart. 'My dear, you gave us a fright – LOOK OUT!'

Something swings low in front of me and Sara screams.

'Jesus!' Angie shouts, her caramel skin pale. 'Fix that fucking thing to the wall, guys!' Another policeman, by the door, mutters something.

'What the hell—' I say. I can feel my whole body shaking, and yet when I look down I'm totally still.

'Nice rig-up,' says the policeman. He glances at me, recognises me, clears his throat and then carries on, his voice suddenly low and serious. 'So, uh, yeah. Whoever did it knew what they was doing. Fixed it up to swing at you when you opened the door. They'd have killed you.'

My eyes fix on something hanging above me. The fire extinguisher, looped up and around over a hook on the ceiling, is swinging gently, as though it's caught in a breeze.

I look up at it. 'What?' I say.

'Someone drugged Angie,' Sara says. 'She should have been listening for you to come back. Kim told her you were back at the hotel but she didn't reply. Kim's new. She should have done. But because she didn't, she saved your life.'

'Well, no,' Angie says. 'If you'd have gone straight back to your room –' she avoids my gaze – 'I'd have come in and got this thing in my face.' She rubs her eyes. 'I didn't wake up till ten. I was on the floor in my uniform. Someone must have spiked my tea.' She looks round. 'I don't understand.'

'How did you – find it?'

'I woke up and I couldn't get the interconnecting door to work. I called Sara and she couldn't either. We called Nicola and got her to let me in. She opened the door and this swung at her. If she'd been two inches taller she'd be dead.'

'I normally wear heels, too,' says Nicola, who is rather short. She gives a nervous, near-hysterical giggle. 'Girls, eh?'

I shake my head. I still don't understand.

Then I see it.

310

Directly in front of me is what I would have seen first when I opened the door, written in some kind of marker pen, in the mirror of the hideous seventies wardrobe:

YOU THOUGHT I WOULDN'T FIND YOU

There's a white rose, taped to the door.

Alec stands up and comes over to me. 'It's OK, darling,' he says, putting his arms round me. 'It's just some drunk idiot with a grudge. We'll find them, don't you worry.' He kisses my head, as the others watch us, ridiculous in our dressing gowns. I remain still, watching the extinguisher swing on the thin rope above me, creaking like a hanging man in a gale.

CHAPTER TWENTY-FOUR

'LISTEN TO ME,' Artie yells down the phone, as the car eases along the gravel drive. 'You don't get out of that car, you do what they tell you, you go straight to London. I'm coming tonight. I'm nearly at LAX. I'll see you tomorrow. OK?'

'OK, Artie, but there's no need. The police are covering it, and I've got security everywhere I look.'

'What the fuck use was security before, hey? HEY? She fell asleep, for fuck's sake!'

'She was drugged. Someone knew what they were doing. It's not her fault. They got past security last time, remember? They're clever – whoever he or she is, they're clever.'

There's the sound of muffled shouting. 'I'm in the car. I'll see you soon.'

'Artie, please,' I say. 'I'm fine, I don't need you—'

'I'm coming anyway,' he says awkwardly. 'I have a few meetings with Patrick and some producers for his next project. He's in town for a premiere, you remember? I told you. We were gonna have you guys go together?'

'No,' I say. 'You didn't tell me.'

'I did. This is crap, this is total BS! I've been trying to get a bunch of stuff through to you the last couple of weeks and you never return my calls.'

'What stuff?' I say. 'What are you talking about?'

'I think your assistant needs some fine-tuning, is what I'm

saying. We'll talk about it. Don't worry, honey. I'll see you tomorrow. Stay cool, take care of yourself.'

We're on the main road, driving east towards London. It's late afternoon and the sun is beating down on my neck as we head into the woods beyond the hotel. I look out of the window, at the countryside I know so well and have come to love as the trees close around me. I think about Mum; I haven't told my parents I'm leaving. As the trees flash and flicker sunlight I can't see my face, and when I jump with a start at a branch clattering against the window suddenly a reflection appears and Sara is staring back at me. I gasp and then realise it's not Sara, it's me. My fringe, once my most recognisable feature, has started to grow out and I brush it to the side or pin it back. Anyway, we could be sisters.

She cried as she said goodbye to me at the hotel. 'I feel like I've let you down. I'm supposed to be watching out for you. I'm supposed to know everything about you.'

I'd hugged her tight, not really knowing what to say. 'No one could watch out for this, Sara. Don't be ridiculous.'

She'd gripped my arms. 'It shouldn't be like this.'

I stared into her eyes and I thought it then, how alike we are. She had a Breton-style navy-and-white striped top on; I have the same, but hers has a red trim. I've seen it somewhere before I'm sure, and I can't remember where. How cruel life is that she, a Californian girl with her perky smile, her natural talent and her slightly intense drive to succeed, to be good, to be liked, would have been better off if she'd been me. Her personality in my body.

'You shouldn't have known anything. I don't know anything. It's fine.' I'm strangely calm as I'm saying this to her.

I look in the glass again, at my reflection, looking for Sara's face, remembering the night long ago when she persuaded me to let Bryan cut my fringe. It occurs to me for the first time that I think I slept with him that same night after he did it. How strange that she was the one who helped me all those years ago and I still haven't helped her at all, unless you count hiring her which, really, is not some great act of friendship on my part, is it? Did she know I slept with him? . . . I'm going mad. I'm seeing stuff that's not there. She's not me, I'm not her. I sit back, my mind racing, and bite on my thumbnail, lines of dialogue racing through my head. What's real, and what isn't?

'Go away. She shouldn't have sent you. I'm Rose. Eve's been dead for forty years.'

Her parents were dead.

A Girl Named Rose.

I'm Rose. I'm Rose. I'm Rose.

My face in the mirror, Sara's face this morning, her top, that stripy top, the face at the door . . .

And suddenly, I see it all.

I scream, as we emerge out of the wood and into the bright sunshine. Jimmy swerves, Gavin looks over his shoulder, one big square hand on the dashboard.

'What? What's up?'

'Jimmy.' I lean forward. 'I need to go to Eve Noel's house again. I've just realised something—'

Jimmy corrects his steering but doesn't turn round. 'What's this? My instructions were to take you straight to London, Soph—'

'I don't care.' My knuckles are white, gripping onto the headrest. 'You have to take me there. I'm sorry. I'll be ten minutes, no more.' He looks in the rear-view mirror. 'It's really important, Jimmy,' I say. 'Trust me. I wouldn't ask you if it wasn't. You trust me, don't you?'

Gavin says, 'I'm not letting you go somewhere I ain't called them up about—'

'You can call the police, let them come in with me – you can come in with me. I promise it's not dangerous.' Now I see it clearly, I know it's OK. One side of the mystery, at least. 'There's nothing there to be afraid of.' I turn back to Jimmy. 'Please, *please*, Jimmy. If you don't, I'll get out at the next set of lights and go there myself. I'm not a prisoner, for goodness' sake.'

314

'Fine,' says Jimmy reluctantly. 'Though what Tony'll say about it I've no idea.'

'Tony won't mind,' I say. 'I'll cover for you, honestly. I have to go.'

Five minutes later, we're rolling up the sparse gravel drive once more, towards the dirty white house. The ivy seems even more out of control than last time; it seems to ooze out of the building.

We grind to a halt and sit on the drive, while the engine runs. I get out and shut the door. 'Stay there. I'll call you if I need anything.'

'Ten minutes, then I'm coming in,' Gavin says. I show him my phone is on, and walk up to the front door to the old rusting black letters, and as I stand there I remember the smell of oil and musty age. I can hear a cat mewing, and I ring the rickety bell. I'm just becoming convinced once more there's no one there, when the door opens, without any preceding sound.

She's standing there again.

Those blank dark eyes, the fine, translucent skin, the delicate bones in her cheeks, at her neck. Her hand is clutching the frame.

'What do you want?' she says. Her eyes dart to the black car behind me. 'Why have you come back?'

'My name's Sophie Leigh,' I say. 'I'm looking for Eve Noel.'

She swallows. 'I know who you are,' she says. 'And I told you before. Eve's dead.'

'No, she's not,' I say. 'You're Eve. I know you are.'

She laughs, and shakes her head. Her hands shake. 'You've seen me once. How are you so sure of that?'

A hard knot is forming in my throat. 'I've seen every one of your films hundreds of times,' I tell her. 'I'd know you anywhere. I live in your old house. I'm an actress, not as good as you. But I know how you can hide yourself away if you want, so no one looks for you. And I know sometimes you want to become someone else. You're not Rose. You're Eve. I don't know what happened, but you're Eve. Where's Rose, Eve? Where is she?'

She inhales, with a long, soft hiss, and I feel my skin prickling.

'No.' She bares her teeth. 'No,' she repeats, her voice rising so it's a wail, long, ghastly, animal-like. She makes to push the door shut.

But I put my foot in the way. 'I'm not here to upset you,' I say. 'I won't tell anyone. I just – want to know.'

'Why?' She gives a little laugh, pressing against the door, squashing my foot tighter. For all that she's tiny, she's surprisingly strong. 'What business is it of yours?'

'None, none at all,' I tell her. 'But . . . I loved Eve. I know you didn't want to be her any more, but . . . I know you're not Rose.' I take a deep breath and ask again. 'Where is she?'

A soft voice behind her says, 'Eve. Open the door. It's all right, dearest. It's all right.'

I am very still, praying the men in the car don't move, make a sound. The door opens wider with a slow creaking sigh and I step back, my mouth falling open. Because even though I'd realised this must be the truth, it's still a shock.

There's two of them, standing in front of me. They are almost identical, but Eve is slighter, more uncertain. Her eyes are blank. The woman standing next to her holds open the doorway. She nods at me. Like she's been expecting me.

'Hello, Sophie. I'm Eve's sister,' she says, her quiet voice firm, her gaze steady. 'I'm Rose.'

I LOST THE baby that night. The night of the Oscars, the night I found out that Conrad killed himself. I didn't really want to talk about it much, and I still can't. I started bleeding and it wouldn't stop. I went to hospital, and the next day something slipped out, after contractions that wracked me like a tide that goes in and out. She was a girl. I thought she would be. But she was dead.

I never saw her. They never let me see her. I don't know what her face looked like or . . . what kind of person she was. I couldn't keep her alive, because I wasn't good enough to look after her, to be able to do anything right, to stand up for myself or for others, and that's why she died. But I wish I had seen her. Just once.

In the hospital it was calm and white, and people talked about me in low voices, and they wore white too. They kept me sedated afterwards. I knew this because when I was awake I'd start to cry, and they'd give me something to drink, chalky, curiously dry, and then I'd fall asleep again.

But I kept on waking up and crying, and I kept on shouting, and trying to climb out of bed, to leave. I didn't know where I was going, I just remembered feeling that these things were important, and the voice in my head that was the real me

317

kept saying I had to leave, to go back to Rose. I'd had the letter about Rose, and it was important. But then I realised that, perhaps, I *was* Rose, and it made sense. I'd left her behind in England, a ghost, and taken on this new person, and the new person was fake, she had to die.

When I wouldn't stop screaming and clinging onto things, when I scratched a nurse and bit through the cardboard clipboard that a doctor had in front of me, then they changed. They were impatient, im-patient, like they wanted another patient. They moved me somewhere, in an ambulance van, the windows blacked out. It was a large building high, high above the sea – I know because I caught a glimpse of the ocean as they loaded me from the stretcher, wriggling under the straps that bound me like a fish caught on the ship's deck. My stomach was still swollen, a dome, like something was in there, but there was nothing, nothing at all.

They said my body was too hot, so they packed me in ice. I couldn't make Rose fly out of me and watch from the ceiling to call out, tell me what was happening, tell anyone else. But who was there to tell? Once, a nurse said it was to lower my temperature, but I didn't know why and she wouldn't tell me. I was asleep, most of the time, but when I was awake I screamed again. They fed me raw eggs. I saw them beating them up. I bit my tongue in a rage, and I remember the blood everywhere.

All I wanted was someone to come, someone to help me. A friend. But no one came. So then it became a blur, and by the time they put the pads on my temples I almost welcomed it. I was mad by then. I was three people, me, Rose me, Eve me. Which one was I? I knew what they were doing, and I hoped that perhaps it would stop everything, make it clearer which was which. Because there was no one else around, no one. And that's when I realised I had to help myself. And as I tried to remember the things that hadn't been shocked out of me, I remembered the panel at the back of the wardrobe.

The electric shocks left burn marks where the electrodes had been. There was one every day, but I don't know how many days. Still today, when I touch my temples, I can feel the memory of it, the bone moving under the singed skin.

Two months after the night of the Oscars, it was mid-June, and they told me I could come out of the clinic, and go home. It happened because people stopped taking notice of me, because I stopped screaming and drawing attention to myself, and other people arrived who were screaming, and I finally got my head back enough to remember what I'd learned before: if you just make no noise and fade into the background then you're not a threat any more. I should have remembered earlier. Perhaps I wasn't the actress I thought I'd been.

A car came to pick me up, and I didn't know who the driver was, or where it was from, but I got in it anyway, because I knew if I didn't they might change their minds and I'd been waiting for him now for two days. I was slow at walking – I was still sore from my baby's birth. And the burns made me confused; the sunlight was unexpected. The gates were painted black, very ornate, higher than the tallest ladder. There were palm trees lining the drive. A lady in a white hat was crossing the lawn behind me as we drove away, pushing a man in a wheelchair. She jabbed him sharply on the shoulder, and he sat upright as she said something to him. Yes, I was right, the ocean was below us, and we were high up.

The driver was friendly, I thought. He smiled at me, but I didn't know if I could trust him or not so I stayed hunched in the back. I didn't ask him where we were going. But he took me home. We sat in the drive and I looked at my house, at the blue shutters and the creeping jasmine.

'Here you are,' he said.

I didn't know what came next and I sat there, biting my fingers, while I tried to think.

'Could you wait here five minutes, please?' And I got out and went inside.

I knew Victoria of course, but she stared at me as though she didn't know who I was. Perhaps it was my hair; it had been shaved off at one point so I wouldn't pull at it, and now it was short and tufty like a boy's. She stared and then she cried. But though I didn't remember much, I remembered she had turned away and left me with Gilbert, the night I lost the baby. Her tears were crocodile's. It was strange, being back there. The house smelled different: flowers of summer out everywhere, a different kind of cleaning polish perhaps. I didn't know what it was. Anyway, I didn't have time.

I'd been keeping a list in a special code since they told me two days before that I was going home again. My actress's brain could remember scripts, still, no matter what was done to it, and I clung to that tiny bit of evidence that I might be able to save myself. I had memorised where everything was in my room. Nothing had changed. The clothes were beautifully pressed and evenly spaced out. The crystal scent bottles and my hairbrush set were polished and sparkling as if I might use them at any time. I didn't stop to look, though; I murmured the list under my breath, methodically putting the items I'd planned into a bag. Then I reached into the back of the wardrobe, where the wood came away from the beam holding it together. I took out the two letters from England, and I reread them. I understood now. Then I took out the purse. I'd stuffed it with money over the years, at first just dollar bills in case I ever needed change, then lately bigger notes that I'd saved up and exchanged, at the studio, at the bar, at a gas station. *Do you have a fifty for this change? I've got so many darned bills it's driving me crazy! Oh, thank you, thank you so much.* I knew I had to have something kept by. That went in the top and then I came back out again.

'Miss – where you going?'

I had the scarf tied over my head, the big sunny sunglasses that made me look like Eve. Who was Eve now, though? I smiled at Victoria. 'Mr Travers wants to take me to lunch.' I raised the bag. 'I have to bring him a couple of things. I'll see you later, Victoria.'

She looked nervously at me, and her eyes had tears in them. 'I'm so sorry for your loss, Miss Eve.'

I couldn't talk about the baby, not think about it, not think about it at all, otherwise I would lose myself completely. I thought about the sea, the horizon, the sky.

'Thank you. I'll see you later, Victoria.' I repeated it like a parrot.

She stepped forward, her pretty face full of concern. 'Oh, Miss Eve—'

'That's not me any more,' I said, loudly, in case anyone else was listening, and I swung the bag into the car. The driver was still there. I shut my eyes tight tight tight tight as we left the house. I didn't want to have any last sight of it, I didn't ever want to see it again.

'Just drive around for a while, would you?' I called tentatively into the front.

As we went down the winding roads and then onto Hollywood Boulevard, I looked out about me. There was Grauman's Chinese Theater, where my handprints were preserved for ever, next to Joan Crawford's: '*Luck and love, Eve Noel x*'. There were the stars on the pavements. My star was somewhere, I think outside a pizzeria. There were tourists peering at the ground, their huge cameras around their necks, families laughing in the sun. They couldn't see me. A little boy shuddered in excitement and opened his hands, then watched in slow-motion display as his ice-cream cone fell on to the ground, *splat*, like Tom and Jerry. His mouth opened wide and he screamed. I was glad I couldn't hear it. The car kept on going.

After a while, I said, 'We're going to the airport, please.'

'Yes, ma'am,' the driver said.

I saw him as his eyes snagged on mine in the mirror.

'Who paid you to collect me?' I asked him. 'Who do you work for?'

He hesitated. 'I work for Monumental Pictures, Miss Noel. I drove you a few times for *Lanterns Over Mandalay*. You won't remember.'

I shook my head; I couldn't remember, couldn't remember anything much about it, even what happened in it. 'I'm sorry. I've been away and my memory is not good any more. What's your name?'

'My name's Jack, Miss Noel.'

'Who's the – what did they want you to do with me?' I asked curiously. 'They sent you to pick me up?'

'Yes, ma'am. To take you home. Make sure you got home. Not take you anywhere else.'

'Oh,' I said. We were heading towards the freeway, the afternoon sun hanging yellow over Venice Beach. 'So – why are you doing this for me, then?'

There was a long silence.

'Because . . .' Jack paused. He looked in the mirror and I met his eye for the first time. He glanced at me for a fleeting second, then back to the road. 'I like your films,' he said. 'My wife and I, you see . . . First time I ever laid eyes on her was outside the movie palace, waiting to go in to *Helen of Troy*. We was set up on a blind date. And we ended up seeing that film four times!' He laughed.

I laughed too. 'Even I haven't seen it four times.'

'Well, it's worth it, I tell you. Alice loves you, Miss Noel. *A Girl Named Rose* – well, she says it's just a crying shame you didn't win that Academy Award. And . . . well, we've been worried about you. You know, I knew you was having that baby . . . we knew you was having a tough time. You hear things on the studio lot, rumours, you know. And you can't trust people these days.'

I didn't say anything, just gave a tiny nod.

'But I didn't believe it. Me and Alice, we always thought you were the best. We always said if we had a daughter, we'd call her Helen! And we did!'

'Really?' I smiled. 'How old is she?'

'She's two, Miss Noel.'

He cleared his throat, as though he was suddenly embarrassed, and then he said, 'When I was driving you, you were real nice. Polite. You always said, "Good morning, Jack", "Good afternoon, Jack", "Thank you very much". A lot of stars . . . they treat you like dirt. Make you feel like you're beneath them. So when they asked me to come today, I reckoned – if I can help her in any way, I will. After all, she helped me to find Alice. So that's what it is.'

I met his glance in the mirror. At last, a friend was here, someone to help me, and I didn't even know him.

'Thank you,' I whispered. 'Thank you so much.'

'Well, we're nearly there, miss. What you going to do when you get to the airport? Got a flight going somewhere exciting?'

My fingers stroked the roll of bills in my bag. 'I'll wait for one,' I said. 'I'm leaving today, no matter what happens.'

Jack didn't question me beyond saying, 'Where will you go?'

'I'm going home,' I said. I clutched the bag close to me. 'And I'm never coming back here.'

We were almost at the ocean. I could see the Santa Monica Pier, the ferris wheel, the sandy beach, and then the horizon, blank and empty and waiting for me.

PART THREE

CHAPTER TWENTY-FIVE

'HOW DID YOU know?' Rose asks.

We are in the dark, warm kitchen, a kettle boiling on the hob. The room is tidy and clean but decrepit: damp on the walls, and ivy inside the windows. I stare at the two women standing in front of me.

How did I know? There's no simple answer. Just that something has been propelling me here, pushing me towards the two of them and their secret.

'I don't know,' I say. I look at Eve. 'I've always been interested in you. Because we come from the same part of the world, and I live – I live in your house.'

'You live where?'

'In your old house. In Los Angeles. Casa Benita.'

'Oh, I see.' She watches me, still as an owl, and suddenly I see that her dark eyes are swimming with tears. I feel like a fraud, an imposter. I have to make them trust me. I can't hurt her.

'I don't know why I put two and two together. I've been wondering more and more about you the last few months. I love everything you've been in – it's so cheesy but it's true, I really do. You were interested in meeting us, then changed your mind. And it sounds crazy but when we came before, I could feel there was someone else, close by. It suddenly came into my head, on the way here today. Eve, Rose . . . There might be two of you.'

'You were right about that day.' Rose appraises me frankly. 'I was in the next room. I wanted you to come in.'

'You did?' I glance from one sister to the other, trying to work out the role each plays here. Eve steps behind her, concealing her face, but Rose moves away and says, almost impatiently, 'I was the one who rang Melanie Hexham. I wanted Eve to do the film, you see. Melanie has never met her, so she doesn't know her voice on the phone. It's been so long now.' I watch Eve, to see how she is reacting. She's staring at her sister's back, eyes on the fabric of her black dress, as if she's somewhere else entirely, head in another place. My heart twists with sadness. I can't believe it's her.

'I've always wondered what happened to you,' I say, raising my voice slightly and addressing her. 'You know, plenty of people do.'

'Do they?' Rose asks. 'I'm never sure. We hear very little, tucked away here. We have the radio, and an ancient television, though we don't watch anything but old films on it. Really we've been here now so long, sometimes . . .' She falters, then gathers herself with a smile. 'It's hard to imagine what the rest of the world is like.'

The kettle screeches into the quiet house. Eve starts bustling around purposefully with cups and teabags. I shift on my seat, looking at them both. There's so much I want to know. Why are they here? Who else knows? What do they do? What will they tell me?

'Can I ask you a question?' I say. 'Does anyone else know you're here?'

'Only one other person,' Rose says. She looks at her sister, then at me. 'Just one.'

'Who?' But they both shake their heads instantly. I try another tack, all the time thinking of Jimmy and Gavin outside, ready to come in and whisk me away.

'But – who . . . How – do you go to the shops? Go out together?'

'We take it in turns. No one can tell the difference. People don't look at little old ladies,' Eve says. 'We wear the same clothes, we look so similar, our hair. Easy for me to pretend to be her, you see. We use the bank account in Rose's name, all the bills are in Rose's name.' She chews the inside of her mouth, as if she's having difficulty explaining, remembering it all. 'Apart from my royalty cheques and I transfer them straight into Rose's account. They pay for everything. Every time they show *A Girl Named Rose* on the television, or re-release the DVD, I receive a residual payment. I do for all of my films,' she adds. 'Of course. But that one is the one that keeps us afloat.'

'More than afloat,' says Rose. 'If it weren't for that film things would be very tight.'

'It's my favourite film,' I say, almost shyly. 'You must hear that all the time. I've seen it about a hundred times. It's just wonderful.'

Eve inclines her head slightly, her intelligent dark eyes resting on me. 'I don't hear that, not any more.' She gives me a faraway smile. 'It is a wonderful film. I was very happy, you know, when I made it.'

'Were you in love with Conrad Joyce?' I ask impetuously. She's here, in front of me, and I have to ask her. I've always wondered. 'Is that why you were so sad? Because he killed himself?'

But she bats me away with her hand and her eyes cloud over and she's vague, uncertain again. 'Oh, no,' she says. 'He was a fairy. He liked boys. I loved him, but then . . . then he betrayed us.' She shakes her head. 'You know, I can't quite recall it all, but I think I killed him really. As sure as if I'd pulled the trigger.' She looks up at her sister. 'That's it, isn't it?'

Rose frowns. 'That's what you told me. But you didn't kill him, dearest. He killed himself.'

'I know.' Eve is impatient. 'But it was my fault. And I just have to get it straight in my mind – it's often not clear. Poor Conrad.' She's staring into the distance again. 'It wouldn't

329

happen now. Maybe it would. I don't know.' She runs the tea towel through her fingers. 'I don't think I could have prevented anything that happened to me, you know,' she says, after a moment's pause. 'I don't think I could have stopped my baby dying, any more. But I think I could have saved Conrad. That is my guilt. That's the guilt I carry around with me. I came back and saved Rose, but I should have saved him too.'

My mind is struggling to unravel it all.

'What did you save her from? How did you save Rose?'

There's a silence, and the atmosphere in the room changes, thickens. They look at each other anxiously.

'We don't like to talk about it,' Eve says.

'No,' Rose says. She looks down at the floor, steadying both her hands on the back of the chair. 'They lied to Eve. Our parents, they—' She stutters, suddenly. 'They – they – they, yes, they lied to us both. Eve remembers me falling into the stream. They told her I'd died. But I hadn't. They sent me away.'

'Why on earth?'

To my horror Rose's eyes fill up, and without warning her face folds into a ghoulish parody of laughter that I realise is a silent cry of pain. Tears slide down her cheeks and fall onto the table, bleeding into the wood. Like a pattern, one drop here, another there. She brushes her face angrily with the back of her hand, not making any noise, shaking her head, her mouth pursed up. It is awful to see. Eve comes over to her sister, puts her head on her shoulder, and they are very still, their dark dresses melding into one, their grey hair mixed together.

'No,' Eve says firmly. 'It's all too much. Later.' She moves away from her sister, hands me a cup of tea. 'Drink this.' Her eyes are swimming with tears too. Her expression is fierce as she sits down, pulling Rose onto the chair next to her. 'You see. This is what I told you would happen if we go back into it all.'

'But we can't live like this any more,' Rose says. She takes a cotton handkerchief out of her pocket and blows her nose. 'I won't do it.' Through the nose-blowing she gives me a half-smile. 'Sorry.'

'No—' I say, feeling hot with mortification. 'I'm sorry – I shouldn't have—'

Eve sits down at the table, next to me, and pats my hand. 'We don't entertain much, as you can see,' she says drily, and I glow, thrilled at her touch.

'Perhaps I shouldn't have come. I just felt I had to find you. Please believe me, I won't tell anyone about this.'

'It's my fault,' Rose says. 'Eve wants us to stay here, ivy wrapping itself around us for ever, but I don't.' She stands up again and gives a shuddering sigh. 'That's why I told Melanie you should come. I want us both to go back into the world. I want my life to start, you see. Eve has a life. I haven't.'

'But I don't.' There's a note in Eve's voice I haven't heard. Cool, determined. 'I want to stay like this. You've got it all wrong, dearest. I don't want this girl here.' She looks down at the table, at her sister's tear stains. 'Forgive me, Sophie,' she says. 'I don't mean to be rude. In a strange way, you know, you remind me of . . . a little of myself. Isn't it curious.'

Rose says to her fiercely, 'I thought she'd be right. I thought she'd help you. She wanted you for the part, because she thinks you're good. Don't you?' She turns to me. 'Isn't that why you're here? Isn't that what we're doing this for? Someone likes you, someone remembers you, Eve. They're here because they remember you. Lots of people do, Miss Leigh said so herself.' Eve is shaking her head. Her sister's voice grows louder. 'Lots of people. Not just him. He's real, they're all real. The world's full of nice people too, you know. You loved him once, Eve—'

Eve puts her hands over her ears. 'Stop it.' She curves over, into herself, and my heart pulls again. I put my hand on her arm.

'Who else knows about you two? Who is it?'

She looks up at me. 'Don Matthews,' she says. 'Don knows.'

The name is so familiar, the memory is almost there at the front of my brain. 'Who's Don?'

'Don Matthews. He wrote *Too Many*—'

'*Too Many Stars*!' I break in, excited. 'And *A Girl Named Rose*! You knew him? Of course! *Too Many Stars*, oh, my gosh. I must have seen that almost as many times. I used to act out the orphan's speech to the stars on my bed every night. What a script!'

'You remember him,' Eve Noel says. 'Oh, that's just wonderful. You remember him,' and for just a second I see her eyes flash, and she is young again, and beautiful, and everything in this damp quiet cell of theirs recedes and I can only gape at her, at her beauty. And in that flashing moment I understand now why they called them gods and goddesses in the golden age. This woman is a goddess, and I am lucky to be in her presence. I see why people plucked her out of obscurity and made her a star.

'He was the love of her life,' Rose says. 'He's over eighty now. He's coming to England and he wants to see her again. After all these years. And she won't meet him.'

'It's been too long. I'm not the same person, and he wouldn't – oh God, Rose. I'm sick of talking about it.' Eve pushes herself up, her voice throbbing with anger. 'You may have forgotten what it was like when we first came here. I haven't.' She rubs her eyes, and then catches sight of me again, and her mood abruptly switches. She sounds cross. 'You too, why do you keep coming round to bother me? Today, yesterday, the day before. All these visits and I keep saying no.'

'One visit,' I say quietly.

She blinks again. 'It's not one visit. It's two, three.'

'No, only once before,' I say.

'Yes,' Rose says. 'She came once before, with the man from the film company. You remember?'

'No. I know I get things wrong, 'cause of the shocks. I'm not wrong about this, though.'

'What shocks?' I don't understand her.

'The treatment. My treatment after I lost my . . .' She shakes her head. 'No. Sophie, you came before. Or a girl who looked

332

like you.' She seems uncertain. 'The day it was so hot. You had your hair—' She sweeps her hands up behind her head, miming a ponytail.

I can feel icy water running through my body.

'No,' I say. 'That wasn't me.'

She looks at me steadily. 'You think I've made it up? No, it's true. She was real.'

'I don't think you made it up.' I try to think. 'Just that it's very strange. Who . . . Have you thought about who it might have been?'

Eve moves her chair a little closer, so she's right opposite me. 'I'm afraid she reminded me of you.'

'You're afraid?'

'Yes. Because she scared me, and I want to like you. She brought white roses, too.'

I can feel my blood run cold again, and I know something is happening, something that will take me closer to whatever or whoever it is that is in my life, in hers, creeping around, suddenly lashing out in violence.

'It wasn't me, I swear,' I say, but it sounds unconvincing. *Was it me? Have I gone mad, do I not remember?*

She stares at my face, and Rose watches her. 'No, she was similar to you but it wasn't you. Like when we take it in turns to go out, and we're almost the same person. I see it now.'

'Can you tell if her accent was English or not? Could she have been American?'

'Maybe. I just don't know. I thought she was English but . . . she sounded strange.'

I shift uneasily in my seat. 'Eve—'

There's a crash from outside, and we all jump.

'What the hell—' I get up but Eve is faster. She moves down the long, damp corridor, scuttling fast. I wonder what's been troubling me, and I look around the kitchen. I hear a voice, a man's voice.

'. . . told her . . . pick her up . . . Nothing for half an hour . . .'

'Jimmy!' I shout. I get up and run down the corridor. A

mouse runs across the floor in the front room, piled high with boxes that sag with damp. 'I'm here, I'm so sorry – I forgot all about you.'

Jimmy's tapping his watch. 'You said ten minutes. I need to get you to town before seven. That's what I told them. Never going to happen at this rate.'

'It's fine, Jimmy. Give me five more minutes. I'll be out then. I promise.'

'Gavin says he'll come get you himself, if you ain't out soon. Right?'

'OK. Just a bit longer. It's fine.'

Eve shuts the door firmly, with a thud that sinks dully into the velvety silence of the house. The lines from *My Second-Best Bed* that I was learning on the way over come back to me, something Anne says to Shakespeare that he uses in a play later on. *I am gone though I am here. There is no love in you. Nay, I pray you, let me go.*

We go back to the kitchen and I look at my watch. 'Sorry,' I say. 'They want me to go to London. It's a long story.'

Rose gets up. 'I'm going upstairs,' she says. 'I usually have a bath around this time, so I shall leave you two.' Eve looks uncertain. She reaches out to pluck at her sister's dress, but Rose shrugs. 'She might understand, better than I, Eve dear. Sophie, it has been extremely interesting meeting you. We know that you are busy and I'm very glad you came.' She takes my hand for a moment. 'Please come back. Soon.'

I watch her go. It feels very quiet after she's left.

Eve gestures for me to sit down. The two of us face each other at the table. 'What do you keep in the boxes?' I ask her, shy now we're alone.

'Letters,' she says. 'My letters. And things I've written down. My time there. Memories I've had when I dream. I have terrible dreams, since they shocked me.' She touches the side of her head again, blinking.

'What happened to you?' I ask her softly.

'I'll try and explain it. I think I need to work it all out myself, too.' She puts her hand on my arm. She has long

334

slim fingers. 'Sophie, I should have said so before but I am glad to meet you, you know. I hear about you, on the radio, on the television. I've always noticed because you grew up not so far away. I felt as if you might be me. Forty, fifty years on. Now I see you properly, we're not so dissimilar, are we?'

'Maybe,' I say, and I can't help smiling, because it might be the nicest thing anyone's ever said to me. 'But I don't think so.'

'That's sometimes what keeps me going, after everything that's happened. We were good. What we did was good, Don and I—' She looks at me.

'Tell me about it,' I say, moving my chair closer to hers. Her mouth opens and her clever, dark eyes search my face.

'You don't have time. But I want to do something. Let me give you some things to read.' She looks around the room. 'I'll give you a box of papers. His letters, and some pages I've written about . . . about it all. I wrote everything down.'

She gets up and leaves me, and for the next couple of minutes I hear her moving about in the next room, the rustle of paper, the creak of furniture. She reappears with a box which seems too big for her small frame.

'Here. Take this.'

'I can't take all of this,' I say, looking down at the pages of neat, black inked writing, the letters postmarked *USA*, dog-eared, worn with folding and refolding, and carbon copies of her own pages, a few scraps of smooth fax paper.

'This is just a selection,' she says. 'A random selection. There are hundreds, maybe thousands of letters in that room. Come back and we'll go through them if you enjoy them. Some of them won't make sense . . .' She is holding out the box, her frail arms outstretched. She looks like a little girl, asking for approval. I hesitate, and she steps away from me, as if assailed by doubt. 'Oh dear. Maybe it's crazy. Do you want to read all this?'

'Of course I want to read them.' *I want to make a film about you one day, Eve. About you and your sister, and your life. But I have to know the truth first.* I know this box is only a fraction of the story.

She gives that funny, wry smile again. 'Well . . . then – take these and I hope you find them interesting. Like I say –' she gestures behind her into the huge room I passed earlier filled with boxes – 'the story's all back in there. We'll go through it one day.'

I shake my head. 'Why are you giving them to me?'

Eve's big black eyes lock with mine. She leans forwards, touches my hand and says, very quietly,

'Something needs to change. Someone else needs to know.' She's nodding, and as she blinks a tear slides down her cheek, splashing onto my hand. We both stare down at it. 'Sophie.' She rubs her throat, as though it hurts. 'It's just I'm still scared. Of what's out there.'

'We all are,' I say, as softly as I can. 'I promise you we all are.' I take the box, gently. 'I promise I'll take good care of them. They'll be safe with me.'

'Of course. Come back soon and I'll show you everything in that room. It tells the story. But mostly it's up here –' she taps her head. 'Ah –' she spreads her arms out and then hugs herself. 'Wonderful.'

In her tiny, withdrawn world she has a contentment I'll never have, because she has Don, and Rose, and because Eve Noel knows someone, somewhere is enjoying one of her films, that she's made something good. We're facing each other on the small kitchen chairs. She is appraising me, blinking slowly. 'Do you know, I was so sure that girl who came to see us was you. But now I look, she can't have been. You are lovely, you know.'

I hear the sound of footsteps on gravel. I know our time is up. I take my phone out of my pocket and fiddle with it for a moment. 'Miss Noel – Eve. Before I go, I have to ask you something. Someone is after me. They're trying to kill me, I think. Or – they have a grudge against me, and they want to hurt me.' I flick through my phone, and then turn it round so she can see. 'Can you remember, was this the person who came to visit you?'

She stares at the small screen, the light reflecting on her face. 'Oh, yes,' she says eventually. 'That was her. I'm sure of it.'

Excerpts from the Correspondence Between Eve Noel
and Don Matthews
1970-2012

> *April 4th, 1970*
> *Dear Rose,*
> *I have no idea whether you'll get this letter. I've written*
> *you so many times over the years, and I don't ever hear*
> *back. If you know that, you'll throw this one aside. 'The*
> *stupid fool, why doesn't he take a hike?' I wrote you at*
> *your house, the studio . . . I even found the village you*
> *came from and fired off a letter to the doctor's house there.*
> *Your dad was a doctor, right? But then I had a brainwave*
> *I hadn't considered before: that I should go through your*
> *UK agents. Who'd have thought. A mere two-week trawl*
> *of movie agents in London, and I finally get one who says*
> *she looks after you, though she's never met you. I don't*
> *know, Rose – is this the gal you want handling your career?*
>
> *I'm being flippant, forgive me. The truth is I think you*
> *might just read this letter this time, and I feel so damn*
> *nervous at the thought it's difficult to decide what to say.*
> *I don't know where you are, how you are, why you've*
> *disappeared. I do know I have to apologise for everything*
> *that happened, but I hope you'll understand, too. It seems*

a nightmare, doesn't it? Gosh, I wish you were just in front of me and I could look into your beautiful black eyes and tell you everything, tell you how stupid I've been, how much I regret not letting you visit me in jail, how ashamed I felt, how much I miss you and think about you, all the time.

Anyway. I sure wish you'd write back and tell me how you get on. I haven't heard anything of you for the longest time. When I ask friends in the business what happened to you they shrug. 'No idea. She went mad, didn't she?' But then every woman over thirty-five in this town who has an opinion is apparently mad, so I don't pay much attention.

A few facts about me: I haven't had a drink for seven years. There wasn't a great deal of it to be had in jail, and I started up again after I got out but then quit. For good, I hope. I'm in New York. Still working, but for TV this time. I write for <u>The Janet Berry Show</u> – we're number one and it's going into a third season, so I guess it's not just a fluke. I have a third-floor walk-up near the park. There's a great Italian around the corner, it does out-of-this-world cannoli and they play Sinatra on a loop. I think of you whenever we go there. But I think of you often, anyway.

Write me, if you want. I really hope you're well.

Yours,

Don

4th June 1970

Dear Don,

It was nice to hear from you.

I am well, thank you. I live in the countryside now, and I don't act any more. The agents are there merely to pass on mail and residuals. Thanks to you I live in a little comfort from the money <u>A Girl Named Rose</u> brings in.

I can't remember a lot about that time. You said you were going to come for me. I will lift up mine eyes unto the hills, from whence cometh my help. I looked all the time but you never came. Why didn't you come for me?

Eve

September 12th, 1970

Dear Rose,

Forgive the tardiness; I only got your letter yesterday, though it's dated June. Maybe you forgot to mail it? Or maybe the US postal service is doing its usual bang-up job.

I didn't come for you because they arrested me. I said I'd do a favor for a friend, give him an alibi, and I was set up. Moss knew what he was doing, I was the easy solution, no one'd miss me. A drunk writer, and without Jerry I was nothing and he knew it. It's all in the past now, but I couldn't come for you because I was in jail and that was the worst weekend of my life, knowing you were waiting for me.

It was very hot, all the weekend we'd made our plans around. I could see out the window, up to the hills. I could picture you pacing up and down, growing impatient, looking at your watch. And then gradually giving up hope, thinking I was just another louse out to stiff you. It wasn't like that. You know it wasn't.

But like I say, it's all in the past now.

You sound different, kind of distant, and I don't blame you. Where are you living in England? Are you by yourself? Are you acting at all? Can you tell me a little more about your life? Or just tell me straight out if you want me to stop writing.

I'm glad A Girl Named Rose is providing you with some comfort. It's the best thing I ever did, and I did it for you.

Don

1st January 1971

Dear Don,

I have good days and bad days. Your first letter arrived on a bad day. I couldn't remember who you were, then I could, then I couldn't. It comes and goes, like a mist, and the trouble is I don't care to hold onto the memories, because so many of them were unhappy ones. You see, you were the one good thing in my life, and then I lost you. And I'm scared to remember it all again. I've spent a lot of time trying to forget. But I have to stop being stupid and remind myself you were the good part of it all, and to separate you out from the bad. Today's a good day. (I'm sorry to sound so black and white, good and bad. I'm childlike sometimes, and don't talk or write much.)

So yes, I'll tell you what you want to know. I live in Gloucestershire, where I grew up, very close to Shakespeare country. It's beautiful. I live in a white house. I'm trying to train ivy to climb up the side, but it's reluctant to grow. I'm a terrible gardener. I've never really tried before.

When you ask these questions, you make me think it through again, and I have to make some sense of it in my mind, before I answer, which is why my letters are late. There's so much I don't remember. I tried so hard to get to you before you went to prison, Don, afterwards, too. I waited round the corner when they took you out of the courthouse. I didn't see you, just people jostling. Then . . . I spent the next year holding on, I suppose. I shut myself down, waiting for you. But on the inside I was starting to think I was mad. I couldn't look in mirrors. I couldn't remember my name. I kept having dreams about my sister. She drowned when I was six, and I never saw her and that's when it all started, my madness, the different parts of it all began then. You see they took her away and I didn't see her, they wouldn't let me see her. She was my sister and when I lost her, it's as though I lost a piece of my mind too.

Our parents died, Don. They died when I was in Hollywood, and I can't remember much about it. They

340

had influenza; my father had a heart attack, then my mother caught the influenza. I think she was already very weak. She always had been, her faith was what sustained her, not food, or real life. We weren't close, you see. They let me go and when I went it was as though I was like their other daughter, dead to them. I was seeing things in my mind by then, things I didn't understand, and I don't think it particularly sunk in that they'd gone. Then I knew I'd started my baby, and at the same time I got the letter about Rose. I think they hid it from me. Gilbert – whoever it was – all of them.

I can't think about what happened, not today, anyway. Maybe another day.

I'm sorry if I caused you any upset. I am fine, just different now.

Happy New Year, dear Don. I wish you all happiness for the year ahead. Today, this first day of the year, it means a great deal to me to be sending you back this letter. There is frost on the ground and a tiny robin jumps about in the hawthorn beyond my window.

Eve

January 8th, 1971
So what happened? When you can next remember, write me. I'll wait.
Don

4th April 1971
Dear Don,
This is the first anniversary. Your letter was dated 4th April 1970 and I'm replying to you now, late again, I'm afraid.

It's spring here now, and the frost is long gone. But it's still cold, I shiver at night. Do you remember the first time we met? We looked at the stars together, at that party in

Beverly Hills. You gave me an avocado. It was a long time ago, wasn't it? Fifteen years. What a baby I was and I was so impressed with you. You were kind, and handsome, and funny. You still are, I'm sure.

What happened to me? I think I had a breakdown. I've been piecing it together, writing it all down for you, tearing it up and starting again.

Conrad killed himself. I think that's also what I couldn't remember and when I do I feel so sad. I think of his death and how I heard of it and it is often the last thing I remember before everything goes blank. I think he killed himself because of me. He hated himself anyway, and was so ashamed of what he'd done to you, Don. He couldn't see a way out. I was his friend and I was not his friend then, and for that . . . I think, yes, I think I was very guilty.

I listen to the radio a lot. It is my link to the outside world, other than the infrequent trips I make to the shops in my nearest town. I heard Jerry talking about his new film, only the other week. Hearing his voice was very strange, so immediate. Do you ever see him? He is, I understand, in New York too. I hope he has made amends to you for what he did.

I lost my baby girl. I was pregnant, she was moving inside me, Don. Then Conrad killed himself, Gilbert and I had a fight, he scared me, and I remember feeling as if my head was ripping in two. As if Eve and Rose were fighting to be inside my head. One is the film star who's in control, who never complains, who's always loyal to the system and does what she's told; the other is the strange, terrifying child who was always disobeying our mother, our nanny, everyone around her, and that's why she drowned, you see. I didn't know where Rose had gone. You are the only person who calls me Rose.

They took me to hospital, and that's where the baby was born, though she was never really born, not as they should be screaming and kicking. She didn't move. I never saw her. I never even touched her. I wish I'd touched her skin, just once, Don. I don't know where they took her afterwards and it hurt me so much, not just the pain of having her, the pain of losing her was much, much worse. They put me under and they took her away.

I was out of control, apparently. When I came around two days later I scratched and bit and hit and wouldn't stop screaming. So that's when I went into the clinic and they shocked me. I can feel the marks they left, now. One person to hold me down, another to strap the pads to my head, one on each side.

ECT is a terrible thing. I have to live and try to be happy, to know I have conquered the shocks they gave me. Because it meant I couldn't remember, it changed the way I think, the person I am. It made me confused and terrified. There were marks on my temples, I can still feel them, I touch them when I don't realise, sitting up at night reading in my room, if an animal howls in the woods and it sounds like a child, or – all sorts of things. And when I touch them, it's the memory of sense that takes me back, and I can feel the gel before it went on, and the straps that burnt my skin as I writhed and struggled to break free, and the soreness in my throat from screaming and screaming and begging them to let me go. When people break you with their strength a piece of you remains broken, I think.

I was all alone, you see. I wanted someone to come so badly and no one came.

Now I'm not alone. Rose is back with me. It's strange but it makes sense, that's why it's strange. I'll explain another time.

Take care, dear Don.

Rose

April 8th, 1971

Dear Rose,

I don't know what to say except I'm sorry. You poor darling girl. I wish I could have helped you. I'm angry I

343

couldn't. I have let you down, partly through circumstance, partly through my own fault. I'm sorry about the baby. And how you were treated. Dear Rose, what an awful time.

I'm coming to London in the summer, to meet with a few people, and we're going to stay on and have a holiday. May I come visit you? I could bring my wife, Hannah, I know she'd love to meet you. Or she can stay behind, whatever you feel comfortable with. She's an actress on the show, and always asks me about you. We've been married four years – guess I should have mentioned that, but you know us guys, we ain't so good at giving out information.

I don't know who the other Rose you mention is. Have you seen a doctor, someone to talk to about the effects of the ECT? I guess you don't want to. I just wonder if there's something that can be done. Anyway, it's not my business. But while we're on the subject of what's absolutely not my business, I think your life sounds too solitary. You were always good at being alone, Rose, you didn't need those acolytes who make a living out of leeching – you liked your own company, a good book, a beautiful view. But it sounds like you've become too good at it, or is that hokum? Would you ever consider stepping out of that life, coming back into the real world at all? There are so many people who miss you, who ask me what happened to you. People really did love Eve Noel.

Thank you for telling me what happened. I am so sorry.

I send you my love, dear Rose. Let me know about the visit. And think about getting some help.

Your friend Don

1st May 1971
Dear Mr Matthews,
I have been asked by my client Miss Noel to request that you cease and desist from writing to her. She asks me

344

to tell you that she has no need of your friendship and no
longer wishes to hear from you.

With my best wishes,
Yours sincerely,
Andrea Neaglewood

4th April 1974
Dear Don,
It's been a while, hasn't it? I don't even know if you're
at this address any more.

I just wanted to write and say hello. I don't want to
see anyone or talk to anyone about what happened, but
that doesn't mean we can't be long-distance friends. So
what I am trying rather ineptly to say is, I'm sorry if I
seemed rude.

Can we be long-distance friends? I'd like that.

I'm very glad to hear you're married again. Hannah is
a lovely name. She is a lucky girl. How did you meet?
Yours,
Eve – I think you should call me Eve now.

June 10th, 1974
Dear Eve,
Well, well, long time no hear. Great to hear from you
now. I'm really pleased you're OK. I was going to write,
I was worried about you, but that Andrea Neaglewood
broad has a tone of rebuke even in a letter; I didn't want
to risk it.

I'm sorry, Rose. I'm sorry I pried. It's not my business
what your life's like.

Hannah is an actress on <u>The Janet Berry Show</u>; I think
I mentioned I was a writer on that show. As it happens
I'm not anymore, but she's still working there, and doing
a fine job. We met because I tipped a drink over her dress.
Do you remember how I drenched your gloves in liquor,

up at Big Sur? Anyway, the dress was houndstooth tweed, and she was not at all happy about it. The summer of love passed Hannah by, I always think. She's like a girl from the '50s – I guess that's why I fell for her. We have been married now for coming up to five years. She has black hair and a beautiful smile. She's from Long Island.

It's great being married again, except I'm not working at the present time and she's all day and night at the studio. I hear you asking why I'm not working – it's the old demon again, Rose, drink. I fell off that wagon, hard. A few things were getting me down, and I wasn't as strong as I needed to be. I don't seem to be able to be, these days. Not to get our long-distance friendship off on the wrong step, but I knew I could do it, give it up, for you. It was hard, but not as hard as all the other times, because you were the reward. Hope that's not embarrassing to hear. Here, there's so much temptation. The bar on the corner, the drinks trolley in the writer's room, the guys disappearing into an old speakeasy on their way home. And I feel old, Rose, past it, ridiculous. I see them looking at me, thinking, What's that old fella doing, here with Hannah? Oh, that's the drunk. All the usual stuff, except now at my back I always hear time's winged chariot hurrying near, as the song goes.

Don't know why I'm telling you all this. Yes, I do. I always could tell you anything. Hope you feel the same way too.

Thanks, my long-distance friend.
Don

24th June 1974
Dearest Don,
I'm so sorry to hear you've been having a hard time of it. I'm sorry I didn't write back, that I behaved like such an idiot.

You understand good days and bad days, and I'm even

sorrier to hear you're having too many of the latter yourself. Don, nothing's worth falling off the wagon for. You know it. Oh, how bossy and glib that sounds. As you know I loathe nothing more than well-meaning people telling me what's best for me. The doctor who said I should move into a community – as if I were eighty and infirm, instead of not quite forty. The man at the village shop who bit his lip for four years and only last week asked me if I had someone to telephone. To telephone for what? I wanted to shout. I need no one out here.

So I'm going to tell you a story. To take your mind off your own troubles.

I want to tell you the real story of a girl named Rose. I write everything down when I remember it. I even use carbon paper sometimes, to keep a copy of the letters I write to you, so I know what I've said. My memory isn't good any more as you know. And I want to write this one down. I know you liked stories from my English childhood. Well, there was a little girl, and her sister, and they liked to play together in the woods by their house. Now, the little girl was naughty, and she sometimes made her parents extremely cross. She would roar and scream, and go rigid, and drum her feet on the ground. She'd stop listening and go stiff, pointing one finger out to hell, as if someone else had taken control of her body. Someone evil.

This little girl didn't mean to lose control, but it kept happening. Once, she kicked a maid so hard she fell down the stairs, and she broke her leg. Another time she knocked her mother out. She didn't know how to stop being like this. She thought she was mad, that someone made her do these things because the devil had got inside her. Her little sister was good, why couldn't she be good too? She was too young to understand it and her behaviour grew worse. Her parents stopped wondering if she was merely naughty and started to think she was possessed by some-thing, something evil. Her mother was a fervent Christian, and she believed the devil was testing her, that he had possessed her daughter. The servants left one by one, they didn't want to look after a devil-child. The doctor from the hospital in Gloucester told them it was most likely something evil had got into her head and he advised them to put her away. That is what they believed.

So one day, when the little girl was eight, she and her younger sister were playing in the river by their house. It was spring. They had been told not to play there, for though the river was thin and low, it wasn't quite a stream, it had a strong current. Suddenly Rose stared at her sister, and her eyes rolled back in her head, and she started to shake, and jerk, and she slipped in the water, screaming and flailing, and hit her head. She was apparently dead, and her little sister didn't know what to do – should she stay with her, or run for help?

She ran for help, but afterwards her parents told her it had been the wrong thing to do. They told her Rose was dead.

But it wasn't true. She was spirited away the same night. Unconscious, this time drugged, but as she left the house by the river she screamed, and the screams woke her sister up, and though she remembered the sounds afterwards, she never understood what they were.

Rose was taken to the home that night. She lay still for two days, and when she woke up, she was bound to her bed. A nurse told her she had nearly killed her little sister with her pranks. That she was evil, best left alone, nasty and foul, and she wouldn't ever see her family again. Oh, Don. She was eight years old. She stayed in that home until she was twenty-eight, and I came to take her away again. For twenty years all she knew was the home. They starved her, beat her, kept her locked up to her bed in a room by herself for a week after she had a fit.

She stopped having the episodes when she was around nineteen – apparently this is common in childhood epilepsy. After that she was allowed to paint, to walk in the garden, to go on drives; it stopped being quite so much of a prison. But no one came for her, no one at all. Apart from her parents and the people at the home, everyone else thought she was dead, and she didn't know where she was. She didn't understand why no one ever came for her. How could she have known?

I found out later that all that time she was only five miles away from her family's house. Five miles.

She would have stayed there for ever, maybe. But her parents died, one soon after the other. They had provided for her care in their will, she was to stay at the home indefinitely: that's what you did, even then. You locked them away, out of sight.

They wrote to tell the next of kin that the arrangement would continue. The next of kin, a younger sister, living far away now, never replied, and another year went past. But some kind soul at the home wrote to them again. She said that Rose was here, and that she needed her. And when that letter arrived it might have been kicked under a mat or hidden from her sister like the first letter, but it just so happened that she saw it. But her sister was ill too, maybe because all along her mind was trying to tell her something. She kept the letter secret and when she was better, she came to England. She found the home and one sunny afternoon she walked up to her sister, tapped her on the shoulder and said, 'Rose, I'm here. I've come to take you away.'

My sister Rose is alive and well, and we live together here. Our parents' house is nearby. It is derelict; neither she nor I had done anything about it since their death. We don't ever want to go back there. One day nature will take it over, and eventually perhaps nothing of it will remain.

You're the only one who knows all this. We are both happy now. She can't hurt me, and I can't hurt her.

I hope that's given you something to think about!
Eve
Hannah sounds beautiful. I am very happy for you.

July 1st, 1974

Dear Eve,

My love to you both. Many things make sense now. You said to me once in Big Sur you felt she was still with you. You were right. It makes me sad to think how unhappy you've both been. Oh honey. What can I say? I'm so sorry. My God, it must be hard.

Love to you both. I hope to meet your sister one day. Don

November 24th, 1977

Eve,

Thanks for your last letter; I did enjoy your description of the cats and life at home. I'm writing this on Thanksgiving. We're back from the Macy's parade and treating ourselves to some eggnog (not me; I'm having milk, with a little nutmeg. It looks like it could be eggnog and that'll have to do). We have folks from our building over. Thanksgiving makes me think of home, my home. I grew up in the Depression, and there wasn't a lot to go round, except on Thanksgiving. My father always had the day off school and he'd make us play football out on the front lawn, me and my sister, even if it was raining. The Matthews Annual Touchdown, he'd call it. Bridget hated it, but I loved it. We'd eat, and Mom always told us the story of the first Thanksgiving, how we came to live here, her ancestors all the way from Holland, would you believe? And Dad's, all the way from Galway, back when he was called Flaherty, not Matthews. How each set of grand-parents met, one pair in the milk bar on Avenue A, the others at Ellis Island, just off the boat. We'd listen to the radio, we had a big set in the den, and when the music came on he and Mom would dance. I can see them now in that old house, swaying in time, holding onto each other, while we watched. They seemed so perfectly in step and it was as though we weren't there, just the two of them dancing around the room, past my mother's china figurines on the little shelf by the window, past my father's easy chair, the slippers, the pipe, everything as it should be. It felt like a home, that place, always did, and I think of it on this day every year. I don't know why but I've never come anywhere close to recreating it. I'll be fifty in a couple of years, Rose. Seems a waste of a life, that's all, and I know I still have a lot to be thankful for.

I'm thankful for you in my life and for the fact I can tell you anything. Hope that's OK.

Don

7th December 1977

Dear Don,

Of course you can tell me anything. That's what these letters are for, aren't they? I feel like I am sane, my old self, me, when I write to you. The rest of the world is like alien life on my own planet, but this makes sense.

This is my Christmas letter to you, and I hope it reaches you before the 25th. I don't like Christmas much. It's the one time of the year I want to be gaudy and gay, and then I think about how one might do that and I shrink from it. Ask Miss Torode the choir mistress from the church in for a sweet sherry? The novelty might finish both of us off. We've been here now for over fifteen years, and I guess I'm feeling a little antsy, for perhaps the first time. Rose is out, getting supplies. It's very cold here.

Someone wrote to me last week about re-releasing A Girl Named Rose on its eighteenth anniversary. Can you believe it, Don? Eighteen years ago next year. They want me to go up to London, introduce a screening at the National Film Theatre. I said no, of course, and then I wished I hadn't. But we wouldn't get any peace again, and I have peace now – sometimes too much, when I can hear the carol singers in the village below and I know they won't visit us, because they're scared. And when I lie in bed on Christmas morning, and think about the old times, in the house not ten miles from here, where we had Father's rugby socks as stockings, green and blue striped. I remember one year there was an orange, some chocolate, a new ribbon for my hair, a little enamel brooch of a rose, a dancing wooden man with string in his legs and arms. I was so happy. We bounced on our parents' bed, shouting, laughing, shouting again. I gave the brooch to Rose, of course. I wanted her to be good, and she was that day. It was a good day. Many things that came afterwards were terrible. We have been through a lot to find this peace, and I'm scared of giving it up. Do you understand?

Well, enough of this. Happy Christmas, dear Don, to you and Hannah. I shall think of you, with love, as I always do. Please don't drink.

Eve

24th September 1984
Dear Don,
Did you see Joe Baxter died? It was on the radio this morning. I burnt the porridge, and then I threw it in the bin and burst into tears. Rose thought I'd gone quite mad: well, she's probably right. He must have been eighty, if he was a day. Vile, vile, vile man! They interviewed someone from the studio, I can't remember who it was, an old movie star. She fawned over his memory as if he'd been Mother Teresa, not a lecherous, repressive, dishonest old bastard. The obituary in The Times *was no less fawning. I came as close as I ever have to writing to a paper about it; but can you imagine the letter?*

Dear Sirs: further to your obituary of Joseph Baxter, I would like to add a few comments of my own. Yes, he was at the studio while Redbeard the Pirate, Dawn Patrol *and* A Girl Named Rose *were made, amongst others, but the writers on those films were due the*

352

credit, not he. To my knowledge none of them has ever received the royalties due them nor the recognition. Yes, he spotted talent, but to say he nurtured it so that it could flourish is entirely false, unless you call rape of a minor nurturing, or blackmail, or homophobia, or false imprisonment, or perverting the cause of justice.

He had excellent taste in ties, however. I believe that was him and not his wife or his mistress.

Yours, Eve Sallis
Once known as Eve Noel

Whaddya think? I might send it off later today.

My sister sends her regards. She is knitting a pair of gloves for me. Cherry red, they're delightful. Perkins came home safely, thank you. He had a dead mouse and was covered in cobwebs, so I suspect he'd trapped himself in a cellar somewhere. So the house is full to bursting again.

Love Eve

August 2nd, 1989
Dearest Eve,
It's late, almost two in the morning. I'm preparing next semester's classes and one of the topics the professor professes we teach is Heroes and Villains, and one of the movies on the list is <u>Dare to Win</u>. I'm alone, Hannah's up at Martha's Vineyard with some friends. Manhattan is a soup, tourists, heat, sweat. Perhaps it's the nostalgia, perhaps the night, or the loneliness, but it got me thinking about Gilbert, and you, and I hope you don't mind me writing you about it, in the dog days of August. He's almost forgotten now, and it seems so strange that he had any success. He was always seen as the perfect English gent, when he was one of the most unpleasant human beings I've ever known. Even before he hurt you. You know the reason he did so well in wartime was he was suited to it – he loved killing, hurting, maiming. I guess we should be glad he was on our side not theirs. I was thinking all this

353

over, perhaps for a class on how you write a hero in a screenplay, and then I realised, it's all crap anyway, isn't it? You get stuck with an image and that's it. The studios make you, and the fans insist you stay that way. But who remembers Gilbert Travers today? No one, except film students and old men.

Makes me think about you, anyway, Rose. The number of people who ask me about you since I started teaching at NYU – well, it's just terrific. And double that – they love the characters you played, but they loved the person they felt they were seeing. I just wanted you to know that, I've never said it before. You may feel alone at times, but I know for a fact people all around the world still thank you for your films, years after. I wonder why no one tries to track you down more often than they do.

So I think about you anyway, you know that. I want you to know what I could never say out loud but I can write very easily: you were the love of my life. You still are. You always say you've changed, that I wouldn't love you anymore, that we have our own lives, and I can see that. I'm not intending on acting on it. It's just sometimes the desire to see you again, hold you in my arms, kiss your soft creamy cheek, it overwhelms me and I have to stop myself running right to the airport. You're Rose, you always will be to me, and I love you, and I'm sorry for this letter: It's not a confessional, just something to reread occasionally, if you need reminding that you are, and always will be, loved.

Don

15th August 1989

Don,

Gilbert was a brute, you're right. But he was a sad, angry man. It's best illustrated by the fact he would never agree to a divorce. He was of that generation of British men who can't admit failure. Though he died a long, lingering death, incredibly painful, and he was all alone.

I think there was no one there at the end and he hated being alone. The trouble was, fame was everything to him. He loved it, it became the driving force in his life. I think that's why he married me and why he couldn't see anything was wrong.

Darling Don. I have reread your letter so many times. I keep it with me. Writing to you every week has come to be the moulding into which I fill the rest of my life here with my sister. Such as it is. If I see or hear anything particularly interesting or noteworthy, I think 'I'll tell Don,' not, 'I'll tell Rose.' I'm happiest when I'm writing to you. My brain works, my thoughts flow. I know what I want to say to you and how. I know you'll understand me. Often I can't work out what to say, to Rose, to the chemist, to the dentist. I get confused still, but never with you.

I wrote you a lot of letters, when I was first here, in the early days when everything was at its worst. I didn't send them. I was less sure of who I was and rereading them is painful. And even though my sister is my life here now, you saved me, Don, darling Don. It may be decades now, but you are still with me, in everything I do. I wake up in the morning and the day ahead is full of things I want to tell you. I feel you're with me, all through the day. I think about you all the time, worry that you're eating enough, hope you're not drinking, laugh at the jokes we've shared, wonder what you make of some story on the news. It's like you're here, with me, and I love you too.

Eve

October 4th, 1996
Dearest Eve,
Am I right in thinking today is your 60th birthday?
Many, many happy returns. The fax is a wonderful thing, isn't it? I hope you have a great day, and that Hudson makes you a beautiful cake, or at least a mousy tribute.
All my love, Don

355

PS *The news is brief here, yes. Classes have started. Hannah and I reached a settlement and I hope the final papers will be signed soon. She wants to be married to her new guy before Christmas, and I'd like to be able to help her do it. I think he's right for her. He works at NBC. That's more than I could give her . . .*

2nd January 2000

Happy New Year, new century, new millennium, dear Don. May it bring you everything you want.

They showed <u>Too Many Stars</u> *on BBC2 last night, or rather this morning. What a great film. We enjoyed it so much. It's still my favourite of yours, apart from* <u>Rose</u>, *of course.*

<u>Rose</u> *went out today for a cup of tea with a lady from the church whom she has met several times in the village. By herself. She said it was a new millennium and time for a new start. I was very against it, but she pointed out that I have you, I can fax you as much as I want and I often do, and she has no one. But it makes me so nervous, this idea of her engaging with someone else. I know why, and I wish I could stop myself. The truth is, we're more different than I'd realised. I've become used to this life. I know its parameters and it makes me feel safe. I don't think I'm strong enough to try something new. Rose is the opposite. She likes our life together, but she wants more. I can't blame her at all, but it makes me so nervous. The thought of it . . . that I might lose her again. Irrational I know.*

You always ask how it is no one wants to track me down, the old, film star me, I mean. The answer is simple – if you don't draw attention to it, most people simply aren't interested. People don't notice old ladies and Don, I'm afraid to tell you that's what I am, these days. In the village, we're Rose Sallis, if we're anything. We're the old witch that lives in the overgrown house at the top of the hill and rarely goes into town. That's quite enough for them. I don't need to alarm them by telling them I know Professor Donald Matthews of the NYU Film School, who has a retrospective coming up in the spring, and who is the cleverest, and best of men. I'm no show-off.

Love Eve

March 28th, 2000
Dear E,
Well, the opening was a bust. The guy introducing me called me 'Den', not 'Don', there were rows of empty seats, and then they loaded the wrong film and we got five minutes of <u>The Godfather</u> before someone changed it back to my second film, <u>Mr Taylor's Test</u>. The trouble is, five minutes is enough to remind you how great <u>The Godfather</u> is. No one wanted to switch over to Taylor – they, like I, wanted to stick with Brando in the study and the guests dancing in the garden to Johnny Fontane.

Frances was with me. She's my new squeeze. She's a teacher here too, lives on the Upper West Side. Our first date was a Woody Allen movie. We're quite the cliché, aren't we?

I think you'd like her anyway.

Watching <u>A Girl Named Rose</u> for the retrospective made me remember what you were like. Goddammit, Rose, you were so good. Wouldn't you ever consider stepping back into that world again? Or just out into the world in general? Don't get mad, but I have to say it. A day trip to London? Would you ever consider meeting me if I came to town?

My love
D

4th April 2000
Professor Don,
You know it's thirty years ago today you wrote to me? April 4th, I never forget it. I'm glad we don't email – well,

357

I couldn't even if I wanted to, technology having somewhat passed me by other than the blessed fax. I'm glad. Means I can have a look through a selection of our letters, just between you and me, when I'm feeling down. Just now and then drop a line, as they say.

I think too much time's past for me to suddenly go back into the world. The London I see on the television is thrilling but too terrifying. As for acting – I'm too old! No one wants a sixty-three-year-old. You ask why no one looks for me – times have moved on so much, who cares about some old film star? And believe me, I'm happier this way. Rose would say different, but my sister is a stubborn old (older) thing.

I think Frances sounds wonderful. And I'd always rather watch <u>Mr Taylor's Test</u> than <u>The Godfather</u>. Marlon Brando is the most overrated actor in the world, it is a fact, I swear to you. As for the screenplay: pah. You're the master, you always were.

With love as always,

E

July 2007

Dearest Eve,

I apologise for my handwriting. I can't see the date, anywhere, it's hugely frustrating. Some days I think my sight is playing tricks on me. What's the point of the Internet if I can't tell my best friend what films she should be watching?

But Jan from down the hallway tells me that tomorrow afternoon you have the choice between <u>Kind Hearts and Coronets</u>; or a terrible film starring someone from <u>Cagney and Lacey</u>, and an old James Bond. May I urge you, with all possible force, to watch the former? 3.20 p.m. on something called Channel Five. Do you get that on your cable-free television?

D

6th November 2008

Darling Don,

We stayed up all night watching the television; a first in our house. Congratulations on Obama, that's wonderful news.

I was sure I saw you last night. They interviewed someone in a coffee shop in New York about the election and there was an extremely distinguished gentleman behind her. Was it you? Do you own a salmon pink jumper? As I write this I'm laughing; no, of course you don't. But he reminded me of you.

E

June 12th, 2009

Hello dearest,

I'm enjoying my role as your cinematic advisor with a little help from others. Tomorrow's televisual treat for you is either Genevieve (3 p.m., BBC2), Wife vs Secretary (TCM 2 p.m.) or Last of the Mohicans which is in the evening on Channel 4, along with The Holiday and Shaun of the Dead on ITV2. Am I alone in thinking ITV2 shows The Holiday on a near-constant loop? I cheered when you bought the Free View box, but what is the point when they only appear to show the same four movies in a row.

Have a wonderful day. Can't wait to hear from you later.

D x

September 3rd, 2010

Hello,

Another residuals check came through today for the 50th anniversary release of A Girl Named Rose; and did you see Moss Fisher died? Ninety years old, knocked down by a tour bus on Sunset Boulevard. Excellent news on the former, and I knew you'd want to know the latter. Can't help feeling there's some kind of cosmic retribution implicit there.

Don't argue with Rose, dear girl. You want different things, but her heart's in the right place. Same place as yours. She wants you to act again and she's right. Who cares if you're older or not? You were Eve Noel! You don't keep a diamond in storage just because they found it a while ago. You let it out and you let it shine.

Anyway, you know what I think; I've told you enough damn times over the years. Oh, by the way that review arrived; thank you. I can't see it but I'll get some help to read it.

Love D

Jan 2011

My third fax of the day to you so I'm sorry to waste your paper. I just had to tell you I'm moving a few things around as Rose is complaining there's no space. One whole room is papers for you. Your letters, letters I wrote you when I was ill and never sent you – oh, so long ago! Things I've written down over the years, little chapters of memories to remember what it was like back then, and our faxes. All of them! I reread some of them, a lot about Conrad and Jerry. Poor darling Conrad. Oh, Don. I know what he did was wrong but my God, he paid for it, poor boy. He was good, sweet, kind – until he betrayed you he would never have hurt a fly and I think for years I blamed myself for his death. It was the system, not me. Has anything changed, now? I do hope so. Gosh, it's painful to remember and sometimes I can't bear to but it gets easier with time, doesn't it? How did we – all of us, how did we let ourselves be duped by that system? Do you wonder sometimes what might have been?

E x

Rose, Rose Rose Rose. Red rose. White rose.
I'm sorry, it's late and I've had one or two.
You're my best friend and I love you. And I miss you,

so much. This is ridiculous. I'm saying it now, and you'll be cross, and I shouldn't drink I know it I KNOW IT but things aren't good sometimes, you'll understand one day. I wish I could explain but I can't, not like this.

All my love Rose, my real rose.

D

15th July 2012

Don, something strange happened today and I don't know what to do about it. Rose was out again, shopping in town and meeting her friend. It's raining here, it has been for weeks, and I was emptying out the water butt again. I heard someone walking up the drive and so I rushed inside and peered through the spyhole in the front door, to see who it was.

There was a girl standing on the doorstep. She was very pretty. I opened the door, more out of curiosity than anything. She looked rather surprised, I suppose I forget my witchy appearance. She said, 'Hi, I'm Sophie, I came by last week? You remember?'

Which is rubbish because she didn't. I remember the film people coming to try to persuade me to do the film. I haven't changed my mind, I'm afraid, Don. And this girl was like the other girl, but not quite the same – oh, I can't explain it, it's my bad memory too, and I only know I sound absolutely crackers when I do.

Still I have to try to get it right, so I can write it down. She smiled politely and her eyes opened wide, really wide, and she said, 'Don't do the film.'

I said, 'Why? I thought you were keen. You were the one they said had the idea for it.'

'No. No. I'm not. I'm not.' And then she said, 'It'll ruin everything if you do it. Please don't.'

I told her I didn't understand.

Then her expression changed, rather as though she'd lost the elastic that was holding her face together. Her

361

mouth drooped. Her eyes took on this awful, hunted quality. She said, 'She's supposed to be making a fool of herself. It's supposed to be a disaster. It's all wrong.'

I said, 'Who? Who's making a fool of herself? Who are you talking about?'

And then she said something that made my blood run cold. She said: 'My dad started out at the clinic where they took you. You hate white roses, don't you? My dad was there. He said you used to scream all night that you hated them. I hate them too.'

I don't know how she knows that. I'm still sure it wasn't the girl from last week. But I can't be 100 per cent positive, Don.

She just smiled and said, 'I'm so sad you're not doing the film but I think it's the right decision! Thank you for your time!'

'Who are you?' I asked her.

'I'm Sophie Leigh,' she said. Then she started to look around her, past my shoulder. I was scared then, because I felt she was close to realising about me and Rose, and I didn't want her to find out.

Then she flashed her big white teeth – she must have been American with teeth like that you know – and said,

'Make sure you don't do that film.'

And she walked down the drive. She was singing to herself.

Very strange indeed. My sister would just say stuff and nonsense and I should do the film. But . . .

E

July 16th
Sorry: I was out of town and I just got this. I think you should do the film too!

But seriously, I also think that girl sounds cracked in the head. I know movie stars these days are all crazy but

362

that's too much. Call the movie producers or the film company, or get your agent to do it.

Listen, Rose, I'm coming to London. Finally. In a couple weeks. An old projectionist is restoring one of my films, and the Arts Council is paying for me to come meet with the guy and talk him through the last section. They're paying! I'll be here three days, I'll let you know the details when I'm booked.

We've both changed a lot. I have some things I want you to understand. It's very, very easy if you want to say no and I won't be surprised. But this time I'm really coming and so I'm going to ask you again. Can I meet you again?

My love

Don

PS Reread this. I don't like it. I think there's something kinda strange going on. Be careful, Rose, my love.

CHAPTER TWENTY-SIX

A GIRL IS cycling along the road by Hyde Park as we drive towards the Dorchester. She has a red-and-white flowered dress on, scruffy grey Converse, a bright green helmet jammed over messy curls, and a brown leather satchel slung over one shoulder. She slides calmly in and out of the traffic, the evening sunlight filtering through the trees in the park and flickering on her dress. As she moves past us I watch her through the blacked-out windows, glad she can't see me. She's so free.

I can't stop thinking about Eve and Rose. And Don. The letters lie beside me, read and reread, now neatly stacked in their box. But they're not just letters, or faxes. There's three whole exercise books full of stories, scenes from her life back then. How she met Don. How she came to Hollywood. What she remembers about the day Rose died. She writes so clearly and beautifully as if she is excising something. I want to know when I can go back to the house, read some more of the letters and see them again. How do you live so quietly when you should be so angry? I suppose because of what I saw in Eve before: that she has a contentment I, for example, don't. She knows the confines of her life, though my eyes burned with angry tears as I read about Rose's imprisonment, or Don's sad, wistful declaration of love to her. She has to meet him again! She has to. It's crazy . . . The moment I get to the hotel, I'm tracking him down, telling him he has to come see her anyway. She's persuadable, I know that much. Yes, I'll get Sara to . . .

Sara. It brings me up short. What comes next. I touch the letters, like a talisman. I stare out of the window again, wondering where the girl on the bike is going. Into town, to meet up with friends? Where would someone like her hang out in London, what would she do?

I lived here for three years doing *South Street People* and I don't know it at all any more, except as a series of luxury hotel suites. Back then I was nineteen, and I thought I was it, with my flat in Shepherd's Bush with the IKEA sofa, my knee-high black boots, my *Heat* magazine party album I played on my brand-new iPod, the series of crusty pubs, tapas joints and pizzerias in St Christopher's Place I used to hang out in with the rest of the cast and crew. I liked *South Street*, for all that it was silly at times (one Halloween episode had me blacking out and dreaming about marrying a goblin). I played a girl called Nina, she was a trainee doctor in an A&E ward and she was cool, I loved being her. That was the time of Alec Mitford, when I realised I liked living like this, away from Mum, doing this job that I knew how to do and was good at. Before my life became like this. This . . . *thing*, totally separate from who I am.

From the front seat, Gavin is issuing instructions into a tiny black headset.

'Bayswater Road incoming. ETA three minutes. Thank you.' He turns around and nods at me. 'So this is how it's going to work, Sophie. No one knows you're going to the Dorchester. The photographers don't even know. There'll be no one outside, so we'll get you straight to your suite. It's been swept and it'll be on lockdown. Only people with security clearance admitted.'

'Who's that?'

He stops, confused at being interrupted. 'I don't know. You. Me. Your assistant – what's her name?'

'Sara,' I say. 'It's Sara.'

He looks at me. 'You don't want her coming in? That's fine, I'll get her struck off. You and me, then.'

'No, make sure she has clearance,' I say. 'I think . . . yeah. I think I have to see her.'

He nods, uninterested. 'Fine. You film the final two scenes at Pinewood this week, three guards with you at all times. Then we fly you home – the studio will pay for a jet.' He sees my expression. 'It's covered by their insurance. You will not go out of the hotel unless accompanied by myself and two others. The police say they have several leads they hope will result in arrest.'

'That's not true,' I can't help but say. 'Seriously, if they knew who it was they'd have got them by now.'

Gavin cranes himself around even further so he can make eye contact.

'I know it's unpleasant. Look, this will all be over soon. You just need to do as we say till then. Is that clear?'

I watch the girl on the bike as the road opens up and she flies away. Her dress flutters and her legs pump up and down, furiously. 'Sure,' I say. 'I – Gavin, can we –'

'What?' he says. His eyes narrow.

I look at him. Think everything through. 'You know what, it doesn't matter.'

He turns back, and I lie against the seat and look out of the window. I'm sick of being driven around in cars. I want to walk down the street myself, like Alec can. I'm sick of men with earpieces surrounding me wherever I go. I want to sit in a cafe and read a magazine, without some photographers trying to get a shot of my tits. I think I know how I can make this all go away. I just need to handle it myself, and maybe, just maybe, I've got it right, and I can start to look at my life again in terms of what I want to do, not what I can't do.

I check my phone again. There's a text from Alec, like I called him up by thinking about him.

Really hope you're OK. This is all a little freaky. I'm fine, hope we're cool. I need to clear my head for a bit.

I'll catch up with you later, lovely. Be brave, be strong, OK?

Oh, fuck off, Alec, I want to reply. But that's exactly how I would have expected him to have behaved, if I'm honest. I'm more annoyed with myself, for allowing myself to think even for one moment that we could be more than just a one-night stand. I feel like I fell for the oldest trick in the book, like someone holding out their fingers and then waggling their thumb on the end of their nose when you go to shake hands. He's always been like that: I wish I didn't care. Something he said last night is in the back of my mind, troubling me, and when I can, I need to pluck it out, think about it, work out what to do.

We pull into the forecourt of the Dorchester. My eyes flick up, and I frown, as Gavin swears under his breath, 'What – what the fuck?'

A great horde of people is standing outside the doors. Young girls, some boys, and a throng of photographers in their black puffa jackets and caps, their huge lenses pointing at the door. They see the car arriving and turn towards us. Gavin is shouting into the headset. 'How the fuck did they know she's here?'

Two burly guys are standing on the steps, holding their arms out and yelling at the crowd. A third guy dashes forward, opens my door. I wish I didn't feel so scared; I grab Eve's papers in their box and he almost yanks me out of the car. 'Clear space, please, incoming,' he's yelling, as the crowd surges nearer. The girls start screaming, the photographers are pushing them out of the way, swatting these young things to the ground to get closer to me.

'Patrick!' 'Patrick!' 'I love you, Patrick!'

I stand up, look around, blinking in the evening sun, and the first burly guy pushes me towards the door.

'Oi, where's Patrick?'

The photographers keep snapping, but the girls and boys have stopped screaming, arms down, some folded. The doors open and Sara bursts out onto the steps.

'You've been so long!' she says. Her jaw is tense, her eyes wide. She reaches forward to take my arm and I pull it away instinctively.

'Hey, Sara.' I give her a small smile. I don't know what to say to her.

She scans my face. She does look worried. 'I was . . . I really was concerned there for a while. Come inside,' she says, and they're pushing me up the steps.

'This is shit,' one of the girls is shouting. 'Where is he?'

'Let's go inside, Miss Leigh,' says Gavin.

'Sophie Leigh,' says someone. 'It's Sophie Leigh! Oh, my God, that bitch. I can't believe she just turns up here like *that*. After dumping him and like running away?' She starts sobbing. 'Oh, my God, poor Patrick!'

The revolving doors have stopped working and we're stuck on the steps. I want to laugh – it's so ridiculous, the whole thing. I don't care any more. I turn around and watch the crowd. The photographers start snapping, I'm smiling, I feel an uncontrollable urge – which I resist – to lift up my arm and point at my armpit. Or to shout something totally nuts.

'What the fuck is going on?' says Sara, pushing at the immobile door. She bangs on the glass, almost hysterical. She's on the edge, this is taking its toll on her. I start to listen to what's going on around me.

'I read somewhere she was being lined up to go out with Tom Cruise but he says no, she's well ugly?'

'That film she's making, it's supposed to be *shit* and she's *soo* all I reckon myself.'

'I bet he dumps her. They ain't together no more.'

'I don't like her dress. It's like a sack.' All of this is bellowed in the charming way people have of speaking within earshot of famous people like they're deaf.

Two girls are crying. 'I have to go home now, I've missed him,' one of them is wailing to her friend. 'I can't believe it? This is so shit? And I hate Sophie Leigh, she's so not right for him? I want to die?'

'Welcome back, Miss Leigh,' the doorman says suavely. 'My colleague is releasing the door manually. It appears to be stuck.'

I'm hugging the letters to my body but I release one arm and wave at him. I feel safe out here, that's the weird thing. Too many people. Too many harmless lunatics around.

'Oi – hey, miss? Will you sign this?'

The first crying girl steps forward, hands me a pink biro, and then turns over her hand. 'Miss Leigh. Come this way.' One of the guards has me by the arm.

'It's OK. Look, I'm not signing the back of your hand,' I tell the crying girl, feeling like a Victorian schoolteacher. 'Haven't you got a piece of paper or something?'

'Nah,' she says, giving me a hard, angry look.

'Jackleen,' one of her friends says. 'Here, have this, you *lesbian*.'

Jackleen thrusts a magazine at me. 'Sign it? Yeah? To – I don't know, put "Wishes and dreams come true" . . . No, "May your wishes and dreams come true, Yours sincerely, Sophie Leigh". Yeah?'

I wedge the box under my arm and take the magazine. There on the front cover:

SOPHIE: FAT AND FRIGHTENED:
Dumped by Patrick for Amanda?

There's a photo of me with my mouth open, yelling at some premiere, facing a photo of Patrick, arms crossed and looking sad, walking alone on a beach.

I start to say something and then stop. There's no point. It's all just stupid. Gavin's pushing me from behind. 'Let's move inside,' he says.

I sign the cover, awkwardly, and hand it back. 'Are you going to eBay this?'

'Yeah,' she says.

'And who are you waiting for?'

Jackleen's friend, the magazine-thruster, says bossily, 'Er . . . don't you know? Patrick? He's staying here, tonight? His like manager told us?'

'Who?' I say foggily.

They look at me like I'm a total loser. 'Your boyfriend, Patrick Drew?'

'She doesn't even care where he's been?' One of them starts crying. 'OH, MY GOD, poor Patrick, it's awful?'

'I'm not going out with him,' I say. They stare at me.

'Eh?' Jackleen says. 'Yeah, you are.'

'I'm not—' I begin, but two of them cross their arms. I can't compete with the truth as laid out in red and pink on the front of a magazine.

Sara touches my arm. 'Come on.' The doors start turning. 'Yes, of course,' I say, recalled to the present. 'Look – see you later. Er – thanks,' I add, not sure why I'm thanking them. They turn away, utterly indifferent. One of them lights up a cigarette, another peers inside her Topshop bag.

I wave goodbye to Jimmy, who's leaning against the car, watching me. He blows me a kiss and I go inside, feeling light-hearted, I don't know why. The fact that they knew who I was but literally couldn't have cared less is somehow comforting. Plus, I'd forgotten teenage girls are hilarious. I don't mind any more, that's the thing. If I'm right about what's been going on – and I must be, mustn't I? – then pretty soon, it'll all be over. I just need to carry on going through the motions. Stay relaxed, and just keep on wheeling in and out of the traffic, like that girl in the red-and-white dress on her bicycle.

CHAPTER TWENTY-SEVEN

A NERVOUS YOUNG man in a too-big suit shows me to my suite on the top floor. The view stretches west, across the park, framed by the white stucco enclaves of Bayswater and South Kensington. The last rays of the sun are bathing the city in an amber glow.

'Artie's on his way up,' Sarah says. 'You're . . . OK?' she says anxiously. I turn and see her face. She is pale, her eyes have delicate blue circles under them, like she's not slept properly.

'I'm fine,' I say. I put the box of Eve's papers on the bed.

'What's that?' she says, curious.

'Stories,' I say, because I don't know how else to explain it.

'Why were you so late, then?' she says. 'Sorry. I really don't mean to like, pry? It's just, I was so worried . . .'

'The car got a puncture. We were on the M4 for an hour. Didn't they call you? I told them to give you a message.'

'No,' she says. 'A puncture?'

I nod. 'Yep.'

'That's really strange.'

'Yes, it is,' I say. 'But then a lot of messages haven't been getting through lately, have they.' She looks up again, not sure what to make of it. 'Never mind, we're in town now, things'll be much easier. I'll be done here soon and then I can go home, get out of here.'

Sara curves her plastic hotel key card between her fingers. 'Right,' she says. The card is almost bent double, the sides touching, like a teardrop. I watch, in an agony of suspense, to see if it'll break.

She's weighing up what to say and eventually she says, 'Sophie, can I ask you something?'

'Sure,' I say. I sit down on the bed.

'When you get back – what – have you decided . . . is Tina coming back to work for you?'

I turn to her. 'You know what's going to happen, Sara.'

She is about to speak but the door swings open with such force that it bangs against the mahogany desk behind it and Artie strides in, arms outstretched.

'Sophie honey, hello. How the fuck are you. Give me a hug. Come here. What the fuck. How are you.'

He pulls me into a hard, almost painful, grasp, then grips my shoulders and pushes me away from him, looks me up and down like I'm a life-size doll.

'How you doing?' he says. 'You look good, great in fact. You been eating?'

'Not much,' I say. It's true.

'Your skin is great.' He turns around. 'All that rain. Sara? Be a doll and get me a diet Coke from downstairs, will ya?'

'There's some in the minibar, would you like me to . . .' She trails off.

Artie stares at her.

'Did you hear me? I asked you to get me one from the bar. I don't want some fucking minibar shit.' Spittle flies from his mouth. 'Did you not hear that's what I asked?'

'Artie, don't talk to her like that,' I say. Sara's eyes are fixed to the ground. 'Is that OK?' I ask her.

'Sure . . .' she says quietly. 'I'm sorry, Sophie.'

'She working out OK?' Artie watches her go. 'That Lynn's assistant? The one who was obsessed with you, had all those postcards of you up over her desk?'

I swing round to look at him. 'She what?'

'Sure,' Artie says, scratching his beard and looking out of

372

the window. 'Nuts about you. It was a joke. Shelby told me about it, the girls used to laugh at her. I told you.'

'No . . . you didn't,' I say, looking wonderingly at him. 'Why—'

But Artie's moved on. 'Listen to me. What is going on with you? What the fuck's been happening? I told Tommy he ought to fire himself, if he's in charge of your security. It's one fuck-up after another, honey – not any more, anyway. I'm gonna see to it. It's gonna be OK though. You shoot two more scenes, we have you here, secure, you fly home, they'll catch whoever did this shit, bam. OK?'

Bam. I look at the table, covered with glossy magazines. *Paris Match* at the top. *SOPHIE: SE MARIE?* on the front, and one of the photos of me and Patrick Drew having coffee. While I've been living in the Forest of Arden for the last few weeks, in some alternative celebrity universe Sophie Leigh is on the verge of marriage or break-up with Patrick Drew. Those photos must have had a good old airing, if that's all they've got to go on, not that they need actual pictures to make up stories. They just do it anyway.

'Where are they getting this stuff about me and Patrick from?' I ask Artie, who's sitting down and tearing at the little cellophane packets of complimentary biscuits.

'No idea. We have a conference call with Ashley later on. Let's ask her.' Artie rips off the corner with his teeth. 'It's complicated – who knows where they get their ideas from.' He raises his hands to heaven, thus admitting guilt and also dispensing with the topic. 'I wanna talk to you, honey. Feel like I had to get on a plane to do it. You've been elusive and I'm concerned about you.'

'I was angry with you after the whole *Bachelorette Party* thing,' I say. 'But I haven't been elusive.'

'Yeah, you have. The number of messages I've left with that damned assistant – she says you'll call back right away, and you never do.'

I close my eyes. 'Yeah. Well, that's going to be sorted. Don't worry.'

'Never returning my calls, etc., etc.' He slams his meaty hands across his thighs. 'But it's fine, I love ya, you're my number one gal, aren't you? So let's talk. And I want us to nail down your next project. We got great feedback on you in *Second-Best Bed*. You're doing some amazing work. Really great. It's gonna get you an Oscar nom.'

He says this nonchalantly. I blink. 'Seriously?'

'Oh, yeah. I'm working on it. It's what people want from you now. We made a good call with this movie. If they get Eve Noel it'll be huge. *King's Speech* meets *Shakespeare in Love*. Meets . . . I don't know. Yu-huge. *Cleopatra*? *Citizen Kane*?' He spreads his arms wide. 'I want my diet Coke.'

'She'll be back soon,' I assure him.

'OK. Now you know, and I know, these kind of movies ain't tent poles. But they go on and on. And it gives us a calling card. "She's shown you what she can do. Sophie Leigh can do anything."'

'You said it'd be a big mistake.' I don't look at him. I move around the suite picking up ornaments, putting them down again. The sun has almost disappeared.

Artie blinks, throws another tiny biscuit down his throat. 'I said that? I don't remember it like that, honey. So what's next? OK, so we couldn't go down that road with *The Bachelorette Party*, but I have a lot of interest in you for Patrick's next film. It's a great role. Lot of heat. A *lot*. Really it's a beautifully written part, and that's what's made me think I have to talk to you about it first, too, then you and Patrick should hook up and talk it through.'

'Great,' I say. 'What's it called?'

He laughs, then wrinkles his nose. 'Are you ready? Huh? Are you ready for this?'

'Yes.' I am surprised to find I'm annoyed. Bored, almost. Is that crazy? I wish he'd go.

'You're ready! OK.' Artie pushes up one jacket sleeve, then the other. '*Surfer Dude 2*. It's kind of similar to *Surfer Dude*, in fact. OK, so he's a surfer, and he won't grow up and commit, he's totally obsessed with the waves, hanging out around

374

Pismo. He has this girlfriend, and she wants to get married, and he's like – no way – and he goes to Australia with his friends for one massive final party.' Artie chuckles. 'Hilarious. Kind of the *Hangover* meets . . . *Point Break*. It's great.' He nods at me. 'So we need to get you signed. They'll start shooting after Labor Day.'

'Sorry, what's my part?' I say.

'You're his girlfriend. You are like the moral heart and compass of the film.'

'Do I go to Australia?'

'No, you're at home. Like . . . calling him up and giving him hell!' Artie smiles. 'You know how to do that!'

'The long-suffering girlfriend,' I say.

'Sure, but it's more than that, honey. She's a clever woman, she's educated, she's totally focused on her career . . . she's pretty humourless. It's almost a dramatic role, in fact . . .'

I stand up and smile at Artie. 'No, thanks.'

He picks some more biscuits off the plate. 'Are you serious?'

'Totally.'

'Nine out of last year's top-ten grossing pictures were sequels, Sophie.' He eats a biscuit whole. 'They're offering five mil and it's only for three weeks' work – it'll be the biggest movie of 2013. You get five mil for douche-all, we get you back up there, people know you're a player again.' He wipes his forehead. 'Plus there's rumours, you know. You're cracking up, that's why you dropped out of *The Bachelorette Party*. You've made up the whole stalker thing.'

'What?'

He's shaking his head. 'I know. It's crazy. But that's what they're saying. Think about it.'

I laugh. 'I've already thought about it, Artie. I'm serious. I don't want to be the girlfriend any more. I want to be the person in my own right. I'm sick of being defined by someone else. Every single movie I've been in.'

Artie's jaw clenches. 'You – what? Honey, that's not what I'm saying—'

'I'll dance in mud and fall over, I'll eat fake shit and make out with a horse – I don't have a problem with any of that. I don't mind looking stupid, I'm just not doing shitty films about drippy women any more. Sorry.'

'What the hell are you talking about? What's made you start talking like this?' Artie demands, as the door opens and Sara comes in bearing a tray.

'I've been talking to some people.' I'm almost laughing. 'Artie, don't worry. I just want to know there's something better out there.'

'There isn't.' He slaps the coffee table promptly. 'OK?'

I smile – I'm not anxious or tense. Like I say, I don't care any more. I know it's nearly all over for me. I know sooner or later they're going to get me, and whether it's a knife or a gun or a 0.1 per cent rating on Rotten Tomatoes or being booed at the MTV Movie Awards, I can see my time's up in some way. It's been working towards this and it took seeing Eve and Rose for me to realise: sometimes you don't have any control over what happens. You have your own mind and that's it. And if you can sleep at night that's fine.

Sara puts the diet Coke down on the table. 'Is there anything else?'

'Sure,' I say. 'Sara, while Artie's here I thought it'd be best to tell you. I think I'll be going back with Tina when we're in LA.'

I face her, watching her eyes move. 'I know that's not a surprise—' I hesitate. 'She's keen to carry on. I just wanted to thank you for everything.'

Artie's flicking through his BlackBerry, occasionally darting glances up at me as he does. Sara looks at him, then at me. She smiles. 'Fine,' she says. 'I thought so. I hoped not but – hey, you can't blame a girl for trying.'

I walk towards her. 'Look,' I say. 'You're really talented. I want to get Artie to help you. Set you up with an agent, get you to some auditions again.'

Artie is half listening. 'Sure,' he says. Then he stops. 'What? No.'

'Artie, as a favour to me,' I say. 'She's really good. You'll thank me. She could be in *Surfer Dude 2*, no problems. She'd be better than I ever could.'

Sara inhales sharply. Her eyes dart over me. 'Serious?'

I nod. Swallow, painfully, in the back of my mouth.

She steps away from me. 'I don't know if—'

A shrill ringtone makes me jump. Artie looks at his BlackBerry. 'Jeez. I have to take this. It's Patrick, honey. He'll want to know you're here! I'll be one second.' He steps outside, and we're alone. I turn to her.

'I know it's what you want.' I keep my eyes on hers. My voice low. 'You should be me. It's fine. I think you could. It's not too late for you.'

A curious expression comes into her tired eyes. 'It's too late for me,' she says.

'No, it's not,' I say. 'You're good. Just – no more crap any more, OK?'

'What do you mean?'

I clench my hands into fists at my sides. 'You know what I mean.'

'No, Sophie, I don't, I'm sorry.' She's knitting her fingers together.

'I know it's you who's been doing this stuff. I know you messed up the house, and I know you set up the trap at the hotel. I know you've been leaving the white roses.'

Sara's back teeth clack furiously together, like she's chewing, a little rabbit movement. 'That's not true. How do you know that?'

'The cops showed me the CCTV from my security gate, the time the first rose was delivered. I didn't put two and two together. It was you, wasn't it? You convinced Denis to let you in, you were dressed like me. I remember he said, 'You're back so soon,' when I arrived home that first time. It didn't make any sense, and then I remembered, earlier today, when we said goodbye. You were wearing the same top today as the girl on the CCTV. Striped. Red trim.'

'That's all you've got?' She's laughing. 'Seriously?'

'No. Eve Noel. She recognised you when I showed her your

377

photo. And she showed me a fax she wrote to . . . a friend. All about your visit to her.' I shrug. 'I don't have any proof, and I don't know how you did it all. Just a feeling. I think you're angry about everything and you're taking it out on me. You want me to fail because you don't think I deserve it. And you're right, you should have my career, I'm sure you're a better actress, but I can't help it, it's mine. LA screws you up if you don't know how to handle it, but it's not my fault, OK?'

Sara rubs her eyes. 'This is crazy. I love you. You're amazing. Why on earth would I want to hurt you, Sophie?'

'I don't think you do really want to hurt me,' I say, holding my sweating hands behind my back. 'I think you've been festering away for so long that now you've got what you wanted, you don't know what to do with it. You don't know what to do with the plan now it's in action.'

She laughs. 'This is stupid.'

'I'm not going to tell anyone,' I say.

'Yeah, right.'

'I'm not. I made a lot of mistakes. I was a cow to you too. That summer, at Jimmy Samba's? When I slept with Bryan . . . he was properly your boyfriend, wasn't he? I only just realised recently. I'm sorry. I didn't really get it, before, didn't notice. It must have hurt you a lot. I was selfish.'

Sara brushes something imaginary away from her cheek. 'Oh . . . wow.' She looks down at the floor. 'Well . . . yeah. I was really into him. You just – you never realised, you didn't see the effect you had on people. You just waltzed in with your accent and your "I don't care, I've got nothing to lose" and it was so weird to me. So weird when that's all I've ever wanted. I suppose . . .'

I interrupt. 'I'm sorry. That's the thing – when you get your own way all the time you start to think you can't be wrong about anything. Well, you've done a lot of stuff wrong. But so have I. When we're both back in LA I'm going to arrange for you to see someone. Someone who can help you. I'll help you get an agent but . . . you need to see a professional

therapist. And then I reckon it kind of cancels out. Just . . .
stop it. OK?'

I haven't thought this through. I don't know what she'll
say. I bend down and unfasten the straps on my shoes, buying
her some time. I can hear her breathing, rapid, shallow. I look
up again and think, *She does look like me.* I smile.

'What's funny?' she says, almost impatiently.

'We – us. You look like me,' I say. 'It's true, everyone always
said it. But you do.'

In her eyes, I was the lucky one, she wasn't. I had a pushy,
nightmarish mother who got me here. She didn't. So I don't
blame Sara, I tell myself. I blame the system that spat her out
and made her like this.

'What do you think?' I ask her.

'OK.' She says this after a moment. It feels like hours. 'OK.
Wow. Yeah. OK.'

The door bangs open again and Artie claps his hands. 'Sorry,
ladies,' he calls. 'Sophie, my apologies. Patrick's on his way.
He wants to say hi—'

He trails off, as he realises Sara and I are still facing each
other.

'Girls, what's this about?' Artie holds out his hands. 'Is Sara
causing you problems? Is—'

I wave him away, pick up my iPad and hug it to me, then
turn to Sara again. 'Nothing. I'm going to have a bath. We're
OK here, aren't we, Sara.'

She nods slowly. 'We are.'

'Great.' He isn't interested. 'So, Sophie. Hey. Where do we
go now?' He chews his lip. 'Honey, honey. Let's say – I'll catch
up with you later. There's a lot of people want a little bit of
Sophie! We got game, we got fuckin' game, let's use it, OK?
We'll talk later.'

I nod, and he kisses me on the cheek.

'I'm going down,' says Sara. 'I'll come with you.'

Artie gives her a non-committal grunt.

'So, bye then,' she says to me. She shoots me one last look
as they leave.

'Bye, Sara,' I say. The door opens and I catch sight of the two big guys outside, black suits, sitting on black chairs, either side of the door before it closes again and I am all alone.

It's only then I realise I am dead, dead tired. Fatigue washes suddenly over me and I can barely stand. I lie down on the blessedly cool, smooth, cotton duvet cover, roll onto my side and stare out of the window at the park. A helicopter flies over the trees in the distance. There's the faintest sound of car horns and traffic. I hear one of the security guards chatting to the other, then nothing. I close my eyes and sleep, for how long I don't know.

When I wake up it's night. The lights of London are red and white outside and it's dark in my room. It's very quiet; I can't hear anyone in the corridor. I'm the only person on this floor. I wonder what Sara's doing. I check my phone. It's ten-thirty p.m. Rubbing my eyes, still half asleep, I wander into the bathroom – coral, grey and gold, like a Moroccan riad. Hot-pink peonies everywhere. I'm going to have a bath. Yes, that's it. A long, hot bath, and an early night. And maybe, just maybe, I'll sleep now. I'm getting one of the guards from outside to stay in my room though, just to be sure.

There's a huge bottle of Jo Malone grapefruit bath oil on the side and I pour it in, breathing in the citrus tang as it roils around the steam. The mirror fogs over, the water rushes. As I lean forward to inhale the sweetly sour fumes my head spins; I'm still knackered. It's been a long day. This time yesterday I was getting ready for the night shoot. I hadn't slept with Alec. I hadn't seen Eve again. Nothing really had happened.

I wonder how Eve and Rose are, in their cold damp house. I wonder if today is a watershed for them, as it hopefully is for me. I need to tell the police I think it's all over. Should I do that? How do I do it? My tired brain keeps short-circuiting. *Get some sleep and think about it tomorrow.*

Instead I'll do something constructive. I make up my mind to call Don Matthews. I'll get hold of his number and tell him to come over and see her. Tell him she wants to see him.

She's just afraid, and she doesn't realise she's got nothing to be afraid of . . . nothing at all. I take out the phone number I'd asked Sara to get for me and dial it.

There's a long, long connecting crackle, about thirty seconds, and for a while I think it's just not going to go through, that the number's wrong, and then it rings, for ages, and again I think, no. Oh, dear. They're not at home.

But suddenly a voice answers. 'Hello? Who is this?'

I walk backwards and forwards. The connection in the echoing bathroom, with the sound of water roaring around me, is rubbish. 'Hello?' I call. 'Hello!'

'Yes. I can hear you. Who is it?' It's a thin, dry voice, slightly quavering.

'My name's Sophie,' I say. I think I hear a sound behind me and I whirl around; it's nothing. I clear my throat. 'Is that Don? Don Matthews?'

'Yes,' says Don Matthews, though he sounds uncertain. 'I'm having a nap. I'm extremely old, you know. What do you want, dear?'

'Oh gosh. I'm so sorry . . . I'm calling from England . . .'

'Right. Well, give me your cell, and I'll make sure and call you when you're fast asleep.'

I laugh, I can't help it, his tone is funny. I turn into a corner, away from the bath, and unzip my dress.

'I'm sorry to bother you. It's just I wanted to talk to you. It's important. About Eve Noel,' I say.

There's a silence. 'What?'

'Well, I saw her today,' I say. 'She told me – about you.'

'Who are you?' he says, sounding cross and old at the same time. 'Why are you ringing?'

'Listen,' I say. 'I'm not trying to do anything. I just wanted to tell you not to listen to her. You have to see her when you're over. She—'

The water is roaring loud and so I don't hear her coming in.

Don't hear the door close.

The blow comes from behind, and the phone drops to the

floor, smashing into pieces. I fall, slipping on the marble, my knee tearing and burning. She stands over me, as I look up at her, and she's laughing.

'You stupid, stupid bitch,' she says. 'Did you really think that'd be it? Do you seriously, honestly, think you've forgiven me and that's it?'

She stamps on my face, and I scream. I hear a crunching sound and I can't see anything. I scream again. The pain is unbelievably, elementally bad. I curl into a ball, but she stamps on me again, my face, my shoulder, and she's laughing as she kicks me against the bath, like you'd kick a rag doll. She is very strong.

'Guess we won't look similar any more after this,' Sara says, laughing, and before I can find the strength to reach out and catch her leg with my other arm she raises her foot above me one more time, and brings it down, and everything goes black.

accept one's fate

OUR ROUTINE WAS basic, and tedious. Get up. Breakfast, two cups of tea for me, coffee for Rose. Clean and do household chores – in a desultory fashion, it must be said. Read a little. Have some lunch. Then a nap. Rose would go for a walk, or to do the shopping, if needed. I would write to Don. Have some more tea. At 6 p.m. every day Rose had a bath, while I listened to the news and made our supper, then we ate supper, read some more or watched television if there was a film Don had recommended, and so to bed. I slept a lot. I read a lot. And most of all I wrote things down, about my life then. Or I wrote my faxes to Don, who was my life now. On the rare occasions I had to venture into the village or to town, I'd go in the morning, rather than the afternoon, because there were fewer people around. Once in a while one of us would attend church. That was the only variation to my routine. The biggest dramas of my life of late were the visits from those film people, and my ear infection, which required a trip to the doctor's. I hadn't been for ten years and though I wanted Rose to come with me, of course she couldn't. It took me a week to get over it. People – waiting rooms – the pain in my ear – a doctor asking me questions I didn't want to answer – until I realised she didn't care that much, only wanted a solution to the problem so she could move on and treat the next patient.

Two days after Sophie Leigh had been to see me, I was standing in the kitchen, opening a tin of soup for lunch and thinking about Don, as I always did. I'd told him about Sophie's visit, just as I'd told him about the girl who'd arrived on the doorstep the week before. He was quite strange about it, wanted to know what they both looked like, and then at the bottom of his fax he'd written:

> *Dammit. I really must see you. I can't come this way and not see you again. My Rose.*

You see, it was that that was making me so nervous. I hadn't asked for Sophie to barge her way in here with her strangely direct questions, but she'd come and now she was gone, and in a curious way her coming meant I hadn't had any choice in the matter. This, this question of seeing Don, it was my choice, my decision. I didn't want to see him – oh, I did, more than anything, you must understand me – but at the same time, I knew, I *knew*, that if I did it would be the end of everything. Letters are words, they can persuade you of anything. Actions are what have hurt me, all through my life.

So until I turned on the radio that Friday morning, I'm afraid I assumed that this drama was really all about me.

> 'The Metropolitan Police are urgently appealing for witnesses after the actress Sophie Leigh was found unconscious in her hotel room, having been subjected to a severe and vicious attack.'

The can buckled as it landed on the ground; lumps of glutinous potato, sand-coloured blobs on the cracked linoleum. I looked down in a daze and stepped over them, to turn up the volume.

> 'She remains in a critical condition in hospital. She was discovered on Wednesday night in the bathroom of her room at the Dorchester hotel by her assistant, Sara Cain,

who alerted police. It is understood Miss Leigh was under close guard already because of specific threats made against her by an unknown person. Police are questioning the guards who were absent from the scene, responding to another security breach, when Miss Cain arrived at the room to check on Miss Leigh. Sophie Leigh is one of the most successful actresses working in Hollywood today. Though she was born in a small town in . . .'

'Rose!' I shouted. '*Rose!*'

They went over to a juvenile-sounding reporter who had some rubbish about the 'Hercule Poirot nature of the crime' – and I stood there, staring at the kitchen floor without really looking at it. My first thought was, *I'm not going to ring them.* I could easily just not have heard the whole thing.

Then I thought of Sophie's beautiful face, rather bolshie and so funny when she wanted to be, how kind she'd been, how confused she seemed. I was surprised to find myself clutching the table; I found I couldn't bear the idea of her in pain.

'Rose!' I called again, and as I did I thought again of that girl who'd come to see us the week before Sophie came back, with the mad, raving eyes that searched over my shoulder, peering into the house. *'My dad started out at the clinic where they took you,'* she'd said. *'You hate white roses, don't you?'* The clinic I was taken to after I lost the baby. Where they shocked me. Who was she? She wasn't Sophie, I knew that much, but . . . what could I do? Perhaps it had nothing to do with anything, I told myself. If I rang the police, what would they say? How would I be helping? After all, my involvement with this world today is minimal, and I thought that I preferred to keep it that way.

You gave her your letters to Don, you gave her your pages about what happened to you. You trusted her, she trusted you. She needs you. Why did you do it if you didn't want her in your life?

I don't know why. *I don't know why.* I mopped up the soup, crossly, and opened the cupboard to take another tin out.

And I looked at the cans, lined up so neatly. Ten a week, half a tin each per lunch, our lives stretching out in front of us in cans. Tomato, potato, Scotch broth soups. I thought about that girl who was so like Sophie and yet never could be. Her eyes, staring at me. '*I hate them too.*'

'What's wrong, Eve dear?' Rose said, appearing in the doorway.

'Sophie,' I said. 'Sophie Leigh. Someone's attacked her. They don't really say how she is.'

'What?' Rose stood stock still. 'Why?'

'I think I know why,' I said. 'I think I need to go to the police. Will you come with me?'

Rose rocked back on her feet and her face grew pinched. The way it used to. When she trusted no one, because she'd been lied to and cheated on so many times. Anyone in authority terrified her. For years after I found her, she had nightmares about the police finding her and taking her away.

I realised then in that moment that perhaps, in many ways, I was the stronger one. Perhaps I always had been. Rose flew out first, and her wings melted in the sun and she fell to earth. I had followed, cautiously, and carried her up in my arms.

So I took a deep breath. 'It's all right. You hold the fort here,' I said, and we looked at each other and smiled. I walked down the corridor to the hall, where hung my summer mackintosh. 'I think I might see if the car wants to work, just this once, and take me to the train station,' I said. 'I think I ought to go to London.'

Rose followed me through and out of the door. 'Good for you, darling.'

But the car wouldn't start. I hadn't driven it for a long time, and I knew it was leaking something rusty, from the bottom. I sat in the car, thinking. If I rang, who would I call? I didn't know who to speak to. I'd spent so long cutting myself off I'd become really very good at it. And after all, what use would I be to Sophie, I asked myself. Some eccentric old biddy turning up talking rubbish about murderous assistants with crazy eyes. No, better to accept one's fate and stay here with my little slice of life: the soup and the mice, the rest of the letters and faxes from Don and the memories, and dream about what might have been. I could spare those letters – I had enough. And she didn't need me. She had lots of people who'd help her. I went inside, ignoring Rose's expression, and closed the door.

CHAPTER TWENTY-EIGHT

THERE'S A GREEN stencil of a flower, like a rose, on the window of my room. That's all I remember, of the two, three, four? days after the attack. I've lost all track of time but whenever I look up it's there. Sometimes I think I'm awake, sometimes I know I'm asleep and it's better that way. There are a few other things I recall, with varying degrees of terror or bemusement. The ferocious clang of the pale blue metal bin lid in the hospital room, white cloth and tissues stained blood-red disappearing into its jaws before it snaps shut. A doctor, or someone, talking very loudly right next to my bed, voice blaring like a foghorn into my soggy mind. Someone sobbing, a voice that I know well. I can't reach out to remember what I feel about the voice and its owner. The pain. The pain closing around me before the cold rush of morphine washes me again in its cool relief.

My first actual memory afterwards is in the middle of the night. I know it's night because it's dark. That sounds stupid, but in hospital for a long time you lose your sense of day and night, hot and cold, who you even are. I wake up, look around, and try to move. But when I do it's agony. I don't know why I'm there and I start to cry, howling great sobs. My right side doesn't do anything. It feels heavy, cold, fleshy. My face throbs. I try to lift my hand up to touch it but I can't feel skin. I try again, lifting my left hand, and it falls onto a mass of cotton dressing. Like a mummy. I trace with one finger, feeling for my eye socket, my cheekbone, but they're covered up. I can't feel anything. Then I remember her, remember Sara's face over me. I scream, hollering so loud my throat hurts. A door swings open, someone comes in, and soon I'm asleep again.

I dream about her. I can hear the words, see her face, the bared teeth, the horrible rictus smile.

'You stupid bitch. You think it's over because you decide it's over?'

She kicks me, in the stomach, and I howl. When you see it on film, it never looks that bad. It is agony, and I curl up as tight as I can.

'*I* decide. *Me. I'm* in charge now, not you. You understand that?' She's so strong. She pulls me up by my hair, thrusting my head back and forward, so I can hear the bones in my neck crunching and I think she might break my neck. Then she throws me back on the floor and starts talking, her mouth open wide, flecked with spittle.

'You remember the day you went into the studio to talk about *Goodnight LA*, and you threw a hissy fit because they made you read, and you thought you were too fucking big to audition any more? I bet you don't remember. It's just another day to you. Well, I was the girl after you. That's when I started to get mad. Watching you, staring at the rest of us outside the room like we were *dirt*, 'cause you'd made your crappy ditzo films and you thought you were a star . . . You're not a star, Sophie, you're just a stupid bitch who got lucky, and I was the girl due to read after you, and I smiled at you but you didn't remember me. I should have had that part, that movie sucked with you in it, you made it tacky, you make everything tacky, everything you touch, you skank . . .'

Her voice is a hissing, rapid monotone. 'And then that day I saw you in the lobby at WAM and I deliberately elbowed you in the tits, because you know what? You did the same thing to me when you came in for the audition. And you just looked at me like I was fucking scum, like you could have me fired, because you're the one who got lucky and I'm the

389

girl who should have had the nose job who didn't get her break and the truth is I deserve it, you'll never act the way I do . . . It should have been me. You had no idea who I was, and that's when something inside me said, *This girl needs to be reminded that she's nothing.'*

She puts her shoe on my chin, pushes my face up. I don't fight her. I'm trying to gather my strength. Slowly, quietly, I breathe in and out. 'You were so desperate for company, it's tragic. You don't have any friends, do you? How totally sad is that?' She makes a boo-hooing sound, and laughs. 'It was so easy to make you believe I wanted to hang out with you. You, you're like the total symbol of what I hate about this town. You're no good. I'm better than you! It should . . .' She pauses and swallows saliva. 'It should have been me, not you.

'I could cope when you were on the trash heap making shitty films, because that's where you belong. But you convinced yourself you ought to be a *proper* actress, making *proper* films.' She's shaking her head, eyes wide open. 'How fucking stupid you sound! You! You're so bad in this movie, and no one's telling you, because you got them the funding, and they're too shit-scared to admit you're ruining it! And you can't do it again.'

'Shut up,' I say. I reach out to take her ankle in my fingers and she glares manically at me, the huge whites of her eyes almost swallowing the irises. I think she might explode.

'Shut up, Sara,' I say again. 'Shut the fuck up. You're tragic, you know that? You're living in a—' With all the strength I can summon, I try to sit up, but when I put weight on my shoulder I realise something's wrong. A white shaft of pain drives through me and I fall on the ground again.

I call out for help, screaming at the top of my lungs, but the water's still running and it's so loud.

She laughs. 'They're all downstairs. I got lucky, there's some drunk guy on the floor below and I told them he was behaving erratically and asking about you,' she says, stepping lightly on my chest with her foot like a victor, mocking me as I lie on the floor, sobbing quietly. The pain is so bad, I hope I'll just pass out. 'No one knows it's me. I'm out of here, and you'll never be able to prove it. The CCTV in your room is disconnected, isn't that weird? I noticed it when I went to check everything was OK in the security booth earlier. You gave me clearance, remember?' She starts kicking me, short jabs all over my body, laughing.

'That's what's so funny. You worked out it was me, and you're so arrogant you thought you could just have a little word, make Sara go away, calm her down? Yeah, right. You're going to be so ugly when I've finished with you . . . You won't act again, and that's the only way to get rid of you. You thought you liked Eve Noel, didn't you? You don't know anything about her. If you did you'd know she hates white roses. My daddy worked in the clinic where she lost her junk all those years ago, he watched her get the shock treatments, he told us all about her, how all she said all day was, "Take them away, take them away." That's why I kept sending them to you, I knew you'd never know. I just liked the idea that your idol was crazy in the head, and the thing you thought you knew about her, you were wrong about, because she hated them, and now you hate them too.

'Your face is *fucked*.' She stamped on my face again, and I cried out in pain, in huge, huge pain. Not sharp, stabbing needles, like before, but internal, agonising, gnawing, heaving pain, the kind that makes you pass out. She did it once more, wiping her lips with her hands, so the lipstick she was wearing smeared across her face, and her eyes were staring at me. I knew she was mad – even then I clung to that – but it was me who'd sent her that way, I was the trigger, and I couldn't help thinking as she did it again, and I prayed to just give up and pass out, that she was probably right – I had done something, somewhere along the way, to deserve it.

But the next time I woke up in my hospital bed three days later, there she was. Standing there, smiling demonically. And when I started to scream again I realised I wasn't making any sound. Just the quiet beep of the monitor. The hum of the strip lights. The gentle murmur of low voices outside.

'Hello, Sophie,' she says, and I open my eyes wide, and realise I can only see out of one, and that I can't move, can't seem to move my face at all.

CHAPTER TWENTY-NINE

SHE STARTS TO walk towards me, with that crazed smile on her face, the huge white eyes, and then her guard slips and I think it saved my life. She glances behind her, just for a second, and I know it on a basic, primeval level: *She's scared. She doesn't know what comes next.*

I can't yell so I act. I flick my one good eye behind her towards the door, looking alarmed. Sara turns around again, on edge and I take a deep, painful breath, reach over, summoning up the last little bit of strength I possess, and with my left arm I pull out my drip.

All of a sudden, things start happening very fast, and because I'm still half out of it, it isn't until later that we piece it all together. The door swings open. A doctor comes in, and a security guard with two policemen, followed, incredibly, by Eve Noel and Patrick.

Patrick Drew. I stare at him. He stops at the sight of me.

The security guard grabs Sara, as Eve steps towards her. 'There.' She points at Sara. 'It's her.'

The guard and one of the policemen pull her arms behind her back, and she struggles. I close my eye, so I can't see if she's looking at me. I don't want to see her any more. She starts screaming as they haul her out of the room, her voice high-pitched, like an animal. *'No! No! No! It's not fair! Leave me alone! No! LEAVE ME ALONE! It's not fair!!'*

The doctor is tiny, pretty and flustered, with a halo of back-combed hair that's escaped her tight ponytail. She presses a button beside my bed and holds up my arm, whipping the stethoscope deftly from around her neck and into her ears. Two people in blue scrubs burst in. I look over at Eve, leaning against a wall, looking pale. Patrick Drew takes her by the arm.

'Would you like to sit down?' he says.

As the doctors start hooking me up to the drip again I watch him helping her into a seat. 'Thank you so much,' says Eve, smiling at him, as if this were totally normal.

'Eve, what are you doing here?' I begin, and then I realise the sounds I'm making don't relate to the words I'm trying to say. I stop.

'It's OK, Miss Leigh.' The doctor looks at the monitor next to me and flicks a biro on my arm. It hurts. I jump. She smiles. 'You've been in a bad way, but you're getting better, you see?'

I can hear Sara's voice receding down the corridor, until it's no more than a tiny, faraway cry. It could be something else entirely. An animal, something in pain, a coyote out in the hills at home. I listen, my eye half closed.

My mouth is thick, heavy, stuffed with something, and I can't feel my face when I reach up with my left hand to touch it. I turn to the doctor. 'What's wrong with me? Why can't I speak?'

But it sounds like rubbish.

'I'm sorry—' The doctor smiles politely. The remaining policeman, pathetically young, shifts uncomfortably, as if the raw, shifting emotion in the room is too much.

'Here.' There's a voice beside me. It's Patrick. He hands me a notebook and a chewed pencil. 'Write it down.'

I've never been more glad to be left-handed. I write, *It was her. She did it. What's wrong with me? Why are you both here?*

But the letters are crazy, wiggling up and down on the page, like I'm drunk.

The doctor looks at Eve and Patrick, unimpressed. 'You should go. We don't have visitors. I need to examine Sophie again.'

The policeman says calmly, 'We'll need to ask you two a few questions, madam and . . .' He addresses Patrick. 'Sir. Can we go somewhere . . .'

I bang my hand on the sheets, shake my head. I write down, *Please, can't you just tell me why you're here first?*

I hold up the pad. Eve turns to the young policeman and says: 'Let me explain, my dear, and then we'll go. A couple of weeks ago, Sophie came to see me. I wouldn't let her in. Then, some time afterwards, another girl purporting to be Sophie Leigh arrived on my doorstep. I live a quiet life but I knew enough to know they weren't the same person. As you see, she resembles Miss Leigh somewhat but it wasn't her. No sparkle. Strange look in her eyes. I have no idea why she came.' She looks at me. 'I think she was lonely. I think she wanted to prove she was as good as Sophie, she could play her, control her destiny, if she wanted.' She lowers her voice, and smiles at me. I try to smile back but I can't. The room is silent; I look at her, so poised and beautiful, and realise she is almost relishing the audience.

'I told Sophie this when she visited again a few days ago, and then I didn't hear anything more until this dreadful business was on the news yesterday. This morning I realised I might be able to help and that . . .' She falters. 'I ought to help. I should have come last night, I know.' She gives me a small, quick glance of apology. 'I came to London, and my agent met me off the train. She took me to the Dorchester, to inquire as to where the police investigation was based so that I might give them my evidence. While I was waiting in the lobby of the hotel, this young man –' she gestures to Patrick – 'approached me, and asked me if I was the actress Eve Noel, which I am.'

The larger, older policeman has re-entered the room. He jerks his head back, as if someone behind has him on a string. I can see him thinking, 'That's it!' The younger one looks a little blank.

'We fell into conversation. I explained the situation to him. He told me the young lady in question was at the hospital with

Sophie. That no one had realised yet it was she who was responsible. We came here with all possible haste. In fact, it seems as if we arrived in the nick of time.'

Patrick nods. 'How the hell did she get away with it?' He turns to me. 'Sophie. Wow. I'm so sorry.'

His kind eyes, his beautiful face: I stare at him, realising I'm probably off my head on morphine and I shouldn't try to speak again. He feels like a benign presence, here in this brightly lit room, cluttered with steel and plastic and machines that beep. I think back to that coffee, on that sunny LA afternoon, when the biggest concern of my life was appearing in public with a sweat patch under my armpits, and how he thought it was kind of ridiculous. He was right.

I hold out my hand. 'Thank you,' I try to say, to him, and to Eve. She nods, then mutters something into her lap and stands up. 'I have to go, I have an appointment,' she says. When she looks up, her eyes are full of tears. She kisses my forehead. 'Thank you,' she says.

I write down, *What for?*

'Bringing me out of myself,' she says. She looks years younger as she says it. 'Though I am afraid it has been at great cost to you.'

I shake my head. I look at her. Then I write, *You should come back to your old house some day. Come and see me.*

She gives the faintest of smiles. 'Maybe. Maybe I will. I wasn't very – happy there.'

That's why you should come back, I write, pleased with myself. She smiles.

I scribble quickly, *What about your letters, your stories? I loved the avocado tree.*

She shakes her head and strokes my cheek, a tiny gesture but the skin to skin contact makes me glow. 'Oh, darling girl. Keep them for now. I've got more than enough.'

'Miss Leigh should get some rest,' the doctor says. I look at her name badge, but I can't read it; the letters are jumbling in front of me and I realise I'm awfully tired. I had something to tell Eve, something about a phone call I'd made for her,

and now I can't remember what it was. I remember the phone
. . . I remember holding it in my hand, talking and then
– nothing.

Eve clasps my good hand. They usher Patrick out after her.
He turns and says, 'I'll come see you again soon, Sophie. Hang
in there.'

Through the open door I look out and see two, three more
guards, thronging the narrow corridor, nurses pushing past them
on their way somewhere more important, a gaggle of patients,
three or four, their mouths hanging open as Patrick Drew walks
past, his arm through Eve Noel's. Then I see Gavin, striding
towards the door, and then he catches sight of me. He winces
and takes a step back, and I recall Patrick's expression when he
first arrived and understand what it means. That little moment,
more than the high drama, the blood, the pain, tells me all I
need to know.

CHAPTER THIRTY

AFTER THREE MORE days in hospital, they transfer me back to the Dorchester, as though it's my home: the release papers have my address as *The Dorchester Hotel*. I will be there for a few days before I fly back to LA. But I need a place to stay so the police can interview me again, somewhere secure and near the hospital, and the hospital doesn't particularly want me there if it can be avoided – I'm out of danger, but there's too much craziness. Two reporters broke in through a ground-floor window, and there's been an increase in 999 calls asking to be taken to St Mary's Paddington, people wanting to rubber-neck Sophie Leigh and her mashed-in face.

I don't care where I am, really. I don't care about anything and it's almost a relief. I don't even know if I have a cheekbone left yet, so I'm not going to worry about whether my hair looks OK or if I should call someone back. But I'm lonely. They keep me in splendid isolation, and Sara was right about one thing, I've realised. I keep thinking about it: I don't have any friends. Sure, there's people I've made movies with who I'd have dinner with, but no one I can call and say, *Can you come over? I need you. I'm in trouble.* They told me Mum was here, when I was under. It's a blur. I'm sure she's coming back. Mum was never going to be the kind of person to deal with it all, though, to draw a curtain around me and her, tell everyone else to get lost. She never was, though she did it for the best.

My good eye gets tired and I have headaches if I try to read or watch TV. So I lie in bed and think. I wonder about Casa Benita all the time. I can't stop wishing I was back there, with my own things, in the sunshine, where avocados grow on trees and the jacaranda flowers in May. I wonder about Deena, if she's still at the house. Has she nicked anything? I think about her often, in fact. How ridiculous she used to seem to me. 'We've got more in common than you realise,' she said. And I was horrified, but now I see what she was talking about. I don't want her to have to make her living that way, then I realise how patronising that sounds. Maybe she likes it? Maybe it's what she wants. Perhaps when I get back I should just ask her what she wants and how I can help her. Things are going to be different when I get home, whether I like it or not. Perhaps this is my chance to make some things better.

Then I catch myself thinking like that and it makes me slightly nauseous, whether because I sound like one of those fake Hollywood do-gooders I always used to despise, or because I'm secretly so shit-scared of what comes next I can't bear to think about it. Not yet. So I lie in bed and think about stuff I do like, until my mind wanders again.

I miss the ocean. I miss California. Maybe I just don't love LA any more. I wish I could move Casa Benita, like Dorothy's house in *The Wizard of Oz*, lift it up and place it down along the coast, towards Monterey and Big Sur, near a pier or that beach Patrick talks about. Somewhere I could sit and watch the sea, curl up on a sofa when an old film comes on the TV, go hiking. Or back down on the beach, near Venice, my old stomping ground where I spent my first summer in America, that summer I first got to know Sara.

She's in custody a few hundred yards away, at Paddington Green police station, which is also where they hold terror suspects so it has breeze blocks and crash barriers outside. I find this comforting. She's saying it's not true. That we've made it up, that she's being held against her will. That someone else attacked me, that she found me on the bathroom floor, that had it not been for her I'd be dead, that I've got a grudge against her and fired her, that she'd come back to fetch her things, she was worried about me, etc. She didn't have a plan, I know it. I think she just thought she'd freak me out, and then it got out of control. Because she's mad. She must be mad, to have done that. Her father has lined up two different psychiatrists to interview her, so she can plead diminished responsibility, serve her time in some US facility for rich people. I don't think she'll go to jail, and I'm not sure I want her to. She needs help.

I can't believe I thought I'd be able to sort her out by myself. Idiot. She was lucky too – there *was* a strange-looking guy on the floor below, some weirdo running around with what looked on CCTV like a gun, so the guards outside my room were right to run off when she came up and told them. Turns out it was some European royal in town for a big party coked off his head and chasing some girl up and down a corridor with a champagne bottle. Idiot.

It's so crazy it almost works, and she's so perky and sweet people believe her. That's the trouble. And there's no one else to back it up. Sure, there may be other people who thought she was a bit strange, but that's not evidence, is it?

We've got the CCTV footage from the house, first time she delivered the rose – just walked right in and left it on the bed, then drove out again, bold as brass, but it's hard to prove that wasn't me. I suppose her confidence is what convinced people, has done all along. So if it wasn't for Eve, willing to swear in court that Sara came to her house and tried to impersonate me, it'd be a lot harder. Oh, they'd get her eventually, I'm sure. She's plain crazy. But without Eve it'd be a lot harder. It's strange, how the two of us are linked. She thinks I saved her, and I know she saved me. I've made a lot of mistakes, but the day I bought Casa Benita, and connected my life with hers: that was a good day, for both of us.

We came in through the back entrance, but after they've got me upstairs and settled me into bed, I realise I can hear the scrum outside – photographers, cameras, rubberneckers, all jostling for a view, a piece of me – from my room. There are helicopters overhead and when I flick onto E! there is a shot of the Dorchester with an inset picture of Elizabeth Taylor and the celebrity reporter saying, 'Not since Dick and Liz has this hotel had so much amazing notoriety, thanks to Sophie Leigh!' in tones of total hysteria. Like getting my face bashed in was an amazing career move, for me and the hotel.

I'm exhausted and so I sleep. When I wake up again, I look around the lovely, sunny room. Gavin is next to me, flicking through *Gun Mart* magazine. And there's someone else, at the end of the bed. I open my mouth to say something, and then don't. I can't remember where I am, or who might be nearby. I swallow, and cough a little, and the person at the end of the bed turns around.

'Sophie? Oh, great.' It's Tina. She gets up. 'Hi there,' she says shyly, her eyes scanning my face. She looks different. Lighter, somehow.

'Hello,' I say, but it sounds strange again. 'How are you?' She nods. She doesn't understand what I've said. 'Where am I?' I say. She shakes her head, her expression fearful. I lick my parched lips and say, as clearly as I can, 'Where am I?' I feel my lips touching on the 'm' of 'am', my tongue working. I stare, confused, at the domed brass lamp base, searching for my reflection, and can only see a whirlpool of human flesh.

'You're at the Dorchester,' Tina says. 'I – ah, I got here yesterday. I figured you'd want me.' She smoothes the sheets, like a nurse in a film. 'Artie told them I could come in. You'll be able to speak soon, it's just your jaw's numb and your tongue too. All that swelling, it'll go down in a day or two, and when it does, we'll see what to do next.' She smiles gently at me, and picks some papers off the side of the bed. Gavin turns around slightly and then goes back to reading his magazine.

I can't find my pad. I pat around for it on the duvet and after a few seconds I say, as clearly as I can, 'Tina . . . You look great.'

She shakes her head, politely, but without pity or a slight look of horror like most other people. 'Sorry, Sophie. I don't understand.'

I repeat myself. 'You look *great.*' I wind my finger around my face. I touch my lips. It's so crude, and yet it's the only way she and I can communicate now, and it's crazily simple.

She closes her eyes and shrugs. She does look great. Her lips are unremarkable. Her face is . . . normal. Beautiful, in fact, and the kind of sad weariness she always wore around her only adds to her melancholic beauty.

'Thanks, Sophie. I'm glad I had it done. It was great to get away. But I blame myself, I shouldn't have left you.'

'I think I had it coming,' I say, but she doesn't understand me, so I ask, 'Why did you come back?' She looks confused.

I repeat it, slowly, and she shrugs her sloping shoulders. 'I figured you needed someone to help.'

She and Gavin, are here because I pay them to help me. I can feel tears of self-pity welling up in my eyes, and they sting. My muscles ache. I ache all over, in fact. I give a great big sniff and she turns around. I shake my head and reach for the pad she's holding in her hand.

In the still of the room, the only sound the faint roar outside of people, traffic and helicopters, I write, *I'm glad you're here.*

She gives a small smile. 'Thanks.'

Tina, can you get me a mirror?

'Um – I don't know, Sophie.'

I push aside the duvet, the golden silk covering.

'Give me a mirror,' I say, as clearly as I can.

Tina smiles. 'Um – well.' She and Gavin exchange a glance.

My arm is in a sling, and there's a massive elastic pad over it. My stomach aches, from being kicked repeatedly. I still can't feel down one side of my face either. Just the sensation of something not being there and I don't know what it is.

'A MIRROR.' But the side of my face is frozen when I touch it, and my tongue sits heavy in my mouth and she looks blank. Panic suddenly overwhelms me and I start to shout, a strange, howling moan. I rock forward in the bed, backwards, forwards, clutching the sides of my head. What the hell has happened? Why am I here? *How bad is it?*

She hands me a mirror, from the dressing table. It's wobbly on the bed, but I hold it in both hands and bring it up to my face. I blink my good eye, and I stare.

At first I can't even make out what I'm looking at. Then I realise that thing there, that's my mouth. Tina is standing next to me. I look up at her, at her beautiful, blemish-free face.

'OK,' I say. I nod.

'The doctor's coming back in an hour,' she says. 'With a plastic surgeon. Artie too.'

'Why's it like that?' I point to my jaw. She shakes her head. 'This,' I say, jabbing at my jaw.

'You broke your jaw.' She corrects herself. 'I'm sorry. *She* broke your jaw. And shattered your cheekbone.'

'I can see that,' I say sarcastically, but it comes out as 'I han heeha.'

I can't stop staring at myself in the mirror, my hair falling into my face. Its greasy but shiny chestnut-brown perfection is almost funny, a doll-like rebuke to the rest of my battered, horrifically ugly face. It's all on the right side. My eye is black and swollen shut, though I can see a little out of it now. I'm covered in cuts and scrapes, and purple and yellow bruises. One of my teeth is chipped, broken off. It's my cheek, and all the bone around my eye, that I can't see. It's covered in dressing, from the nose to around my ear, and my jaw too. When I touch my cheek, I can't feel anything.

You wouldn't recognise me. I don't recognise myself. Honestly, I look like a monster.

There's a silence as I stare and stare, and Tina watches me. 'Facial injuries heal quickly but they always look worse than they really are,' she says hurriedly. 'They told me that.'

'*Phantom of the Opera* mask, please,' I say to Tina, and by a miracle she understands me and smiles.

Then she says, 'It's nice to see you, Sophie.'

The doctor is old and posh, called Mr Marsden. In fact he's a maxillofacial surgeon, he tells me, and I write this down carefully on my pad. He's upbeat, jovial, but slightly ill at ease.

His voice is a little too loud and he rocks on his feet, glancing from Tina to Artie, clearly wondering what their roles are. This will all heal, he says. The double vision will go, and they'll use veneers on the teeth. The clavicle fracture is a clean break and should mend itself with supervision. And it's pretty simple to fix a broken jaw inside the mouth. No scar visible.

'There will be some residual damage, perhaps, and it's somewhat painful, but Sophie, you seem to me to be a brave girl.'

He smiles down at me and I try to nod.

He carries on and I pretend to understand what he's saying and write it down. We can reconstruct the cheekbone. Something about a vermillion border and how my zygomatic arch is broken. They'll make a cut in the hairline and use it to elevate the bone.

'Kinda like she'd be having a mini-facelift?' Artie says.

I look at him and try to smile at the joke. And then I realise he's not joking.

'No, Mr Morgan,' says Mr Marsden. 'This is a major operation.'

'I know, I know. I'm just saying – if you're in there anyway, would it be something you'd consider as a by-product of the procedure? You see?' Artie spreads his hands out wide, the old gesture. *I'm an open guy. Trust me!*

Mr Marsden looks at him, then me. 'Why would you want to do that?'

'I don't know . . .' Artie looks baffled: *Why would you? I know!* 'Hey, no idea. It's just a thought, because of her career, people are gonna ask her these things . . .'

'Your career?' Mr Marsden says. He leans forward. 'I'm sorry. Are you worried about your appearance from a professional point of view, then?'

He smiles at me kindly.

'She's Sophie Leigh!' Artie says. I can hear Tina swallowing repeatedly.

'I'm sorry—' says Mr Marsden.

It turns out he's never heard of me. Artie can scarcely

believe it. 'She's *English*!' he keeps saying after they have tried to explain it to him. 'She's from *England*, she's your biggest star!'

Mr Marsden looks apologetic. 'I'm awfully sorry. I don't go to the cinema much, you see.'

Artie can't fathom that a client of his who makes him this much money isn't known to him, but I get Mr Marsden. He's like the patrons of the Oak hotel. Why would a sixty-something guy have heard of the star of *The Girlfriend* and *A Cake-Shaped Mistake*?

'You're a film star?' he says again, for perhaps the fourth time.

I write down on my pad, *Been over here shooting a film about Anne Hathaway and Shakespeare. With Alec Mitford.*

His face lights up. 'Alec Mitford! Wonderful actor. I saw him in this terrible costume drama, still my wife and I . . .' And then his expression sags. 'Oh, dear. Oh, dear me. Of course. You're an actress. A film actress. My dear, this rather changes everything.'

I look up at him.

'I'm afraid I can't be quite so optimistic that you'll make a full recovery, not to the level you'd require, I assume. You will heal and have a completely normal life, except you may limp for quite some time – your ankle has been quite badly shattered, you will need extensive physiotherapy for that. And you will have headaches, I expect, you usually do with this kind of head trauma. Pretty bad ones, but we can prescribe you something that's jolly effective. But as for appearing on film, I'm afraid your injuries will be noticeable.'

I nod. I write, *How?*

He says, 'It's relatively simple to mend a broken jaw without scarring. The cheekbone however . . . The surgery can leave you with an asymmetry.'

'What's that?' Tina asks quietly.

He turns to her and says, 'The shape of the face is altered. One eye may appear higher than the other. The broken collarbone will have a rather unsightly bump for a couple of years, which you could have surgery to remove, but then you're left with a scar. I'm afraid the cuts around your eyes mean you will have noticeable scarring there. This will all fade over time, some more than others. But . . . . I'm afraid . . . You won't look the same. Perhaps it doesn't matter though!'

'We live in an HD age,' Artie says, irritation in his voice. 'It does matter. Listen, this sucks.'

Mr Marsden's voice gets that high-pitched arrogant tone that public-school British men do so well. 'I'm sorry, but with this level of trauma to the bone—'

Artie interrupts. 'You don't touch her, OK? We're going back to LA tomorrow, we'll get a second opinion, and you don't go near her. You know who this girl is? No!' He shouts. 'You don't know who she is, you have no fucking idea! Jesus, this country! I don't wanna hear that she's gonna have one eye higher – what the *fuck* is that about? Some kind of freak? One eye higher than the other?' He's shouting. He turns back to me. 'Honey. Don't worry. You don't worry at all. This is gonna be fine. We're gonna be fine.'

He walks out of the room. Mr Marsden ignores his exit. 'Sophie, I feel I have to be honest with you. You understand me?'

I nod and write down: *Totally understand.*

At least I know.

CHAPTER THIRTY-ONE

MUM IS ON her way to see me, Tina says. She's phoned to ask Mum when she'll be here, in case I'm sleeping, but can't get hold of her. Dad is out of the country, golfing in the Algarve. He's coming to visit on his way back, he's told her. He's texted me:

Darling Sophs, keep your chin up. Don't let the bastards get you down! Will come and visit you on my way back from sunny Portugal. Big kisses to my little girl, Dads xxxx

So I wait, basically. I wait till I can get on a plane and go back to Casa Benita. I can't ring Eve, she doesn't have a mobile and I don't know her home number, besides which I make no sense at the moment anyway. I've written to her, thanking her for everything instead.

Tommy, bless him, sends me a huge food hamper, full of nice soft gooey stuff, and a personal juicer. My own personal juicer, yes. A guy called Keith who has a programme on some obscure home shopping channel comes to the hotel and juices whatever I want. He is bright orange with extremely curious blue eyes and has the fanaticism of a cult leader. He keeps telling me juice will make me better.

In addition to this Tommy keeps trying to Skype me. I am sure this is because he wants to get a look at my face, see how damaged his goods are. I've lost all track of time, spending the last six days in hospital or in a hotel room, but I've stopped looking myself up on the Internet, which I'd started doing again, just to see what people were saying:

Sophie Leigh Attack Imperils Bard Pic; Canyon To Lose Out; Star's Career A Wrap?

That was the *Variety* headline. I know, cheery.
The *New York Times* report said:

Though Miss Leigh only had two more scenes to shoot and it thus might have been possible to work out some compromise in order to complete production, the picture was already in danger due to the illness of Cara Hamilton, the actress playing the older Anne Hathaway. Miss Leigh had, in recent weeks, been attempting to persuade the reclusive actress Eve Noel to take on the part. Miss Noel was seen at the hospital shortly after the attack. It is not known, however, if she has agreed to return to the screen for the first time since Triumph and Tragedy *(1961). It seems likely these combined casting problems may lead to the shutdown of* My Second-Best Bed.

I'm sitting up in bed drinking one of Keith's juices, a couple of days after I've returned to the Dorchester, when there's a knock at the door. It's Tina – it's always Tina – and I nod at her. She peers around the door, looking nervous.

'There's someone here to see you,' she begins.

'Is it Mum?' I put down my glass, trying to peer behind her.

'No, it's me. Tell me if you want me to clear out.' Patrick looks around the door. 'I just wanted to check up on you. I'm flying out later today. Hey, you're doing great. Looking so much better.'

The swelling is starting to go down on my face, and it's not frozen by painkillers. I can speak more clearly, with difficulty, but I have no idea if people understand what I'm saying. I pretend to be tidying up the mess on my bed, to hide my confusion at his appearance. 'Thanks. Sit down. Want some fruit?'

I gesture to one of the ever-present fruit platters at the end of my bed, and put my good hand up to my hair, then let it drop, almost amused by my vanity. What's the point? He's seen me far worse, anyway.

'How's the pain?' He sits down on the edge of the bed.

'It's OK. I don't feel it most of the time. The foot and the cheek are the worst. But it's getting better.' I smoothe the sheets.

Patrick watches me, a worried crinkle between his eyes.

'What's Artie say?'

'Well, he's back in LA. Actually I haven't heard from him in a couple of days,' I say carefully. 'He told Tina he was working on my options.'

Patrick shrugs. 'He's kind of a tool.'

I can't help but laugh. It sounds like a donkey braying. 'He's your agent too!'

'I know, but I don't like him. I want to take some time off, go to film school, spend some time with my folks. He wants me to make him money. Maybe we're not right for each other.'

I smile and nod. 'What about *Surfer Dude 2*?' I write the rest down. *He wanted me to be in it. Are you going to drop out?*

'No, I can't, it's too late and I'm carrying the picture, I can't do that to them. I'm gonna make it, but it'll be so, so bad no one'll ever want me again. I've got my own plan, you see.'

'It's better than my plan,' I say. 'Having your face kicked in by a psycho.'

'I'll let you know,' he says, and he smiles. 'Wow, Sophie. I'm glad to see you. I can't stop— I'm sorry you've been having a crappy time.'

'Don't want to talk about me,' I say. I sit up in bed a bit and write slowly, with difficulty, *So all that stuff, coming out of nightclubs and vomming, being a dufus – what's all that about?*

He shrugs and takes the pen out of my fingers. 'We've all upchucked once in public, haven't we? That was eight years ago and they're still showing it. I hate the way they try and put you in a box. And the way they behave like I'm important. I'm *not* important.' He's drawing on my pad.

409

'No, you're not,' I say.

Patrick stops doodling. He laughs and slaps my knee, then looks horrified. 'Oh, jeez, Sophie. Did I hurt you?'

I shake my head. 'No. Honestly. Go on.'

'I was thinking about it, you know. My mom's friend Janet, she saved an old guy on Pfeiffer Beach last fall. It's my dad's birthday and I'm up in Big Sur, we were all just hanging out on the beach, catching some waves, and he's drowning. Doesn't make any noise, either. Just laying there, slipping in and out the water. And she knew what to do. I wouldn't know what to do if that happened, that's all I'm saying. She saved his life. That's important. Being some guy in a movie, that's not important.'

'It's because you're gorgeous,' I say fuzzily.

He says, 'I'm sorry, I didn't catch—'

I take the pen back and write it down. *You're gorgeous. People like looking at you.* Patrick shakes his head. There's a strange silence between us. He is blushing, and I would if I could.

Thanks for the other day. You saved my life, you know, arriving when you did.

'I didn't. It was Eve Noel, not me. She's amazing. Get her to tell you about it some other time. And anyway . . . it was my pleasure, Sophie. You just need to rest up and get better. Here. Want a banana?'

I hesitate. 'I can't eat—' I begin. He gets a fork and a bowl from the untouched food on the tray they brought up earlier, and starts mashing the banana up.

'Bananas are so great, man. When my dad got in a motor-bike smash and had his jaw like pretty much wired shut I fed him bananas for about two months solid. Have some.' He taps at my mouth with the fork, I open it obediently, and he shovels it in. It's slimy and cold, but sweet.

'Thanks a lot,' I mumble. He nods.

'No problem.' He gives me another forkful. 'So you pretty much shut the hotel down for a while, did you know that? Isn't that cool? They had to cancel our press junket, so I owe you for that big time.'

I smile, or try to smile at him. 'Good,' I say slowly, 'Don't stay if you're going to be late.'

'I've got a couple of hours. I thought I'd keep you company, if that's OK? I'll just stay here and you can do whatever you want, sleep, whatever.'

I stare at his face, thinking again how perfect he is, like a Greek statue, breathing, twinkling at me. I think of the years I've spent trying to keep my beauty intact to please other people, grooming it and treating it like a pet, and how it was probably a waste of time. And I realise how little Patrick would care if his face was messed up. I don't think he'd even notice. Alec, on the other hand, would go into a terminal decline. It hurts to smile, I realise now.

'What do you want to do?' Patrick says. 'Play a game?' He reaches over for my iPad. 'I'm amazing at Scrabble, you know? Want to play?'

I hesitate, and then I nod. Then I write down, *Won't you be late for your plane?*

'Ah, I'm all right for a while.' He grins, takes off his jacket, and sits opposite me at the end of the bed.

An hour later, we're both bored of Scrabble, and I'm bored of losing especially. It's the painkillers, I tell him, they're messing with my mind. I look at the alarm clock by my bed and he follows my gaze.

'I've been here way too long. I ought to leave, let you get some rest.'

I clutch his hand, in a frenzy of panic that overwhelms me and I don't know why. 'Don't go. Please don't go.'

He stares down at me. 'Sophie – it's OK. Hey.' He strokes my hair and cups my chin very gently in his hands. 'Hey, there. Don't cry, honey.'

'It's just – I feel OK when you're around.' I grip his other hand in mine. I don't care what's cool and what's desperate any more, don't care if it's the wrong thing to say. I know he doesn't either, never has done.

'There's plenty of people to look out for you, Sophie. Listen to me. I have to catch a plane.' He waggles his fingers inside my iron clasp. 'I'll come see you back in LA. Yes?'

I let his hand drop and turn my head away. I know I'm being ridiculous. 'Sure,' I say. 'I'm back the day after tomorrow, if they let me. You mean it? You'll come see me?'

'Er – sure.' He stands up. I feel a dead weight plummet within me. I can't talk to people any more. Of course he's not going to come see me. I'm being insane. He's Patrick Drew. He doesn't want to hang out with some clingy freak who he'll have to feed mashed-up banana to. He looks at his watch again. 'Listen, I'm glad . . . I'm glad you're all right. Hang in there, OK? I'll come see you soon. I promise. Maybe we'll have another coffee, yes?'

He smiles. I lean back against the pillows, trying not to cry. 'I'm sorry, Patrick. I'm being stupid. I just want to—' I begin, but there's a knock at the door and then it opens.

'Love – oh, Sophie, love—' It's Mum. She bursts into the room, carrying a fistful of shopping bags, dumps them on the floor and stares at me, holding both her hands to her face in shock. 'Look at you,' she says. 'Oh, my dear girl. Sophie . . .'

She rushes over and hugs me, and I scream out in pain because she's grabbed my shoulder. I lean back, shaking my head, and my eyes fill with tears. 'No,' I say to her. 'No, no.'

Poor Mum, she doesn't know what to do. She flushes red, then stands back and turns impatiently to Patrick, who's by the bed. She looks at him angrily.

'Hello?' she says almost rudely. 'I'm Sophie's mother. Who—'

'I'm Patrick, ma'am, I'm a friend of hers,' Patrick says, holding out his hand, and my mother stiffens for a moment, then melts.

'Of course you are! How lovely to see you,' she says in her best Sybil Fawlty voice, clasping his hand in both of hers. 'Well, well! Patrick! How nice of you to come and see her. Are you in town for a film?'

'Yes, we had a premiere last night and I'm staying here

412

too. Lucky coincidence.' He's so polite. He glances round. 'I'll leave you guys—'

'Oh, don't go because of me!' Mum cries. 'Please stay!'

'I'm going to try and make my flight. I would stay otherwise but I think Sophie's probably pretty tired.' He nods at me briefly. 'Take care of yourself, OK, Sophie? You hear?' and with a hand raised at my mother he's gone.

I watch the door close and smile at her, though I want to cry. She comes and sits on the bed next to me. 'You poor thing. Oh, my goodness, you poor thing,' she says, patting the coverlet.

I stare at her. The vision in my right eye is cloudy – it comes and goes. I blink in annoyance. 'Tell me what happened,' she says, brushing out the creases in her linen trousers with one plump hand. Her rings cut into her tanned, freckly skin. I try to tell her, but she doesn't understand me. I write it down and she shakes her head as she reads the scrawling script, frowning at me, then glancing away. She can't really bear to look at me and she doesn't know what to do. There's nothing we can do to help each other. Eventually she stands up, and goes over to the pile of plastic bags she's dropped on the floor.

'Well, you look better than you did on Saturday, love. Last time I saw you I wouldn't have known you. I've been up since Saturday, you know. Staying with Julie. She's in Teddington. I would have come up again on Sunday but you were just coming out of it and there didn't seem any point.'

'Course not.'

We're both silent.

'Well, I did a bit of shopping on the way. Here you are,' she says, thumbing through the layers of plastic and handing me a Gap bag. I wedge it between my legs and open the drawstring top. There's a pink vest with a ribbon around it, and matching pink checked pyjama trousers with the same ribbon. 'For you, darling, in case you run out of nighties and . . . other things.'

'Thanks, Mum,' I say, holding them to me. My eyes fill

with tears and I remember again that it hurts when I move the muscles in my face to cry, and I try not to, but it doesn't work. She watches me.

'Are you crying? Oh, you poor thing,' she says, coming close to hug me again, but she stops in front of me, then pats my good shoulder and moves away. 'Now,' she says. 'What do you want me to do? Do you want a bath? Shall I wash your hair? It's a bit dirty.'

I can't help giving a snort of laughter out of one side of my mouth. 'No, Mum. It's fine. Not supposed to get it wet.'

'Oh.' Her restless hands flutter back into her lap. She looks at her watch.

'You don't have to rush back to Teddington. We'll get you a room,' I say.

She doesn't understand, so I write it down, and she smiles and says, 'Oh, I'd love to, dear. I won't stay tonight though – I'm off to see *Jersey Boys* with Julie a bit later. She got a two-for-one deal in the *Mail* last week. Great seats.'

I write down, *So glad I nearly got murdered so you could catch up with shows in the West End!*

She reads this and looks upset, for a fleeting second. 'Oh, Soph dear, don't be like that. Anyway, Patrick said you needed to rest, didn't he? You know I was never any good with you when you were ill. I'll come back tomorrow.' She pats the silky coverlet again.

We're quiet together in the room. I don't have anything to say to her. I remember the silence in her spotless kitchen, how I couldn't get away fast enough.

It's not that I want her to stay, because honestly, I don't. I remember back to when I was about ten, and I'd been in bed for two days with the flu. Drinking Lucozade and listening to fairy stories on my shiny silver tape-cassette player, curled up in bed feeling very sorry for myself. The third day though, there was an audition for an ITV children's series, down in Bristol. Mum got me up, bundled me in the back of the car, wrapped in a duvet, and outside the studios she slapped some blusher on me, wriggled me into my new shoes and cute

414

pinafore dress and sent me in there to audition, raging temperature, sweats, wobbly legs from not eating for two days, and all. I didn't get the part, of course. The producers must have thought I was a weird little girl.

I look at her now, her freckled face with the coral lipstick smile, her perfectly highlighted ash-blonde hair. Her clothes so neat, her handbag shiny and new. She'd always have tissues in her bag, always have lipstick and a compact to hand. She taught me so much about being on time, not complaining, getting on with it and working hard. She taught me not to need anyone. She was trying to give me what she couldn't have. She did try, I know that.

She says suddenly, 'I heard from Deena the other day.'

I look up. Nod. 'Yes?'

'She said to say hello. She told me that George director fellow you were seeing turned out to be a nasty piece of work. You never mentioned. I hope he wasn't nasty to you.'

George. Another lifetime. I shake my head and mumble, 'Maybe it all worked out for the best.' She looks pleased.

'So do you think you might work with Patrick Drew again? Or do something . . . do something different after this film?'

I shrug. 'Don't know,' I say. 'Don't know if they can sort this out yet.' I point to my face.

Mum looks aghast. 'Really?'

I nod again and write, *My cheek/collarbone/jaw fractures might not heal. Cheek and jaw need ops. Will have scars on face for a while.*

She stands back and looks at me. 'But what will you do?' she says.

I shrug again. 'No idea,' I say, and it doesn't feel that bad. When she's gone, I run my hands over the Gap pyjama set, stroking the comforting fleece. Somehow that makes me feel much worse. I cry then, trying not to move my swollen mouth so it's just fat tears, dropping onto the soft cotton.

415

I am strong

AFTER I LEFT the hospital, I said goodbye to Patrick. What a nice young man – when you're my age, you can resort to clichés. He reminds me of Rose. He really doesn't care what people think of him. I don't believe he should be a film star at all, though it's probably why he's so successful – he can cope with it.

'May I walk with you a while?' he asked. He pointed to his feet. 'I got my sneakers.'

I laughed, put my hand on his arm. 'You lovely boy. Thank you, but I'll be all right. I want to go by myself.' Having been brave once I rather wanted to try carrying on being brave. 'And I'd like to clear my head.'

'She'll be OK, you know,' he said, though I rather thought he was talking to himself. And I don't know yet that she will be.

We bid farewell and I walked. I walked and walked for what seemed like a long time, through Mayfair, towards Soho. You see, I hadn't been to London since I came back home for the *Helen of Troy* premiere. As I waited for the traffic lights to change I stood still and counted it on my fingers. Fifty-four years. Almost unbelievable and yet, with my life, everything seems to have taken place in the past, a long time ago through a glass darkly, or whatever the saying is. I was nineteen when they came to Central School of Speech and Drama, Mr and Mrs Featherstone, and sat in on our Shakespeare class, and talked afterwards, very seriously, to Hermia Gauntly, my vocal teacher. I remember watching her, the disdain for them writ so large over her expressive face; she couldn't hide it. *Film people. Vulgar, Hollywood types.* In the mezzanine above, we stood and watched her.

'They're casting for a film, someone said,' Clarissa, my flatmate, had whispered, pushing her black ballet pumps over her slender feet: ballerina fashion was all the rage that winter. 'They're looking for a new star. Someone fresh. Someone who can act.'

'Someone who can act, in Hollywood?' I laughed.

It's funny, I remember that so clearly. I remember Clarissa's big satchel, borrowed from her brother, a rugby player called Mike. I remember her shoes and the windows and the smell of beeswax polish. All these little details. My disdain matching Miss Gauntly's. And then they called me over, and Clarissa said she'd wait, but by the time they'd finished with me she'd given up waiting and gone home and I emerged alone, head throbbing with promises, into the evening gloom.

My legs are awfully tired, and my brain is gently humming; though the quiet streets of Marylebone are surprisingly empty, when I cross Regent Street and head into Soho I'm terrified again, until I find a quieter route, one that takes me through Georgian townhouses and deserted, dirty back streets that I start to recognise. It's funny how the city feels the same, underneath it all, but yet it looks so different. Bright awnings and signs everywhere. Black tarmacked roads covered in yellow and white markings, information screaming at you wherever you look: it is overwhelming. Of course, I've seen it on the news, on television dramas. I watched the Royal Wedding looking for signs of old London, not the first sight of the bride. But to be here is very different. I'm pleased to see Bar Italia is still standing. It looks exactly the same. The nights we spent there, arguing about the stage, Olivier versus Gielgud, whether the National Theatre was a Good or Bad thing, what Art meant and how it tied into Commerce. Goodness, how repulsive we must have been! I wonder what happened to Clarissa Mackintosh, whom I last saw in the Hampstead flat off Flask Walk, as I hugged her goodbye and promised to be back by Christmas. And Richard, my Central boyfriend, who was big and gentle and fumbling, and with whom I think I would have been perfectly happy. Richard acted for a while; I used to hear his voice on the radio, afternoon plays and all that. But I've no idea where he or Clarissa are now. Perhaps I could find out. Perhaps, now I've broken out of my own prison, there are many things I could do.

I wish Rose was here. I determine to myself that I'll bring her back here, soon. I'm not afraid any more. In this huge sea of humanity I see something important – I don't matter very much.

This morning at about eleven, Melanie had picked me up from Paddington station – Andrea retired years ago now and Melanie is my agent, a curious woman, very keen and excitable, eager to please but oh, my! so young. In my day, agents were fat old men who ate and drank a lot, not eager young girls who wave mobile phones around and wear high heels and carry coffee in paper cups. In the taxi – they're the same, that's good to know – trundling the short distance to the Dorchester, she asked me why I was here, why I had to come down and help Sophie. I couldn't tell her, didn't feel it was her business yet.

I remember her curious dark eyes, looking to check I hadn't noticed anything about her. Desperately uncertain, yet her voice was strong and clear. I had shivered as grey buildings scrolled past us, cars moved in thick ribbons alongside us. I jumped at little things, not quite able to believe I was in London again, after all these years. I was beginning to think how awkward this was, maybe a mistake.

'You know,' Melanie said nervously, as we approached the hotel. 'If you ever wanted to work again – I could put the word out. People would fall over themselves. *My Second-Best Bed* – they still haven't found anyone to play old Anne. I should say, the senior Anne. The film's on hiatus till they know what's happening with Sophie. They'd love to have you. And there's a Miss Marple just starting, they need a—'

'Me? No, dear girl,' I said gently. 'I don't act any more.'

'I know you don't but I thought I should ask you anyway,' she said boldly. 'You see, I might never meet you again, Miss Noel. Don't you miss it?'

She sounded genuinely curious and so I said, 'I've never really thought about it. I left Hollywood a long time ago. I didn't ever want to go back.'

'Just because you're not there doesn't mean you can't act anywhere else.' Melanie sounded suddenly embarrassed. 'Forgive me. But you're – you're seventy-five. That's not old.'

'It is old.' I can't help laughing.

'It's not, not to an eighty-year-old. Oh, don't worry. I was told by my boss that I mustn't pressurise you. Just remember the door's open if you want it. *Upstairs Downstairs*, that sort of thing. Lady Bracknell—' She waved her hands vaguely and I watched her. 'There's lots you could do, you know. People remember you. *A Girl Named Rose* is my mum's favourite film ever. If she knew you were appearing in something on the Beeb, well, she'd cancel all her plans for the next six months just to make sure she didn't miss you. Here we are.'

I walked north out of Soho towards Bloomsbury, tiring a little. I recalled my farewell to Sophie.

'*You should come back to your old house some day,*' she had said. '*Come and see me.*'

And I had said, '*Maybe. Maybe I will.*'

At Goodge Street I got onto the Tube. That was terrifying, after all these years. Some kind girl gave me her seat, and I sat clutching my handbag on my knees as we swayed in time through the dark tunnels and the near-soporific commuters hung onto handles, scanning their *Evening Standard*s. I looked down at my hands, peered at my face in the glass opposite, as the seats cleared.

I didn't know what I was doing, or whether I should be doing it, but I knew I had to try.

When I emerged at Hampstead, the early-evening light was beautiful. High up above the city, the pale blue sky was scudded with creamy, fluffy clouds, like a Hogarth painting, the clean above the dirty. I found the bench I'd agreed, beneath the old black-and-white road signs, smelling the roses from the old houses on the quiet walk above me. I closed my eyes, trying to remember what it had been like all those years ago. What it would be like now. I must have drifted off; I heard a tapping sound, crunching feet on sandy gravel, and then, 'Rose?'

There was a light tap on my shoulder. I didn't look round. I stayed still.

'Don?' I said. 'Are you here?'

'Yes, I am,' said a voice behind me, warm, smoked with rye, kind, heartbreaking. 'I'm here.'

I didn't move, I couldn't move. I heard a tapping sound again. I looked up.

Don. It was Don. He was standing next to me, feeling for the bench. His eyes were clear but unfocused; he had a stick in his hand. His dear, dear face, still so handsome, only a few lines; his tall, rangy form, remarkably upright; his smile; the neat line of his parting, his hair thick; but his eyes were unseeing. He took my fingers in his, and at his touch I gave a little cry.

'It's you,' he said. 'After all these years, Rose, it's you.'

He sat down slowly next to me, I holding his elbow. 'Tell me what you see,' he said.

'I see you,' I told him.

'And?' he said. 'You know I always wanted to come here. Wanted to meet you here.'

'Don—' I said, trying to keep my voice steady. 'What happened?'

'I'm old, and I'm diabetic, and I drank and smoked too much,' he said. 'I could never get up the nerve to tell you. I can see a vague shape, you know, with this eye.' He pointed to his left eye. 'I can see that I'm next to someone. And I can hear that it's you.'

I wanted to cry, with sadness, with happiness. Suddenly I wished, ferociously, that he could see me, could see how the years had taken their toll. How wizened and mean and curious I had become.

But he said, as if he heard my thoughts, 'You're still the same.

Oh, I don't know what you look like, and I don't care. But you're the same person.'

'I tell you, I'm not,' I said.

'I've written you every day for over forty years. Until my sight went a couple of years ago I could read everything you said, and now I have software that can do it for me. I tell you, you are.'

I squeezed his hand instead, and put my head on his shoulder. 'I can't believe we're here.'

'Darling Rose.' He kissed the top of my head. 'We'll always be here. And from now on, we'll always be together.' He paused. 'We will, won't we?'

I nodded, and said softly, then more loudly, 'Yes. Yes. Oh, yes.'

'What about your sister?' He laughed softly. 'I sound like a teenage boy at a party. I meant, I'll have to meet her. I'd love to meet her.'

'I can't wait for her to meet you.' I looked around, the old red brick glowing in the sun, the sky blue and clear. 'It's funny, I thought everything had changed. But some things stay the same. The important things.' I squeezed his hand. 'Don't ever leave me. Ever again.'

'Rose, I—'

I interrupted him. 'No. Eve. Rose is Rose, I'm Eve again. It's my name. It's time to stop hiding and come out and say it.' Suddenly a great thrill of joy rose up within me, bursting out as though I could sing. 'Oh, Don. Stay here. Let's stay here. We have some time. We'll have a little garden flat here. We can walk on the Heath like I used to when I was a student. I can go into town, or anywhere, if I'm needed, if I want to work again.'

He smiled. 'Yes. I'll do that.'

'What, you won't even think about it?'

'No. It's the best way to make decisions. Too much thinking's bad for a man. Let's decide it here, right here.'

I kissed him then, unable to believe his darling face was in front of me, unable to trust that he was mine again, that I'd look after him like I've looked after Rose all these years, that I could have some happiness, even for a short while, because already I felt as though it had wiped everything out, the years of guilt, then misery, my dead baby, my breakdown, the years of slowly mending, Rose and I clinging to each other in our small house with our small life in the woods, until Sophie decided to track us down. And now I was ready.

'What about Rose?' Don said.

'I'll call her right now. I can't wait to tell her. She'll live next door. Or around the corner. It doesn't matter. She'll be nearby.' I took his hand again. 'Don, if I've got you it doesn't matter if I have one more day or a year, or ten, twenty more years. This, us sitting here, now, it's a lifetime of happiness.'

'It may only be a year, darling. Do you really want to take me on?' He moves away a little. 'I'm not even sure I should move. What if—'

'Life's full of what-ifs. What if you'd said no to Jerry. What if we'd gone home together from Big Sur. What if I'd won the Oscar, what if I hadn't lost the baby, what if Rose hadn't fallen in the stream, what if Sophie hadn't moved into my house, what if. You can live your life with what-ifs.' My fingers squeeze his hand so tightly he smiles. I kiss his dear face. 'I'll look after you. We can go to New York, visit your friends, we can spend a few months here, a few months there, we don't have to make any decisions about this or that. Just live, Don, live for today. Oh darling, we can do what we want.' The world is opening up to me, peeling off layer upon layer. 'When I had to, for Sophie, I ran up to town, got on a Tube, walked through Soho, strolled into a hotel and then a hospital bold as brass, didn't I? All in one day. After years of . . . of nothing. A weekly trip to the shops, to the library maybe. Well, if I can do all those things . . . I can pretty much do anything. And I won't go on without you. If I've got you, and Rose, and you've got us, and she's got us, that's more than most people have.'

He is very still, then he feels for my fingers and takes them in his. I love him, I love him so much. 'What about this movie they want you for?' Don says. 'Will you do it?'

I put my hand on my chin. 'Just maybe,' I say. I give a little smile and turn to him. I don't know how much he can see at all, but Don smiles too. And I feel the years drop away from me, the sun on my hair. His warm hand in mine. We sit in silence on the bench. He puts his head on my shoulder. I am strong.

CHAPTER THIRTY-TWO

I FLY INTO LA, two days later. I'd forgotten how funny the city looks from the air. The mountains, the ringed ocean, and draped over the land a sprawl of humanity, arranged with no thought or planning. As we land, I gaze across the ocean to the horizon. I'm back.

It's strange, but when they announce they have to disembark a passenger with medical needs first, everyone applauds.

'Why are they clapping?' I say, as one of the medical attendants, impassive-faced, lays me back on a stretcher.

Tina says solemnly, 'I think they're glad you're OK.'

As I'm carried out of the plane (I'm sure I could walk, but Tina has way overstated my medical needs to the insurance company, clearly) people appear from further down the plane, calling out to me. I'm still the number one celebrity news story. No one's got a picture yet, but they certainly are trying.

'There she is.' 'Don't crowd her.' 'Hey, Sophie.' 'You look great.' 'Feel better, Sophie!'

Some guy has a phone out, and takes some photos. A woman in her thirties admonishes him. 'Put that away!' she shouts, as I descend the steps. I look up, and there are faces at every oval window, waving, clapping, and I can hear stamping of feet too. A little girl right up at the front blows me a kiss.

T.J. is waiting in a blacked-out jeep for me on the tarmac.

He and one of the nurses help me into the car. I watch the people at the window of the plane, still confused.

'That's so weird,' I say. 'Why are they doing that?'

From the front of the car T.J. shakes his head and says, 'You're crazy. They're doing it 'cause they like you, Sophie.' He shrugs and then reaches back and pats my hand. 'Hey. It's good to see you. Let's get you back home.'

As I stand in the hall, looking around my house, the jasmine climbing up the clapboard outside, the old pool clear turquoise, everything pristine and beautiful, I can't help but think of Eve. On the flight home I reread the pages she gave me, the day I found her and Rose. Her letters to Don, his to her. Her essays about her time in Hollywood. How she came back here once more, only to leave, and never return. Now I am back, and everything has changed, and she's the person who would understand.

Two helicopters throb constantly overhead and even though all the doors are shut the sound is penetrating, a constant whirr drilling into my head. I limp slowly into the den, to make sure the doors onto the terrace are closed against the noise. And I stop, and stare.

The room is filled with flowers. Not white roses, this time. Flowers of every colour, bouquets, plants, bunches tied with string, a huge riot of colour. There's even a row of lavender bushes shaped into an S. They hide the furniture in the room.

Tina sneezes. 'I'm going to make sure your bags are OK,' she says. 'Oh, by the way—' she points to the corner of the room. 'Carmen and Deena have been sorting some mail out for you. You might want to check it out.' She gives me a little smile, and walks out.

I look over to where she's gestured and stare. I hadn't noticed what else is on the floor. Like Santa's grotto, there are ten or so sacks, all filled to the brim, cards, postcards, letters spilling out onto the carpet. I kneel on the ground, my fingers fumbling on the envelopes, as I tear them open: more bad news, more hatred? Give it to me now. I can take it. I open the first one, written in crazy felt-tip pen writing, every letter of my name a different colour. I swallow. I don't know if I want to read this.

Dear Sophie,

My name is Sophie too. I love The Bride and Groom. I want a dress like yours wen I am older. I am sorry you are ill. I love your films, you are pretty. Get well soon love Sophie aged 8 and a half

I pick up another.

Dear Sophie,

I've never written a letter like this before: I just wanted to say that I was really sad to hear about your accident and I hope you get better soon. My friends and I have a Sophie Leigh club where, no matter where we are, we meet in New York when you have a new movie out, and then we go drink rose wine (<u>has</u> to be rose) and catch up afterwards. Last time my friend Selina flew in from Buenos Aires just to see The Blue and Gold Dress with us. I guess we all really love your movies, and you've brought us together. Every time I'm feeling down, if I switch on the TV and one of your movies is on I always feel better. So take care of yourself, and get well soon.

Yours,
Melissa Fitzpatrick

Hi Sophie,

My daughter was extremely ill last year and spent a lot of time in hospital. The only thing that cheered her up was watching DVDs of your films on her laptop. She is back at home now and getting much better every day, but when she heard about your accident she, and I, wanted to write to give you our love and send you our thanks. What happened to you is terrible. If you ever want a break, please come to Bournemouth. You'd be very welcome.

Love from Joyce and Eliza Darling

Hello lady,

I love your films, you're funny. It sucks what happened to you. I want to send you love and strength. Remember what Martin Luther King Jr said. 'We must constantly build dikes of courage to hold back the flood of fear.' Peace.

Lila,

Long Beach

Tears run down my face, and I brush them aside, smiling. I seem to spend my whole time in tears, lately. I pick up the next letter. There must be a thousand pieces of mail here. How am I going to answer them all?

Hi Sophie,

Can you send me a photo of your face? My Friend Misha says it is messed up and you will never see again and all the bones have been Sucked Out of It. Get Well Soon Zac

Yeah, Zac – maybe not.

I'm looking up and smiling again, and then something outside catches my eye.

I scream. There's someone lying there. At the noise Tina comes rushing in, to find me laughing, clutching my face, a sack of letters spilling out onto the carpet behind me

It's Deena. She is asleep on the terrace. She's dragged my favourite rug – sourced from Turkey by a specialist LA interiors company – out by the pool and there she lies, her nut-brown, stick-like body almost naked and immobile, glistening with oil in the midday sun. Her mirrored shades are the blue of the sky.

'Oh, my God,' says Tina, dashing forwards and shaking her. 'Deena! Deena, you can't be here. What are you doing here? I told you to leave.'

Deena doesn't move.

'Deena!'

She shakes her one more time. My heart contracts, my stomach lurches.

'Deena!' I call, and I hobble forwards, ignoring the helicopters.

We crouch down beside her. I pull off her glasses. Her eyes are closed. And then they open, slowly. Tina and I groan with relief.

'Hey, kiddo,' Deena says. She pulls the shades back over her face. 'You're back.' I nod, and she grimaces as she looks at me. 'Wow. OK. They really messed you up.' She closes her eyes again. 'So how you doing?'

I shake her. 'Deena, are you OK?'

'Sure . . . Sure . . .' she mumbles. 'Tired.'

'She's out of it,' Tina hisses.

She bends down and touches Deena's shoulder lightly.

'Leave her,' I say. 'She's sleeping it off. Whatever it is.'

Deena props herself up on her elbows, and looks up at the helicopters. There's two overhead, one lower than the other, lights twinkling in the sun. 'Hey, guys,' she says, looking upwards. She raises her middle finger. 'Sit on this, you fuckers!' she yells. 'Screw you! Screw the hell out of you you fucking idiots!'

Tina and I turn away from the cameras, but Deena calls to us, 'They won't use that, trust me. It doesn't go with their story.' She stands up in one fluid movement, opens the miniature fridge that stands under the canopy and pulls herself out a beer. 'You guys want one?'

Tina and I stare at each other, then we nod. 'Great,' Deena says. 'Then we'll go inside. Douches.'

She cracks the lids against the grey stone wall and the caps fly off, leaving a chalky line on the stone. I notice several similar marks that definitely weren't there before.

'Use a bottle opener, Deena,' I say, holding the door open. 'If you're going to stay here . . . OK?'

'Sure,' she says. She hands us each a bottle and we clink the rims together, in the cool, calm room. 'Welcome back, kiddo,' she says. 'So you got burnt, hey. You'll be all right. You're a clever kid. Welcome to the scrapheap. I think you'll like it.'

I look out onto the pool, out to the hills and the houses and the valley below, the helicopter juddering just above, blades slicing into the sky like it's clinging on for dear life to something we can't see. We drink our beer in silence.

EPILOGUE

Three months later

WHAT HAPPENED NEXT? That's what you always want to know at the end of a film, isn't it? Did they live happily ever after? You don't want to see the wigs and fake eyelashes being peeled off, the cranes being dismantled, the set being taken down, the shop signs in the studio's fake city streets being painted over so they can be used as backdrop for a new legal drama, or a thriller, or another romcom starring another perky, hopeful girl like I once was, or Deena, or Eve. Or Tina, or even Sara.

There'll be another one. Thousands of girls every year, piling into this town with the old dream of fame in their eyes, to be exploited in a thousand different ways. Some of them will work out how to use whatever it is they have to their advantage, but most won't. Maybe some of them won't even notice, and might not mind.

Alec Mitford came last week. He stayed here, in fact. We had a blast. We recorded some new dialogue, did the looping for the last couple of scenes for the film. The studio's throwing money at a digital solution using unused footage of me mixed with my voice.

I have to hand it to Alec; he was great. He came in, stared at me and said, 'God, you look fucking awful.' Not for him

429

the vast hand-tied bouquets, the gift baskets, the trinkets and baubles that keep arriving, weeks after it's happened. He gave me a turquoise-and-grey Liberty scarf, wrapped in beautiful purple tissue. 'I didn't know how mashed up your face was. I thought you might need something pretty to hide it behind,' he said and I burst out laughing. I was wrong when I thought I had no friends. Deena is, bizarrely, my friend. And Alec's a friend. He really is someone you're glad to have in your corner. I realised something else, too, what had been bothering me all along: I'm sure he's gay. I wanted to ask him, but I didn't have the nerve. Maybe that's what he was trying to tell me before we spent the night together. I'm sure he knows it. In a way I hope he's not. Because if he is, he's hiding it, and I hate to think things are the same as when Conrad Joyce killed himself, over fifty years ago. Nothing does change much in Hollywood, does it?

But it was great to have him here. At night when the helicopters had given up we'd sit out on the terrace, candles surrounding us, and talk for hours, chatting about the film, about who he'd seen out at the Ivy the previous week, how he'd said hello to Jason Isaacs, what he'd heard about various industry people we both know, but mainly about how great he was for coming to see me. When I said, 'What do you think they'll do about me, in the film?' he said, 'Darl, haven't you realised? It'll be box office gold, now. Your last film before – all this. Eve Noel's first film for half a century.'

'Is she great? Tell me she's great.'

'She's amazing. She's got T.T. on his toes all right. Never misses a cue, or an angle. Knows everyone's names, polite as anything. And she looks extraordinary. She glows. The camera wants to snog her, it loves her so much. I'm telling you, she's stealing the film from right under you. Better get that face mended and get back out there, love.'

I smiled and changed the subject.

So my face? My face is not great. The injuries will be unnoticeable again in a few years they say, maybe five to ten. I have to have three more operations, one on the cheekbone,

430

something about a comminuted fracture around the eye and one for my jaw which is kind of uneven, and one on my ankle. I'm still limping. And I get tired, really tired. I don't go out much either; I'm afraid. I don't know what I'm afraid of. I suppose it's the future, but lying in bed all that time in hospital has taught me to be afraid of what might happen that's out of your control. I hate myself for it, because it's kind of self-indulgent. I'm not Rose. I didn't have my life completely, wholesale taken away from me like that. So what if a girl who used to be beautiful isn't any more? What does she lose? Adoration? Well, I had that, and it wasn't much to write home about. Money? I've got all I need. Fame? I've had fame and I know it doesn't bring you anything really worth having. But still, I'm scared. Scared to be a different person from the Sophie I used to be, even though she's gone now, she doesn't look like me any more.

Artie has 'let me go'. He thinks I need someone with more dedication than he can give to me and that I have a 'different focus to his'. That's fine, to be honest. I think we were going different ways long before all of this began. It's a relief, not having to fold myself into the person he wanted me to be. Tommy's on my side though, in fact he's raring to go. He's lined up several TV interviews, a *People* magazine front cover, and a huge book deal, just waiting for when I want to do them. The thing is, I'm not sure I want any of that. I don't want to be tragic Sophie Leigh. I want to be Sophie Leigh who does something great and oh, by the way, one eye is slightly higher than the other and she has a couple of scars and a very slight limp – she was attacked years ago but it's well in the past now.

Sara's trial is set for early next year. In a strange way I'm looking forward to it. I want to look at her, hear her try to explain why she did it. I'll be scared, but I think it'll be good for me to go through these last four months again and work it all out. I hope she doesn't end up in jail. It won't help her. At the same time, I don't exactly want her free to roam the streets again.

What else? Well, the other new thing is scripts. Tommy's

starting his own production company. He's begun giving me scripts to read and make suggestions on, because I'm stuck in the house and bored, and I've already given notes on one that's got a big development deal from Twentieth Century Fox, thanks to me. It's easy when you know how, and all those years watching movies and making movies has taught me how. Elevate the next draft so it's less mumblecore and more JenAn. Reconfigure the leading man so he lost his wife two years before. Lose the subplot and make the heroine's sister a closet lesbian – that's how you get to the third act. Have the star of the picture go to England and find herself and her real-life heroine. How does it end? Like I say, I don't know.

So three months after I came back to LA it's coming up for Thanksgiving and I'm sitting in the garden, wrapped in a blanket, scribbling on a pad again. My handwriting is extremely fast since the accident, it had to be. Now I write all the time. It's early in the morning, and a little chilly for LA. I'm talking to Tony Lees-Miller.

'I'll see you next week,' he says. 'We can iron out the details then.'

'No first-look deals,' I say. 'They're awful. And could I have the scripts messengered over here every morning? I can't read on an iPad yet, it does something strange to my eyes.'

'It's done,' he says.

I hesitate. 'Are you going to announce it?'

Tony laughs. 'Sure we are. But low-key. This isn't novelty. It's business. We'll just say, "Canyon Pictures' new head of US development is Sophie Leigh, taking a break from starring in movies herself to developing and producing them." We'll do it after they announce the Oscar noms. People'll see it but they'll move onto other things.'

'OK,' I say. 'I hope you're right. I hope they won't laugh.'

'I think they'll hope like me that one day you'll go back to acting. It's not over for you. You just need a break from it, a chance to do something else. You're good. There'll always be parts for you.' I can hear him chuckling on the other end of the phone. I picture him in his large corner office over Leicester Square, late autumn light flooding the pedestrians below. 'Besides, you know, the one thing I've learned in life is that people are much less interested than you realise, Sophie.'

'I know it, believe me. I'm the least interesting person in Hollywood these days. Not a letter or a helicopter or even a fruit basket for weeks now. They've moved on.'

We say goodbye and I pick up my work tray, then wrap myself up in the blanket again, looking out at the view. Morning is my favourite time now. I don't sleep so well any more and so I like to get up, read, do something, to keep me from thinking too much. I have a portable desk, like a break-fast tray, that I bring out onto the terrace with me when I'm reading, and write things down. And I write things down all the time now, like Eve. Maybe one day I'll tell my story too, as well as hers. There's a photo attached to the corner of the desk. I've had it laminated so it doesn't get ruined. It's of two little girls, Rose and Eve, arm in arm and squinting at the sun. They are in matching dresses and their hair is curling black, flashes of silver in the light. On the back Rose has written:

We have each other and we have you, Sophie dear.

I like the fact there's a photo of the two of those girls in this house now. It feels right.

I take a sip of my coffee. As I'm reaching for an apple, my phone buzzes.

'Hello, Miss Leigh,' says Lance, the new, scary security guard, six foot three, shaved head, hails from Montana. 'Someone at the gate for you.'

I stay still. 'Who's there? It's not even seven yet.'

'Uh . . . ma'am, it's Patrick Drew. Can I let him in?'

I start and my coffee cup flies out of my hand. 'Who?' I look down, almost surprised to see the black liquid from my cup staining the cream blanket.

'Patrick Drew.' There's a crackle. 'He says . . . Ma'am, he says he won't stay long. He's just coming for coffee.'

I begin to laugh as I'm dousing the blanket with water. There's something about this man: I can't see him without having some accident in some way, whether it's perspiration, coffee spillage, or full-on hospitalisation. 'Sure,' I say. 'Let him in.'

It's about a minute until he appears, but it seems like an eternity. He comes straight towards me and we stand awkwardly, facing each other.

'Hi,' he says. I drink in the sight of him, his firm jaw, dark brown eyes, the broad shoulders, the slightly uneven brows that give his beauty its charm and distinction. 'What happened?'

'Sorry – I had an accident,' I murmur, and sit back down, covering myself up with the stained blanket.

'Another one?' He drops his hand onto my hair, lightly. 'It's good to see you, Sophie.'

'And you. What are you doing here? It's barely light.'

'I've been up for hours,' he says. 'Drove back down from my folks late last night and I haven't slept. I had this idea, and I thought I should come ask you about it.'

Carmen hurries out from the kitchen. 'Hey. Sophie. Morning. You want some breakfast?'

'Hey, Carmen. Yes, please, scrambled eggs and bacon. Patrick?'

'That sounds great.' He turns to Carmen. 'Thanks.'

Carmen actually rolls her eyes at him and blows him a kiss. He smiles; he must be used to it, mustn't he? After she's gone he turns back to me. 'Your face is healing well. I didn't know what to expect. How's your ankle?'

'It's fine. I have some operations soon. We need to let the cheekbone knit together to see how it's going to settle down. I say "we". I mean "people who know what they're talking about" obviously, not me.' I am used to talking about my injuries now, but I have to do it in this way. Slightly jokey. 'And I'm walking short distances again.'

Patrick sits down and pulls the chair so he's next to my lounger. He puts his hand on the armrest, and says lightly, 'You know, you're different.'

I laugh. 'Well, duh.'

'No, I mean, like you've changed. You're a different person.'

'Well, that's being stamped in the face for you.' I'm trying to keep my voice light; there's a ball of something hard in my throat.

Over in the guest house I see one of the windows opening. There's a vague sound of swearing as something clatters to the floor. Deena is awake. Patrick takes my hand.

'It's going to be OK, you know. You were that person before. You still are.'

'I wasn't like this. Scared of everything, sad about everything. I can't watch the news, or think about the future.' I shift away from him, suddenly cross. 'So don't talk like you're in a movie, Patrick.'

He flinches like I've slapped him. 'I'm not, Sophie.' A faint flush creeps across his face, but then he grins. 'I never remember my lines anyway – I can't quote from any movies I've been in. You know when we had that coffee? We both talked about wanting something more. I just thought it'd be me who gets out first, 'cause I'm lazy. You're not. And I suppose . . . I don't know, there's something about meeting you properly that day . . . every day since then, you're all I can think about, and I wish I'd had the balls to come up here and tell you, but then you disappeared, went to England and I never got the chance to say it.'

My heart is racing. I reach up and touch my cheek.

'I don't just want that life any more,' he says. 'I want something else. Something that's . . . that's good. Like Eve, you know? When I left her that morning she was going to find Don, she was going to make a life with him and who cares if they only have a short amount of time left. Because just one day with the people you love, no one can take away from you. And if you're lucky, maybe you'll get more than one day. Maybe years – years and years of happiness.'

'I don't know,' I say, and the weight of not saying what I want to makes my voice crack. 'I don't think that's how it works, Patrick. Not any more.'

'Yes, it is,' he says. He leans forward; we're side by side, the sun creeping over the hills, the whole of the city spread out before us. *I will lift up mine eyes unto the hills.* 'You make it yourself, that happiness, not someone else. It's up to you. You have to be the one who chooses it. I choose it, you should too.'

A tear runs down my cheek. He shakes his head. 'You mustn't cry. You mustn't cry. When I said you were different, Sophie – do you know you're more beautiful now than you ever have been?'

I laugh. 'You really are a hippy, Patrick.'

He shrugs and grins. I grip his hand, clutching onto it as if he's about to be swept away. 'Well, so what. That's what I've realised I am. I'm going to do something different. Head upstate, go back up Route 101. Maybe open a bar, help my folks out. Take my time and do something right, anyway.'

'You're not making movies any more?'

He nods. 'Nope. Told Artie yesterday. He fired me on the spot. He was mad.'

I can't help but smile. 'Two clients in three months. Wow, there must be a lot of happy actors out there.'

We're both silent for a moment, watching the view. It's going to be a beautiful day. Patrick clears his throat.

'So Sophie . . . I wanted to ask you something. What are you doing for Thanksgiving? Any plans?'

I shake my head. 'Maybe I'll go over to Tommy's. Anita makes a delicious turkey, but it'll be full of industry people and I don't—'

His hand is warm. My hands are cold, stiff in the crisp morning sun. 'Come to Big Sur with me,' he says. Come stay with my mom and dad.'

'Big Sur?'

'Sure,' he says. 'We'll hike into the hills. Walk on the beach. You can get some fresh air in your lungs. See some otters! My dad does an amazing grill. It's famous at Thanksgiving. We'll hang out, maybe come back on the bike if you wanna . . .'

'A motorbike?' I stare into his brown eyes, push the hair away from his forehead, touch the little scar by his eye. 'Are you mad? Why the hell would I get on a bike, after everything I've been through?' I feel panicked and I don't know why. Like I want to let go of something, and I can't, I can't, it's too hard. 'Look, I think perhaps I'll just stay here. Go to Tommy's.'

'Are you sure?' he says. ''Cause I was thinking, I won't go. Not without you. I'll stay here with you if you want. We can just get some takeout, then. Watch an old movie together.'

I smile up at him, and warmth floods through me. Something fighting inside me gives up. 'Well, if you put it like that . . . thank you. Thank you very much. I'll think about it.'

I slip my hand into his and we stay still, watching the sun creep higher in the sky.

ACKNOWLEDGEMENTS

Writing this novel was a protracted affair. I had a baby in between and I had the help of many people, not just delivering the baby but the book as well. Firstly, I would like to thank amazing edimama Lynne Drew for shaping it into a much better novel, and then Thalia Suzuma who was so helpful, thorough and reliable, and is brilliant too. The title is her idea and it's wonderful. Also big thanks to Kate Elton, for her special help and support, and everyone at HarperCollins, especially glittery Liz Dawson, Ann Bissell and her trousers, Roger Cazalet, Martha Ashby, Lucy Upton, Katie Sadler, Liz Lambert, Oli Malcolm and everyone else who worked on the book.

Thanks for help with research to Fred Casella, for his advice and lunches and map-gifting. To Simon Mulligan and Lance Fitzgerald for their East Coast/West Coast coffee knowledge. To Doctor Jon Mutimer for explaining facial injuries in gruesome detail and answering my odd questions. What the people passing me on the stairs of the London Library thought as I sat there discussing shattered jawbones, I have no idea. To Reb for her swing-bys and her friendship. Finally, huge thanks to James Coleman. For his help with LA and Hollywood, and for always being a wise sounding-board.

To Jonathan Lloyd, Lucia Rae, Melissa Pimentel, and all at Curtis Brown: my gratitude and love. And to Kim Witherspoon and David Forrer and my US publishers Simon & Schuster, especially Louise Burke, Jen Bergstrom and Karen Kostylnyik. To Christine Steffen-Reimen at Droemer Knaur, and to Frederika van Traa at Uniboek (and little Rosa!) thank you for sticking by me and for being such great colleagues.

I also want to say thank you to everyone at Hopes and Dreams nursery, especially Amanda Little and Sarah Payne. You, as much as anyone, have helped me finish the book because I never worry about her when she's with you.

And I want to thank my dad, who has better taste than anyone, for passing on to me his love of films, especially the way they used to make them.

Lastly thanks to the Boss and Chris *waves arms in the air*. You're just too good to be true.

Read on for an extract of another
brilliant Harriet Evans novel,

Love Always

PROLOGUE

Cornwall, 1963

If you close your eyes, perhaps you can still see them. As they were that sundrenched afternoon, the day everything changed.

Outside the house, in the shadows by the terrace, when they thought no one was looking. Mary is in the kitchen making chicken salad and singing along to Music While You Work *on the Home Service. There's no one else around. It's the quiet before lunch, too hot to do anything.*

'Come on,' she says. She is laughing. 'Just one cigarette, and then you can go back up.' She chatters her little white teeth together, her pink lips wet. 'I won't bite, promise.'

He looks anxiously around him. 'All right.'

She has her back to him as she picks her way confidently through the black brambles and grey-green reeds, down the old path that leads to the sea. Her glossy hair is caught under the old green-and-yellow towel she has wrapped round her neck. He follows, nervously.

He's terrified of these encounters – terrified because he knows they're wrong, but still he wants them, more than he's wanted anything in his life. He wants to feel her honey-soft skin, to let his hand move up her thigh, to nuzzle her neck, to hear her cool, cruel laugh. He has known a couple of women: eager, rough-haired girls

1

at college, all inky fingers and beery breath, but this is different. He is a boy compared to her.

Oh, he knows it's wrong, what they're doing. He knows his head has been turned, by the heat, the long, light evenings, the intoxicating, almost frightening, sense of liberation here at Summercove, but he just doesn't care. He feels truly free at last.

The world is becoming a different place, there's something happening this summer. A change is coming, they can all feel it. And that feeling is especially concentrated here, in the sweet, lavender-soaked air of Summercove, where the crickets sing long into the night and where the Kapoors let their guests, it would seem, do what on earth they want . . . Being there is like being on the inside of one of those glass domes you have as a child, visible to the outside world, filled with glitter, waiting to be shaken up. The Kapoors know it too. They are all moths, drawn to the flickering candlelight.

'Hurry up, darling,' she says, almost at the bottom of the steps now, in the bright light, the white dots on her blue polka-dot swimming costume dancing before his eyes. He clings to the rope handle, terrified once more. The steps are dark and slippery, cut into the cliffs and slimy with algae. She watches him, laughing. She often makes him feel ridiculous. He's never been around bohemian people before. All his life, even now, he has been used to having rules, being told when to wash behind his ears, when to hand an essay in, used to the smell of sweaty boys – now young men – queuing for meals, changing for cricket. He's at the top of the pile, knows his place there, he's secure in that world.

He justifies it by saying this is different. It's one last hurrah, and he means to make the most of it, even if it is terrifying . . . He stumbles on a slippery step as she watches him from the beach, a cigarette dangling from her lip. His knee gives way beneath him, and for one terrifying moment he thinks he will fall, until he slams his other leg down, righting himself at the last minute.

'Careful, darling,' she drawls. 'Someone's going to get killed on those steps if they're not careful.'

2

Shaken, he reaches the bottom, and she comes towards him, handing him a cigarette, laughing. 'So clumsy,' she says, and he hates her in that moment, hates how sophisticated and smooth she is, so heedless of what she's doing, how wrong it is . . . He takes the cigarette but does not light it. He pulls her towards him instead, kissing her wet, plump pink lips, and she gives a little moan, wriggling her slim body against his. He can feel himself getting hard already, and her fingers move down his body, and he pushes her against the rock, and they kiss again.

'Have you always been this bad?' he asks her afterwards, as they are smoking their cigarettes. The heat of the sun is drying the sweat on their bodies. They lie together on the tiny beach, sated, as the waves crash next to them. A lost sandal, relic of someone else's wholly innocent summer day, is bobbing around at the edge of the tide. The cigarette is thick and rancid in his mouth. Now it's over, as ever, he is feeling sick.

She turns to him. 'I'm not bad.'

He thinks she is. He thinks she is evil, in fact, but he can't stay away from her. She smiles slowly, and he says, without knowing why he needs to say it, 'Look, it's been lots of fun. But I think it's best if—' He trails off. 'Break it off.'

Her face darkens for a second. 'You pompous ass.' She laughs, sharply. '"Break it off"? Break what off? There's nothing to break off. This isn't . . . anything.'

He is aware that he sounds stupid. 'I thought we should at least discuss it. Didn't want to give you the—' God, he wishes it were over. He finds himself giving her a little nod. 'Give you the wrong impression.'

'Oh, that's very kind of you.' She stubs the cigarette into the wet sand, and stands up, pulling the towel off the ground and around her again. He can't tell if she's angry or relieved, or – what? This is all beyond him, and it strikes him again that he's glad it will be over and that soon he can go back to being himself again, boring, ordinary, out of all this, normal.

'It's been—' he begins.

'Oh, fuck you,' she says. 'Don't you dare.' She turns to go, but as she does something comes tumbling down the steps. It is a small piece of black slate.

And then there is a noise, a kind of thudding. Footsteps.

'Who's there?' he says, looking up, but after the white light of the midday sun it is impossible to see anyone on the dark steps.

In the long years afterwards, when he never spoke about this summer, what happened, he would ask himself – because there was no one else he could ask: Who? His wife? His family? Hah – if he'd been wrong about what he'd seen. For, in that moment, he'd swear he could make out a small foot, disappearing back up onto the path to the house.

He turns back to her. 'Damn. Was that someone, do you think?'

She sighs. 'No, of course not. The path's crumbling, that's all. You're paranoid, darling.' She says lightly, 'As if they'd ever believe it of you, anyway. Calm down. Remember, we're supposed to be grown-ups. Act like one.'

She puts one hand on the rope and hauls herself gracefully up. 'Bye, darling,' she says, and he watches her go. 'Don't worry,' she calls. 'No one's going to find out. It's our little secret.'

But someone did. Someone saw it all.

4

PART ONE

February 2009

CHAPTER ONE

It is 7:16 a.m.

The train to Penzance leaves at seven-thirty. I have fourteen minutes to get to Paddington. I stand in a motionless Hammersmith and City line carriage, clutching the overhead rail so hard my fingers ache. I have to catch this train; it's a matter of life and death.

Quite literally, in fact – my grandmother's funeral is at two-thirty today. You're allowed to be an hour late for dinner, but you can't be an hour late for a funeral. It's a once-in-a-lifetime deal.

I've lived in London all my life. I know the best places to eat, the bars that are open after twelve, the coolest galleries, the prettiest spots in the parks. And I know the Hammersmith and City line is useless. I hate it. Why didn't I leave earlier? Impotent fury washes through me. And still the carriage doesn't move.

This morning, the sound of pattering rain on the quiet street woke me while it was still dark. I haven't been sleeping for a while, since before Granny died. I used to complain bitterly about my husband Oli's snoring, how he took up the whole bed, lying prone in a diagonal line. He's been away for nearly two weeks now. At first I thought it'd be good, if only because I could catch up on sleep, but I haven't. I lie awake, thoughts racing through my head, one wide-awake side of my brain taunting the other, which is begging for rest. I feel mad. Perhaps I am mad. Although they say if you think you're going mad that definitely means you're not. I'm not so sure.

7:18 a.m. I breathe deeply, trying to calm down. It'll be OK. It'll all be OK.

Granny died in her sleep last Friday. She was eighty-nine. The funny thing is, it still shocked me. Booking my train tickets to come down to Cornwall, in February, it seemed all wrong, as though I was in a bad dream. I spoke to Sanjay, my cousin, over the weekend and he said the same thing. He also said, 'Don't you want to punch the next person in the face who says, "Eighty-nine? Well, she had a good innings, didn't she?" Like she deserved to die.'

I laughed, even though I was crying, and then Jay said, 'I feel like something's coming to an end, don't you? Something bigger than all of us.'

It made me shiver, because he is right. Granny was the centre of everything. The centre of my life, of our family. And now she's gone, and – I can't really explain it. She was the link to so many things. She was Summercove.

We're at Edgware Road, and it's 7:22 a.m. I might get it. I just might still get the train.

Granny and Arvind, my grandfather, had planned for this moment. Talked about it quite openly, as if they wanted everyone to be clear about what they wanted, perhaps because they didn't trust my mother or my uncle – Jay's dad – to follow their wishes. I'd like to believe that's not true, but I'm afraid it probably is. They specified what would happen when either one of them died first, what happens to the paintings in the house, the trust that is to be set up in Granny's memory, the scholarship that is funded in Arvind's memory, and what happens to Summercove.

Arvind is ninety. He is moving into a home. Louisa, my

mother's cousin, has taken charge of that. Louisa has taken charge of the funeral, too. She likes taking charge. She has picked everything that Granny didn't leave instructions about, from the hymns to the fillings in the sandwiches for the wake afterwards (a choice of egg mayonnaise, curried chicken or cucumber). Her husband, the handsome but extremely boring Bowler Hat, will be handing out the orders of service at the funeral and topping up drinks at the wake. Louisa is organising everything, and it is very kind of her, but we feel a bit left out, Jay and I. As ever, the Leighton side of the family has got it right, with their charming English polo-shirts-and-crumpets approach to life and we, the Kapoors, are left looking eccentric, disjointed, odd. Which I suppose we are.

Cousin Louisa is also in charge of packing up the house. For Summercove is to be sold. Our beautiful white art deco house perched between the fields and the sea in Cornwall will soon be someone else's. It is where Granny and my grandfather lived for fifty years, raised their children. I spent every summer of my life there. It's really the only home I've ever known and I'm the only one, it seems, who's sentimental about it, who can't bear to see it go. Mum, my uncle Archie, Cousin Louisa – even my grandfather – they're all brisk about it. I don't understand how they can be.

'Too many memories here,' Granny used to say when she'd talk about it, tell us firmly what was going to happen. 'Time for someone else to make some.'

Finally. The doors wobble open at Paddington and I rush out and run up the steps, pushing past people, muttering, 'Sorry, sorry.' Thank God it's the Hammersmith and City line – the exit opens right onto the vast concourse of the station. It is 7:28. The train leaves in two minutes.

The cold air hits me. I jab my ticket frantically in the barrier and run down the stairs to the wide platform, legs like jelly as I tumble down, faster and faster. I am nearly there, nearly

9

at the bottom . . . I glance up at the big clock. 7:29. Like a child, I jump the last three steps, my knees nearly giving way underneath me, and leap onto the train. I stand by the luggage racks, panting, trying to collect myself. There is a final whistle, the sound of doors slamming further along the endless snake of carriages. We are off.

I find a seat and sit down. My mother doesn't drive, so I know the ways of the train. The key to a good journey is not a table seat. I never understand why you would get one unless you knew everyone round the table. You end up spending five hours playing awkward footsie with a sweaty middle-aged man, or surrounded by a screaming, overexcited family. I slot myself into a window seat and close my eyes. A cool trickle of sweat slides down my backbone.

This is the train I took every summer, with Mum, to Summercove. Mum would bring me down, stay for a few days and then leave before the rest of her relatives arrived, and sometimes – but not often – before she and Granny could row about something: money, men, me.

It was always so much fun, the train down to Penzance when I was little. It was the anticipation of the holiday ahead, six weeks in Cornwall, six weeks with my favourite people in my favourite place. Mum would be in a strangely good mood on the train down, and so would I, both of us looking forward to diluting our twosome for a few weeks, away from our dark Hammersmith mansion flat, where the wallpaper peeled away from the walls, and in the summer the smell from the bins outside was noticeable. Bryant Court didn't suit summer. The noises inside and out got worse, scratching and strange, and the cast of characters in the building seemed to get less eccentric and more menacing. The hot weather seemed to dry them out, to make them more brittle and screeching. We were always euphoric to be out of there, away from it all.

Once, when we were on our way to Paddington and my mother was dragging me by the wrist towards a waiting cab,

10

bags slung over our shoulders, Mrs Pogorzelski hissed, 'Slut!' at Mum, as she opened the door. I didn't know what it meant, or why she was saying it. Mum bundled me into the black cab and we sat there grinning, surrounded by luggage, as we rolled up through Kensington towards the station, both of us complicit in some way that I couldn't define. That was also one of the times Mum forgot her purse, and the cab driver let us have a ride for free after she cried. She forgot her purse quite often, my mother.

She is at Summercove already, helping Cousin Louisa sort out the funeral and the house. She is convinced Louisa has her eye on some pieces of furniture already, convinced she is controlling everything. Archie, Mum's twin brother and Jay's dad, is there too. Mum and her cousin do not get on. But then Mum and a lot of people don't get on.

The train is flying through the outskirts of London, out past Southall and Heathrow, through scrubby wasteland that doesn't know whether it's town or countryside, towards Reading. I look around me for the first time since collapsing into my seat. I want a coffee, and I should have something to eat, though I'm not quite sure I can eat anything.

'Tickets, please,' says a voice above me. I jump, more violently than is warranted and the ticket inspector looks at me in alarm. I hand him my tickets – thankfully, I collected them at Liverpool Street, knowing the queues at Paddington would be horrendous. I blink, trying not to shake, as the desire to be sick, to faint, anything, sweeps over me again, and slump back against the scratchy seat, watching the inspector. He raises his eyebrows as he checks them over.

'Long way to be going for the day.'

'Yes,' I say. He looks at me, and I find myself saying, too eagerly, 'I have to be back in London tomorrow. There's an appointment first thing – I have an appointment I can't miss.'

He nods, but already I've given him too much information,

and I can feel myself flushing with shame. He's a Londoner, he doesn't want to chat. The trouble is, I want to talk to someone. I need to. A stranger, someone who I won't see again.

I haven't told my family I'm coming back tonight. Growing up with my mother, I learned long ago that the less you say, the less you get asked. The one person I would like to confide in is being buried today, in the churchyard at St Mary's, a tiny stone hut, so old people aren't sure when it was first built. In the churchyard there is the grave of a customs officer, one of many killed by desperate smugglers. There is a lot about Cornwall that is still kind of wild, pagan, and though the fish restaurants, tea shops and surfboards cover some of it up, they can't entirely conceal it.

Granny believed that. She was from Cornwall, she grew up near St Ives, on the wild north coast. She saw Alfred Wallis painting by the docks, she was born with the cry of seagulls and the wind whistling through the winding streets of the old town in her ears. She loved the landscape of her home county; it was her life, her job. She lived most of her life there, did her best work there, sitting in her studio high at the top of the house, overlooking the sea.

There are so many things I never asked her, and now I wish I had. So often that I wished I could confide in her, about all sorts of things, but knew I couldn't. For much as I loved my granny, I was scared of her too, of the blank look she'd get in her lovely green eyes sometimes when she looked at me. My husband Oli said once he sometimes thought she could see straight into your soul, like a witch. He was joking, but he was a little scared of her, and I know what he meant. There are some things you didn't ask her. Some things she wouldn't ever talk about.

Because for many years, Summercove was a very different place, centre of a glittering social whirl, and my grandparents were wealthy, successful, and it seemed as if they had the world at their feet. But then their daughter Cecily died, two months short of her sixteenth birthday, and my grandmother stopped painting. She shut up her studio at the top of the house and, as far as I know, she never went back. I learned from a very early age never to ask why. Never to mention Cecily's name, even. There are no photos of her in the house, and no one ever talks about her. I know she died in 1963, and I know it was an accident of some kind, and I know Granny stopped painting after that, and that's about it.

We're going past Newbury, and the landscape is greener. There has been a lot of rain lately, and the rivers are swollen and brown under a grey sky. The fields are newly ploughed. A fast wind whips dead leaves over and around the train. I sit back and breathe out, feeling the nauseous knot of tension in my stomach start to slowly unravel, as a wave of something like calm washes over me. We are leaving London. We are getting closer.

Happily Ever After

You can't escape the
ties that bind. The past
catches up with you
no matter how far
you try to run...

This is a story of a girl who
doesn't believe in happy
endings. Or happy families.
It's the story of Eleanor Bee,
a shy, book-loving girl who
vows to turn herself into
someone bright, shiny and
confident, someone
sophisticated. Someone who
knows how life works.

But life has a funny way of catching us unawares.
Turns out that Elle doesn't know everything about love.
Or life. Or how to keep the ones we love safe...

Absorbing, poignant and unforgettable,
Happily Ever After is a compelling
story of a fractured family and a girl
who doesn't believe in love.